SAVING SERENA

HAWK SECURITY

ERIN SWANN

ISBN-13 979-8341281165

Edited by Jessica Royer Ocken

Proofreaders: Jen Boles, Victoria Straw, Jennifer Herrington of Fresh Look Editorial

The following story is intended for mature readers. It contains mature themes, strong language, and sexual situations. All characters are 18+ years of age, and all sexual acts are consensual.

❀ Created with Vellum

CHAPTER 1

SERENA

AT THE LIGHT, I TURNED RIGHT ONTO THE FEEDER ROAD, NOTICING THE BIG, BLACK SUV in my mirror—it made the same turn.

Today had been my first trip into the field since my promotion was announced last week, and it had been eye-opening. My blood boiled, recalling the meeting I'd just had with the people at Knife Creek Chemical. How could they be so flippant about their inability to show me their latest outflow-monitoring results? The meeting had been scheduled in advance. They should have been prepared.

On top of that, their COO, Aiden Pons, had propositioned me for dinner on the way out. *"I think you'd enjoy the view from my hilltop mansion."* Back in the car, the first thing I did was pull out my wet wipes to clean off the slime from his handshake.

Maybe since Knife Creek had hired the likes of Pons, I shouldn't have been surprised that they weren't prepared with their data. I pitied the executive assistant who had to work with him.

In contrast, the company I'd visited before them, Excalibur Plating, had been as pleasant and professional as I could have expected. Larry Pollock had uploaded their data to our server without complaint.

When I'd gotten this promotion, my boss, Edward Powell, hadn't been happy. He'd wanted his pet, Remy Laurent, to get the promotion instead. But Katelyn and Nick, coworkers from my office, as well as Remy and I, had all applied. And the merit review board had chosen me. So tough shit, Remy. Office politics were the worst.

And things were no picnic in the field either. If very many of the companies in this area were like Knife Creek, I'd have to grow a thicker skin.

The SUV again followed when I made a left onto the main road heading back to the city. Maybe it was just the color and the tinted windows that made it look ominous. The fact that we were both turning toward town shouldn't have alarmed me.

My real problem was that I was on the road back to the office with nothing to show for my visit to Knife Creek. *"Have the data ready for me at our next meeting,"* I'd told them, which hadn't been what they wanted to hear. Well, tough fucking shit. I represented the Environmental Protection Agency, and the EPA didn't have to take shit from Knife Creek or anybody.

Katelyn, the closest approximation to a friend I had in our department, would probably laugh at me when I came back empty-handed. She'd been an external auditor for a year now and would have been the one at that meeting this morning if I'd agreed to the swap she wanted because the territory I got was closer to her home.

Maybe I should have invited her along. She probably knew what to say to get them to comply, and we'd have the data now instead of nada, zilch, zero.

I could have said, "Hand over the data, or else."

But then "Or else what?" might have been the response.

That's where my bravado ran out of answers. I was in auditing, not enforcement. I wasn't Dirty Harriet. The most dangerous thing I carried was a ballpoint pen. Yeah, when I got back, I'd ask Katelyn how she would have approached it.

But then again, maybe I should wait a while to ask for her help.

The sound of an incoming call came through the speakers of my government-issued car. At least they'd included Bluetooth in the fleet for safety purposes. My friend Grace Brennan's name showed on the screen.

"Hey, girlfriend," I answered. "What's up?"

"I'm sorry, but I'm not getting back into town until the end of the week. Can we put off cooking until next Wednesday?"

"Got you down." Every few Wednesdays we got together for joint cooking sessions where we tried out new recipes. Ever since we met in group therapy, it had been our thing, a way to relax. Having shared our trauma stories gave us a special bond.

"Good," she said. "Your place this time."

I nodded. "You bet."

She sighed. "See ya then."

When we ended the call, I checked behind me and didn't see the ominous black SUV. I breathed easier.

Not a minute later, the phone rang again. This time, it was my brother Zach.

"Joey's Pizza. Today's special is a family-size pepperoni with three colors of bell peppers," I answered.

A laugh and then, "Serena, since when does a pizza joint have road noise in the background?"

"It was worth a try. What's up?"

"Mom wants to know if you're joining us for her barbecue."

A glance in the mirror showed the big SUV was back again—or still back there? Maybe I hadn't looked close enough last time. "Why doesn't she call me herself if she wants me to come?" I shifted left a lane and sped up.

"She said she called three times, and you didn't answer."

"It was two times," I corrected. I'd answered the second time. "And I'm still not interested in getting back together with George." I left off that I'd yelled an angry *hell no* at her, and a few other choice words, when she'd asked me to give the guy another chance. I'd get over it, but the call still made me angry.

Zach laughed. "He comes from a good family," he said, parroting Mom's logic.

I added the kicker. "And Dad has a joint venture in the works with George's father." Yes, Mom wanted grandbabies, and Dad wanted business advantage.

George Kittleman, my boring ex-boyfriend, had been bugging me about getting back together ever since he returned from his stint in Paris. He hadn't been this attentive before leaving for a job offer *he couldn't pass up*.

Zach laughed again. "Dad didn't actually say that, did he?"

"No," I admitted. "He probably just thinks George is stable and safe." What was and wasn't safe for me had consumed Dad since the dark time in my life.

Zach laughed again. "And ready to have kids."

"That's not funny. Why aren't they busy setting you guys up instead of always picking on me?"

The silence on the line spoke volumes. I had four brothers, all too busy out sowing their wild oats to settle down. But Mom wanted grandbabies, and that meant convincing one of her daughters to get serious and stop the birth control—with a man of appropriate breeding, of course.

Kelly's move to Washington, DC had stymied Mom's efforts with her, which left me as the only daughter within reach. Unfortunately, at this stage in my career, I had to endure her matchmaking attempts. I couldn't take Kelly's escape hatch and move away from LA yet.

I relaxed after checking my mirror again. The SUV was now way back there.

"Are you still there, Serena?" Zach asked. "What do you say about Saturday?"

"Sure, I'll show up if you guys are going to be there, too. I'm not going if it's only going to be me and Mom and Dad and George."

3

"I've always got your back, you know that," Zach said. "And she may not be ambushing you with George, anyway."

"Right," I added, heavy sarcasm to my tone.

"Bring a date, then, as protection. Just in case."

That was a nonstarter. I hadn't gotten past the second-date stage in over eighteen months.

"Shit," I muttered, gripping the wheel tighter. The creepy SUV was two cars back again. It must have been hidden behind a truck.

"What's wrong?" There was honest concern in my overprotective brother's voice. He, and the others, always tried to shield me from the world. It had been cute when I was twelve. Now, it was annoying.

"It's probably nothing." His silence prompted me to elaborate. "I'm heading back from the Valley, and there's a lot of traffic. I hate it when these big SUVs ride my ass." It was true, just not today's truth.

"Don't do anything stupid, Serena, like brake-check him. I don't want to see you become a road-rage statistic. Here's what you do—"

"I'm smarter than that, and I can handle myself," I reminded him. I was a grown-ass woman, not a kid.

He powered through my complaint. "You don't want to provoke guys like that."

When protector mode became dictator mode, I got pissed. Time to end this conversation. "My battery's getting low," I lied. "Gotta go." I always had to exude confidence, or my brothers would try to swoop in and fix things for me.

"See you Saturday."

I dreaded these setup attempts by my mother. But she was family, so I couldn't exactly refuse every meal invitation. "Saturday," I agreed before ending the call.

A little while later, searching my mirror, I didn't see the SUV. He might have turned off back there, and I missed it.

A few miles ahead, the road through the hills peeled off to the right. I could use it to prove I was imagining things. And if he did follow, there was a fire station a few miles in that would be a safe place to stop.

Mentally, I congratulated myself for planning ahead like Dad had taught me. Changing lanes again, I sped up. When my turn appeared ahead, I still hadn't spotted the SUV. I considered not turning off, but if I was wrong, the scenic route would only cost me a half hour.

The nervous twitch in my left leg proved I wasn't as confident as I wanted to be, and I pressed on my knee to calm it. Nervous equaled weak, and I was not weak. *Be proud, be bold.* I'd gotten the tattoo to remind myself every day.

When I reached the fire station, I breathed a deep, easy breath and continued. All my mirror checks showed no scary SUV. A weak woman would have stopped

4

and dialed 9-1-1 from the safety of the fire station and then endured questions from the highway patrol officer about why I felt threatened when I hadn't even seen the SUV follow me onto this road.

The officer would shake his head all the way back to his patrol car, marveling at what a weak little girl I was.

I wasn't weak. I was proud and bold, so I drove on by. There was no reason to stop. Besides, it was a nice day to enjoy the winding road through the hills.

Music. That's what I needed. Something light to cheer me up. I could do this job. Next time, I'd show those creeps at Knife Creek who was boss. As I tuned in a station, I told myself there was nothing to worry about, not even Mom's pending Saturday barbeque.

Aretha Franklin's "Respect" came bursting through the speakers, and I sang along. A little R-E-S-P-E-C-T was what I needed, all right. I'd moved up from data analyst to pollution-control auditor, and all on my own—without my dad's help. I was done being the sheltered little girl in the billionaire's family. I was on my own and proud of it.

When a melancholy breakup song from another artist started, I switched off the radio. That wasn't my cup of tea today. How could I relate to a melancholy breakup song when splitting with George Kittleman last year had been the best thing for me?

Then, a shiver ran down my spine when I looked back to find the evil-looking SUV behind me, gaining fast.

I hadn't checked the mirror in a while, so maybe it was a different black SUV driven by someone in a hurry. There had to be hundreds of them in the LA area, if not thousands.

But then he got close, too close. I pressed on the gas. Sweat beaded on my forehead. My nerves about this SUV had been right. *Why didn't I mention it to Zach?*

The SUV accelerated with me.

I hoped my little EPA sedan could handle the curves better than he could. I took the next corner faster, my tires protesting a tiny bit. My left leg trembled. I relaxed my death grip on the wheel when, as expected, the SUV lost ground in the corner.

Then, on the straightaway, he surged forward. My chest tightened as adrenaline rushed through me. God, I wished I'd driven my car. At least it had an engine. Like most government cars this one only had three hamsters on a wheel under the hood.

I knew the road well enough to keep the accelerator on around the long bend leading to the tight corner. My heart raced as I took the car nearer to its limit than I wanted.

The asshole matched me again. This was getting serious fast. Why hadn't I been smart and stopped at the fire station?

I laid on the brakes for the corner. A second later, he bumped me hard, throwing my head back against the headrest.

We were going too fast. My rear tires squealed, and the tail of my car pitched out. Dad's words, *"Steer into the skid,"* echoed in my head as I adjusted the wheel and recovered at the very edge of the pavement, just as he'd had me practice on a rain-slick parking lot years ago. *Thank you, Dad.*

I had to create distance between me and this maniac, so I floored it, exiting the turn with the little engine screaming in protest. I shot forward and checked the mirror. No, my car didn't have more get-up-and-go than the big SUV.

When I yanked my eyes forward again, it was almost too late. I saw the deer bounding into my path and swerved right to keep from hitting him and sending three hundred pounds of deer and antlers through my windshield. I still clipped him, and I put my arm up to shield myself as I headed for the edge. Hitting the guardrail sounded like a gunshot as the airbag slammed my wrist into my throat and hit me in the face. My eyes shut instinctively. I was weightless for a second as we hurtled over the edge.

I was thrown side to side like a rag doll as the car rolled down the embankment. When we stopped, I hung upside down from the seatbelt, listening to the whine of the revving engine, then it went silent. My shoulder throbbed to the fast beat of my heart.

Dazed and disoriented, I pushed against the airbag. Man, was it hot, and it smelled of smoke.

Phone.

I needed my phone. It had been in the cupholder next to me. I didn't see it anywhere now, but I was hanging upside down and dazed.

Fucking shit. The smell of gasoline joined the smoky smell. I fumbled around until I found the seatbelt release. I bumped my head hard on the roof as it let go, and it took some contortions to get untangled from the steering wheel.

Bluetooth. I could use the car's Bluetooth. I pressed the call button. "Call 9-1-1."

Nothing. Pressing the start-stop button got the engine to turn over, but not catch. Of course the thing wouldn't be able to start upside down. Pulling the door handle got me nowhere. *Trapped.* This could get worse in a hurry. I searched again for my phone.

Then, through the windshield, I saw a man in a black leather jacket at the top of the embankment. "Help me," I called to him. My throat hurt. It came out hoarse, but loud enough to reach him through the broken passenger-side window. Unfortunately, the roll had crushed the roof on that side enough to make it impossible to get out in that direction.

6

Black Jacket Guy started down the hill—black pants, black boots, all black. He just needed to find a rock to break the window and get me out.

He smiled at me. *Odd.*

"Call nine-one-one," I screamed. He pulled something out of his pocket as he made his way cautiously down the hill.

I looked for my phone again and then back uphill. Black Jacket Guy was flicking a cigarette lighter as he calmly approached. The fucker smiled at me. "You're going to tell me where the stick is," he yelled. He had an accent.

What stick? My heart stopped. *This morning's note on my car.* I'd thought it was meant for my neighbor.

Put the USB stick under the red bush or else.

Crash, gasoline, lighter. This was not good.

Even if I knew where the stupid stick he wanted was, I'd seen enough movies to know how this ended.

I couldn't die like this. My last words to my mom had been angry ones.

CHAPTER 2

Duke

We arrived at Cardinelli's in Westwood fashionably late for lunch.

I ushered my client, Ariana, and her lunch date, Missy, inside without incident. This was *the best* white-tablecloth restaurant if you wanted good Italian in this part of the city.

I scanned for threats as I followed them and the maître d' to their table.

"Sorry for the delay," Constance said over my comms earpiece. "I'm on the way now." Constance Collier, a new addition to our team, over from Hanson Security, was supposed to be my partner on this job. Then her doctor had called and moved up her appointment.

"Copy that. No issues here." I'd told her to skip this and go. This was a simple lunch gig, nothing I couldn't handle alone.

"But we want the VVIP section," Ariana complained. The daughter of a Russian oligarch, she was the epitome of a spoiled, entitled Hollywood brat. She didn't settle for VIP status. Everything had to be better than her competition.

Her real name was Zoya Zolotarev. Try saying that three times fast. And so, with Daddy's money, a nose job, and a boob job, Ariana Harmony had gotten her start in Hollywood. Her big break came when her father financed a film that then cast her in the lead role. Her bouncing tits in the plentiful nude scenes did the rest. Now, she was on the reality TV show *Real Models of Beverly Hills*, which of course had no reality in it whatsoever.

The maître d' gave the girls the pick of two other tables.

8

Ariana chose the one by the courtyard window. She didn't seem to notice the maître d's eye roll as he left.

I knew for a fact that there was no VVIP or even a VIP section here.

As the girls ordered drinks and looked over the menu, I scanned the room, assessing and determining threat levels. In a high-end restaurant like this, the maximum threat was usually a two on a ten-scale.

Technically, my job was to keep my client safe from kidnapping, assault, theft, and harassment. With Ariana, it usually amounted to keeping overzealous selfie-seekers at bay, regardless of how innocuous they seemed.

And then there were the paparazzi. I hated dealing with the paps, they were all pricks.

While the girls discussed the menu, I opened my phone and checked on Constance's location. The icon on the map showed she had a long way to go.

"Asian chicken salad, medium rare," Missy ordered.

The server nodded with a wry smile, knowing enough not to comment on the airhead's apparent desire for undercooked poultry.

Ariana also ordered salad, typical fare for actresses out in public.

What the public didn't know was that as soon as she got home, a bucket of hot and spicy Kentucky Fried Chicken would be on the way. After that, she'd go into the bathroom and puke it up. Also typical Hollywood.

Having grown up with very little food on the table, I couldn't understand it. Eating and then barfing it up didn't compute for me.

Standing by the wall and smelling all the food I was not able to taste made this part of my job annoying, but at least I was done having to worry about road-side IEDs. Plus, I got to sleep in a bed instead of on a dirt floor in a country where I didn't speak the language.

As boring as it could be, guarding a celebrity was a lot easier than dealing with the rock groups that came through town. Trouble sought those guys out, and they were always high, or drunk, or both. It was worse than herding cats, and my ass was on the line if trouble got past me.

"Cobra, get our waiter," Ariana said, moments after their food had been delivered. "I don't like this dressing."

Cobra was the code name I'd carried over from my time in the military. On assignment, I preferred it over my legal name. Having a client look me up after an assignment could get problematic.

I didn't see the server but kept an eye out to flag him down.

"Yeah, Cobra." Missy giggled. "Go get our waiter. Chop, chop."

"No," I answered without even turning my head in her direction.

"Why, Cobra?" Missy asked.

I ignored her. Missy got my protection at this lunch because of her proximity to my client, but that was all.

"You can tell her," Ariana prodded.

I turned my head and gave her the stare. "A cobra strikes without warning and is deadly."

Missy's eyes bugged out when I added a hiss.

"Cool, huh? And he's not allowed to leave me," Ariana whispered. "Rules."

My comms earpiece came alive with colorful cursing from my pal Winston Evers. Our ace tech guru, Jordan Hawk, my brother, was getting a tongue-lashing. And this time, it sounded like he deserved it.

"It's not marked that way," he tried. Jordy had been giving Winston directions to follow a target and had messed up by trying to send him the wrong way down a one-way street. The target now had a quarter mile of separation.

"Jordy, save it for later," said my brother Lucas, our boss, cutting off the bitch session. "Give him a parallel route to catch up. And Winston, pedal to the metal until you get back in position."

I clicked off my comms. The boss had it handled, and I didn't need the distraction.

Missy nodded toward me. "Does he ever smile?"

"Nope. Probably also against the rules." Ariana took another dainty bite of her rabbit food just as I heard a series of camera clicks.

The pap scooted out through the kitchen door so fast I couldn't have the pleasure of chasing him and *fixing* his camera for him.

"Want to take this seat so they get a better shot?" Missy asked Ariana.

"Good idea."

They traded places. Staged casual shots were another Hollywood staple I didn't understand. But reality-TV stars like Ariana were zero percent real. The nose, the boobs, and the tan were all fake.

I reconsidered that and decided on ten percent real. The Russian accent and the on-screen temper weren't fake.

Incoming. A giggly pair of teenagers with phones in their hands headed our way. I left the wall and intercepted them, holding my arms out like a fence. "Hey, girls, give us some privacy. They're here to eat. She's not doing selfies today."

"Cobra," Ariana said from behind me.

The girls' eyes went wide.

"It's okay," Ariana said.

I let the girls pass. When my phone vibrated, I checked the alert I'd set. The picture of Ariana and Missy at lunch had already been posted on ZMT with a caption that gave everyone the location. That meant fans were on the way, and our exit would be a zoo.

I stood back as the giggling girls took selfies with Ariana and Missy.

Why people put up with this shit, I would never understand. They never got any privacy. I knew firsthand that Ariana couldn't do any normal things a girl her age might want to do, like go out to a movie, visit a pizza joint, stop at Baskin-Robbins for a cone, or sit outside Starbucks sipping coffee and watching people walk by.

After the giggleygirls left, Missy poked at her salad and made a face. "Don't you just hate it when they put all the croutons on one side?"

"Yeah, that's like rude and unusual punishment," Ariana agreed.

The conversation only got more childish from there.

When they'd finished complaining about everything under the sun, I prepped for the exit by peeking out the front window while they paid. The fan swarm had arrived, along with two paparazzi I noticed.

"It's a madhouse out there," I told them at the door. "We're going to make a rush to the car." Today, I was driving the armored Suburban instead of one of the Porsche Cayenne Turbo GTs Lucas had chosen for us.

"Right." Ariana nodded.

The group mobbed us as soon as we got out the door, demanding autographs and yelling questions. The fans were even more aggressive than the paparazzi, shoving their way to the front.

"Sure," Missy said, accepting an invitation to sign a guy's chest when he pulled up his shirt and offered a Sharpie.

Ariana had started this two weeks ago. The internet went crazy, and now it was her thing. She took selfies with the girls and signed the guys' chests. Marketing genius or perversion, I didn't care, but it had made the crowds larger and rowdier.

The cascade began when other guys copied that one idiot's move.

Not wanting to be one-upped by her friend, Ariana pulled away from me and took a Sharpie to a different guy's chest, then a selfie with the girl next to him.

I stayed close to my client and tried to keep an eye on the crowd, looking for any crazies. In a crowd this size, there was almost always one who needed to be kept away.

I reconnected to comms. "Constance, we've left the restaurant, and it's getting a little busy here. I could use your help."

"Traffic sucks," she said in my ear. "I'm still fifteen out."

"Make it ten. Cobra out."

The paps were snapping away, loving the free-for-all as the girls entertained more fans.

Then I saw it, a knife protruding from a guy's pocket. If Constance had been here, I would have corralled the guy while she kept watch, but she wasn't. Escape from the threat became the only option.

I pulled Ariana away. "We have to go." With my other hand, I yanked hard on Missy's arm and pulled the two toward the car.

The swarm of fans followed us.

"Let go of me," Missy complained.

"I'm not done," Ariana hissed.

"There's a guy with a knife," I said. "It's not safe here."

You'd think the mention of a knife would have scared her into complying, but no, not Ariana. She planted her feet. "You're not the boss of me."

Missy copied Ariana. "Me either."

A fan pushed in and held out a camera, trying to get a selfie. Another lifted his shirt. "Do me."

I tried logic. "You're not safe here."

Ariana took a pen. "I said I'm not done." She inked the idiot's chest.

I tried calm and insistent. "We have to leave now."

"I told you. You're not the boss of me," Ariana said, posing for a selfie with her tongue sticking out.

"We have to go."

"I'm sick of this," she said. "You're fired."

This was new. Nobody had ever fired us before. "You can't fire me," I snarled.

"Papa said I can, and I just did. Now get lost." She made a shooing motion. "You're ruining the vibe." When I didn't move, she raised her voice. "Leave. I don't need you, and I don't want you."

A chorus of *yeah, get lost*, rose from the crowd.

I walked away. She didn't want me or need me, and if her father gave her the option, I certainly didn't need her attitude. On my way, I grabbed the guy carrying the knife, disarmed him, and tossed the knife down the storm drain.

The idiot opened his mouth to complain, but I cut him off with a pointed finger and one word. "Don't."

He took off.

I double-clicked my comms. "Constance?"

"Still five out," came her reply.

"We're not needed anymore. This assignment is terminated."

"What do you mean?"

"The client has terminated the engagement. I'll see you back at the office."

A silence followed before she acknowledged. "Copy that."

"You're not the boss of me." Ten-year-olds were more eloquent—and nicer.

CHAPTER 3

SERENA

BEEP... BEEP.

I cracked my eyes open to the sight of wires, tubes, and machines. *I'm in the emergency room,* I reminded myself.

As soon as I closed my eyes again, the awful scene from the hillside repeated in my head. Black Jacket Guy had come down the hill with a lighter in his hand, while I was trapped in the car with the smell of gasoline. I'd watched enough *CSI* episodes to know they would have had to use dental records to identify me. I shivered in spite of the warm blanket over me.

Beep, beep, beep. The machine registered my distress at the memory.

Then, I'd seen and heard a second man. *"What happened?"* he'd called from the top of the hill.

Black Jacket Guy had put away the lighter and yelled back, *"Call nine-one-one. There's someone in the car. She ran off the road."*

"On it," my savior at the top of the hill had confirmed.

"Where is it?" Mr. Black Jacket had then demanded.

"Where is what?" I'd croaked.

"This isn't over." He'd retreated up the hill.

Beep... beep. My heart rate steadied again.

The firefighters had used the jaws of life to extricate me. I'd wheezed and tried to tell them about the accident as they pulled me free.

13

"Don't talk," the paramedic had said as he put an oxygen mask on me. *"Relax. I've got you."*

The whole time, I'd kept an eye out for Black Jacket Guy. I hadn't seen him again. With all the time it had taken to be freed from the car and get to the hospital, I'd peed in the ambulance.

Here at the hospital, they'd CAT scanned my head, since I'd bumped it on the roof of the car and probably the window when the car rolled, and also my throat because it didn't seem to be working. I'd tried to talk but could barely get a sound out. An x-ray of my shoulder was scheduled next. And the nurse had promised to get to the cuts on my face as soon as she settled another patient.

I glanced around my tiny space in the emergency room while I waited for the nurse to return, or better yet, for the doctor she'd promised to arrive. Through the gap in the curtain at the end of my exam space, I could see people walking by. I could hear other patients complaining, some in obvious pain, and several nurses.

Then, a man in a black leather jacket walked by. *Beep, beep, beep, beep.* The machine announced my distress. *It's him.* Black Jacket Guy was here.

I had to get out of here. I was a sitting duck. Why hadn't I recalled all the movie scenes before? The assassin who missed his target always went to the hospital to finish the job. If the victim couldn't tell him what he wanted to know, a syringe of something went into the IV line, and the machines stopped beeping —game over.

He hadn't found me yet, but as soon as he did…

The curtain opened. *Beep, beep, beep, beep.* The nurse entered. "X-ray has an opening for you now."

That was my chance to get past him. I nodded and used the breathing technique that had gotten me through worse than this. *Beep… beep.* My heart rate slowed.

"Oxygen mask, please." I held my hand out. "I feel a little faint."

The nurse obliged and started the oxygen flow.

I held up a thumb and secured my hair behind my head, adjusting the pillow to hide as much of it as possible.

After unhooking the monitors, the nurse unlocked the wheels and split the curtain to wheel me out.

I draped my arm over my face.

"Are you all right?" the nurse asked.

"The lights are bright."

Eventually, she stopped the gurney and set the brake. "The technician will be right with you. You're next."

I removed my arm and looked around—no sign of Black Jacket Guy.

She handed me a hospital gown. "They'll want you to take off your top for the x-ray. You can put this on after."

I nodded and accepted the gown.

As soon as she turned the corner, I ripped the tape off my wrist and yanked the IV needle out of the back of my hand. I didn't care that it hurt, or that it bled.

My heart thundered as I hurried down the hallway, hoping I'd picked the right direction and wouldn't run into Black Jacket Guy.

Ignoring the technician who called after me, I escaped through the ambulance entrance and took off in a painful run toward the street. When I reached it, nobody was following, so I slowed to a walk, although my pounding heart didn't get the message.

I turned left and walked with my head down. No phone, no purse, no money, and no plan. I was fucked ten ways from Sunday. The TV episodes I could remember were my only guide. I couldn't go home. I needed some place safe. *Then what?*

"You okay?" a man asked.

When I looked up, he wasn't Black Jacket Guy. "Yeah," I rasped. Realizing my appearance said exactly the opposite, I improvised. "Being the victim in acting class sucks."

The man nodded and walked on. That's when I saw the answer. The Covington Industries building rose up ahead. I'd find a friend there—and safety.

Once inside the tall building, I did my best to compose myself. But the looks I got said that bloody, dirty, and having peed on myself, I didn't belong here. If they kicked me out, I was really up a creek.

I straightened. "Gus—" I addressed the security guard at the desk by his name tag. "—I need to see Bill Covington."

"Sure you do."

Yup, the dirt and blood on my shirt and the wet pants screamed more home-less than heiress.

I sighed. "Look, I didn't have time to change after acting class. Tell him Serena Benson is here to see him." I normally avoided throwing my family name around, but this was not one of those times.

He didn't move for the phone. Instead, he pulled out his wallet and offered me a five. "Promise me you'll use it for food."

Time for another approach. "Call his wife, Lauren, then. She'll vouch for me." He put the money back in his wallet.

This was the worst possible time to learn that appearance mattered more than substance. I hoped a personal story would convince this guy I knew the Coving-tons. "We're close friends, and Lauren told me the first time she met Bill, she spilled coffee on him in front of the elevator and didn't even know who he was."

Gus's eyes brightened. "I was here for that." He picked up the phone and dialed. "Mrs. Covington, Gus downstairs. I have a Serena Benson here to see Mr. Covington." He hung up. "She'll be right down."

I nodded. "Thanks."

"Sorry, I thought—"

I raised a hand to stop him. "I know. It's supposed to look realistic."

"My God, what happened?" Lauren's almost shriek when the elevator opened drew more attention than I wanted.

"A man ran me off the road," I confessed, looking around the lobby.

"That's terrible."

"Can we talk upstairs?" I asked.

She pushed the button again and held the elevator door open as I joined her.

"Car accident," I explained when the door closed. "I need your and Bill's help."

"You should go to the hospital."

"I already did." The door opened on the top floor.

"They didn't do a very good job," Lauren said as she pointed the way.

The woman outside Bill's office—Judy, by her nameplate—smiled when she saw Lauren. "He won't be long. He's interviewing the candidate for the Boston job." Her face changed when she took in my appearance. "My goodness."

I was having that effect on everybody today.

"This is important," Lauren said as she opened the door and ushered me in.

I silently slipped into the office behind her, then stopped in my tracks when Bill's guest turned around.

"What the hell?" my brother Vincent exclaimed as he rushed over.

"Ouch." I winced at the hug he gave me.

He backed off at my reaction. "What happened?"

"Car accident. Sorry about my voice. I got hit in the throat."

"I'm taking you to the ER. To get checked out."

Serena do this. Serena do that. I pushed away "I can take care of myself. I've already been. Nothing's broken. It's just bruises. Really."

He scanned me up and down, about to argue, but didn't.

I sat down, and my leg started shaking again. I'd already mentioned being run off the road to Lauren, so there was no avoiding the discussion.

I gave my brother my best glare. "You can't tell Dad about this."

Lauren gasped. "Why not?"

Vincent shook his head, but I knew he understood the source of my reluctance. "Serena... Sometimes you have to get over this constant need for independence and let family help."

"It's important. We just can't," I said. Dad would lock me up forever if he thought I was in danger.

Bill's brows drew together.

"Let's all have a seat and talk this through," Lauren suggested, taking my elbow.

"A man ran me off the road," I explained.

Bill straightened. "Why?"

Vincent nearly fell out of his chair. "You said it was a car accident."

"It was," I insisted. Swallowing, I turned to Bill. "I'm not sure, but I found a threatening note on my car this morning."

Vincent cocked his head. "What did it say?"

"Can I see the note?" Bill asked.

"It's in my purse, which is… After the accident, I don't know where it is."

Vincent motioned for me to keep talking.

"It said, *Put the USB stick under the red bush or else.* I thought somebody had the wrong car."

"What stick?" Bill asked. "Like a USB drive?"

I shrugged. "That's my guess, but I have no idea."

Bill shook his head. "I'm going to have to tell Lloyd."

"No," I said firmly. "You can't tell my dad." I pivoted to Vincent. "You either, and that's not up for negotiation. I just need a safe place to stay for a while."

"Of course," Lauren answered instantly.

I shook my head. I didn't dare put her and her child in danger.

"I've got room at the other place," Vincent offered. "Are you sure it wasn't road rage?"

"Maybe you cut the guy off and he got mad," Bill suggested. "And it has nothing to do with the note."

I shook my head. "I'm sure. This wasn't road rage. No way. The guy tailed me all the way from my appointment in Thousand Oaks up into the hills, where he rammed me off the road. Then, after the accident, he asked me where the stick was, and when someone else showed up, he said we weren't done and disappeared."

Bill steepled his hands. "And you don't know who this guy is or where this stick is that he wants?"

I shook my head. "No clue."

"She has to go to the police," Lauren said.

Bill's jaw worked. "That's not the best idea. Without a direction to start looking, they'll give up and move on pretty quickly."

"I'll stay with Zach, if Dennis isn't around." I looked at Vincent. "No offense, but you're in and out of town a lot."

Bill shook his head. "If you crack a crown, who do you go to?"

My mouth fell open. *What?* I couldn't track this change in direction.

"You go to a dentist, because he's the professional," Vincent said. "We love

17

you to death, Serena, and we'd do anything for you. But you need professional protection."

"I could leave town for a while," I offered.

Bill shook his head. "Not at all. That wouldn't be safe."

Vincent's brows drew close. "Why not?"

My leg bounced.

Bill held my gaze. "You'll only be safe when we find out who he is and what he wants. Otherwise, you'll be looking over your shoulder forever."

I liked Bill's use of *we*. I definitely needed help.

Lauren and Vincent nodded in agreement.

I attempted to still my unruly leg. "And how—"

"Protection and investigation," Bill said, cutting me off. "A security firm that has the people to keep you safe and the resources to find out if someone is after you."

What the hell? If *someone was after me?* Bill didn't believe me. I straightened. "Look, I know what happened. I didn't imagine it. If you don't believe me, maybe I should just go."

"I believe you." Vincent had always been a rock for me.

Lauren shot her husband a warning glare. "Of course we believe you. Don't we, Bill?"

"Absolutely," Bill agreed. "What I was trying to say…" He glanced at his wife. "…is that I know the best firm in town. Hawk Security's crew is top-notch in every way. Their people are ex-military, Secret Service, FBI, CIA—they have it all. Lucas Hawk's people will ferret out who this is and what they want."

His mention of Lucas Hawk made my throat go dry. I'd met the man at my lowest and owed him my life. The chest that held those memories rattled, threatening to spill open.

"If you think they're the best, we'll gladly use them," Vincent decided for me.

Be proud, be brave. I nodded. "Sure. They sound fine." What else could I say? Lucas Hawk was central to secrets I couldn't share. I mentally wrapped another chain around the chest.

Bill nodded slowly. "Good."

"To be clear," I emphasized, "we're not involving Dad." Getting my father involved was the one sure way to lose all my hard-fought freedom. "Or anyone else," I clarified, looking at my brother.

He nodded.

"Understood," Bill said. "I'll arrange it with Hawk and make the introduction."

I nodded and took a deep breath of relief. For now, Dad wouldn't know.

"I get that you want to handle this by yourself, but I'm available for anything you need, you know that." My brother pointed a finger at me. "But let me be clear. If the Hawk folks tell tell me you're being reckless and not following their procedures, I'll have to get Dad involved," Vincent added.

And he would too. I nodded. "I understand." *Be a good girl, Serena. Do what you're told, Serena.* I was so sick of it.

Bill picked up the phone.

"They're good people," Lauren assured me while Bill dialed.

"Hi, Lucas, Bill Covington. I have a top-priority job for you. A dear friend of mine has been attacked... Yeah, both protection and investigation to find her assailant... That's great. We'll be right over."

Vincent stood. "I think I should come along."

"That won't be necessary," Bill said, standing. "Lauren can tell you more about the opportunity while I'm gone."

Lauren nodded. "Glad to."

"I'll be back in thirty," Bill added. "We can finish the interview then."

Uncharacteristically, my brother backed down. He clearly wanted the job Bill had available, whatever it was. We each had our own method of escaping Dad.

CHAPTER 4

Duke

I returned to the Hawk Security offices after grabbing lunch. I'd rationalized that a Whopper, fries, and a shake were a higher priority than explaining to my boss and brother, Lucas, that the client had fired us.

Actually, that was a copout. In reality, Lucas was on the very short list of men who could scare me. I wouldn't enjoy his dressing down about how protection meant staying in the background and that my leaving the background had led to this.

I stopped by my other brother Jordy's office with his dozens of screens that made it resemble a NASA control room. "Any word from Brett?"

Jordy didn't bother looking up. "Not yet."

Our fourth brother, Brett, had been called back to active duty for an above top-secret mission, and I missed him already.

Winston Evers looked up from his computer when I entered the office space we shared. "Done already? Got your princess tucked safely away at the castle?"

"I'm done," I confirmed. "You should apologize to Jordy," I added, changing the subject.

Winston was ex-FBI and a crack investigator. If I gave him a single crumb to run with on Ariana, he'd have figured out what had happened faster than I could recite the alphabet backward.

"Already did," he confirmed. "I just got a little heated because I didn't want to screw up the tail." Naturally, Winston wanted to make a good impression with my brother because he was the other person we'd recently hired when Hanson Security closed down.

"Constance back yet?" I asked, wanting to circle back with my partner. Ariana had been a pain in the ass. I was sure Constance would be relieved to be rid of her as well. We were ready for something other than babysitting a rich, spoiled princess.

"Said she's on the way, and she promised to take Jordy out to get a cup of coffee."

I nodded. "Smart move to enlist her to smooth down Jordy's feathers for ya."

His smirk confirmed my guess. "My girl Constance has the touch."

"If you value your balls, I'd be careful about calling her a girl to her face." It was a lesson I'd learned quickly. Constance was ex Secret Service and tough as nails. You had to be to join the First Lady's protection detail.

"Noted." Winston looked back at his screen.

The blinds in Lucas's office were pulled, which didn't happen often.

I thumbed over my shoulder. "Who's the boss got with him?"

Winston shrugged. "Dunno."

"Singleton and March, maybe?"

Winston shrugged. Again.

I'd referred Jeff Singleton and Zane March when Lucas had said he was looking to add more talent. I'd known both from DEVGRU—known to the public as SEAL Team Six. The guys were still at the top of their game, and would make excellent additions if my brother could stomach bringing in more frogmen.

Lucas was a former Delta operator and Army through and through. He was not shy with his opinion that Delta could run rings around the SEALs all day long.

As a former SEAL, I knew that was total bullshit. Deltas had some limitations —take them out of the desert, throw some water into the equation, and they folded like wet cardboard. There was a reason SEALs had been chosen to take down Bin Laden, and it wasn't because we were second-rate.

Just then, Lucas's door opened.

Winston and I looked down the hall and caught sight of a man I knew we both recognized. We'd done work for the Covingtons before. As Bill Covington emerged, I caught a glimpse of a homeless woman still in the office. I liked Bill, and I lived in the same building as he did, one floor down.

The office door closed behind him, and Winston and I both raised a hand in greeting to Mr. Covington.

He waved back and thumbed over his shoulder. "Take care of her." Then he disappeared down the stairs.

Dumbfounded, I didn't reply. What would he be doing with a homeless woman? And why would we be taking care of her?

"One of our irregulars?" I asked Winston. We had some people on retainer who made good lookouts as they hung out on the streets unnoticed.

"Don't think so." He used a toothpick on his teeth. "Could be an interview to join, I guess."

My phone vibrated. It was Lucas. "Yeah?"

"Get into the office as soon as you can. I have a new assignment, and I need my best man."

His comment filled me with pride. "I'm here now."

"My office," he commanded. "And bring Constance too." He hung up before I could say anything.

I looked over at Winston's questioning eyes. "New assignment. He wants Constance as well."

"I'll tell her."

When I entered Lucas's office, I knew immediately that the woman across from him wasn't homeless.

She didn't look up, but in those clothes and shoes. The dirt, the blood, the twigs in her hair—she looked beaten up, not beaten down.

I sat, knowing enough to let Lucas do the talking.

"Serena, this is Cobra. He's the best we have in personal protection." "Constance is on the way in," I explained, smiling in Serena's direction.

She didn't smile, nor did she look over. She wasn't merely scared. With the way her leg shook and she'd glued her eyes to the floor, she was terrified.

"Cobra," Lucas said. "Somebody tried to kill Serena today. We want to find him, and in the meantime, we need to protect her. Constance will be your number two. I'm shifting you off the Zolotarev girl and on to Serena's case."

I nodded. I still needed to tell him Ariana had fired us.

"Cobra is a former Navy SEAL, and Constance was on the First Lady's Secret Service detail," Lucas explained. "They'll keep you safe."

Serena nodded tentatively as she pressed down on her jittery leg.

Lucas turned to me. "Take her to the Santa Monica safe house for now and keep her there until we get a handle on who is responsible."

"No." Serena's voice was hoarse but firm.

Lucas's eyes narrowed. He wasn't used to being overruled, and Serena's tone said she was doing exactly that.

"I want protection, but I won't go into hiding. That's a deal breaker."

"Cobra and Constance are the best, but if you insist on being foolish, maybe you should choose another firm."

With that, her gaze shifted to assess me. Slowly, recognition shone in her green eyes.

In that instant, I also recognized her. She was no longer the skinny teenager from years ago. Of all the people to walk into our offices, what were the chances it would be her, Serena fucking Benson, the girl I'd never forgotten, the object of a million of my fantasies. Also, the one I could never approach. Her father had taught me that lesson the day he ruined me and killed my dreams. If it hadn't been for him...

"I can afford the best," she said, turning back to Lucas. "And Bill Covington says your firm is the best. Is he wrong? Is my case too difficult for you to take on? Is your only solution to lock me away in a safe house?"

I hid a smirk behind my hand. Her play was a good one, using Lucas's ego against him, and his relationship with the Covingtons as well. The bedraggled look was deceiving. This woman was cunning and strong-willed.

"There's nothing we can't handle," Lucas said. His dark brown eyes became almost black with controlled anger.

She pivoted to me. "Are you really that good?"

I'd never been challenged like that before. "Yes."

After a second, she nodded. "No safe house. I will not be chased away from my home, my work, or my family."

At *family*, I checked her hand. No ring, but that didn't mean anything.

"Okay, not the safe house," Lucas said.

After a single knock, the door opened, and Constance entered. "Lucas, Winston said you wanted me?"

"Yes. Constance, this is Serena Benson, a new protection client."

Constance offered her a hand. "Nice to meet you, Serena."

They shook hands. "You too."

"Serena was run off the road in the hills," Lucas explained.

"Oh, that's terrible," Constance replied.

Serena locked onto Lucas. "I will not be hidden away. I will continue my normal schedule and activities without restriction from you or..." She looked my way. "...or anybody."

Lucas tried to hide his annoyance, but I saw the clench of his jaw. "We will secure your house, and you can continue your normal activities. But this will only work if my team accompanies you when you are out and you follow all their instructions. If they see a threat and think it's necessary to remove you from a situation, you will not object. Do we understand each other?"

I wished he'd said those words about following instructions when we'd taken on Ariana as a client.

"I understand perfectly." Serena turned to look at me. She didn't blink, and her pale-green eyes held a determination I'd rarely seen off the battlefield. Behind the blood and the dirt, she was a strong natural beauty, and I bet she knew it.

For a moment, Freddy's words came back to me. "*You need a strong woman by your side for the long haul.*" Serena struck me as that kind of strong. I blinked away the memory, needing to lock down that shit. After what happened with Marilyn, I didn't want or need a woman long term, strong or not.

Lucas nodded, seeming satisfied that he'd won the round.

"To clarify," she said. "I work at the EPA on Wilshire. It's a secure federal building with armed guards, metal detectors, the works. They won't be able to follow me inside."

Lucas looked my way.

"I'll get an office nearby, and you can notify me when you're leaving the building," I suggested.

"That's a good start," Lucas said. "Constance is technically still a Secret Service consultant. So if we determine we should also be in the building, we can arrange credentials to get her inside."

I looked over at Constance, surprised. She hadn't mentioned that consultant tidbit to me.

"I'd rather play that by ear," Serena said. "I don't want my coworkers to know. Nobody knows."

Lucas nodded. "We'll keep this as discreet as possible."

Serena eyed my boots. "Outside the office, we may also be going places where your current attire doesn't fit in."

"He can adapt," Lucas quipped.

I smirked. "I can even shower if the occasion requires it."

Constance bit back her laugh.

Lucas drilled me with his don't-piss-off-the-client glare. "Should I assume we'll bill your father?" he asked, turning back to Serena.

Her father must have been a previous client.

"No," Serena blurted. "This is my business. You aren't to tell my father anything about this."

Lucas shifted. "That may be difficult."

"Not a thing," Serena emphasized. She straightened in a way that had me noticing her chest, an asset I'd been trying very hard to ignore. She had a surprising amount of spunk. I'd give her that.

Lucas's jaw ticked. "If you don't comply with Cobra's requirements, we'll withdraw and notify—"

"I get it," she said, interrupting what was likely a threat to tell her father.

"Very well." He rose and offered her his hand.

She stood as well, her leg calmer now than it had been, and shook with him.

"I'll let you three get started with the debrief in conference room one, and I'll join in a minute. First group meet at seven."

A whole-group meeting to launch a new client and then regular updates to the group was one of the things I liked about how Lucas ran his operation—a holdover from his time in Omega.

24

Standing, I opened the door for Serena. "You can start by telling us every-thing that happened today. Second door on the right."

As she exited, just her proximity made me gulp. The grime, the cuts, and the blood stains did little to hide the fact that grown-up Serena was a total smoke show.

Lucas was dialing his phone when I closed the door.

Following her down the hall, I couldn't help but notice the sway of her fine ass. She wasn't a cookie-cutter, stick-figure airhead like Ariana. No, Serena was a real woman, intelligent and determined. If it weren't for that entitled attitude… *"I will not be hidden away. I will continue my normal schedule and activities."* Yada, yada, yada. I pulled open the conference room door for her.

She entered and sat gingerly.

I closed the door after Constance.

My partner asked the first question. "Why don't you want us to talk to your father?"

"I just don't," Serena said, wringing her hands. There was a story there that we obviously weren't getting today. "My nickel, my rules."

There was that attitude again. *He, or she, who has the gold makes the rules.* It seemed I was stuck babysitting another spoiled brat from an insanely rich family.

CHAPTER 5

SERENA

THE CONFERENCE ROOM CRACKLED WITH ANTICIPATION.

The Duke Sparrow I'd known from camp had been tall but gangly, nothing like the massive man in front of me today who looked like he could lift an elephant. His dazzling gray eyes looked straight through me with an intensity I wasn't used to. His dark hair was in need of a cut. With a strong jaw and a short beard just beyond stubble, he wasn't classically handsome. Yet Duke exuded a very masculine power that sent a tingle down my spine.

The sixty-four-thousand-dollar question was, did he remember me from summer camp? After their initial questions, quiet had settled over us. "Where do we start?" I asked.

Duke—or Cobra as his boss had called him—opened a mini fridge. "Water?"

"Yes, please."

Constance declined with a wave of her hand. Her bob cut fit my view of a woman in the Secret service, but she was short and I always pictured their agents being tall.

My eyes trained on Duke's strong forearms as he brought the water to the table. It wasn't my fault. I blamed it on him for rolling up his sleeves and flashing forearm porn. With those hands, I'd bet he had a hell of a handshake.

He sat and slid the bottle forward. "It's been a long time, Serena." *Question answered.*

Puzzlement flashed on Constance's face. "Cobra, you two know each other?"

26

I snatched the water and opened it, not meeting Duke's eyes. "We met a long time ago as teenagers," I said as nonchalantly as possible, ignoring the twist in my stomach and remembering the lie. My heart skittered. If he mentioned the note, I was going to die of embarrassment over my teenage crush on him.

He merely nodded.

"Back then, I knew him as Duke Sparrow." I had been Serena Rose. The camp was big on not bringing our backgrounds with us, so our nametags had been first name and cabin name only. I blushed, remembering those times. I'd imagined him as Captain Jack Sparrow from the movie, only more clean cut.

He gave me a slight wave. "It's Duke Hawk, but you can call me Cobra."

"Wait, you're Lucas's brother?"

He nodded. "Guilty as charged."

We needed to move this along. "How does this debrief business work?" I chugged from the bottle.

"Men like your father don't like to be left in the dark," Constance said, a dog unwilling to give up a bone.

I almost coughed up my water at the mention of being in the dark. "Tough," I spat. The room felt suddenly colder, and I wrapped my arms around myself. I was not reliving the darkness, the nightmare.

She continued. "Maybe if you let my boss—"

"No." I slammed the water bottle down harder than I should have. "A hundred times, *no*."

Constance's face contorted. Clearly, she didn't like my answer.

Screw that. I was done, done, done with having my controlling father run things. After a calming breath, I lowered my anger level. "I'm old enough to have my own life. Your boss agreed. We keep my dad out of this. End of subject."

Duke settled it. "Agreed."

If Constance had a problem with that, she kept it hidden.

Duke appraised me for a moment and, thankfully, moved on. "Let's start with why you think you need us." He phrased the question just as Bill Covington had, with the implication that I was a neurotic, scared woman seeing nonexistent threats around every corner.

I felt my face reddening and stabbed my finger against the table, done with men not taking me seriously. "I don't think. I *know*. I was intentionally run off the road, and the guy wanted information about a USB stick he thought I had. He threatened to kill me. He would've torched my car to finish the job if some Good Samaritan hadn't come along and interrupted him."

"Take it easy," Constance urged. "Give us facts."

I ramped up my volume. "Fact one: he fucking ran me off the road." I shivered. "Fact two: the car ended upside down. I was trapped inside with gasoline leaking. Fact three: he started down the hill with a cigarette lighter in his hand, not a cell phone to call nine-one-one. No, a fucking lighter. He planned to roast me." I couldn't stop trembling.

Duke reached over and placed his massive hand over mine. "Serena, we believe you."

I looked over at Constance, and she nodded.

The soothing quality of Duke's voice contrasted with the zing of electricity his touch sent through me. The crush I'd had for him flared back to life like a smoldering fire fed fresh oxygen.

"Serena," he added, holding my eyes captive with his piercing gray ones. "I'll keep you safe. We'll keep you safe." He didn't let go of my hand. "But we have to ask all the questions, the hard ones, the stupid ones, and the insulting ones."

I nodded, gripping his hand like a lifeline. "Well, you got the insulting part right. Now let me help you with a stupid one. I didn't cut anyone off, tailgate, or anything. This wasn't road rage. I didn't flip anyone off."

He nodded. "I understand."

Somehow, his two words calmed me. "If it was you…" I looked between the two of them. "Would you choose the safe house?" Had I been too quick to dismiss it?

Constance deferred to Duke.

"You want the truth?" he asked.

I nodded. When our eyes connected, I saw the same kind eyes from years ago —and something else. I knew he was one of the rare men I could trust.

"Once you start running from your fear, you're condemned to be on the run forever. You have to face it as best you can, because the alternative is never being free of it."

Constance nodded silently.

His answer was different, but eerily similar to my therapist's advice.

I took a breath. "What would you like to know?"

Constance started. "Do you know of anyone who would want to hurt you?"

"No." That wasn't precisely correct, but Harvey Fox had been locked up in jail for years.

"Did you see his face?" Duke asked. "The man who attacked you?"

I nodded. "From a distance, yes, but I don't know him."

"What kind of vehicle?" Constance asked.

"A big, black SUV. I don't know what kind. I'm not a car person."

"Do you remember any part of the license number?"

"It didn't have a plate on the front."

Constance opened a notepad. "Have you received any threats? Phone hangups, anything like that?"

"No." I shook my head. "Nothing—wait a minute. I forgot to mention that I got a note on my windshield this morning. I'd parked on the street, down a few houses from mine, and I thought somebody had mistaken my car for one of my neighbors'. The note said to leave the USB stick under the red bush or else. Almost everybody has a red bush, and I had no idea what *the stick…*" I added air quotes. "…meant, so I ignored it."

"Can we see the note?" Constance asked.

"It's in my purse."

"Which didn't travel with her to the hospital," Duke added.

Constance took down a note. "Have you noticed anybody following you, lurking around, anything out of the ordinary in your neighborhood recently?"

I'd already asked myself the same thing. "No."

Duke sat back. "Run us through your day."

It confused me how much I wished he was still holding my hand. "I started in the office on Wilshire, the same as any other day. Well, not exactly the same, because I just got a promotion, and this was my first day out in the field." I explained my previous position and how I'd been selected by the merit review board for my new job in external auditing. "Which means I go out into the field now to check on companies."

Unlike Constance, Duke didn't take any notes.

The door opened, and Lucas Hawk joined us, taking a seat next to Duke. With a buzz cut, dark brown almost black eyes, and a deep voice that cut through you, he was scarier than I remembered, a lot scarier. But that circumstance had been very different from today.

Thankfully, Lucas didn't acknowledge having met me before. "What did I miss?" he asked.

"The incident was definitely intentional," Duke said. "She saw him but doesn't know him."

That relaxed me a little. At least Duke believed me.

"But she hasn't received any threats," Constance added. "Or have any reason to suspect anyone in particular. So we don't have a suspect yet."

"Nope." I shook my head.

"Go ahead," Duke urged me.

"Right. I had two meetings in Thousand Oaks. After I finished the meetings, I started back to the office." I explained when I'd first noticed the SUV, my call with my brother, how I'd considered stopping at the fire station but didn't, and how the SUV had finally run me off the road. Then I explained what I remembered from after the crash—the man in the leather jacket and then the other person who stopped at the crash.

"Back up a second," Lucas said. "Are you sure it was a lighter he was holding and not something else?"

"Positive." I'd already reviewed that part in my head. "He flicked the flame on and off as a threat and he yelled about telling him where the stick was."

Lucas's brow creased. "And what was that about a deer?"

"I had to swerve right to keep from hitting it. Deer collisions cause two hundred deaths a year in this country. I didn't want to be one of those."

"And this was when?" Lucas asked. "In relation to going off the road?"

"Right before," I admitted. From Lucas's look, it was clear where this was going.

Great. He didn't believe me about the lighter, and he didn't think my crash was related to me being chased and hit by Black Jacket Guy either. He thought I was just a girl who couldn't drive. He'd ignored the part about the guy demanding information from me.

After a knock at the door, another man poked his head in. "Vladimir Zolotarev is on the phone, and he doesn't want to wait."

"Thanks, Winston," Lucas said, looking a little relieved. "I need to take this. You guys carry on without me." A second later, he was gone.

I looked back at Duke and Constance. Even I wasn't sure where things stood now. This day could not get any worse. *Are you sure, Serena? Maybe you're being paranoid.*

❧

DUKE

THE BOSSMAN LEFT TO TAKE ZOLOTAREV'S CALL. ARIANA HAD PROBABLY CALLED Daddy to complain about how I hadn't given her enough freedom to interact with her fans, but thank God she was no longer my problem.

"Duke," Serena prodded, pulling me back to my current assignment.

The defeat in her eyes made me want to hold her and tell her it would be all right. Because of the deer question, she thought Lucas had written her off. But I knew better. My brother hadn't gotten where he was by jumping to conclusions with zero hard information.

Serena sighed. "What now?"

I held out my hand. "Let me see your phone. I'd like to review your messages." Prior communications often held clues in a case like this.

"The car rolled, and I couldn't find it after the accident."

Constance wrote a note. "I'd like to take you to the med center to get you looked at. It's a good idea after an—"

"I've been there. CAT scan was negative," Serena said, looking down.

"Why didn't they clean your cuts?" Constance asked before I could.

Emergency care had gone to shit if they let her out looking like this.

Her leg started trembling again. "I checked myself out early."

"Why?" I asked.

"I think I saw him."

"The guy with the lighter?"

She nodded. "Yeah."

"It's certainly too late now," Constance commented, anticipating my train of thought. Hospitals didn't do security cameras inside—patient privacy.

Winston opened the door. "The boss needs you both."

Must be time to listen to Ariana's father rant about how rude I'd been to his daughter. I forced a nod. "Winston, would you mind cleaning up Serena's wounds?" We'd circle back to what she saw at the hospital.

Serena's eyes widened. She was a skittish one.

I patted her hand since that had seemed to settle her earlier. The zing of contact with her was a warning that, after all this time, I hadn't forgotten the suggestion of her note. I pulled my hand back. That memory lane was best not traveled. "Excuse us while we go talk to our boss," I told her. "Winston will take good care of you, and we'll be right back."

She blinked before nodding acceptance. What she'd been through had clearly terrified her.

Constance handed her a pen. "If he gets out of line, stab him with this. That's what I do."

That pulled a giggle and a warm smile from her.

I wished I could see more of that smile.

CHAPTER 6

SERENA

MY EYES LINGERED ON DUKE AS HE WALKED TO THE DOOR WITH CONSTANCE. THE man he'd become was even more magnetic than the boy had been. I rubbed my hand, still feeling the echo of his touch.

After they left to visit with Lucas, the large man who'd been sitting across the hall stepped out a moment and then returned with a huge first aid bag. He set it on the table and opened it up. "Hi. Like Cobra said, I'm Winston."

"Serena." I left off my last name, as I usually did. "Is it a job requirement that you guys all be six-three and two-twenty or something?"

"Sometimes it helps, but Constance stands five-three, and she can sometimes kick my ass. I don't dare ask her weight."

Appropriately chastised for making generalizations, I nodded and stayed quiet.

He retrieved glasses with a magnifier and flipped on the attached bright light. I relaxed as he took his time examining my injuries. I was safe here. He sat back after finishing. "Car accident?"

I nodded. "Is it that obvious?"

He tapped the bridge of his nose. "A cut from glasses being hit by the airbag is not uncommon. You should've gone to the emergency room."

I didn't appreciate the lecture. *Serena, you should have…* I tried truth for a change. "I did, but was too scared to stay."

"Ahhhhh," he drew out the sound. "Cobra and Constance will keep you safe."

"Is he that good? I mean, are they?"

"Yup. The best." Winston nodded and pulled out tweezers. "Just don't tell Cobra I said that," he whispered.

I liked this guy's easygoing approach. "Deal."

He brought the tweezers up to my face. "Close your eyes and hold still. You have some debris I want to remove."

I did as I was told and only felt two light pricks.

"This will sting a little," Winston said.

When I opened my eyes, an antiseptic pad hovered near the cut on the bridge of my nose. I nodded and closed my eyes.

It did sting, but not as much as all the accusing eyes and questions had today. *Serena, that doesn't make sense. Are you sure, Serena?* I'd heard every variation of the comments and questions. You'd think I had something tattooed on my forehead that said *believe at own risk*.

After my nose had been addressed, I opened my eyes to watch. "That's a pretty big kit."

Winston wiped my next cut. "In this line of work, we need more than the usual office does." He carefully applied antiseptic ointment and a bandage. "Shirt off." The next cut was on my side.

I heard the word *deer* come from Lucas's office and tensed up. I knew what I had to do. I'd been a young girl the first time I met Lucas Hawk, and he still saw me that way. They didn't believe me, none of them. "I think I'd rather have a nurse—"

He backed away and raised his hands. "If you'd prefer a woman, that's okay."

I improvised. "Cobra said to go home, but I don't have any money on me. He said you could get me an Uber?"

Winston zipped up his bag. "I'll set up the Uber to take you by the emergency room first and wait to take you home. That wound needs to be treated."

"Thank you." Anything to speed up my escape.

A MINUTE LATER, OUTSIDE THE HAWK SECURITY BUILDING, I CLIMBED INTO THE BACK of the Uber Winston had called and closed the door. It had been a mistake to tell them about the deer. Now, I needed to start over again and find a replacement bodyguard service.

As the car pulled away from the curb, my heart raced. I couldn't help but look behind us for the black SUV. It might not be rational, but fear gripped me. Yes, I felt Bill was right that I needed professional protection, but I wouldn't work with, couldn't work with, someone who treated me like a little girl and didn't take me seriously. *Serena are you sure that's what happened?* I was sick of it.

The driver checked me out in the mirror. It only took her two blocks to ask, "What happened to you?"

Why was my life like Groundhog Day, everybody asking me the same questions over and over? "Car accident." It sounded more believable than *escaped a murder attempt.* That's what it was, though, right? I discarded that thought. I couldn't let Lucas's skepticism cloud my judgment.

"Ah. That's why the hospital first."

"No. I changed my mind. Home, please."

She shook her head. Everybody was judging me today.

I tried deep breathing. It didn't help. My heart felt like it wanted to burst out of my chest. How had Black Jacket Guy known to follow me up onto the hill road? Had I just not seen him? Was I paranoid? Fuck no, I'd been scared out of my wits—almost dying tended to do that to you.

As we drove, I thought back to being in the meeting room with Duke. The moment our hands touched... How could such a big man's touch be so gentle? It brought back memories of summer camp—not that I'd had his hands on me back then. But I did remember the kindness of his smile, the kindness in his eyes. Kindness was a trait that fit him. That's why I'd written the note. Yes, up until that last day, it had been a good summer.

∼

Duke

I COULD SEE THAT LUCAS WAS ABOUT TO LOSE IT. HE'D BROUGHT CONSTANCE AND ME in to listen to Mr. Zolotarev rant about us "walking away" while his daughter was attacked, and I'd calmly explained my side of the tale. But then just as it seemed like the Russian was winding down, he ramped back up again.

"How can you let this happen?" he exploded through the phone, his accent thicker than usual. "She has cut on face. How can actress work with cut on face?"

"She fired us when I tried to pull her out of a dangerous situation," I explained again. "She told me you said she had the power to fire us and told me to leave, so I did."

"She not hire you," Zolotarev yelled. "I hire you. I fire you."

Now I was getting pissed. He had no right to talk to me that way.

Lucas leveled me with a stare. "I'll put a different man on her."

34

"No." The word was loud across the phone line.

"Mr. Zolotarev—"

"I say no. I find others. You filth."

"Then have a nice day." Lucas punched the squawk box off. "Fucking asswipe, calling us filth. I should have never taken him on." He shook his head and turned to Constance.

"She had nothing to do with this," I explained. "I told her we'd been fired from the account and to come back to the office."

"Right." Lucas was back to shaking his head. "Before I forget—about the new girl, a deer?" he asked. "What do you make of that?"

I shrugged. "Too early to know for sure, but I believe her."

"Seems fishy to me," Lucas said.

"It does, but if she wanted to lie, wouldn't she choose something more believable?"

Lucas shrugged. "Probably."

The desk phone rang.

"Zolotarev again," Lucas said wearily. He accepted the call and put it on the squawk box. "Hawk here."

"What you do to punish this man for he not protect my daughter? He needs pay."

Lucas's face twisted into a snarl. "How I deal with my employees is my business, not yours."

"Your man will pay for letting this happen my daughter, and you will pay."

"Mr. Zolotarev, you are no longer a client of ours. Do not call again." Lucas punched the phone hard to end the call. "That's one angry mother." He looked up at me.

The full weight of his glare landed on me as his scary-motherfucker face took shape. There was a reason the name *Lucas Hawk* struck fear in anyone who knew him—or of him. "That is not acceptable. Protection means you protect at all costs, and the last person you let scare you away is the client. You don't need to like her. You don't need to respect her. I don't care what her father told her. You need to stay and protect her no matter what until I—" He punched the table with a finger. "—say not to. Me and nobody else. Am I clear?"

I nodded. "Yes, sir," Constance and I said simultaneously.

I prided myself on not being scared of anybody, but right now, my brother was the exception. When his voice took on that tone, the former Delta operator could scare you to death without raising his deadly finger.

Everyone in the spec ops community knew the story. It was a documented fact that he'd once killed an enemy with a single, well-placed stab of that finger. The battlefield was littered with men who'd underestimated my brother.

His voice grew louder. "If you're not strong enough to stand up to a little woman who tells you to piss off, I don't need you. You get me?" he said, pointing.

"Yes, sir. Sorry, sir." I'd never felt worse for letting a man down.

"Duke, don't ever pull out of an assignment again. You sure screwed the pooch. And you'd better watch your back. That is one pissed off Russian father, and in my experience, they can be fucking unpredictable."

My stomach churned. "Understood." This was not the kind of lecture you survived a second time.

He looked between the two of us. "Now. Moving on, keep the Benson girl safe and find the asshole. This job is important to both the Covingtons and the Bensons, so do us proud. They are not families I want to be on the wrong side of."

"Copy that," I said, standing. Both families had infinite money and powerful connections.

"Yes, sir," Constance echoed.

Once out of the office, I sighed. Lesson learned: stick with the client, period.

"Do you need to change your pants?" Constance asked with a giggle. "I don't have spare men's underwear, but I do have some sweats in the desk and wet wipes."

"Very funny." It had gotten close to being that bad.

"What the hell did you do?" Winston asked in a hushed voice when we reached his desk.

"You heard that?"

"Hard not to when he's pissed."

I opened the door to the conference room. It was empty. "Where'd you stash the girl?"

He lifted a shoulder. "She said you told her to leave, so I arranged an Uber to the hospital and then home."

"Fuck. Text me the home address. Constance, you've got the hospital." I ran down the hall.

Fuck me. A few minutes into the case, and I'd already lost track of my new client. Lucas was going to skin me alive.

Once I was in the car and on the way, I called Winston. "Hey, man, find out where they towed her car. We need to check it out. Serena said she was hit from behind and swerved off the road because of a deer."

"You don't believe her?" he asked.

"Lucas is skeptical, so we trust but verify. It was in the hills, so—"

"Start with the sheriff's office," Winston said, continuing my thought. "Also, paint transfer might give us a clue once we narrow down the suspect pool."

"Exactly." I loved that we were often on the same wavelength in investigations.

"On it."

I pressed the gas pedal harder. I was getting eyes back on Serena pronto before she did something stupid and got herself hurt.

~

SERENA

MY GARDENER'S TRUCK AND TRAILER WERE IN FRONT OF MY HOUSE. OTHERWISE, IT was eerily quiet when the Uber stopped. I checked both directions down the street for that black SUV, then thanked the driver and exited.

Marco, my gardener, came out of the side gate, pushing his mower, and immediately stopped, his mouth falling open. "Miss Benson, what happened to you?" I was going to get a lot of that today.

"Car accident," I explained.

He rushed over. "Can I help?"

I shook my head and waved him off. "I'll be fine. How are things with Angela?"

He brightened. "She forgave me. That spa day gift certificate idea of yours did the trick." Marco had had lost his wife to the horrors of cancer. Even though he was a very nice guy, he hadn't had any luck dating until he met, Angela, a thirty-something cashier on a late-night visit to the grocery store.

"I'm glad." My suggestion had been to go beyond flowers. I told him every girl liked some pampering now and then.

"And that other thing…" He blushed. "…She loved it."

I'd recommend a foot massage to make up, since I guessed she spent a fair amount of her time on her feet. "That's great."

He pointed to the pile of bark on my driveway. "Oscar is sick today. Can we spread it next week?"

I nodded. "Sure. No problem."

After he loaded his mower and drove off, I checked both directions down the street for that black SUV, before walking to the side yard, lifting the fake stone, and pulling out the spare key my brother and I kept there. He only stayed here occasionally, so it made things easier. And at least one thing had gone right today —I didn't have to break a window to get back into our house.

Closing the front door behind me, I flipped the deadbolt. Finally, relief settled over me. I was safe. I froze when the landline rang. We almost never used it, but Dad had insisted we have it in case of an earthquake, power outage, or dead cell phone battery.

I picked up when the caller ID indicated my brother Zach. "Hello?" I answered tentatively, in case it had been spoofed.

"I heard you had an accident," Zach said. "And you're not answering your cell. What happened? Are you okay? Do you need anything? I could loan you a car."

I waited until the barrage of questions ended. "That fink Vincent told you, didn't he?" I was going to get back to him for not keeping this to himself.

"He worries about you. We all do. So what happened?"

"Car accident in the hills. I'm a little banged up, but nothing time won't heal, and it was a work car, so my wheels are fine. The only thing you can do to help is make sure it doesn't go any further. I don't want Mom or Dad to hear about this."

"I get ya. They won't hear it from me," he promised. Zach had seen Dad's smothering first hand.

"I gotta go, Zach. But everything's good. Thanks for calling."

"Later."

I put the phone back in its cradle. Yes, I was safe here, but I had to figure out my next steps. I needed to call work. That was a given, but inhaling some food was higher on my priority list.

I checked the fridge and decided a yogurt was the quickest way to take the edge off my hunger. My shoulder hurt, and a peek inside my shirt showed I was going to have a nice seatbelt bruise as well.

Dad's advice echoed in my head, "*First things first.*" The question of why me didn't have an easy answer, so it would have to wait. I needed to get cleaned up and call work. Plus, I needed to get my purse and phone, and get my life back on track.

Scraping the bottom of my yogurt cup, I pondered that. Maybe it hadn't been such a great idea to escape the hospital in a rush. Would my things be there, or in my car at some junkyard, waiting to be stolen?

After that would come the search for protection. Of all my brothers, Dennis and Vincent were the most likely to help me without tipping off our parents, but I now knew Vincent was negotiating for a job in Boston working for Bill Covington. He could be leaving any day, which made Dennis my best choice.

Since he was away on business, it probably made more sense to call Dennis this evening. *A Benson always picks herself up and gets on with life.* I'd learned the hard way that I had to face my fears and live. But I was safe here, and getting on with my life could wait a few hours.

Maybe a nice hot bath…

Ding.

The loud ding startled me, sending the almost empty yogurt cup and my spoon to the floor. I froze in place, my heart racing.

It was the front yard sensor—somebody was walking up to the house.

There had to be one or two good reasons for somebody to be at the door, but the one very bad one dominated my mind—I'd walked away from protection, and my pursuer had found me.

CHAPTER 7

DUKE

WHEN PRESSING THE BUZZER AND KNOCKING ON THE DOOR GOT NO RESPONSE, I bellowed, "Serena, open up." She had to be here. This was the address she'd given Winston for the Uber driver.

Nothing.

I opened my phone and found a message I hadn't heard.

> WINSTON: Her things are at the Temple substation.

I sent a reply.

> ME: Who is the property owner of this address?

I waited.

> WINSTON: Two Benson Castle LLC

It figured. Opaque property ownership was a gimmick of the privileged, and she'd run to one of her father's properties.

After three more tries, a faint "Go away," came through the door. It was Serena's voice. At least I was at the right house.

"Open up, Serena." I stood back to look less imposing if she used the peephole.

"I'm going to use somebody else. Go away." Her voice wavered.

"No, you're not. I'm assigned to you, and you know it. No other firm would dare poach one of our clients." It sounded good, even if they'd have to know she was our client for it to apply.

"Consider yourself fired."

This time, I knew better than to listen. "You can't fire me."

"I just did. Can't you get that through your thick skull?"

I shook my head. "Until my boss tells me otherwise, you're my assignment. End of discussion. So let me in."

"No." After a pause, she added. "I'm going to take a shower. You better be gone when I'm done."

For a second, I imagined her naked in the shower, and my cock responded inappropriately. Wait, why was I reprimanding myself? She'd been the one to mention a shower. "Open the door, Princess."

"I'm nobody's princess." Her voice was angry now. She banged on the door. Yup, that pushed a button. The princess angle at least got her riled up enough to keep talking.

"Then stop acting like one."

"I'm damned well not letting you in to watch me shower."

I shifted. My dick liked the fantasy of her in the shower, the warm water caressing her body, flowing over her full tits and down to… *Get it together, Mr. Hornypants.* "You can't get your bandages wet."

"Leave, or I'll call the cops," she threatened.

I laughed as I adjusted my aching cock.

"What's so funny?"

"You won't do that."

"Wanna bet?"

I rolled out the nuclear option. "If you do that, your father will hear about all of this."

An exasperated sigh came from behind the door, but then the deadbolt clicked, and the door swung partially open.

She looked somewhat better, with bandages where earlier there had been raw cuts on her head and neck. "You would call my father, wouldn't you?"

"May I come in?"

She pulled open the door and stepped to the side. "I'm still ending your services."

I entered, careful to not crowd her. "That's above my pay grade. You'll need to talk to my boss about that. And he also said if you didn't follow protocol, he'd have to go to your father."

"I hate you." She groaned.

"Get in line." Hating me, but following procedure and staying alive, was better than the alternative.

The blood stain on the side of her shirt had grown. She apparently hadn't followed Winston's instructions and gone to the hospital.

I moved inside from the foyer and started with the room to my right, ignoring the blood soaking through her shirt. That would be next.

"What are you doing?"

"It's called clearing the house. It's standard procedure to make sure there isn't a threat inside." I pointed behind me. "Lock the door." I heard the deadbolt click as I moved to the next room.

She followed.

In the kitchen, I found a yogurt container and a spoon on the floor and tapped the counter. "Stay here while I finish the rest of the rooms."

After clearing the upstairs, I called Constance.

"She hasn't shown up here," Constance answered. "And nobody's asked about her either."

"I found her," I announced. "At her house. I've got her secured. Why don't you hang out there to see if the perp comes back looking for her?"

"Sure thing. I just love hospital vending machine food. How is she?"

"Stubborn, in denial about the threat." I didn't add *hot as fuck*.

I returned to the kitchen and pointed at the yogurt mess she hadn't cleaned up. "What happened?"

Serena scooped up the items and grabbed a paper towel. "Sorry. You scared the shit out of me. I thought you were..." Her words trailed off.

I filled the silence. "I know how stressful it can be to fear for your life."

"No. You don't."

Stopping, I turned. "I may not understand your particular fear, but trust me, I've been shot, mortared, and in situations that would make anyone soil their drawers."

"Sorry. I just meant... Never mind." Once again, she held something back. There was a particular fear that likely wouldn't come out today.

Her side needed to be treated. "Stay right here while I get my med kit from the car."

She *tsk*ed. "You sure are bossy."

I ignored the dig and returned quickly with our standard first aid kit, which was as full as a paramedic's bag.

Her eyes widened. "Are you expecting a war to break out or something?"

"It's good to be prepared. Now, shirt off." I tapped the dark granite kitchen island. "Hop up."

She huffed. "I can take care of this myself."

Nope, she sure didn't like orders or relying on anyone.

"It's my job. Now, shirt off."

With a sigh, she removed it, revealing a mouthwatering amount of cleavage in a black lace bra. She winced when she placed her hands on the surface to lift herself up, so I grabbed her hips and boosted her, putting my face way too close for comfort to her tantalizing tits. I turned her to the side so I could deal with the wound without having them in my face, but my cock had already noticed. Yes, Serena Benson had grown up to be a very beautiful woman and quite the temptress.

She gasped as I touched her side.

The gash wasn't deep, but it was long and already starting to redden. Half the bra strap had been sliced through as well.

She eyed me and snorted as her eyes slid lower. "Like what you see?"

Busted. "No. That's going to be quite the seatbelt bruise."

She glanced down at the diagonal mark. "Oh."

"And you should have had this cut cleaned earlier to avoid infection."

"I didn't…"

Down, boy. Of course my cock was still reacting to the lusciousness of her tits, but now was not the time to be thinking of that. I backed away and folded my arms. "I also see a woman who is taking headstrong all the way to self-destructive. A woman who won't listen to good advice."

It was her turn to fold her arms over her chest. "I am not. I was afraid he'd be at the hospital looking for me."

"Then you should have asked Winston to take you, or waited for me and Constance to get out of our meeting. Any of us would have taken you. You made a bad decision."

"Okay. So I got that wrong. That hardly qualifies as self-destructive."

"You also shouldn't have come back here alone." I prepared antiseptic wipes. "Winston told you to go to the hospital to get this cut looked at. Did you?" I added sarcasm. "No, of course not, because a princess like you knows better."

I wiped the lower section of the cut with antiseptic to clean it.

She pulled away. "Ouch."

"Don't be a baby." I dabbed at the cut more gently this time, then gave her the bad news. "I'm going to have to undo your bra to get at this."

"First take off my shirt, then my bra, what's next?" she sassed.

I wasn't touching that question. The obvious answer would have been, *Everything so I can check you thoroughly.* "I can still take you back to the hospital, if you want."

She shook her head. "No. Go ahead."

I undid the clasp and removed the shoulder strap on this side. Mentally I thanked her as she gripped the cups to keep from flashing me while I cleaned the gash. My dick couldn't take it. Then I took up the tweezers. "Lift your arm a little farther."

"It hurts." Her lips formed a pouty O, and my mind wandered to what those lips would feel like against mine, or wrapped around me.

I coughed to clear my head. "I have to get the tree branch out. Or do you want a piece of wood embedded in the scar for the rest of your life?"

"Tree branch?" she asked with a laugh.

"Fine. Keep it. It'll make a great conversation starter when you wear an evening gown to one of those swanky parties."

She lifted her arm even higher than I needed. "Go ahead." She sighed.

"That's good. Thank you." It took a few tries to dig the offender out. She flinched but didn't complain. "I got it." I brought the tweezers around to show her the splinter.

Her brows winged up. "That's big."

I nodded. "You can lower your arm now. Cross it over your chest." The margins were already an angry red. "You really should have gotten this cleaned and closed earlier."

"You said that."

I wiped the cut some more and located my glue. "Then you ran to this house without one of us."

"I'm safe here. This is my house."

"Wrong." I leaned down and examined the edges of the cut. "A little farther around with the arm. Squeeze your other breast with your forearm."

"Why?"

She was argumentative to a fault.

"I'm going to glue the cut shut, and we need the skin properly aligned to avoid a visible scar."

"Oh."

When she didn't get it right, I repositioned her arm over her boob. "Hold it there."

"Why was I wrong to come here?" she asked as I worked on the cut from back to front.

"Shh..." I'd finished half the cut. "Your attacker left a note on your car. He knows what you drive and where you live. He would also know his best chance was to catch you here, rather than risk guessing wrong about the several possible hospitals you might have gone to."

She gasped. "You're saying he could have been here waiting for me to come home?"

"Exactly." A chill ran through me. It could have gone that way, and I could have lost her.

I felt her shiver.

"Now, hold still while I finish." I completed the gluing, and it was a damned good job—well-aligned.

She sniffled. "I'm sorry. I was upset that you didn't believe me about the attack, you know, with all the questions about the deer."

"I believe you."

"Your boss doesn't." Resentment tinged her voice. "He's already judged me to be an emotional female making shit up."

"That's not true. Now you're the one jumping to unfounded conclusions."

Her eyes narrowed, but she didn't reply.

I applied antiseptic cream and a bandage. "Now you can go clean up and change, but washcloth only, no shower. You have to keep the bandages dry. Don't stretch the skin."

"Yes, sir," she spat with attitude as she slid off the island.

"And no bra. You don't want to rub that wound." I blinked twice to clear the vision of a braless Serena in a tight, thin T-shirt, nipples clearly visible, that popped into my mind. *Concentrate, man. Concentrate.*

She stopped and turned with a mischievous smile. "Are panties okay, or do I need to leave those off as well?"

She was killing me. "It's a medically based suggestion, nothing more."

After she left, I dialed Terry. Terrance Goodwin was our security system specialist.

"Cobra here. We have a new client who needs a whole-house system installed." I gave him the address.

"Sure thing. Do you want audio as well?"

"The works. Group meet is here at seven."

"Lucas mentioned it. Catch you then. I'll order the pizza."

After disconnecting, I cleaned up my bandage and wipe wrappers. Locating the trash bin under the sink, I found a surprise. A bouquet of red roses had been tossed, and they were fresh. I fished out the card that had come with them, then added my trash.

We need another chance. You know we belong together.
-G

Who the fuck was G, and why had she tossed these?

When Serena returned, she'd washed up and changed into jeans and a long-sleeve button down, and yes, she'd followed my braless suggestion. She spotted the two roses I'd laid on the counter along with the card.

"Going through my garbage, I see."

"When did these? Tell me about this guy. Could he be behind this?"

"He's my ex. It ended a while ago, but he's back in the country." She threw her hands up. "My dad and his have some deals together, so Dad thought… It doesn't matter. I'm over him, and he's having trouble understanding that."

"Last name?"

"Kittleman. But it's not him. I would've recognized him."

"Is he rich enough to hire someone to do his dirty work?"

Her mouth dropped open for a solid three-count. "His family is. But the stick question doesn't make any sense."

I agreed with that and moved on. "Is this your house?"

"Yes. Why?"

"I saw men's clothes when I cleared upstairs. Who's living with you? A boyfriend?" Why did I dislike that idea? Because it would make it harder to protect her with another person around—yeah, that sounded like a good reason.

She laughed. "No. Those are my brother Vincent's clothes, but he's not here much. Although on paper, the house is technically Dad's."

"Two Benson Castle LLC?"

She rolled her eyes. "It was a compromise to get released from Dad's house. I had to live with my brother, and Dad had to approve the neighborhood and the house." She shifted to a mock baritone. *"It's not safe for a young woman to live alone in this city."*

I nodded, not because I agreed, but because I'd begun to understand her efforts to put distance between herself and her overbearing father. My disgust with him grew with every word.

Serena was an adult, but her father treated her like a child, and that would grate on anybody. Picking out a dipshit boyfriend for her, dictating where she lived? This strong woman deserved better.

Leaning against the counter, I stuck my hands in my pockets. "You could have moved out and told him to stick it."

"And be accused of breaking up the family? No thanks. That would devastate my mom."

I found it interesting that she put her parents' feelings ahead of her own. "Do you feel well enough for a drive?"

"I guess." She was probably running on fumes, but I couldn't leave her alone.

"You lost your phone in the accident. How about we start by going to retrieve it and your purse from the sheriff's office?" I wanted a look at her message and call history for clues.

She perked up. "My purse?"

I nodded. "I expect so. They would collect obvious personal items of value. I also want to see that note."

That spark reappeared in her eyes. "Good. I can't lose my wallet."

"Go find some shoes, and I'll take you." With all the money her family had, why was she worried about a few bucks in her wallet?

~

THE VIEW FROM THE PASSENGER SEAT OF DUKE'S TALL SUBURBAN WAS SO MUCH better than from my low car. As I'd told them, I wasn't a car person, but I'd read the emblem on the door. As the traffic went by, I crossed my fingers that my wallet would be at the sheriff's station. Then, I looked over at my driver. When he returned my glance, I saw eyes that had softened from the warrior eyes he'd worn when he'd first barged into my house, determined to root out any intruders. Yes, Duke Hawk was a man of many facets.

The city went by in a blur as he drove us through the streets of west Los Angeles, and the episode with Mr. Black Jacket Guy played out in my head on repeat. I kept checking the mirror on my side. *Any black SUVs behind us?* No, but I did spot a half dozen in other colors.

The car search kept me from rehashing Duke's reaction to the flowers and to having seen Vincent's clothes upstairs. There'd been a flash of something akin to relief in his eyes when I'd explained about dipshit George and my brother. Maybe it was his professional reaction to reducing the suspect pool, or just maybe it wasn't. At some point, we'd have to talk about the note I'd given him that last day of camp.

I went back to watching the cars around us. What if the guy had taken his SUV through a car wash and rinsed off the watercolor black paint, leaving it blue or brown underneath? I'd seen a movie where the bank robbers did that, so it was possible.

Or I was paranoid. That was also possible. The telltale shake reappeared in my leg.

"What are you nervous about?" Duke asked.

"He's still out there. That's what."

"And what about that makes you nervous?" he asked.

"Don't you ever get scared?"

"Sure, everybody does. I didn't mean you couldn't be nervous. I'm just curious what you're nervous about." He seemed determined to use *nervous* instead of scared, a word choice clearly meant to be soothing.

"Do you think he'll try again? I mean, he came pretty close last time."

"Are you nervous that I won't be able to stop him?"

I hadn't considered that my insecurity was insulting. In Duke's presence was the one place I shouldn't be scared. "I didn't mean…"

He laid his hand over mine on the center console. "I'll keep you safe. You can count on that."

47

My leg calmed. I didn't know whether to attribute that to his words or the strength his touch conveyed, but my tension eased. Instead of pulling my hand away, I turned it over to grip his. He was suddenly my anchor.

I shifted my focus from what was outside the vehicle to what was inside—or rather, who. Years ago, the kind eyes of the boy I'd known had intrigued me. His touch now was so much better than my teenage fantasies.

He'd changed since then, and not just physically. There was a hardness to him. Obviously, we'd both been through things the other didn't know about.

My eyes traveled to a tattoo that showed on his forearm.

> If knocked down,
> I will get back up,
> every time.

I tapped it with my free hand. "Is there a story behind this?"

He glanced down before returning his eyes to the road. His jaw clenched. "It's a line from the SEAL creed."

"You were a SEAL?"

He nodded. Unlike my dipshit ex, George, who liked to boast about having been a SEAL, Duke was the strong, silent type.

He glanced down again as I ran a finger over his ink. "It's important to you?"

Suddenly, he jerked his hand away, hitting the horn.

I looked up to find a car headed for us. I jammed my feet against the floorboards. Closing my eyes, I braced for my second crash of the day.

CHAPTER 8

DUKE

"HOLD ON," I YELLED. TAPPING THE BRAKES, I WHIPPED THE WHEEL TO THE RIGHT, then the left, and then right again, the tires complaining loudly. "Fuck, that was close."

The tiny car that drifted across the center line missed us by about a foot. Only when the horn got her attention did the young girl behind the wheel finally look up from her phone and swerve back to her side of the road. She probably pissed herself. *Good.*

"Fuck," Serena screeched, looking behind us. "Do you think that was…?"

"Not unless your attacker was a teenage girl watching her phone more than the road." When I glanced over, her eyes told the story.

She was hyperventilating. "Almost killed twice in one day," she gasped. "That has to be a record."

Shaking my head, I gave her the truth. "We would have been fine, but that girl would have…"

"Died," she finished for me.

I nodded, letting out a slow breath. "A toy car like that, head-on against this big truck only ends with bad news for her." I hoped the incident had scared some sense into that kid.

The near miss had rattled Serena terribly. Her telltale leg twitch reappeared, and the hand she put on the console shook.

I should have kept a professional distance and resisted the dangerous invita-

49

tion for physical contact. But I was only human, and seeing her in distress hit a weak spot in my armor. She might be a spoiled brat, but she was mine to protect and to console.

"I understand that scared you, but trust me, I'll keep you safe." I laid my hand over hers again.

She relaxed, which had been my intention. Her skin was soft and warm, and my mind quickly wondered what other parts of her would feel like, which had very much *not* been my intention.

"Thank you." She clasped her other hand over mine, trapping me, unless I wanted to be rude and pull it away.

"For what?"

"For understanding." A few seconds later, she added, "You believe me about the guy, don't you? The guy who attacked me?"

"Yes, I do."

I LED SERENA INTO THE SHERIFF'S SUBSTATION AND LET MYSELF RELAX. INSIDE HERE I didn't need to worry about protecting her from an anonymous man only she could identify. Black pants and a black leather jacket weren't enough to rule anyone out.

"Hey there, Cobra," Deputy Noreen Skagmont purred from behind the counter. "It's been too long."

It had been a year since her first come-on, and a month since I'd last been in here. She wasn't giving up yet.

I nodded rather than agree with her. "Hi, Noreen. This is Serena Benson."

Noreen didn't give Serena a glance. "As I recall, you owe me a dinner, big guy."

"It was lunch," I corrected.

"My goodness," Noreen exclaimed, finally noticing Serena's cuts. "Did he beat you up? I can arrest him for that."

"Really?" Serena asked, bringing a finger to her chin.

"Yeah, but he might like the cuffs." Noreen giggled.

I leaned against the counter. "Serena was in an accident up in the hills today," I explained, trying to get us off the crazy train. "They transported her to UCLA. I'm told you have her belongings?"

"On North Sepulveda," Serena supplied.

Noreen's brow scrunched. "You know, with interest accrued, lunch should now be dinner."

Serena shifted, an amused look on her face.

Noreen didn't move to her keyboard, as I'd expected. "Do we have a deal?" she asked.

Serena nudged me.

I wrapped an arm around Serena's waist and looked down with my best smile. "What do you say, honey? Will you let me go to dinner with Noreen?"

"No." Serena melted into me, playing it beautifully. "Sorry, Deputy," she said with syrupy sweetness. "He's taken."

Noreen eyed us suspiciously.

Serena's warmth against me ignited an urge to pull her closer, an urge I gave in to, telling myself it was only a subterfuge to get out of a dinner with Noreen. It made sense.

Serena looked up, and I swore a hint of desire lit her eyes. She lifted up on her toes to press her lips to mine.

I leaned into the kiss, feeling the softness of her lips, the slightest moan as my tongue slid across them. I then brought my hand up to run my thumb along the underside of her breast.

Serena's whimper as I teased her breast was Oscar-worthy. Her hand locked behind my neck, giving her leverage as she deepened the kiss, seeking more, exploring more, the ultimate temptress. Noreen's exaggerated cough reminded me to break it off. This was just for show. At least that's what I told myself as my heart sped into full-blown attraction speed.

Serena blinked rapidly as I pulled away. Had she only meant the kiss to throw the deputy off, or had she wanted to follow up on that note from years ago?

It didn't fucking matter. She was a client now and nothing more, acting and nothing more, the daughter of the man who'd ruined my dreams and nothing more. *Nothing the fuck more.*

Noreen huffed. "You could have just said she was your girlfriend." She clicked her mouse furiously. "North Sepulveda?"

"That's right," Serena said.

I kept a possessive arm around her.

"The make of car?" Noreen asked.

"I don't remember. White sedan, government plates," Serena answered.

Noreen checked her screen and stood. "We did get a government car in today." She held her hand out. "ID?"

"My purse was in the car." Serena stated the obvious. "That's why I'm here."

Pulling my mind away from the kiss and back to the case, I volunteered, "I'll vouch for her identity."

Noreen scowled. "Your credibility is zilch, big guy. Let me check the box to see what we have, but if her ID isn't in there, I can't release anything from the car." She wandered away, muttering under her breath.

I released Serena from my arm. "Thanks for the save."

She elbowed me. "If I don't get my stuff, I'm going to send you on that dinner date."

I rolled my eyes.

"You owe me big time," she said, tugging my earlobe—hard. "You hear me?"

I rubbed my ear. "Loud and clear."

Another deputy, a man I didn't recognize, arrived at the counter and eyed Serena. "Can I help you, miss?"

When his gaze lingered way too long, I answered for her. "Thank you, but my girlfriend's already being helped."

He didn't leave until I gave him the glare that said she was mine.

Noreen returned with a plastic box and set it on the floor behind the counter. "I gotta make sure this is really your stuff. You understand? Describe your purse."

"It's black leather," Serena said. "A Gucci shoulder bag with a horse bit on the side."

The handbag that cost a month's rent was more confirmation that she was a spoiled little rich girl.

Noreen rummaged in the box. "And the phone?"

"An iPhone in rose gold."

Noreen rummaged around. "And what do we have here? What's the title of the book?" Noreen prodded.

Serena turned beet-red. "*Secretary to the Bazillionaire*," she mumbled.

I smirked with just the shortest chuckle.

Serena elbowed me. "Don't judge. It's a good book."

Noreen held it up. A bare-chested guy on the cover confirmed what I'd suspected from the title. "You say it's good?"

"If you like spicy, yes," Serena said. "The author is terrific."

Now, I was getting uncomfortable.

"I'll order it," Noreen said, hefting the box onto the counter and putting the book away. "I still need to verify your ID."

Serena opened the purse, retrieved a wallet, and pulled out a driver's license.

After a signature, a smiling Serena lifted the purse to her shoulder. "Thank you, deputy."

Noreen nodded toward me. "If he gives you any trouble, let me know, and I'll cuff him faster than you can say *mighty fine ass*." Her eyes moved over me again.

"I'll keep that in mind," Serena said, opening her wallet again. "For the lunch he owed you." She dropped a twenty on the counter and turned to me. "We need to go, honey, if you want to have time to try page two-oh-eight when we get home."

I noticed Noreen writing the number down.

As we walked out, Serena squeezed my ass. That had to be for Noreen's benefit, right?

I waited until we'd cleared the door to ask, "What's on page two-oh-eight?"

"You'll have to read the book."

Fat chance. Real men didn't eat quiche or read that stuff. I also knew better than to ask about the kiss. She'd gotten me out of a jam, and I owed her—end of story.

She checked her purse and let out a relieved sigh when she found a faded photo that she quickly stuffed back into its spot.

I scanned the parking lot for threats as we walked to my truck.

She started scrolling on her phone.

I held out my hand. "I need that."

She held it out of reach. "No. Why?"

I bleeped the locks on the truck. "To check for clues in your message and call history."

"No," she huffed out.

"Yes," I insisted.

Her face hardened. "Remember the ground rules. I get to keep my life, and right now I have to return my dad's three calls and call work. You can have it when I'm done."

I walked her around to the passenger side of the truck and opened the door for her.

She climbed up. "Until then, you just sharpen your knife or whatever bodyguards do."

I shut the door more forcefully than was called for, but that's how this opinionated woman and her constant arguments affected me.

CHAPTER 9

Serena

As Duke buckled his seatbelt, I noticed his forearms again, and my mind went right back to the kiss. The memory of my body pressed against his sent heat to my core. The fire intensified when I remembered that gentle brush of his hand against my breast. It teased what getting to second base with him might be like.

Of course the deputy had eyed Duke like he was a prime cut of steak. The man was as hot as all get out, but tough luck, deputy. I'm the one who got to kiss him.

Duke put the car in drive and glanced back at the station. A slight smile curved his lips. Deputy Noreen stood at the door. Her scowl hadn't changed. That woman did not like me.

Duke turned onto the street. "Don't you have a call to make before I can have the phone to do my job?" he barked.

His tone was a clear signal that the kiss might have affected me, but for him it had been subterfuge to get him out of dinner with the deputy. And I'd initiated it, not him. He'd merely played along. If it had affected him the way it did me, wouldn't he at least be nice?

I selected Dad's contact and called.

"Hey, Munchkin, I've been worrying about you. I called and you didn't pick up."

I sighed. "Dad, I can't always answer, you know that. What's up?"

"How about we meet for ice cream? I have something I'd like to talk to my little girl about."

Right. In his mind, I was still his little girl. "I'm busy with work right now," I said patiently. Being Daddy's little girl was no longer my only occupation.

"Then we can talk at the barbecue your mother has put together."

"I'll try to be there, but I may not be able to make it. I've got lots of work stuff," I lied.

"It's important to your mother."

It sounded more and more like another setup I didn't need or want. "I said I'll try." It wasn't worth complaining about the *little girl* comment.

"Munchkin, I need you to come. We need to talk. It's important."

When he put it like that, there was no way I could refuse. Not after all we'd been through. "Sure, Dad. I'll find a way." I might fight it now, but I could never forget how lucky I'd been to have an obsessively protective father when it mattered. The outcome could have been…

"Good." Dad's voice cut off that depressing train of thought. "How's the new job going?"

"Fine so far."

"You can tell me all about it at the barbecue."

"Sure, Dad." I got off the phone after fending off another ice cream meeting suggestion. That had been our thing when I was little, and he couldn't let it go.

Duke looked over at the next stoplight. "Nice job not telling him about your adventure today."

"He's not ever going to know," I replied as I dialed my boss, Edward Powell.

"Who are you calling now?" Duke asked.

I held the phone to my ear. "My boss."

"Powell." Edward Powell didn't bother with niceties like answering the phone with hello.

"This is Serena—"

"I can see that from the caller ID. Where are you? You missed the daily review meeting."

"I'm sorry. I was in an accident."

"You should have called if you were going to be late." Ever the compassionate boss, he didn't even ask if I was okay.

"I couldn't. The car rolled over, and I lost my phone for a while."

Powell continued, "The protocol is—I have an important call coming in. We're going to have to talk later."

The line went dead before I could explain. I looked at my phone for a moment and then put it in the cupholder.

"It didn't sound like your boss asked how you are."

I let out a long breath. "He had another call coming in."

"That's more important that talking to an employee who just said she was in a rollover accident?"

I shrugged carefully. "I guess." Duke had nailed it. I could have said I'd just gotten out of the ICU, and it wouldn't have garnered a reaction from Powell.

"Your boss is a dick."

Dad had drilled into me years ago that you never badmouthed your boss, so I stayed quiet. "I'm going back to work this afternoon, and that's that." *How's that for standing up for myself, Mr. Cobra?*

"It's up to you, but I'm not a fan of that until we get some vetting done."

I gasped. "Why? You can't suspect my coworkers."

"Until people have been vetted, I suspect everyone." He turned us toward the freeway entrance. "Were your company meetings this morning random visits, or coordinated ahead of time?"

"Both visits were scheduled a month ago."

"Is either of the companies in trouble with your office?"

"No. Excalibur Plating was a fine visit. No red flags. They had everything ready for me. Knife Creek Chemical is full of jerks, but in the past they've always been in compliance." I wished I could put the Knife Creek people on the suspect list just for being assholes, but they didn't have a motive.

"Money can be a big motivator. Can't you fine them or something?"

"If they had issues, we would start with abatement orders before progressing to fines, and we have some companies that are in that category, but not these two." After a moment of silence, I added, "I'm going to work. I have to."

"I don't like it."

Sometimes, the best defense was an offense. "Why do they call you Cobra?"

He sighed. "It was my call sign on ops—the cobra is deadly and strikes without warning."

"Yeah, I just wondered why you use yours at work, and the others don't."

He shrugged. "The bossman's isn't very appropriate in our line of work, and the others aren't military. Winston came out of the FBI, Constance was Secret Service, Jordy is from the CIA, and Terry Goodwin came to us from the LAPD SWAT. It also scares the groupies when a client calls me Cobra—makes the job easier. You never want to use force if words will do."

"And?" I prodded.

"A while back, I was protecting a client who decided she didn't want to let go at the end. She found out where I lived and—"

"You had a stalker," I finished for him.

"I like to keep my work identity separate from my personal one."

"What did she do?"

"Not relevant. What's the address of your office building?"

"Eleven-thousand Wilshire." It didn't seem fair that his stalker was need-to-know only.

Duke hit buttons on the screen and initiated a call.

"Hey, Duke," a man's weary voice answered through the speakers. "What do you need?"

"I need to locate a place to hang out while our new client is at work at the eleven-thousand Wilshire Federal Building."

"Hold one sec… I've got an office for lease on Wellworth, the other side of the parking lot. Four hundred and fifty square feet. No idea what floor it's on or if it faces her building or not. If you don't like that one, next closest is… Let's see… Two blocks farther away."

"The first one works," Duke said. "Get me a showing in let's say an hour or so. I'm looking for space for my satellite law office, and you're my assistant."

"Copy that. Anything else?"

"Nope."

The call ended without either of them saying goodbye.

Since he hadn't offered, I had to ask. "Who was that?"

"My other brother, Jordan, but he prefers Jordy. He's our tech and comms specialist."

I hit redial on the screen as soon as Duke looked out his side mirror. "Now I know why they really call you Cobra. Because you have the manners of a snake."

"What now, Duke?" he answered.

"Hi, Jordy. This is Serena. Duke forgot to say thank you because he's a tough guy who wants to keep his grumpy-badass reputation intact."

Jordy laughed.

"He's very appreciative of your help and thinks you should introduce yourself as his overworked and underappreciated assistant."

Duke glanced over at me, looking like he'd bitten down on a lemon.

"Thank you, Serena. That's very sweet of you. Now hang up and let me get to work on our tough guy's office."

Duke stabbed the screen to end the call. "I'm only asking him to do his job. Besides, he knows I appreciate him."

"Does he?"

His jaw worked, but he said nothing.

A block later, my phone rang. The screen said unknown number, so I showed it to Duke.

"Answer it."

I accepted the call and put it on speaker. "Hello?"

"I want the stick. If you don't hand it over, this is going to get nasty," the creepy voice said.

I looked over at Duke, eyes wide. He nodded. "I still don't have any idea what you're talking about," I told the caller. "You must have the wrong person."

Duke motioned for me to string out the conversation, then pressed his ear and talked toward the window in hushed tones.

"Really, I think you've made a mistake."

"Don't bullshit me, Serena."

There went my hope that this was all a case of mistaken identity. My leg started up big time.

"Hand it over before this gets ugly."

We were beyond *ugly*. My anger boiled over. "Listen, asshole. Whatever it is you want, I don't have it."

"That won't work. I know otherwise. You have one week. I'll be back in touch."

"Fuck you," I spat, and the line went dead.

Duke laughed. "You've got spunk, girl. Did it feel good to tell him to fuck off?"

I held my thigh and prepared to be called stupid. "Not very smart, huh? Telling off a maniac?"

"Actually, that's good. We want him angry."

I was confused, because an angry maniac sounded like a guy considering a chainsaw.

"Angry people often make mistakes," Duke continued. "Bad decisions that give us a chance to find him and stop him."

Duke touched the screen to dial Jordy again. "What did we get?"

"Sorry to disappoint, but nothing," he said. "He used voice over IP and bounced all over. I'm good, but even I can't track a call like that in a few minutes. Nobody can."

"Okay," Duke said and ended the call.

"Are you completely untrainable?" I hit the button to redial.

"What now, Duke?" Jordy said. "You know you're not my only case."

I motioned at the screen.

Duke sighed. "I forgot to say thank you."

"You're welcome, Duke, and tell Serena I appreciate the gesture. She can call me anytime."

Duke grunted. "Bye." He hung up.

"What do you make of the call?" I asked.

He sighed. "Better and worse."

I cringed. It was already pretty damned bad in my book.

"It wasn't mistaken identity, and he's both committed and patient," Duke explained. "Those are not the qualities we want for him. He may not anger as easily as I'd hoped."

"And the good news?" I asked, trying to calm my runaway leg.

"We have some time to prepare for the next contact."

"You're not cheering me up." As a matter of fact, his matter-of-fact explanation had almost made me wet my pants.

"Just giving it to you straight."

As I looked over, I admired the strong jaw. He licked his lips as he signaled a lane change, and I replayed the kiss we'd shared. Why couldn't we have met on vacation, a beach in Hawaii, perhaps, and had the kiss be real?

I closed my eyes, leaned back against the headrest, and imagined that kiss relocated to the warm sand of a Hawaiian beach. I wouldn't have stopped at just a kiss.

Would he have invited me to a romantic dinner or maybe a cocktail by the pool and then back to his place? Or would the no-nonsense former SEAL just lead me by the hand to his hotel room?

I got wet thinking of the possibilities.

What would it be like to be with a man like Duke, the object of a million of my fantasies? Would he be a quick lover, a rough one? What position would he prefer? I'd read enough romance novels to give me plenty of options.

A man like Duke could have his pick of women. What if I didn't kiss well enough to get to the next stage with him? Doubt was a fickle bitch.

The engine stopped. "Serena? We're here."

I opened my eyes. We were back home on my street.

I followed Duke to the door, which gave me a chance to ogle him from behind. Yes, the man had a hell of a set of shoulders, and his jeans hugged a nice ass. The beach would have been great.

"Give me a minute to clear the house."

I rolled my eyes. The house had been fine before leaving for the sheriff's office. But instead of pointing that out, I let him go in first and waited. When I heard the commotion, though, I rushed in after him.

"Hands up," Duke barked.

I froze in place in the hallway, and my gut clenched. *Black Jacket Guy found me.* For a second, my legs went weak, and my vision dimmed. I put my hand against the wall to steady myself. Fainting was not allowed.

"Drop the knife, or I'll shoot," Duke growled.

Reminding myself why I'd gotten my tattoo, I marched in and rounded the corner to the confrontation. I wanted to see my protector take down the asshole and finish this.

~

DUKE

59

. . .

THE GUY HAD BEEN RIGHT THERE, HIS BACK TO ME WHEN I'D ROUNDED THE CORNER to the kitchen. He'd rummaged through one drawer, then another, mumbling, *"Where the fuck is it?"* while I took up position. This was going to be a very short case. I'd leveled my trusty SIG Sauer P226, the same weapon I'd carried as a SEAL.

"Who the hell are you?" he'd demanded. Like an idiot, he refused to drop the knife he was holding even after two warnings.

"The man who's going to put a bullet in you if you don't drop that knife," I'd explained.

Then Serena came barreling around the corner, but instead of stopping behind me like she should have, she kept going past me toward the intruder.

"What the—" she screamed.

I lunged and wrapped an arm around her waist, yanking her back.

"Are you trying to get yourself killed?" Serena yelled.

"Let her go," the idiot demanded as he advanced on me.

Serena struggled to get free. "Let me go. He's my brother."

I released her and lowered my SIG. "Why didn't you say so?"

"Put the stupid knife down," Serena told him. "Before you hurt yourself."

Against my better judgment, I holstered my weapon and extended my hand, though the idiot still had his knife out. "Vincent, I presume."

He nodded and laid the knife on the counter. We shook. "And you must be the bodyguard." Vincent's grip went from firm to very strong.

Two could play that game, so I gave it back to him doubled. "Protection specialist."

The veins on Vincent's neck bulged as his face reddened.

Serena shook her head. "More like guard dog."

I gripped tighter. "But you told the deputy I was your boyfriend."

That drew a startled expression from Vincent.

I used the opportunity for a better grip. Vincent's lips quivered, and his jaw went rigid. He had impressive strength, but I never lost at this, and it would only take a few more seconds.

"For God's sake," Serena whined. "Why don't you guys get a ruler and lay them on the table to measure?"

Vincent laughed and pulled his hand away, giving in. He shook it out.

I smiled and kept my hand still to rub in my victory.

Serena slapped my shoulder. "I told you I lived with my brother. Why did you have to pull a gun on him?"

"He was searching drawers. I thought he could be the guy, and then he pulled a knife on me," I explained. "In my line of work, my actions were by the book."

"For Christ's sake," Vincent said. "I was looking for the spatula so I could make myself a grilled cheese. The knife was to slice the cheese, but I'm not putting it down when a stranger barges into my house."

"My house," Serena corrected. "Now, if you don't mind, I'm going to change for work."

"After I clear the upstairs," I insisted.

Naturally, she rolled her eyes.

CHAPTER 10

SERENA

"Where's your car?" Duke asked as we pulled into the federal building parking lot.

I pointed. "Far corner. I don't want to risk door dings. I only just got it." I directed him until we found a spot nearby and parked. "See? It's just like I left it." My baby was a pretty blue and only three years old, bought used with my hard-earned money.

"I still want to check it out."

This didn't surprise me. Check the car, check the house. What was next, checking my underwear drawer for explosives? *Duke and my underwear drawer—* the thought made my core clench. I had to lock down thoughts like that before they got me into trouble.

"Open it up," he commanded.

I crossed my arms, determined to make a point.

"Please," he added.

With a smile, I pressed the button twice and unlocked the car, then released the trunk for him. I waited patiently as he examined the trunk and the interior of the car, including under the seats and under the hood, before finally getting on the ground to look underneath.

"Satisfied?" I asked as he brushed himself off.

He scowled. "You might have a tracker. I'm going to have Terry check it out."

"Are you kidding?" Suddenly, I felt less confident that his efforts were overkill.

"In the movies, they have blinking red lights. In real life, it's not that simple. Let's go." He waited a few steps before repeating himself. "Until we've vetted people, remember—"

"I got it. You don't recommend I tell anybody the details of what happened today." I used air quotes while reciting what he'd drilled into me at least three times on the drive over, explaining that none of us knew our co-workers as well we thought, and someone slipping up with a piece of information they shouldn't have known sometimes solves a case. "I ran off the road, avoiding Bambi. Oh, silly me," I intoned in a falsetto. I wouldn't like lying to my friends and coworkers, especially Katelyn, but at least the bit about the deer was true.

"See? That wasn't so hard."

"What?" I asked.

"Agreeing with me for once."

I huffed and angled my walk slightly farther away from him.

He adjusted to stay close. "Except for going to work, do you have anything on your calendar for the next week?"

"A barbecue at my parents' house, and before you ask, no, there's no way I can get out of it. I promised. But you can't introduce yourself as my guard dog."

"Protection detail." Duke adopted his sour-lemon face again.

"What? You think the guy will invade my dad's compound to get to me?"

Lemon face still in place, Duke announced, "I'll be sending Constance with you to that. She can go as your friend."

"It's not a bring-a-random-guest kind of party," I countered. Then I remembered Zach's advice about how to avoid hookup attempts. "You can come as my boyfriend. That would work." A little tingle went up my spine.

The suggestion did nothing to improve Duke's mood. "That wouldn't be a good idea."

"Sure it would. My mom and dad are making noises about me getting back together with George, and with you there, it'll totally stop that." I liked the idea better with each step we took toward the building.

Duke shook his head. "You shouldn't go."

"I have to. I promised my dad."

"We'll talk about this later." He pulled me to a stop before we entered the building. "I'll be nearby. I'm getting set up in an office down on Wellworth."

"I know. I'm an adult. I heard you the first two times."

"And call me," he said, completely ignoring my complaint, "before you're ready to leave the building."

I saluted him. "Yes, sir, and I won't accept packages from strangers, or drink or eat anything offered to me by anybody else, or go into any rooms alone, and I'll avoid all dark spaces—"

"This is not a joke," he said, gripping my shoulder.

Once again, his touch seared me through the fabric. *Down, girl.* The way my body reacted to him was unreal.

"You need to take this seriously." He moved closer and whispered in my ear. "Just because this isn't a country road in the hills doesn't mean there can't be danger."

I cringed at the memory of the crash earlier today. "I get it. Begin by suspecting everybody. Trust nobody."

He nodded, backed away, and watched as I went inside and through the metal detectors and security.

Once in the elevator, I waved to him as the doors closed. When the doors opened upstairs, it was just my luck to have my boss walking by.

He checked his watch. "It's about time."

"Sorry, Dr. Powell. I got here as soon as I could." The ostentatious snob insisted on being called *doctor*, which struck me as weird, given that his doctorate was in metaphysical philosophy.

Once, I'd overheard my coworker, Nick, forget the doctor part and call him Mr. Powell. That had not been a good day to be Nick Butcher. He'd gotten a dressing down like he'd missed a week of work.

"If you can't drive without getting into an accident, perhaps we should reevaluate whether or not you're suited to be an external auditor," he clipped out. "I'm not issuing you another vehicle just yet."

That steamed me, but like a good girl, I kept my mouth shut. Since he went left, I turned right, taking the long way to my new double-size cubicle. I'd been looking forward to having a car to drive to and from work. It was newer than my Camry.

Remy stopped in his tracks when I turned the corner. "My God, girl, what happened to you?"

I lifted a shoulder. "A deer ran in front of my car."

Katelyn appeared. "A deer on the freeway?"

She was followed by Nick and several others.

"The freeway was backed up," I explained. "So I got off and took the route through the hills."

They bombarded me with questions about where, when, whether my car was okay, and if the deer had died.

"I barely clipped him," I assured them. "He ran off into the bushes, so I guess he's okay."

Remy shook his head. "Remind me never to drive that road. Jacques would kill me if I hurt a deer."

"Are we having a party?" Powell asked over the top of the cubicles.

The group scattered, and in a moment, it was just me and Katelyn. She had the cubicle across the aisle from mine. She turned away and started on her computer.

Explaining the crash without being able to vent about its true nature had triggered me. My leg bounced in a big way. The memories of what happened played over and over again in my head. I'd nearly died three times, first with the crash and rollover, second with the threat of being cooked alive, and then in the hospital, I'd almost become a surprising fatality. I had no doubt that Black Jacket Guy would've given me a fatal injection, no matter what I said or how I pleaded, if he'd had the chance. In the movies, the villain always cleaned up loose ends, and that's exactly what I would've been.

After a long, deep breath, I pushed back from my desk and headed for the breakroom, with a dollar in my hand just in case. When I got there, the coffee machine looked a lot less appealing than it normally did, so I chose hot water to make peppermint tea instead. The tea basket on the counter didn't contain any peppermint, and when I stretched to reach the shelf with the teabags, a sharp pain erupted in my side. Why didn't I get the step ladder?

Finally, the first sip from my aromatic cup hit the spot. I then fed the candy machine my dollar and indulged in a bag of peanut M&Ms.

Nick walked in, and straight to the coffee machine.

I yearned to get off the accident and back to normal stuff. "How are things with Allison?"

His face lit up. "She's a huge Disney fan, and I'm working on something to surprise her."

I backed away to leave. "I hope it works out for you."

"Thanks." He waved, still smiling broadly.

When I returned, Katelyn was on her phone. "I understand. Bye." She ended the call with a sigh. When she looked up, I noticed tears in her eyes. "Problems?" It was a rhetorical question. I knew the woman had problems up to her eyeballs, ever since her fiancé, Leo Gambino, had died in an auto accident.

Leo had been a kind soul who'd debated EPA policy with me numerous times, slowly coming around to my views on some issues. But then he fell asleep at the wheel six months ago. I missed our debates.

Katelyn shook her head. "Don't ever buy a historic fixer-upper. It means everything is way too old, and it all needs replacing or fixing. And, fixing old shit costs twice as much, and these contractors are rip-off artists. Nothing ever gets done right or on time." The tears started. "With Leo gone, I don't see how I can finish the remodel and keep up with the mortgage. But we did the demo work, so I can't sell it like it is."

"I'm sorry." It was all I could think of to say. Today I could sympathize with her plight—not the money part, but the hopelessness. I'd always had enough money, but now I was faced with a danger money couldn't solve.

She threw her hands up. "And with the distance my section is from home, I can't drop in to supervise the A-holes."

I didn't respond to her obvious plea to switch territories with me. After the way my morning had gone, I knew a request to switch would be all Powell needed to declare me unfit for the job and hand it to Remy. No, I had to stick it out with my current area.

"Maybe we could go out after work," she suggested. "Talk a little bit."

"I can't. I have a…" I was not missing the meeting with Duke and the whole Hawk Security crew this evening.

"A date?" she guessed.

"A meeting."

She narrowed her eyes. "With a guy?"

My cheeks flamed, thinking of Duke.

"By the way…" She wiped away her tears and scooted her chair around to face me across the aisle. "If the car got totaled, how'd you get here?"

I stumbled over my answer. "A friend dropped me off."

"Your face is turning mighty red, girlfriend, so I take it this friend is of the male persuasion, and you're meeting him tonight?"

I nodded, trying to keep from showing any more embarrassment. Duke was definitely all male, and hot as fuck. I couldn't allow my thoughts to go there.

She laughed and waved me off. "Go on your date, girl. We can go out another day."

I was relieved when she returned to her work. I swiveled away as well. What would it be like if tonight actually was a date with Duke? Would he be a quick and rough lover, patient and thorough, clumsy and clueless? No, that last one definitely didn't fit Duke Hawk. But the dampness in my panties every time I thought about him was a dead giveaway that I wanted to find out.

DUKE

Serena's suggestion that I go to this Benson family event as her fake boyfriend had thrown me. If I went as her fake boyfriend, it would probably get me killed, considering how her father felt about me.

I could fight my way out of almost any situation, but Lloyd Benson was not a forgiving man, and he had the resources to hire a big enough army to take me down. He also had the resources to make a body disappear.

In this day and age, weighting down a body and dumping it in a lake or river had too many modes of failure, which then gave the authorities forensic evidence to work with. But someone rich enough to have a body dumped out of a plane a hundred miles offshore stood an excellent chance of getting away with it.

I'd completely forgotten to get Serena's phone from her before she went into the building. Checking her message history would have to wait.

So, I met with the real estate lady and signed the lease for the office Jordy had located nearby.

My first item of business should have been a threat assessment of Serena's message and email history, but without her phone, I was stuck with the mundane task of ordering the basics for my office. Constance had agreed to hang out there tomorrow so at least one of us would be there to receive deliveries in case I needed to leave. Next, I arranged for Jordy to set us up with computers. After that, I was stuck watching the clock and waiting for Serena's call. Twice, I got on Amazon to order the book she was reading to find out what was on page 208. Twice I chickened out.

～

SERENA

I'D JUST SETTLED INTO A GROOVE AT MY COMPUTER WHEN AN INTEROFFICE MESSAGE from Powell appeared on my screen.

Meeting in my office - five minutes

I pulled my mouse over and opened up the files on Knife Creek Chemical, the likely topic of this meeting since I'd failed to get the requested data. Work would cleanse my brain of naughty Duke thoughts.

Sophia Rossi had been the last one on the account, but I didn't find anything from her. Katelyn's fiancé, Leo, had been the auditor before her, and I reviewed his notes on the visits to their facility.

The Knife Creek guys—in particular the COO, Aiden Pons—had been real jerks to me. It was discouraging not to find any mention of assholery in Leo's notes. It could only mean I was the issue. Either Pons disliked having to deal with a woman in authority, or it was my other cross to bear.

I got asked pretty often if I was one of *those* Bensons. When the question came up, it could either work in my favor, or against me. They'd asked during my visit at Knife Creek, and the way things had gone, I'd put them in the not-helpful category.

Going over the prior data, I didn't find anything concerning about the contamination levels of the original spill, or the trends from the monitoring wells. At least getting rolled by them on the latest data wasn't putting anyone in jeopardy, and I could endure Powell's inevitable criticism for coming back empty-handed. All Leo's reports, co-signed by Powell, showed a groundwater contamination site that had been almost completely cleaned up and didn't even extend to the edge of their property.

Delays were the hardest part of this job, as the system we had was slow as molasses and risked endangering children with fouled drinking water or contaminated soil while we gave polluters the time the regulations allowed. But in this case, having delayed data would not endanger anyone other than me.

I pulled their business cards from my purse and dialed the number for Gabriel Woodward, the person I'd been told to interface with at Knife Creek.

It went to voicemail. "You've reached Gabe's phone. I'm probably busy with astronaut training. If this is an urgent matter, take two aspirin and call me in the morning. If you're calling to solicit money, don't bother leaving a message. My ex-wife took it all. Have a wonderful day." At least he had a sense of humor.

I waited for the beep. "Gabe, this is Serena Benson from the EPA. We met earlier, and I was wondering when you'd be able to send over the testing-well data that was missing at our meeting. I'd like to give you guys a passing grade. You have my number and email. Don't be shy." There was no passing or failing grade for me to assign, but he didn't need to know that.

"Benson, my office," Powell bellowed, probably from his doorway. Far be it for him to actually walk the distance to my workspace and say what he had to say at a conversational volume.

Before going, I opened my wallet, pulling out my inspiration for this job—the faded photo of Carmen at age five. My eyes watered. A study partner from college, Marisol, had become Carmen's mother as a young teenager. During our friendship, I'd learned a lot about grit and determination in the face of obstacles as Marisol navigated being a single mother and a college student at the same time.

Marisol's grief when Carmen passed away from bladder cancer at age six had torn at me. Their water had come from a well next to a known toxic site. The company that owned the land had delayed cleaning it up for years. That tragic outcome had led me to join the EPA. I would do everything I could to prevent the death of another child or the suffering of another parent from the effects of contaminated drinking water.

"Benson," Powell shouted again.

"Coming, Dr. Powell." Spine stiffened by the photograph, I wiped my eyes with a tissue, returned the picture to its resting place, and rose. Time to face the music.

CHAPTER 11

Duke

Eventually, Serena called, and I headed over to pick her up after work. Waiting at the employee entrance, I was relieved when the door opened and I recognized her curls. I felt like the luckiest guy in town as Serena graced me with a beaming smile and passed out of the security gate alongside the woman from earlier and a man.

"See you tomorrow, Katelyn," she said.

"How about a drink?" the guy next to her asked. "Jacques will be there."

I growled and advanced. "Hey, Princess. You're late." I sent the guy a withering glare. "She's busy." She was absolutely not having a drink with this guy or any dipshit named Jacques.

Katelyn eyed me before continuing on. "Have fun, Serena."

The guy gave me a wide berth. "See you tomorrow." He followed Katelyn.

I faced Serena again. "I thought you government employees got off earlier?"

She shook her head. "According to my wonderful boss, arriving late means I *get to* stay late. Hospital visits don't count." She took my hand and pulled me toward the sidewalk. "I'm famished, honey."

Honey? She was taking this fake-boyfriend thing to a new level. I didn't do relationships or girlfriends, not since—

"How was your day?" she asked. The words were neutral, but the tone was all girlfriend-ish, if that was a thing.

Her hand in mine felt more natural than it should have. I considered dropping it, but Katelyn looked back at us. Instead, I stopped and pulled Serena close for a light hug, careful of the cut on her side. "I've been thinking of you all day, Princess," I told her, just loud enough to be overheard by the woman. The odd part? It wasn't a lie. I'd done my best to lock down my memories from years ago and stop myself from considering what could have been, but I'd failed.

Her only response was to wrap a hand behind my neck and pull herself up to my ear. "Me, too, honey." She continued holding my hand as we walked to the cars.

"How did work go?" It was a lame line, but Serena had a way of taking me off my A-game.

"My boss sucks, but otherwise okay. They all bought the deer story, and as you suggested, I didn't even tell my friend Katelyn what happened or that I had a bodyguard. She was the one who left with me."

"Good work, baby. Who was the guy?"

"Remy."

I watched him in the distance and growled.

She squeezed my hand. "For your information, Jacques is his husband."

I turned to see Katelyn climb into a Maserati. "Your friend must be well paid."

Serena dropped my hand and pivoted to look. "She has expensive tastes. Her fiancé died in a car accident not too long ago, and… He was rich, and well… She's struggling. Grief and bills, a double hit."

Back at the cars, I held out my hand. "Phone."

Serena was busy scrolling on it. "Why?"

"I need to check it for threats. We've put it off too long."

She huffed. "There's nothing on it. If somebody sent me a text saying I was going to die today, I would have noticed." Back in argumentative mode, she didn't offer the device.

I wiggled my fingers, and she handed it over. It was locked. "What's the pin?"

"Zero-four-zero-four."

"Climb in the car. This will take a minute."

Once she was safely inside, I went through her voicemails first.

While I checked them, I noticed the two coworkers she'd walked out with drive off. Reading the automated transcriptions was faster than listening to them. Ignoring the ones from her family, I didn't see anything of interest until I got to one from *George*, sent yesterday. Feeling suddenly tense, I turned to her. "George is the guy you used to date?"

She nodded. "My *very* ex-boyfriend."

"I thought you said you hadn't gotten any threats."

She shook her head. "I haven't."

"He sent you, and I quote, 'It would be a mistake for both of us if we didn't get back together.'" That one sent a chill down my spine.

"So?"

"That qualifies as a threat. It's exactly the kind of message a stalker would send—not too direct or obvious, easy to explain away if he's confronted, but with a clear undertone of warning."

"Sorry. I guess since he wasn't the guy who wanted to barbecue me, I didn't think it was serious."

"That was a mistake. How do you spell his last name?"

"Kittleman. Two Ts. But it's not him."

I dialed my brother, Jordy, our tech guru. While Lucas, Brett, and I had gone the military route, our nerd brother had decided on the NSA and later CIA.

"Hey, Cobra," he answered. "What's up?"

"I need everything you can get on a George Kittleman, two Ts."

"What city?"

I turned to Serena. "Where does he live?"

"Brentwood."

I repeated this to Jordy.

"On it." The line clicked off. He wasn't big on personal interactions, even with his brothers.

"It wasn't him," Serena said. "I would have recognized him for sure."

"Like I told you, these guys can hire people to do the dirty work."

She cringed. "I forgot about that."

If it was Kittleman, this would be a lot harder. Nailing the guy who pulled the strings was always more difficult than catching the actual perp.

This was getting more difficult by the minute. I handed her phone back. "I'll follow you home."

She nodded, not seeming as confident as she had a few minutes ago. "You think it could be George?"

"Until we know more, it's possible. Now, let's get you home so you can change your bandage before the meeting."

"Yes, honey."

She meant it to poke me, but I could see myself getting used to it.

She pointed. "What's with the keychain?"

I held it, felt the ridges on the metal, and the horrible memory came back. I pocketed the thing.

"What? I don't get to ask you any questions? How's that fair?"

"Not about that. Now get in your car, and I'll follow you home."

"Your dog tags?" She wasn't going to let this go.

I turned. "Not mine. A buddy who died on an op with me. My best friend. He didn't deserve to die, but sometimes bad shit happens to good people."

71

"Yeah, I know."

I blinked rapidly to rid myself of the image of Marilyn. "You've lived in a privileged cocoon your whole life. You don't know shit about hardship. Now get out, Princess. I'll follow you."

She didn't understand true loss. Hopefully, she'd never find out.

Did I watch her pretty ass sway as she strutted to her car? You bet I did. Closing my eyes, I imagined her naked, splayed out on my bed. My cock surged to life, and the horrible memory of Marilyn faded away.

～

SERENA

I'D REALLY STRUCK A NERVE ASKING ABOUT THE KEYCHAIN.

Maybe I hadn't been to war, but I'd visited hell. I slammed the door to his SUV and walked to my little car.

"You don't know shit about hardship." Those words stung. I knew more about hardship than he could imagine. Fuck you, Duke Hawk. You don't know shit about me or my history.

Beeping the door unlocked, I yanked it open, climbed in, fastened my seatbelt, and locked the doors. "You're the one who doesn't know shit, you big oaf." His words still felt like lemon juice in a fresh cut, even if he was a sexy oaf.

After a few more breaths to calm down, I looked his way.

He smiled, and I pressed the start button.

BOOM.

The car shook, and fire erupted from the hood.

Why me?

I pulled the door handle—it didn't open. Panic filled me as smoke entered the cabin. My eyes burned, but I found the unlock button and clicked it, still pushing on the door.

I coughed. The door was still locked.

The smoke thickened. I couldn't see a thing but yelled the one thing I could think of. "Duuuuuuuuke…"

72

CHAPTER 12

Duke

The sound of her car exploding froze me for a split second, then I jumped out and raced around my Suburban. The corner of her hood had bent skyward, and flames shot out.

"Serena?" I yelled.

She hadn't gotten out, and I could see panic on her face as she struggled with the door. I tried the door handle, but it was locked. I grabbed my weapon and hit the glass. It didn't break.

Nothing. Smoke had filled the inside of the small car, and she screamed my name.

"Cover your eyes," I yelled. Releasing the safety, I aimed behind the seat and shot the edge of the window. It cracked, and after that, two strikes with the butt of my SIG and the window gave way.

Serena coughed terribly as I reached in and wrestled the door open. I holstered my weapon and pulled her out and away. She clung to me, continuing to cough.

"Hands up."

Turning, I found two marshals advancing with their guns drawn and another talking into his radio.

I kept one arm around my coughing girl and raised the other. "I had to shoot out the window to get her free."

One of the marshals pulled Serena away while the other took my weapon and frisked me.

Lucas would surely blame me for not checking the car again before letting her —or, in this case, telling her—to get in. It was a rookie mistake to assume that since I'd checked it earlier, it was still clean.

I was not paid to make rookie mistakes.

But none of that mattered. Serena was safe, and that was the important thing. I'd let her push my buttons, and my emotions cloud my judgment. Thinking back to Marilyn had distracted me. I wouldn't let that happen again. I couldn't.

AN HOUR LATER, THE FIRE CREW WAS CLEANING UP, THE MARSHALS HAD FINISHED asking me questions, and Serena's car was being loaded onto a flatbed.

Terry had arrived, and I'd looped Lucas in on the events.

"Wanna tell me why your client had a bomb placed in her car?" LAPD Lieutenant Marcus Wellbourne asked.

I looked up. "You know I can't."

Several years ago, when Lucas had specialized in kidnapping cases, he'd located the lieutenant's wife and *neutralized* the kidnapper. That had made Marcus our go-to guy at the LAPD and earned us the kind of consideration within the department that money couldn't buy.

He shrugged. "The bomb squad says it was tiny—basically an M-eighty meant to send a message, not kill her. The fire investigator says the guy placed it too close to the fuel manifold and the battery. Otherwise, it would have only blown the hood off, nothing else."

"Thanks." *Message fucking received, asshole.*

Marcus offered me my weapon. "I've smoothed things over with the marshals, but next time, have your accident off of federal property. It'll make my job easier."

"Hey, Marcus, one more thing. Don't let this get back to Serena's father."

His brows creased. "Okay, I'll try, but if he finds out, it's your ass in the wringer, not mine. Now get outta here."

I collected Serena from the paramedics.

She snuggled against me. "I can't thank you enough. Now I owe you too."

This wasn't the time nor the place to question her about anything, so I bundled her into my car for the ride home.

SERENA

· · ·

AS WE DROVE BACK, I KEPT LOOKING OVER AT DUKE AND THANKING MY LUCKY STARS that he'd been close. While they were cleaning up, the fire guys had said the explosion was only meant to scare me. *Mission accomplished.*

I couldn't hold it in. "They blew up my car."

"You're safe, and that's what matters."

"But I saved for a long time to buy her." It was an accomplishment I felt proud of. Something I only got because of my hard work and not my family name or family money.

"It's just a car." He didn't understand.

To avoid obsessing, I forced myself to shift gears and consider the barbecue coming up at my parents' place this weekend. Duke clearly did not want to go, but the way I'd felt for just the short few minutes we'd played boyfriend and girlfriend in front of Katelyn convinced me we could pull it off. Bringing him would be perfect.

Would I also feel a little empowered that I got to tell big, grumpy Duke what to do for a change? Yeah, that too.

In spite of his imposing size and gruff exterior, I felt completely comfortable with Duke. No, *comfortable* wasn't the right word, maybe *excited* was better. We all had a first crush, and most of us made a fool of ourselves with them. I certainly had with Duke. But how many of us got a second chance?

We parked on the street two doors down from my house. As we walked up to the door, Duke pointed at the enormous pile of bark in my driveway. "We need to get rid of all that so you can park in your garage. It's safer."

"The gardener is supposed to spread it next week." The pile was the reason I'd been parking on the street for several days, and why I'd thought the note I found was meant for a neighbor and not me.

"Move that up," he commanded.

When we reached the porch, I unlocked the door, disabled the alarm, and stood aside to let Duke enter.

"Stay behind me until we finish the first floor."

I gave him a mocking salute and followed several steps behind as he silently moved through the rooms. Reaching the family room, which faced the backyard, he suddenly halted and raised a fist. Being the avid movie watcher I was, I knew that as the military hand gesture to stop, and I did.

Then he continued, and we ended in the kitchen. He tapped the countertop. "First things first. You wait right here while I finish clearing the house."

"I have an alarm."

"Your system is shit." He didn't say this as a joke. "It would be child's play for anybody who knows what they're doing to get in and hide in a closet upstairs."

I wrapped my arms around myself. That was straight out of a horror movie, complete with big knives, chainsaws, and horrific outcomes. I'd had enough personal horror in my life. Still, as I expected, he returned from upstairs, having found nothing. "Princess, hop up on this island so I can change your bandage."

"I'll change it myself."

"Taking care of you is my job. Now stop arguing."

Just like that, Mr. Bossypants was back.

When I reached the island, my lack of a bra loomed large. "You're just trying to undress me. Won't your girlfriend be jealous?"

His jaw clenched. "I don't do girlfriends." There was a definite story in those four words. He didn't elaborate, merely glared at me. "The damn bandage needs to be changed."

"You want me to undress, then you undress too," I teased, thinking that might get me off the hook. I should have known better.

"If you insist." With one swift motion, he yanked his shirt over his head. It landed on the counter.

"Damn you. My shoulder is sore. I'll need help—"

He took my hips and boosted me up. "Lean forward and put your arms out as much as you can."

When I did, he gently pulled the top over my head. I should have chosen a button down.

I folded my arms to cover up and admired the view before me. Duke wasn't just big and muscled, he was a chiseled-from-granite god with barely an ounce of fat on him, the complete opposite of soft men like George. Glorious tattoos covered his chest and one shoulder. A snake coiled up the arm that didn't have his SEAL Creed tattoo.

"You're staring."

Busted. An instant blush ran up my chest and cheeks. "I like your tattoos." I didn't mention that I also liked his broad shoulders, strong arms, and...

"I like yours too." He'd noticed the words imprinted on my other side. "That's a good motto to live by. Now turn. We better get to this bandage before the guys arrive."

As I adjusted, I noticed a bulge had appeared in his pants. But that probably happened anytime a girl had her boobs covered only by a hand-bra. "Ouch. That hurts." While my eyes had focused where they shouldn't have, he'd ripped the bandage off.

"Trust me, quick is better than slow," he said.

"Typical man. Any girl who agrees with that is a liar," I shot back.

The laugh he gave me was wonderfully full. "Trust me, Princess, if a woman can't find enjoyment in both, she hasn't been with the right man."

"I am *not* a princess, and I thought you were going to re-bandage me instead of brag."

"Darlin', it's only bragging if it ain't true."

My cheeks flamed hot, and I cast my eyes to the ceiling. *Down, girl. He's feeding you unsafe fantasies.*

He touched the tender area on my side. "You've been a naughty girl."

If we were still alluding to sex, I was not participating. I winced when he moved closer to the cut.

"You've pulled a section of the wound open, and it bled a little. Did you raise your arm like I told you not to?"

"I had to reach the teabags," I said. "Sorry."

He worked quickly, and every time I glanced down, his eyes were on my wound, not the generous helping of side boob in front of him.

I inched my fingers away to show a bit more—no response. What did it say about me that I hated that I couldn't crack his professionalism?

He moved back. "Done."

"Thank you. I mean it."

He picked up my top. "Arms forward."

I hesitated.

"Come on. I've got two sisters, so it's nothing I haven't seen before."

I wasn't willing to guess exactly how many pairs of breasts he'd seen. As good-looking as he was, I'd bet plenty of women willingly shed their clothes for him.

"Do you want to wait for Constance?" he asked.

"Don't be silly." My tattoo reminded me to be bold, so I did as he asked and let my boobs fall free. I closed my eyes as the cool air hit them.

He hesitated, then slowly slid my top up my arms and over my head. Had he checked me out? Had I wanted him to? What had he thought?

Do not ask him. I ticked off another first with Duke. I'd held hands with him, hugged him, kissed him. Oh my, that kiss had been off-the-charts hot and made me regret that we hadn't connected before. Now, I'd been topless with the man. Saying all that in my head made me realize exactly how much of a man he was— the total package, a sexy badass who pumped out testosterone like nobody's business. Yes, he was the ultimate panty melter, and I was not immune. Nope, get me a fire extinguisher.

"The gang will be here soon," he said. "Is it okay if we set up in the family room?"

"Sure. Wherever."

He walked into the other room, and I touched a finger to my lips, recalling the kiss.

Duke hadn't said anything about it. Maybe it hadn't meant anything more to him than a way to get the horny deputy off his case. Or maybe I wasn't a good kisser. Maybe both.

"What the fuck?"

Duke's angry yell broke my daydream. "What?" I slid off the island and joined him in the other room.

He'd pulled open the curtains and stood staring out. "Does anyone have a key to your backyard?" he bellowed.

"I don't lock it." Given what had happened today, the admission sounded stupid even to me.

"Dammit, the fucker was here," Duke snarled.

Just when I thought my day couldn't get any shittier, the blood in my veins turned to ice. My attacker had taped a note to the outside of the glass.

You have one more chance. Place the USB stick under the red bush tonight or else. Next time it will be the real deal. Or, maybe we can enjoy each other's company and have a nice long chat.

CHAPTER 13

SERENA

Now Duke's cautious approach to entering the house didn't seem so out of place. The room turned cold. I wrapped my arms around myself. "Are you just going to leave it there?"

"I'll have Winston dust it and get a full forensic workup."

I imagined scenes from *CSI* with dusting powder and UV lights.

"But first…" Duke pointed. "Get in the kitchen and stay there. I'm going to sweep the house again."

"The note is on the outside. Doesn't that mean he didn't get in?"

"You can't trust anything he says or does. He's playing with us, telling you you had a week on the phone and this…" He pointed at the note. "It's to throw us off balance. We don't know for sure that he didn't get inside and leave you a present."

His words chilled me to the bone. "Do you mean a bomb?"

"More likely a surprise. He wants the information on the drive, so you're no good to him dead."

"Maybe I shouldn't have told him to fuck off?"

"It doesn't matter. I would have done the same."

Did a surprise mean a dead rat in my underwear drawer or something worse? An equally good question was why, when I thought of Duke, did I always come back to my underwear drawer?

After Duke finished downstairs and went upstairs, I drifted back to the family room and the note, reading the words over and over.

All was quiet in the house, save the ticking of the grandfather clock.

The red bush the note mentioned was in my front yard—out of range of the motion sensor and the doorbell camera. If the guy knew that, did that mean he'd been here before, or he worked for someone who had? My dipshit ex came quickly to mind.

"Serena?" Duke's yell echoed through the house. "Serena."

"In here," I responded.

Duke charged through the doorway, gun at the ready. "I told you to stay in the kitchen, goddammit."

"Sorry. You'd already cleared the downstairs, and I needed to look at this note again."

"Sorry doesn't cut it," he bellowed. "You needed to do exactly what I told you. Stay in the kitchen."

"Stop yelling at me."

He growled, but lowered his voice. "When I tell you to jump, you ask how high. You don't argue."

"Well, I'm not like all your other bimbos." I had no idea where that insult came from.

"You insolent woman." He stomped closer. "It's my job to decide what to do to keep you safe. It's your job to stay safe by doing what I tell you."

"I'm paying the bills, so I get a say."

"No. I'm the professional here, and I'm the only one who gets a say."

"Typical man," I huffed out.

"Typical entitled princess," he shot back. "Do I have to tie you down to get you to stay put?"

"Tie me down?" I joked. "Is that what you do with all your female clients, or only your bimbos?"

A beastly glint shone in his eye. It scared me. "The question is, since you mentioned being tied down, is that what you'd like?"

We'd devolved into a standoff, neither of us willing to answer the other.

I would not allow a discussion of being tied up, tied down, or anything that could take us to a discussion of the event I never talked about. "Serena, do this. Serena, do that," I complained. "Everybody's always telling me what to do, and I'm fucking sick of it. You have no idea what it's like."

"You're right. I have to work for a living, Princess."

Tears pricked at my eyes. Now it was official, my family's money had entered the discussion. I stomped my foot. "Don't call me Princess." Only too late did I realize that stomping my foot played right into his narrative. "It's insulting. You wanted to know why I didn't want my father involved. Because I'm trying to make my own way in the world, and he's constantly—"

His face changed. "Treating you like a helpless little girl?" he suggested.

His kind words deflated my anger. I nodded. "Yes."

He approached. Taking my hand, he morphed from beast to gentle giant in that way only he could. "I can't fix your issues with your father or anybody else, but I can promise that when I tell you to do something, it's for your safety. That's all. Which means it's important that you follow my directions, for your sake and for mine. You need to understand that I care, and I won't boss you around unless it's a matter of safety."

I felt a little off balance. Looking up, instead of the eyes of the warrior, I saw the kind eyes that had first intrigued me. "I get it. I'll try to be better." But, his current insistence on bossing me around had clinched something else. I was going to make him come to the barbecue whether he wanted to or not. I would not lose that argument.

"Like Yoda said, 'there is no try, only do.'" He rested his hand on my cheek. "Sorry I yelled. Are we good?"

I leaned into his touch and nodded. "We're good." Was it weird that the touch of a man I'd only met today could instantly put me at ease? Sure, I'd known the boy he used to be, but neither of us was a kid anymore.

He was a tempting badass, and I realized I was a woman longing for his touch and so much more. His mouth inched closer to mine as lust entered his eyes. Did he feel what I felt or was I imagining it?

I tilted my head up, rested a hand at his waist, and closed my eyes, waiting for the brush of his lips over mine. Or would they come crashing down? Need coursed through me, sending liquid heat to my core and a zing up my spine—a mixture of anticipation and fear. Was he merely comforting a scared little kitten, or did he want me?

If he did, could I handle a man like Duke Hawk?

My other arm wrapped around his neck, pressing my breasts to his chest and the hard length of him against me, hinting at the answer.

When his lips met mine, I knew. Duke Hawk hadn't wanted teenage me, but he wanted the woman I'd become. He cupped the back of my head and deepened the kiss. He was demanding, but not rough—savoring and exploring the connection. Yes, Duke Hawk could kiss the panties right off a woman, and he wanted me.

I speared the hand on my good arm into his hair. The dance of his tongue with mine was intoxicating, unlike anything I'd experienced before.

His hand slid under my loose shirt. He inched me away from him and cupped my breast. Liquid heat filled me as his thumb circled my nipple, teasing the peak into a hard bud, and the sound of blood rushing in my ears overwhelmed the ticking of the grandfather clock.

Pleasant sensations overwhelmed the pains from the crash as the room melted away. I floated in his strong arms. I shoved aside my worry about Black Jacket Guy's note and felt the warmth of Duke's hard body against mine. Our tongues danced with passion, each learning the other.

He cupped my ass, and there was plenty to grasp. I wished for more contact, more skin, just more Duke. No, more Cobra. Sliding a hand between us, I cupped his erection through his pants.

With a tortured groan, he broke the kiss. "You're playing with fire, Princess."

"I'm old enough to decide for myself, and you agreed to not tell me what to do."

He sighed. "If you're going to be bold," he said, quoting from my tattoo. "Be sure, absofuckinglutely sure." He pinched my aching nipple, sending a zing of electricity through me. "Once we start this, I'm not going to stop."

"Promise? I choose bold," I answered, giving his cock a squeeze.

His mouth took mine again as he tugged at the belt on my pants and slid them off my hips before guiding his hand inside my panties. He blazed a hot trail over bare skin as his fingers traveled down to where I wanted them, craved them.

The sizzle of sensation when he parted my slit was heavenly. I was on a hair trigger, as it had been a long time since any fingers besides my own had explored my sex. I shifted to the side and grabbed for his belt to make us even. I could tell he was big, but how big?

He pulled my hand away. "Not yet," he said firmly before re-engaging the kiss.

Going back to palming his length, I refused to stop working him through the fabric.

His finger circled and teased my entrance, pulling a begging moan out of me before sliding inside. "My God, you're wet."

"It's what you do to me," I breathed. I squeezed him again. "And you're hard as steel."

"That's what you do to me."

He groaned as I yanked on his length. "Careful, or I'll blow."

It drove me crazy to know I had that effect on such a powerful man as Cobra. I wasn't a supermodel, not even close. I repeated the move.

"Stop it." He retaliated by adding a second finger and working my pussy with abandon.

Instinct took over. I couldn't stop my moans or my hips as I gyrated against his hand. It had to be the long dry spell. I'd never been so close so quickly, even with my vibrator.

"You're close. I can feel it."

"Uh-huh," I managed between primal moans.

"I want you to come for me, Princess."

I nearly came undone when his thumb found my clit. The princess comment no longer mattered.

"Look at me," he commanded.

I opened my eyes, and we locked gazes. It felt like he could see into my soul and read my deep, dark secrets—the ones only one person knew.

"Come for me." His torture of my clit became more intense. "Come for me, Princess," he repeated.

I chased my orgasm over the cliff, moaning incoherently, and split apart as the waves spilled over me.

His smile was genuine as he held me through the spasms. "That's a good girl, Princess."

I locked my knees to keep from falling down and leaned against him in the bliss that followed. With orgasms like this, I might complain, but I could endure the Princess moniker. I pulled on his solid length. "Your turn, big guy." Now I would get to see how big.

The loud ding startled me for the second time today.

He yanked his hand away and stepped back. "What's that?"

"The motion sensor out front." I shivered. "Do you think he's back?"

"Stay right here." He sprinted for the front door with a monster bulge in his pants, a bulge I'd put there but not satisfied.

I pulled my pants back up, but this time, I stayed where I'd been told.

CHAPTER 14

Duke

His timing sucked, but boy, was I relieved to see a pizza delivery guy through the peephole.

I adjusted myself, paid him, and brought the food inside. "You're safe," I announced. "It was the pizza guy."

Serena sidled up to me. "Put it down and let me take care of you."

Juggling the boxes, I checked my watch. "We don't have enough time. I'll need time to savor you."

She blushed and rubbed a tit against my arm. "I bet you could be fast…" Her voice was coy.

My phone rang with my sisters' ringtone, killing the mood. "Raincheck? I have to take this."

"You can answer it later," she suggested, again rubbing my cock through my pants.

"It's one of my sisters. She won't stop," I explained as the song kept playing.

Serena shrugged. "Later, I guess."

I accepted the call. "Hello, gorgeous."

Serena smiled and lifted her shirt to flash me her luscious tits. They looked even better than they felt.

"*You're killing me,*" I mouthed silently.

"Got a minute?" Alice asked.

Serena, the minx, broke out in a full-faced smile. Torturing me was exactly her intention.

With a sigh, I turned away to keep from coming in my pants and set the pizza boxes on the island. "What's up?"

"Checking in." My youngest sister had the worst fucking timing.

"What kind did you get us?" Serena asked. She reached for the top box.

I swatted her hand away. "Wait."

"I hear a woman. You're with a woman," Alice stated with obvious glee.

"And you're a detective now," I countered.

"I'm famished," Serena announced, obviously intending my sister to hear.

I tapped the cardboard pile. "It should be a deluxe meat lover's, a Hawaiian, a simple pepperoni, and a veggie."

"Is she pretty?" Alice prodded.

Trapped by my long-ago promise, I answered. "Uh-huh." Complete truth was a commitment I'd made to my sisters when they were young.

Serena pulled two plates from the cupboard.

Alice kept at me. "How pretty?"

"We should talk later," I told my nosy sister.

"I'll start with Hawaiian," Serena announced. She opened the top box and closed it after finding the meat lover's.

Alice was not one to give up easily. "After you tell me how pretty she is."

"She's a client," I added.

Serena slid the top box off the pile and opened the second.

"So? Tell me... Now," Alice said.

With no option, I spit it out. "Yes, my client is a very pretty woman."

Serena's head jerked up, and a blush formed. *Pretty* was an understatement.

"Put her on," Alice demanded.

"No, Alice. Goodbye." I hung up. "Nosy sister."

"You think I'm pretty?" Serena sing-songed.

"Reporting the facts."

She giggled. "Thank you. You're not so bad yourself."

Uncomfortable with where this was going, I separated the boxes and located the Hawaiian for her.

She smirked. "This is where you also say thank you."

I didn't look up as I slid a slice onto a plate. "Thanks."

My phone sang the same infernal Shania Twain song as before, announcing a sister again. I glanced at the screen. It wasn't Alice. "Hello, Emily," I answered. She lived in Portland, and I didn't see or hear from her that often.

"I hear you have a pretty girl as a client." The grapevine had been activated.

"Women are allowed to be clients." They made up the majority of people looking for protection.

"Does she get to boss you around?" She giggled. "I'd love to watch that."

"It's been super nice, Em. Bye now." I hung up with attitude. "Sisters."

Serena slid the second plate toward me. "How many of you are there?"

I surprised her with a quick kiss. "That's for later." Then, I opened the meat lover's box. "Me, three brothers, and two sisters. My other brother, Brett, is on deployment."

"I think big families are a blessing. I've got one sister and four brothers."

Nodding, I picked up a slice of pizza and took a bite. But I almost spit it out when Shania's "Man! I feel like a woman!" started up again. Every time I changed it to a George Strait song, one of them changed it back. I answered, "Alice, I don't have time to talk."

"I wanna talk to her," my bossy sister demanded.

"We don't have time for you to talk to her."

"What are you doing right this second?"

"Eating pizza before a work meeting. Everybody from the company is due here any minute.

"Ah... Sharing a meal is a good first step. Is she really a client?"

"Yes. And we don't have time right now."

Serena held out her hand. "I'll talk to her."

Against my better judgment, I handed over my phone. Then I bit into the pizza and wished it was crispy potato chips so I wouldn't hear what was said about me.

"Hi, Alice," Serena started. "No, it's not a date. I am a client... Yeah, I heard him say that, and I think he's good-looking too. Actually, your brother is the very definition of hot." She smiled, doing her best to make me uncomfortable.

I turned away, feeling a blush coming on.

"No, he wasn't fibbing. We do have a meeting coming up. I'll tell you what, how about we talk later in the week, and you can tell me all his secrets? Let me give you my number." After reciting her cell number, she added, "Good talking to you, too."

After a few seconds of silence, I composed myself and turned around, advancing on her. "The very definition of hot?"

A blush crept into her cheeks as she backed against the fridge, still holding a piece of pizza. "Merely reporting the facts."

I narrowed the distance between us. "Is that right?"

"Is *pretty* the best you could come up with?" she asked, raising an eyebrow.

"As I recall, I called you *very* pretty." A few inches closer, and I'd be tearing her clothes off. "And a woman, not a girl."

Her eyelashes fluttered as her cheeks grew redder. "You're just being kind because I'm paying for your time."

"How can you say that after…" I sighed. "I meant every word. Long ago, I promised my sisters I would never lie to them."

She slid to the side and brought the pizza slice up between us. "Good to know there's somebody you won't lie to."

The spell broke, and I backed away. "Giving Alice your number was not a wise choice. You know they're both going to call you."

She shrugged and ate her pizza. "You can thank me later. It keeps you from having to talk to them," she mumbled through her food. "They know how to push your buttons."

"That they do." It seemed Serena was in that club as well.

The front motion alert sounded again. "That would be the crew. You better grab a second slice of whatever you want before I let the vultures in. I slapped her ass as I went to the door.

She yelped and stuck her tongue out at me before reaching for the veggie box. "You're going to pay for that."

"We'll see. The way I see it, you have to pay for talking to Alice."

She nodded. But she only knew half the story.

CHAPTER 15

Duke

I opened the door for the rest of Hawk Security. As soon as Constance was inside, I passed over Serena's phone and my observations for another pair of eyes on the messages and emails.

"Thanks." She poked my chest. "Next time you get the boring hospital-stakeout duty."

"Next time," I agreed.

Half an hour later, introductions had been made and pizza passed around, and the group had settled in the family room.

Lucas shooed Serena toward the door. "You can wait upstairs."

Her eyes went wide with indignation. "No way. Whatever you guys have to say, I want to hear it."

"No. It may be upsetting, and—"

"I am not a weak wallflower. You, of all people, should know that."

"It's not the way we do things, and if you don't like it, perhaps—"

I cut him off. "I want her in. She may have an insight we'd otherwise miss."

Lucas narrowed his eyes at me but relented.

Serena shifted close enough to me on the small loveseat that our thighs touched, and I willed my cock to ignore her—it only half listened.

The hint of a tremor in her leg told me she was nervous about this. I whispered into her ear. "You can trust them. Don't let the hard questions scare you."

The room hushed as Lucas spoke. "Cobra, it's your op, so bring everybody up to speed."

I started by explaining the morning attack on Serena, including the demand for a USB drive. I told them I'd tasked Winston with checking out her work-issued car, and I mentioned the call Serena had gotten while we drove to her office, followed by the bomb in her personal vehicle and note on the glass.

"That's quite an escalation," Terry noted.

Lucas took charge. "Agreed. Winston, tell us about the work car."

"The most interesting thing," Winston said, "was that it had a tracker on it."

"That's no surprise for a government vehicle," Constance pointed out.

"But this..." Winston held up a small box. "...was a second tracker, in addition to the tracker the government installed." He handed it to Terry.

"What else?" Lucas asked, trolling for trust-but-verify answers.

Winston offered a few hard-copy photographs. "There was damage to the rear bumper and black paint transfer consistent with the vehicle she described, and..." He added another picture to the pile. "...I found fur at the left front hood juncture from the deer she clipped."

Lucas nodded. Trusted and now verified.

Next to me, Serena's leg stilled. "Is the tracker how he found me in the mountains? I was sure he hadn't seen me turn off the freeway."

"Probably," Winston said. "The accident report doesn't give us anything else."

"Serious stalker MO," Constance said, taking the tracker from Terry.

"I emailed you the serial number," he said. "Jordy, let's find out who bought it."

"I'll try," he said. "But that's not so easy with these things."

"If it were easy..." Lucas chuckled. "We wouldn't need you, brother."

The rest of us laughed politely, having heard Jordy's warning and my brother's comeback too many times to count.

Jordy started tapping on his laptop.

"What do we know about the Suburban in the abduction attempt?" Lucas asked.

"The guy's a pro," Winston reported. "He went into several areas with very limited cameras, but so far I've tracked him as far as the valley."

Lucas nodded. "Keep on it."

"Have you noticed anybody hanging around at work, in the parking lot, or around the house?" Terry asked.

"Let's finish the physical evidence first." That was Lucas, always one for logical progression.

Winston held up baggies containing the two notes. "They're handwritten instead of printed, so likely not a professional. The writing is similar between the two. I'll have them into forensics first thing, but I wouldn't count on anything. I dusted the side gate on the way in. Nothing. The guy was careful, I don't even see a partial print on the tape."

"Constance," I said. "What's your feeling about the text messages on Serena's phone?"

"I agree with you," she said. "I'd flag a message like '*It would be a mistake for both of us if we didn't get back together*' every time as a possible stalker."

"Who is this guy?" Lucas asked.

"George Kittleman, her ex, and he sent flowers multiple times," I added.

"How many times?" Lucas asked.

"Three," Serena answered. "But I always threw them out, and I never answered his calls. He's persistent but harmless. He never gave me a USB drive, so there's nothing to want back."

"Serena," Constance said kindly, "the unassuming ones can be the most unpredictable."

"He has the means to hire muscle," I added. Jordy looked up from his laptop and pulled a disgusted face.

"Did he ever give you anything that might have hidden a USB drive?" Winston asked.

That was an interesting angle.

Serena thought for a moment. "No. I never got anything from him except flowers."

I controlled the urge to grit my teeth.

Lucas raised a hand. "Okay, so Kittleman goes to the top of the list. Jordy, we need a digital workup. Work with Winston on that."

It felt good to have Lucas agree with me and Constance.

"I also like the idea that it could be one of the businesses you visited," Terry said. "Those guys probably have money on the line. Can't you put them out of business?"

Serena looked noncommittal.

"But how would a USB drive come into play with one of them?" Winston asked.

"How does it come into play with any of them?" Jordy pointed out.

"Maybe they know she uses a stick to store the data on their inspections, like notes and stuff," Terry said. "Do you do that, Serena?"

"I bring a laptop with me and a notebook," she answered. "But that's not the point. I didn't get any information from either of them."

"This George guy been to your house, right?" Terry asked, shifting gears. "He could have left a USB drive here and maybe you moved it without realizing, like it was in a plant or something."

Serena nodded. "Sure. But he took all his stuff when he left for Europe."

I clenched my fist, but hid it. Serena was a sweet girl who didn't deserve to have a dipshit ex pressuring her.

"I doubt he earns much working at the State Department in the passport division," she continued. "But he has access to family money."

Constance perked up. "Passports? Isn't that in the same building as you?"

Serena nodded. "Different section, though."

"You can't go in to work then," I blurted. I was not letting her go unprotected into the same building as a suspect.

Serena turned, fire in her eyes. "I told you upfront, I'm not stopping any of my normal activities, and that includes my job."

"It's not safe," I insisted, "if that dickwad works in your building."

"He hasn't once come up to my floor," she snapped. "It isn't him."

"If not him, then who?" I snapped back.

Lucas raised his hand, apparently amused at our argument. "Duke, you handle outside the building, and Constance will be on duty inside." He turned to my partner. "Constance, figure out what your cover is going to be so you can stay in close proximity to Serena."

"Sure thing," she said, smiling.

Internally, I fumed that close proximity might not be good enough. But Lucas had made the call, and there was nothing I could do about it.

"People can't know you're there as protection," Serena said. "I can't have it getting out. That's a dealbreaker."

Jordy went back to staring at his laptop, but Winston and Terry looked as confused as I felt. This restriction having to do with her old man was extreme.

"No problem," Constance assured her.

Jordy moved to sit at the other end of the room.

"Where else do we have to secure the client?" Lucas directed his question to me. "Outside of work, what else is on the schedule?"

"Lucas, don't refer to me as *the client*," Serena said. "I'm right here."

Lucas's eyes went wide. "Sorry, Serena. No disrespect intended. What else do you have on your schedule that we should be aware of?"

"I have a family barbecue this weekend that I can't miss."

"That should be a relatively safe space," Lucas said.

"My mom and dad have been encouraging me to get back with George. I wouldn't put it past them to invite him," she added.

"Constance can accompany her," I offered quickly.

"That won't work," Serena insisted.

I braced for it.

"But Duke could come as my new boyfriend. That would be the best thing. It would also be a good reason to avoid my ex, just in case."

"Good idea," Lucas agreed before I could mount a defense. "Anything else?"

"Not at the moment," Serena said sweetly.

Jordy shifted the angle of his laptop, still frowning.

"Okay," Lucas said. "Duke, you and Winston stay here tonight after we bait the trap, and we'll see if this guy was just toying with us or comes by to check the bush out front. Constance, you get some rest before you go undercover inside the federal building tomorrow."

Constance nodded.

"Jordy, we need a spare USB drive as bait to put under the bush out front for this dirtbag."

Jordy typed away on his computer and adjusted how it sat in his lap.

"Jordy?" Lucas prodded.

"We have a problem," he finally said. "There's a Wi-Fi signal coming from the front yard. My triangulation puts it by that tree next to the walk."

"Shit," Terry said as he fumbled through the backpack at his feet.

Lucas beat us all to the front windows, but Terry was the one with the binoculars.

Terry only searched for a second. "We're screwed. There's a camera in the tree pointed at the bush, and it would have caught all of us walking in. No way we catch him picking up the bait."

"What's this mean?" Serena asked.

"It means the asshole was a step ahead of us," I murmured. "We have no idea how long that camera has been there."

"Terry," Lucas barked. "We need a full system on this house, and we needed it yesterday."

"I brought a few cameras with me and planned on picking up the rest of the stuff tomorrow," he said.

"Not good enough any longer," I decided. "We need motion and door sensors tonight. The rest of the package can wait until tomorrow."

Terry looked to Lucas.

"Do it," he said. "Duke is right. Winston, you and Duke take shifts tonight here at the house. Leave his camera in place. Let him think he has the upper hand. Constance, no change. You get sleep for the federal building tomorrow. Good work, Jordy. As you leave, sweep each of our vehicles for a tracking signal."

It would be a long night. And now, with the combination of danger to Serena and Winston being in the house, I wouldn't be getting together with her this evening.

CHAPTER 16

SERENA

THE NEXT MORNING, THE FACE LOOKING BACK AT ME IN THE MIRROR REFLECTED A fitful night's sleep with dark circles and bloodshot eyes. Basically, I was death warmed over, with bandages from the accident thrown in for good measure.

How had Duke possibly called me pretty yesterday?

My various injuries from the crash had made it difficult to sleep—that would be my go-to reason today when people asked. The real culprit was that I couldn't stop thinking about Duke and how he'd played my body like an instrument.

Yesterday had been an unequaled rollercoaster of a day, from the low of the crash and coming whisper-close to being roasted alive and blown to bits, to the high of Duke giving me the quickest orgasm of my life. My God, the bossy man turned me on.

How would he look at me today? We hadn't had a moment alone to talk about it. Was this the start of something, or had it already run its single-night course without even getting to the good stuff? The not knowing ate at me. I hoped for more than an interrupted one-night stand.

I thought about texting him, but in the movies, the techie on the team had access to everybody's communications to coordinate them, and his brother Jordy was no slouch. I couldn't risk it, so I'd have to wait for a chance to talk in person.

Thinking about that discussion tied my stomach in a knot this morning. What a letdown if the moment I'd finally gotten a taste of the incredible man Duke had grown up to be, he decided I wasn't worth more than the few minutes we'd had.

93

Did they have rules about that sort of thing in his line of work, in his company? I doubted it was as unethical as a doctor-patient hookup, but what did I know?

A knock sounded at my bedroom door. "Serena, are you coming down to breakfast?" It was Constance.

"Soon." *How will he look at me?*

I finished dressing. To avoid the cut on my side, I had to choose my low-back bralette. It wasn't often I disobeyed the master chief's rule to always wear an underwire bra.

～

Duke

TUESDAY MORNING, IN FRONT OF SERENA'S STOVE, I MARVELED AT HOW HOMEY HER kitchen was—a pepper grinder with a cat's head, frilly pot holders, and dish towels with funny sayings. Even the spatula I held had a flower pattern on it. It was all quite different to my kitchen of black, white, and stainless.

Since my omelet pan still hadn't warmed enough, I checked the text message that had come in overnight.

Ursula: Want to meet up later?

Ursula had been an almost-world-class gymnast before becoming a flight attendant for Scandinavian Airlines. She was a firecracker in bed and quite the contortionist. Her work schedule also made her a relationship-phobe. In other words, she was the perfect match for me—no expectations, just a nice meal, hot sex, a night here, a weekend there. Ursula was an exception for me. Repeats with her wouldn't lead to a relationship.

Since Marilyn, I'd only hooked up with women interested in onetime encounters. No repeats meant no attachments, no pain, no more nightmares.

But this time, I did the un-Cobra thing and ignored the message.

Constance had shown up just as Terry was walking out the door to take up watch on the street. He'd walked the long way around the tree camera, hoping to get lucky and spot the guy cruising the street. Constance took the same winding path inside. Instead of her favorite leather flight jacket, she wore a professional pantsuit.

With her here, I now had no chance to get a minute alone with Serena.

"What is that?" Constance asked, peering around me into the pan as I poured in eggs.

"What does it look like?" She was new to the company and wasn't aware of all my skills.

"It looks like you may know how to cook a respectable omelet."

I puffed out my chest. "I'm a frogman. Of course, I can cook. In the field, if we can't cook, we don't eat."

"I thought you tough guys subsisted on dry grass, worms, crickets, and MREs."

"You try MREs for thirty days straight. They'll keep you alive if you have to eat 'em, but having to and wanting to are two different things."

"That smells great."

"Yesterday was a pretty rough day for Serena. This is the best way I know to start off a new day. I think she deserves it."

"And here I thought you were doing something special for me." She pouted.

"Your turn will come. Maybe you'll be lucky enough to have a psycho after you someday."

"Yeah, she had a rough day." Constance checked her watch. "I'll try again to get her moving."

"Tell her not to spend an hour on makeup, or we'll be late."

Constance left with a middle finger raised high.

My mind went into overdrive. Now that the passion had worn off, would Serena's anger return? Did she regret what we'd done? Why hadn't she tried to contact me last night?

When two in the morning had rolled around without a peep from her, I'd had to face the fact that I was a big mistake in her book. Would she go to Lucas and file a complaint? How screwed was I?

Now, I waited for her to come down and either smile at me or not, either pull me aside to talk or not. How pathetic was that? As in a game of she likes me, she likes me not, I was powerless to affect the outcome. If I'd knocked on her door last night, maybe we could have talked it out and I could have had a say before she had time to solidify her stance.

Worse than all that, I was now roped into facing the bane of my existence, her father, Lloyd Benson. And this time as the fake new boyfriend of his daughter. That was going to be one epic shitstorm.

If she didn't file a complaint, I could beg off the assignment and leave it to Winston and Constance. Serena would be more comfortable, and I'd avoid saying something that drove her to out me and my conduct. If what I'd done got out, I'd be toast—not only at Hawk but with anyone who knew Lucas, which was a wide net.

"She'll be right down," Constance said from behind me.

I tended my pan and didn't turn around.

"Good morning," Serena said a moment later. "You're here early, Constance."

"I plan on going into the building with you."

Serena gasped. "You managed clearance overnight?"

"Let's just say Bill Covington's uncle, Garth, knows all the right people."

"Wow," Serena noted.

She'd said not a word to me, and that appeared to be my answer. The cold shoulder meant she'd at least put last night in the mistake category.

"I hope you're hungry," Constance added. "Duke has cooked for us."

"An omelet," I said without turning around.

"I'm not really hungry," Serena said. "I'll wait in the front room."

I started to plate the omelets, not daring to look and get the doom stare. I turned around only after adding the English muffins and fruit to the plates.

Serena had left the kitchen, and I had my answer.

CHAPTER 17

SERENA

DUKE TURNED IN AT THE ENTRANCE TO THE FEDERAL BUILDING PARKING LOT.
My nerves had built steadily during the quiet ride as I sat with Constance in the back of his SUV. He'd given me only the briefest of glances in the rearview mirror during the trip.

He pulled to a halt in front of the employee entrance. "Let me know when you're ready to leave," he said.

Constance opened the door. "Copy that."

I followed her after thanking Duke for the ride, as was proper to do.

While we waited in the security line, my stomach took the opportunity to gurgle and announce my hunger.

Constance smiled. "Sounds like you should have had some of Duke's cooking after all."

"Maybe," I admitted.

"He made that omelet especially for you," she added.

My mouth dropped open in a gasp. "He did?"

"He told me you deserved the best after yesterday," she whispered.

Suddenly, the day looked brighter. I nodded. "I'll call and thank him for thinking of me."

"He might growl at you, but ignore that. He'll appreciate the gesture. Somewhere under that tough hide, he's human."

"He's sort of bossy," I observed as we inched toward the metal detectors.

She shrugged. "It's the type, an overachieving SEAL. Be the mirror."

I followed her forward. "I don't understand."

"When he gets out of hand, let it bounce off you and send it right back to him. Don't be a wimp."

Don't be wimpy, I repeated silently to myself. I had to remember that. I'd been wimpy this morning in the kitchen and probably gotten the wrong impression from Duke. Only a conversation would clear that up, and I desperately hoped for the right answer.

"Remember, you don't know me," Constance murmured as we moved forward.

A few seconds later, she was next for the metal detector.

I laid my purse on the conveyor for the X-ray machine. She didn't. Instead, she showed the gun in her holster and flashed credentials.

"What's the Secret Service doing here?" the marshal asked.

"Classified," she said sternly.

He got the message and ushered her through, no purse search, ignoring the beeps. "LEO," he told the marshal behind him.

I'd watched enough *NCIS* episodes to know LEO was their lingo for law enforcement officer. I showed my ID and walked beep-free through the arch. "What's with the Secret Service?" I asked.

The marshal shook his head. "Who knows? They don't tell us crap."

Constance chose the left-most elevator, and I took the one on the right.

When I reached my floor, Constance was nowhere to be seen. I marched on to my cubicle, taking the route away from Powell's office, just in case he still had a bad attitude from yesterday.

Even before I went for my first cup of coffee, I settled into my chair, opened my cell, and dialed Duke. I had to talk to the man, even if the conversation was monitored by Jordy.

He didn't answer, and after a few seconds, I got a text that he was busy and would talk to me later. My heart sank.

"Meeting in the big conference room, everybody." Powell's voice boomed over the space. Yes, the tyrant of our time had struck again.

I got to the room in time to choose a chair far away from the one at the head of the table, otherwise known as Powell's throne. Distance was my friend. The rest of the department filed in, buzzing with questions. "What's the meeting about?" Everyone wondered, but nobody had an answer.

Powell walked in, followed by Constance and Isaac Tramell, the local special agent in charge of our criminal investigative division.

Powell sat. "Get the door, please."

Nick walked over to close it.

Tramell and Constance stayed standing.

"We have a guest who'll be joining us for a while," Powell announced. "Agent Evers is with CID."

Constance raised her hand in a wave. "First, you can call me Constance, and I'll make my best effort to be unobtrusive."

Murmurs rose in the group. CID was the arm of the agency that took down bad guys, the polluters we filed criminal charges against.

"Who are we after?" Remy asked.

Powell deferred to Tramell with a hand motion.

"Agent Evers is on loan to the inspector general's office," he explained. "She'll be reviewing some files and interviewing a few of you as well."

"Why?" Remy demanded.

Constance motioned to Remy. "What is your name?"

"Uh, Remy, Remy Laurent."

"Mr. Laurent." She opened a binder, checked it, and closed it. "Yes, I'll start with you."

Remy's mouth gaped open as he slumped back into his chair.

People shifted uncomfortably and murmured to their neighbors. The inspector general's office concerned itself with internal investigations, not external ones like CID. That meant the office, or someone in the office, was under suspicion.

"I'm on loan to the IG," Constance repeated. "That is all I have to share at the moment."

But Powell wasn't satisfied. "For how long? How long will this interruption continue?"

Playing the part well, Constance answered in true bureaucratic fashion. "That is indeterminate at this time. As soon as I'm settled, I'll start the interviews with you, Mr. Powell." She pointed at Remy. "Mr. Laurent, you are now second."

White as a sheet, Powell stared at the table.

I bit back a smile, as did a few others in the room. Constance had settled the power dynamic with Powell beautifully.

Tramell stepped forward. "I expect everyone to give their complete cooperation to Agent Evers." The meeting ended as he turned and left.

Back at my desk, Katelyn and Nick crowded into my cubicle.

"What do you think they're investigating?" Katelyn asked anxiously.

"No idea," Nick said. "I hope it's Powell's management style."

"Don't we all," I agreed.

Katelyn took the conversation down to a whisper. "Did you see how she put Powell in his place?"

I grinned. "Priceless."

"I don't want to get on her bad side," Nick noted.

Katelyn nodded. "No way. She's armed."

Nick poked his head up to check. "Yeah, that's hot. Maybe I'll ask her out."

"Pervert," Katelyn said, punching his shoulder.

Personally, I agreed with Nick. Duke was armed, and I thought he was hot.

Remy arrived. "The fro-yo truck is due any minute." The group dispersed as that news trumped the gossip.

I stayed, itching to get a call back from Duke.

An hour later, still no word from Duke, but Katelyn had returned.

She nodded toward the small conference room, which had a view of the entrance to my cubicle. "Why did she have to set herself up so close to us?"

I lifted from my chair and with a quick glance saw that Constance had chosen a seat that gave her a direct line of sight down the aisle of our cubicles. I shrugged. "It makes more sense than the large conference room."

"I guess, but she gives me the creeps."

"Me too," I lied. "What do you think she's after?"

"I hope it's Powell."

It was almost lunchtime when I got the message.

COBRA: What do you need?

I dialed his number.

"Cobra," he answered coldly.

Katelyn wasn't in her cubicle, but I whispered anyway. "Hi, this is Serena—"

"I know who it is. Is everything all right?" he asked. "Constance told me she's in position."

So he'd answered her call but not mine. "I wanted to talk," I explained.

After a pause, he said, "It's not a good idea for OPSEC. It should wait until after work."

From TV, I knew OPSEC meant *operational security*. "I'll be brief," I promised. "Still—"

"Thank you," I started before he could object further. This was not going the way I'd hoped, but I couldn't let him off the line without an answer. "Con…" I stopped myself from saying her name out loud in case somebody heard me. "The lady at breakfast said you made the omelet special for me, and I wanted to say thank you. It's always proper to thank people for thoughtful gestures, and yours was very thoughtful." I stopped myself from blathering further.

It was an agonizing second before he answered. "You're welcome."

"Also, I appreciate you taking care of me." It was time to take a chance and see where he stood. "Last night, after the note scared the crap out of me, and before the guys showed up, before the pizza, you know…" That should make it obvious enough.

"I told you, it's my job to patch you up and take care of you, keep you safe."

That wasn't a definite response. Maybe he didn't get the clues, so I laid myself bare. "I don't want to go to the hospital. I want you to change my bandage when I need it. Quick or slow, either way, is good. If you're up for it, that is, with a spoiled princess."

He laughed. "I never called you spoiled." Still not a concrete answer.

"And my bandage? I think you were right that girls who say it has to be pulled off slow are wrong." If he didn't get it, I was going to smack him over the head with a frying pan tonight.

"Anything you want, Princess. I can pull the bandage off fast or slow. You just have to tell me what you want."

I nearly jumped out of my seat with joy. That was a yes. I think. "What I want is for you to stop calling me Princess."

"Too late for that, Princess."

"Serena?" Katelyn called from behind me.

I had no idea how much she'd heard and hoped it had been nondescript enough. "I gotta go. Bye." I hung up and turned.

She cocked a brow. "Your hunky boyfriend?"

Without any other option, I nodded.

"I think Princess is a cute nickname." A hint of wetness shone in her eyes. "Leo used to call me Contessa."

"That is sweet," I agreed. "Maybe I can get used to it, but I don't think my guy means it the same way."

She scooted her chair closer. "What do you call him?"

I shrugged a shoulder. "We're kinda new. I don't have a name for him yet." Then I remembered. "Except for Cobra."

"I hope that's a reference to his size, you know where."

I blushed, afraid to touch that one.

"Leo was sort of average, but it's true what they say about Italian men. They know how to wield it."

My blush flamed hotter.

"What about your guy?"

Yes, what about my guy?

Remy interrupted us. "Watch yourselves," he mumbled. "She's a ball buster." He shifted his eyes in Constance's direction.

"Hey, want to go to Disneyland this Sunday?" Nick asked. "I scored some tickets."

"Jacques and I have plans," Remy said.

"I have to get back to work," I told the pair.

That got rid of Nick, but not Katelyn. "That sounds great. What do you say, Serena? We could make a day of it—the two of us. I mean, when else could I go? I can't exactly afford a ticket since…" Her expression drooped as her words faded.

She couldn't even say *since I lost Leo*. "Please?"

I wanted to agree. It would be nice. But with Black Jacket Guy out there, I couldn't. "Sorry, I've got a family barbecue this weekend." The barbecue was on Saturday, but it was the best excuse I could come up with to not insult her.

"The good kind of family get-together or the other?"

"A mix. It'll be good to see everyone, but my parents might invite my ex—"

"I thought you were seeing Duke the hunk."

I realized I'd stepped in it. I rolled my eyes. "That doesn't always matter. Dad has his own ideas."

Katelyn's face contorted. "Yuck. A meddler, huh?"

"Big time," I agreed.

"Tell him to stuff it. Is it all day? Maybe we could do the afternoon." She was clearly eager to get some time with me.

"Middle of the day and probably go late, sorry."

She plastered on a fake smile. "No biggie." She abruptly turned and left. Clearly, my decision had stung her.

Swiveling back to my screen, I tried to work, but found my thoughts hijacked by a very muscular, very tattooed bodyguard and my hope that we'd be alone tonight. Yes, alone, and with what I'd already experienced with him, I didn't care about quick versus slow, not one damned bit. I just craved more.

An hour later, a message arrived, and my pulse spiked with hope that it was from Duke. Then, I turned over my phone, and dread filled me.

UNKNOWN: You didn't obey. There will be consequences.

I dialed Constance's cell. "I just got a message."

"I know. Jordy is on it. Just go about your day."

My heart refused to slow down. *Just go about my day?* With a psycho after me? One thing was no longer a question—Jordy monitored my phone.

CHAPTER 18

DUKE

SINCE I'D GOTTEN OFF THE PHONE WITH SERENA, I'D BEEN HARD AS A ROCK, contemplating both quick and slow with my vixen. The big problem was going to be getting some alone time to explore each other. I didn't do girlfriends, but that didn't mean I couldn't spend more than my usual night or two with her. Right? Suddenly, my brain and body were all about making deals.

My phone buzzed with a call from Jordy. "What do you have?"

"She just got a text from the same number as the threatening call yesterday."

I tensed, pushing aside my daydream. "What does it say?"

"You didn't obey. There will be consequences."

"Asshole." My blood boiled. "Any luck tracking it down?"

He laughed. "You should know that's impossible if the guy knows what he's doing, and so far, this guy does. Still voice-over-IP bounced a million ways. But Winston is making progress on the car."

"Put me on speaker."

Winston's voice carried anger. "Too fucking many black or dark Suburbans in this town, but with her note that he had no front license plate, I narrowed it down. So far I've tracked him to West Hollywood, but I'm still going through footage and don't have where he parked yet."

"License?"

"Only a partial. It has mud on it."

"Convenient." That was an old-school trick. "Good work, Winston. Let me know when you find it. I'd like to pay this dirtbag a visit." I clenched my fist and visualized breaking somebody's nose, to start with.

"You got it," he said.

"And?" Jordy asked.

"And what?"

"And what about me?"

Remembering Serena's lesson, I dutifully told him, "Thank you for everything, Jordy." She'd already trained him to expect it. Then, I ended the call, leaned back in my chair, closed my eyes, and visualized something better than breaking the asshole's nose—Serena in my bed, her hair fanned out on the pillow and a sheet splayed across her waist, revealing those luscious tits, tits that called to me.

Who the hell am I? It had been one fucking day, one fucking make-out session, or rather one finger-fucking session, and hell, all of her called to me in a way I wasn't used to.

Maybe it was that we'd been interrupted before I got off. That had to be it because this wasn't me. Old Cobra would've been calling up Ursula for a sure thing. Maybe this was like that sci-fi TV show where the alien gave off super pheromones, like a love potion to anyone around.

Yeah, that could be it.

Two hours later, Lucas called. "I'm outside. Let's go. We found the Suburban."

I bounded down the stairs of the office building and jumped into Lucas's Aston Martin DBS. I didn't like the poor visibility in this low sports car, but with a V12, it sure could haul ass. It was even faster than the company Porsche Turbo GTs. The exhaust sounds were music to any car guy's ears. And it made a statement to arrive in a James Bond car.

"Winston didn't call me," I said as he took off going east.

"I told him not to."

"Why the hell not?"

"Because I couldn't have you race off there alone. It's in West Hollywood."

"Do we know who was driving?"

"It's parked behind Babushka Irena's restaurant."

I whistled. "Holy shit." That was Russian mob territory. West Hollywood had the highest concentration of Russians in the country outside of New York City.

"Exactly. We're going to pay Igor Yaroslavsky a visit."

Yaroslavsky ran prostitution and drugs, but a lot of his money came from a protection racket. He laundered the money through his legit businesses—car washes, refuse hauling, laundromats, and beauty salons.

I checked that my weapon had one in the pipe and de-cocked it.

Lucas stated the obvious. "Nobody goes in there alone. Winston will meet us. It's pucker time, and I wish we had Brett along."

I nodded. Lucas could handle any five men all by himself, so it said a lot that he wanted both me and Winston with him. "When's Brett getting back?" Winston was a good man in a fight and a damned good shot, but there was nothing like having our brother, Brett, another tier one operator, at our backs.

"Not soon enough, as far as I'm concerned."

"Copy that." I'd hoped Lucas had more info than I did since he'd been in Omega before Brett, but apparently not.

Brett had gotten the call from the secretary of defense himself, which could only mean Omega needed him. In our family, you didn't say no when SECDEF called. Duty was a part of our DNA.

Mentally, I crossed my fingers that we'd get him back in one piece. It sucked not knowing where he was or what he was up against, but I understood operational security and hadn't insulted him by asking about the op.

A few minutes later, we stopped in front of the restaurant, and Lucas made a call. "You ready?"

When he hung up, we got out, garnering our share of stares with the expensive car.

A pair of sketchy-looking kids walked up. "Nice car. We watch it for a hundred bucks."

Lucas pointed a finger. "You'll watch it for free."

The taller of the two laughed.

"Anything happens to it, and you answer to Mr. Yaroslavsky."

The kid stopped laughing and went pale. His buddy nodded.

Winston pulled up behind us.

"This car too," Lucas instructed.

"The vehicle and plates are stolen," Winston reported as we walked toward the door. "The car is still behind the restaurant."

"Calm and cool," Lucas said. "Let me do the talking. Winston, bring your ID?"

He smiled. "Sure thing."

We followed the boss inside.

Lucas spoke in Russian to the lady who greeted us, though all I caught out of it was *Lucas Hawk*.

She scurried off, and two big goons emerged from the back—one with a buzz cut and the other with no neck. They were both packing. Buzz Cut had his in an obvious shoulder holster, and Idiot No Neck had a Glock tucked into the front of his pants, easy to reach, but also an easy way to shoot your own dick off since a Glock had no safety.

Buzz Cut spoke. "Mr. Yaroslavsky not here."

"I'm Lucas Hawk. He'll talk to me, or we'll have a dozen FBI agents in here in sixty seconds flat."

"You not cop," Buzz Cut scoffed.

"He's FBI." Lucas thumbed in Winston's direction, never taking his eyes off the two.

Winston flipped open his old FBI creds. He'd kept a copy for just such an occasion, and he still trimmed his hair and dressed like he was in the bureau.

Sweat appeared on No Neck's forehead.

Lucas checked his watch. "Fifty seconds. If we don't call them off, they're coming in."

The next ten seconds were tense. Buzz Cut's eyes shifted left and right as a vein throbbed at his temple. He'd get blamed for sure if a bunch of FBI agents joined us, but he'd been told to send us away.

"Come," No Neck said, making up Buzz Cut's mind for him.

Winston lifted his phone and placed a quick call I knew was fake. "Hold fast."

We entered a back room. "Ah, Lucas Hawk," exclaimed the rotund man sitting at a table. "What bring you here?" He made it sound like he and Lucas were old friends. "Sit."

Lucas didn't accept the invitation. "Igor, it's come to my attention that you are bothering someone under my protection."

He laughed. "I bother no one."

"Her name is Serena Benson."

Igor's twitchy eye gave him away. He knew the name.

Lucas continued, "Igor, you don't want me as an enemy."

"I know nothing."

"He's lying," I spat.

Lucas fixed me with a glare and turned back to Yaroslavsky. "Bullshit."

Igor's fist hit the table, and his eyes narrowed. "You in my house."

"You're in my town, Igor."

"Big talk," the Russian scoffed.

Lucas's hand balled into a fist. "You know my reputation. Back off, or you won't like the consequences." Then he raised the finger—the finger of death.

Igor's eye twitched. He'd heard the stories. "I only acquire information and supply car to man," he said, looking away.

That confirmed that these Russian dickheads were involved in the attack.

"Well, you're fuck out of luck because she doesn't have it," Lucas countered, lowering the finger.

"My information say different."

"You should double-check."

"Can not."

What the hell did that mean?

"She lie to you."

Lucas wasn't done. "The car that ran her off the road is behind this restaurant. I want the driver."

Igor twitched again. "Not my business. I only supply information and clean car."

"Who the fuck is the driver?"

"Independent contractor. I don't know him."

"Who? I want a name."

The staring contest lasted five seconds before Yaroslavsky gave in. "I look into it."

I expected Lucas to push, but he only said, "Noon tomorrow or we have a big problem."

I couldn't ask any questions until we were outside and secure in the car. But once the door closed behind me, I nearly burst. "What happened? We should have pushed for the name. Now we have to wait a day."

Lucas shook his head. "We won't have to wait long. He's going to give the guy a head start to get out of Dodge. Anything less and he loses face."

"But—"

"But nothing. We're on his turf, and we got another clue when he said he couldn't double-check his information. His source is either in the wind or dead. Just in case, we'll look for bodies."

I opened my mouth and then closed it. I hadn't picked up on that. Lucas was as smart as he was lethal.

"She's not safe until we figure out what they're after," he added. "Igor is only a middleman. We take him out of the picture, and whoever is behind this gets somebody else."

Winston nodded, exited the car, and drove off in his vehicle.

"You have to find out what Serena knows," Lucas told me. "It'll be some detail she doesn't realize is important."

I nodded as Lucas waved at the two kids and sped away.

Things looked a lot less rosy now than when he'd first told me we'd tracked the Suburban.

A few minutes later, his phone rang. He put it on speaker. "Jordy, what have we got?"

"He made two calls, one to a local burner phone that took the call driving south on the four-oh-five and then went dark."

Lucas grinned. "That'll be our guy. Watch for the phone to go live again, and let us know the minute it does. It might end up in another state. What about the second?"

"He called Miami. I'll have to get back to the office to identify who took it."

Lucas braked for the next light. "Good work, Jordy."

"What did he say on the call?" I asked Jordy.

"Hi, Duke. That would be a major miracle, and I deal in minor ones today. Numbers only."

"Thank you, Jordy."

"You're welcome, Duke." The call disconnected.

"How did he—"

Lucas didn't let me finish. "Howard Hawks once said…"

I waited for another of his corny quotes.

"Fortune favors the prepared." He glanced over and smiled. "I had Jordy set up behind the restaurant to spoof the local cell tower."

Yes, definitely as smart as he was lethal.

SERENA

AT THE END OF THE DAY, KATELYN WALKED OUT WITH ME AGAIN, AND WE RODE DOWN in the same elevator to the lobby.

She pulled me to a stop. "Pinch me. I must be dreaming." She pointed out Duke, who hadn't noticed us yet. "Is he for real? Leo never came to pick me up. Let me know when you're done with him. I could use a man like that."

"Oh, he's real." I didn't address her request. Duke wasn't one to be passed along.

"He's one mighty fine specimen."

"He can cook too," I bragged, although I had yet to taste it. But Constance wouldn't steer me wrong.

"Can I meet him?"

She was taking this pass-the-boyfriend-along thing way too far.

"And let you charm him away? No, thank you. He's mine, and we have to get going." We did because we had to meet Constance on Veteran Avenue to pick her up.

"Okay, already. I get it. See you tomorrow." Past security, Katelyn turned left for the other doors.

I walked up to Duke and planted a kiss on him, pulling back before I'd gotten my fill. "Have to keep up appearances for Katelyn."

"Right." He pulled me back in.

I surrendered to him as my sense of where we were evaporated. The electric feel of his body against mine and the sinful taste of him pushed all rational thought aside.

His arm around me flattened my breasts against him, and I wished for fewer onlookers and a lot fewer clothes between us as our tongues dueled. It was all I could do to keep my hands at his neck instead of cruising over his body the way they craved. I loved that I was making him hard, and I desperately wished my words to Katelyn had been real.

He broke away and stuffed both hands in his pockets. "Is that good enough?"

Dreamily, I nodded. "For now." My heart thumped in my chest, wanting later to come pretty damned soon.

Constance walked by us without a glance.

DUKE

SERENA WAS NERVOUS AS A MOUSE AT AN OWL CONVENTION ALL THE WAY TO THE CAR. "What are we going to tell her?" she finally asked.

"Constance?" I shrugged. "The truth. We had to make it believable for your coworker, that's all."

"I guess."

"Or the other truth," I teased.

"Which is?"

"That you want to test drive my big cock." I laughed.

She punched my shoulder—hard. "You're terrible...and conceited."

"Only if it's not the truth."

She punched me again. "Grow up. I don't talk like that."

I laughed again. "But you think like that."

She joined the laugh and then hauled back and punched me again.

"Struck a nerve, did I?"

All I got was a glare and the silent treatment the rest of the way to the car.

We picked up Constance on Veteran as planned. She chose to ride shotgun, leaving Serena in the back.

"What was that?" she asked as soon as she'd closed the door.

I started us off. "What was what?"

"The kissing, of course."

"Katelyn walked out with me yesterday," Serena explained. "And she saw me with Duke, so I had to explain him away as my boyfriend. She followed me out again today."

"So it's the cover, same as we planned for the barbecue," I added.

Constance poked my shoulder. "Tough gig."

I chuckled. "If you recall, I suggested you be her date to the barbecue. Then you two could make out."

"Not with my family," Serena complained.

Constance made a face. "Yeah, we'll stick with the original plan." Then, she launched into a discussion of what she'd observed today. It seemed we'd gotten past the kiss. "And her boss is an ass."

"Amen to that," Serena agreed.

Constance kept checking our mirrors. "The CID agent in charge doesn't like me."

I changed lanes. "Will he be a problem?"

"I don't expect so. My letter from his boss's boss's boss tells him to stay out of my business. That should cover it." She sighed. "I heard you had an exciting meeting with the Russians."

"Jordy?"

"Yep."

"What Russians?" Serena asked. "Why would Russians be after me?"

I checked my mirrors again. "He said he was only hired to get information—the information that points to you having the USB drive—and then he provided a car to somebody unknown."

"Oh." Disappointment tinged Serena's voice.

I added the good news. "Lucas doesn't want to push him too far, but we did get him to call the perp."

Serena unbuckled and leaned up between the seats. "You found him? Who is he?"

"No name," I said as we reached a stoplight. "But we have a phone number to track. For now, he's keeping the phone off, so we have to wait."

"That's good, right?"

"Put your seatbelt on," I ordered. "If we're followed, the ride could get hairy."

"You don't have to be so bossy."

Constance raised a brow and smirked.

"Serena," I intoned calmly. "Would you please put on your seatbelt? It's for your safety."

She moved back and buckled in. "Was that so hard?"

I gritted my teeth but kept my tongue in check.

Constance turned and did the client-calming for me. "It's very good progress."

"That means I can get my life back soon, right?"

"No. It can take time to find a man like this," Constance explained.

With that, everything in me deflated. Serena sounded like she'd be happy to finish with us and be done with me, all before we'd even started. I had a very unprofessional desire for this assignment to go slowly.

As if to point out my ridiculous feelings, an hour later my phone buzzed with a text.

URSULA: Are you around?

CHAPTER 19

Serena

By the time we made it home, playful Duke had somehow turned into Grumpy Cobra. New cameras had been placed under the eaves, and the front door looked different.

"What's this?" I asked, pointing at the new rectangular glass panel nearby.

"Palm scanner," Constance answered. She put her hand against it, and the door clicked to unlock.

I followed her inside.

"Terry's been busy," she commented, touching the new keypad with a dozen buttons and lights. "Big upgrade."

Duke only grunted.

I went up to my room to change without another word to Mr. Grumpypants.

When I came back downstairs, my kitchen was full of security professionals having a heated conversation.

"I tell you, she won't go for it." That was Mr. Grumpypants himself.

Their discussion stopped when I walked in.

Lucas Hawk's presence dominated the room. He turned over a piece of paper.

The man scared the crap out of me, but it was time to be bold. I walked straight up to him. "I won't like what?"

He didn't blink. "We think we should move you to a more secure location."

I shook my head. "Cobra was right. The answer was no yesterday, and it's still no today."

Terry tried to hand Duke a bill without me seeing.

I speared Duke with a look. "You bet on my answer?"

Duke pointed next to him. "He bet. He lost."

I crossed my arms. "You guys are unbelievable. I said from the beginning that I would not be chased out of my house, and now you want me to leave the same day you upgraded my security system to Fort Knox?"

Duke raised his hands in surrender. "Not me."

Loudly, I let Lucas have it. "I hired you to protect me, not lock me away."

Lucas tried calming hand gestures. "Just a minute, Serena."

I looked him in the eye. "I'm listening. You tell me why you can't handle the job."

"We got a clear enough view of the guy's face from one of the traffic cameras to run facial recognition."

I nodded. This was standard TV and movie fare. "So who is he?"

"We're only at ninety-one percent certainty," Lucas explained. "But we think it's Tony Spinelli. He's a freelancer, a former Special Forces gun for hire to the highest bidder, and a very bad actor. If it were some local schmuck, I wouldn't be recommending this, but this guy is a pro."

"He was a tier-one operator," Duke added. "A guy who's worked with him called him top-notch but unpredictable, which is why he got booted."

Lucas flipped over the paper they'd been looking at. It was a picture of Black Jacket Guy.

My leg started to twitch. "That's the guy who ran me off the road." Now I had a name to go with my fear, a name I'd never forget. *Tony Spinelli.*

Winston looked my way. "I checked with the Bureau, and he's been close to making their ten-most-wanted list for a kidnapping in Georgia that they think was one of many. The woman got away and told a story of multiple other women being held for human trafficking. Word is his brother, Johnson, runs that business. But he's slippery, and they've never nailed down a case against him."

I hated to admit it, but their scare tactics were working. I gritted my teeth to make the most difficult decision of my life. Then Duke's advice came back to me. "If I start running, it will never end," I told them. "If you need to hire additional people, do it."

Lucas looked around the table. "Okay, people, it's all hands on deck for now."

Nods followed. I relaxed.

"You got that, Jordy?" he asked.

"Got it, Lucas." Jordy's voice came from the phone sitting face up on the granite. So, the group had been complete. Jordy was here all along.

I squeezed into the space between Constance and Terry. "What does this mean?"

Terry chuckled. "It means Constance is the only one getting a full night's sleep."

"Duke, Terry, and Winston will split the night-time guard duty," Lucas explained. "Constance stays in the building while you work."

"I want that post," Winston complained.

Constance stuck out her tongue. "You should've stayed a consultant."

Lucas rolled his eyes. "And Duke is on standby while you work, to handle any off-the-premises time."

Duke wore something less than his bite-a-lemon face, but he clearly wasn't happy. He raised a hand. "I know you've been talking to Singleton and March. They're good guys, and they'd fill out the team nicely."

"I was thinking the same thing." Lucas nodded. "I'll see if they're available and ready for trial by fire."

"A frogman is always ready," Duke answered.

It reminded me of his tattoo about always getting back up.

When he met my eyes, it was still with that sour face.

After a moment, I left the group and went upstairs to wait for the Chinese takeout they'd ordered. They continued talking about camera coverage and other things I didn't understand.

∽

HALF AN HOUR LATER, A KNOCK SOUNDED AT MY BEDROOM DOOR.

"Come in."

It was Duke carrying a tray. "I made a plate for you. Not sure what you like, so I've got a little of everything." He shut the door behind him.

"Thank you."

The tray had two plates. "That's more than I can eat."

He smiled. "I thought I'd eat with you."

For a moment, I thought I'd heard him say he wanted to eat me. That's how out of control my hormones were. Scooting back against the headboard, I smiled for the first time tonight. "I'd like that."

He sat cross-legged at the foot of the bed and placed the tray between us. "We should talk about us."

My chest seized. I'd never seen a movie where a conversation that started with those words ended well.

∽

DUKE

. . .

114

Serena looked down, disappointment clouding her beautiful face. "What about us?"

"I thought things would be slower here at the house, and we'd have time to be alone. But…" Swimming a mile in frigid water was something anybody would consider hard. But right now, I'd rather have started a *five*-mile swim than face this conversation.

"You want to call it off? Is that it?" she guessed.

"No."

Her face lit up as she let out a breath. "Good."

The difficulty had just moved to a ten-mile swim. I took her hand. "But with everybody here… We can't…"

Confusion filled her eyes as she yanked her hand back. "Stop telling me what I can and can't do."

"It would look—"

Anger welled up in her eyes. "You're ashamed of wanting to be with me."

I tried for her hand again, but she pulled it away, denying me the physical connection I needed to express what my words kept messing up.

"You should go." Her words cut deep.

Then I did the one thing I shouldn't have. I got up off the bed.

She glared at me. "Coward."

Seething, I launched myself at her, taking her mouth with mine before she could scream.

She fought for two seconds before anger morphed into desire, and she clawed at my hair, pulling us together the way I wanted. Her tongue fought mine for control, and her hand slid down to cup my aching cock.

"I want you," she mumbled.

I pulled away, regaining control, and stood. "No. I don't think—"

"Damn, you're stupid." She crossed her arms over her full tits. "This isn't a time for thinking."

"Dammit, woman." I pointed an angry finger at her. "Stop interrupting and listen for a change."

She grimaced, but for once didn't argue.

"I don't want my team to think less of me, so until I talk to Lucas, we need to keep a lid on this."

"Does—"

"Don't…" I cut her off with a finger to her lips. "Say a thing. I want you, too, but I won't sully either of us by sneaking around. When the time is right, we're doing this in the open."

She nodded with a sigh. "When?"

"I'll let you know." I picked up one of the plates. "Now eat your dinner and know that we're going to keep you safe." I went to the door. "One more thing. It's not safe to call a SEAL either stupid or a coward."

"Sorry about that." She blew me an air kiss.

I blew one back and closed the door behind me.

Blowing air kisses? Since when did I do that?

As I walked down the stairs, fear crept up my spine. That had been dangerously close to acting like a real boyfriend, and I didn't do relationships. I could handle a fling or hell, even a fuckbuddy, but not a real girlfriend. Not since Marilyn.

Then my real fear reared its ugly head. *I'm not good enough for Serena. She may want more than I can offer.*

A long, lonely night lay ahead of me. I knew sleep wouldn't come until I jerked off to thoughts of Serena. Vicarious pleasure would have to do until I got this shit sorted out. And, if I woke up in the middle of the night, I'd have to repeat the process to get back to sleep.

I stopped and considered turning around.

$\sim$

SERENA

THE DOOR CLOSED AND I FLOPPED BACK ON THE BED ASHAMED OF HOW I'D ACTED.

Sure I wanted him more than I could put into words, but I'd acted like a spoiled brat when he'd insisted on being the principled adult.

And the worst part of it was that the integrity he showed in wanting to wait and do the right thing by his team was a quality that made me desire him even more.

Yes, my badass SEAL had integrity and principles.

I rolled to the side of the bed and pulled my toy out of the nightstand. It would have to do.

CHAPTER 20

Duke

On Wednesday afternoon, I picked Serena up after work, same as before. We shared a kiss, but she didn't hold my hand on the way back to the car.

"How was work today?" I asked.

"Oh, same old, same old, except that I'm grounded. After the crash, my boss won't let me go out in the field until he figures out what to do with me."

"But it wasn't your fault."

She shot me the side eye. "And you told me to claim it was."

"Sorry."

"Yeah, everybody's sorry for me except Remy, who's sorry for the deer. I can tell Powell is trying to use this to demote me and put his pet, Remy, in my place."

I beeped the door locks open. "That sucks."

"Tell me about. It's really, really sucked to be me for a few days."

Inside the car, she didn't look my way or offer her hand. We were definitely in Awkwardville after last night, and there was nothing I could do about it because Lucas had been called out of town for the rest of the week. The conversation I needed to have with him couldn't be done over the phone.

"I need some clean clothes," I told her. "Is it okay if we stop by my place on the way home?"

She stared out the window. "Whatever."

As I turned onto Wilshire, she looked over at me. "I'm still supposed to wait, right?"

I glanced over. She was beautiful, and I yearned to touch her. But I nodded. "Lucas is out of town." I turned into the long circular drive in front of my building. "We're here."

"I thought you said we were going to your house."

"I said *place*." She was correct that it was no house. It was a gigantic fucking tower.

"Holy shit. You live here?" Her surprise was understandable, given that this was the premier address in this part of town.

I shrugged. "Mr. Covington's wife named it Battlestar Covington. I just call it home."

"You know Lauren?"

I parked and shut off the engine. "We've done work for several of the Covingtons."

She let me run around the car to let her out.

Before we reached the safety of the lobby, three men stepped out from behind a car. I recognized the two burly ones as two of Zolotarev's goons, Baldy and Tattoo Neck. I remembered seeing them drop Ariana off to meet her father.

This was not good. I stopped us, dropped the bag, and swept Serena behind me with my free hand.

"Stay back," I whispered. I had my phone in my hand, and I wished it was my SIG. But my weapon was sitting in the lockbox in my truck. I hadn't expected to need it in my own parking lot.

Baldy had a Beretta out, and I bet he knew how to use it.

Tattoo Neck flexed his fists. He didn't have a gun.

The shorter man I didn't recognize.

"You," Shorty said, pointing an angry finger. "You hurt my sister." That explained who he was. The idiot brother, Stanislav—the one even airhead Ariana called stupid.

"She never got hurt when I was with her." I kept it simple for rocks-for-brains.

Shorty kept coming. "You walk away. She get cut. Your fault." He parroted his father's faulty logic.

"Not my problem. She fired me." I stood my ground. Distance was not my friend here. With a gun in play, I needed them close to have a chance. Even if I hadn't released Terry for the night, he couldn't have arrived in time. "Now leave. This is private property."

Shorty laughed and then spat on the ground. "We fix you."

They all moved forward.

My adrenaline surged as I prepared. "I'm warning you." Pretending I was scared, I took a small step away and forcefully pushed Serena farther back. "Stay behind me, baby."

Shorty was still flapping his gums but hadn't pulled a weapon, which gave me a chance. "Papa tell you. You not listen. Now you learn." He nodded to Baldy, who stepped forward.

Baldy grinned and swung the barrel back and forth.

Tattoo Neck came up behind him.

"Which knee, pretty boy?" Shorty laughed.

Baldy moved closer, keeping his feet tight together. "Or shoot..." He waved the gun in the air. "Your woman."

Big mistake. "You will not threaten her," I growled.

"Or what, pretty boy?" Shorty snorted.

With his feet together like that, Baldy couldn't quickly move sideways or back.

Tossing my phone, I lunged.

I was almost there when the gun went off.

I PUSHED PAPER AT THE EPA. HOW HAD THIS BECOME MY LIFE?

I felt Duke tense, then he threw his phone and jumped. The big, bald man fired, and my heart stopped.

Duke landed a kick to the guy's gun arm, and the weapon went flying.

The tattooed one moved up to swing, and he missed as Duke landed a punch on his neck and a kick to that guy's midsection, sending him against a parked car.

Bald Guy recovered and swung wildly, hitting Duke in the side. Duke retaliated with a combination of punches to the man's face that made him look like a bobblehead doll before he slumped to the ground.

The tattooed one got up and ran at Duke, who stopped him with a kick to the head. He went down in a heap. Their boss, the short one, watched slack-jawed as my man took out his two thugs. He fumbled at his pocket.

If he pulled out a gun, this wouldn't end well. I screamed and hurled myself toward him.

Duke punched the bald one again when he tried to get up.

The boss was still having trouble with the Velcro on his pocket when I reached him and launched a woman's best offense—a kick to his balls. He didn't swivel enough to escape, and my shoe landed solidly. With a cry like he was dying, he crumpled to the ground and curled into the fetal position.

Duke landed another fist to the bald one's head as the doorman jogged up. The bald guy went limp.

"My goodness, Mr. Hawk. What happened?" The doorman's accent was British.

I wanted to scream that my man was a badass and had just creamed five or six hundred pounds of Russian muscle. That's what happened.

"Oliver, these three jumped us." Duke pointed. "Please get the gun."

I should have thought of that. I watched Oliver scurry over and grab the pistol. He clearly knew how to handle it.

Duke stood. "If any of them move, shoot them anywhere you like."

Oliver grinned. "My pleasure, Mr. Hawk. I'm partial to the stomach. But it's been a few years, and I might miss and hit the groin."

The short guy in front of me moaned, and I gave him a warning glare and cocked my kicking leg back. "Don't move."

"Oliver, this is my girlfriend, Serena Benson," Duke continued. "She is to have full access to the building and my unit."

I blushed. Being Duke's girlfriend still felt almost too good to be true. I gave the old man a slight wave. "Hi."

Oliver tipped his chin. "A pleasure, Miss Benson." He pulled out a phone with his free hand. "Shall I call the police, sir?"

Duke waved a finger. "No need. My company will take care of it."

Oliver nodded knowingly and put the phone away. "As you wish, sir."

A minute later, my badass man had the two big guys zip-tied. "Sorry, I didn't bring enough zip ties for everybody. Oliver, shoot this short little shit if he moves a muscle."

Duke took my hand. "I hope my phone's okay."

I clung to the security of his hold as we searched for it. "Why'd you throw it at him?"

"Not at him. Off to the side."

I admitted my biggest fear. "I thought he shot you."

"Not even close. The eye instinctively follows a moving object. That gave me the advantage." He picked up the phone and with a quick call arranged to have Terry pick the guys up.

"You scared the shit out of me. Please don't do that again. I almost had a heart attack." I kept the other part to myself—that watching him do his badass thing turned me on.

He pulled me close with a possessive arm. "No promises, Princess. I'll do whatever it takes to keep you safe—anything and everything."

Nobody had ever said that to me before, and I knew my protector meant every word of it. I wished even more that I could take him someplace private and show him how much I appreciated him. "Watching you take down those goons was the hottest thing I've ever witnessed."

"Really?" He pointed at two motorcycles as we passed, one a big black Harley and the other a small, sleek machine that looked like a racer. "Ever ridden?"

"No." I'd only dated milquetoast boys who didn't ride badass motorcycles. And Dad had forbidden me to ever ride a bike after Johnny Raskin had shown up with one. I didn't hear from Johnny again after Dad's outburst.

Duke grinned. "We'll fix that after this whole thing is over."

"Yes, please." I pulled myself closer to my badass biker.

"Do you think it's safe to leave Oliver alone with those three?" I asked as we entered the lobby.

Duke chuckled. "Don't let him fool you. He can probably shoot the tail off a field mouse at a hundred yards. He's former SAS."

Ahh, yes. SAS was the British armed forces equivalent of our SEALs.

"Some people say they're even better than our SEALs," I joked. When Duke's eyebrow rose, I quickly added, "Some people are idiots."

LATER THAT NIGHT, I FINISHED BRUSHING MY TEETH, AND AS ALWAYS, DOUBLE-checked the nightlights before getting into bed.

Accepting that I had poor willpower, I reached into my nightstand for my vibrator. It was nothing to be ashamed of. Probably Duke was taking care of business as well. All guys did that, didn't they?

I couldn't wait for Duke to clear this up so we could be together. It was noble of him to want to handle things professionally with his team, but honestly, we were adults and didn't need anybody's permission to take things beyond platonic.

Switching on the toy, I settled back and spread my legs. Soon, I was moaning his name.

CHAPTER 21

SERENA

FINALLY, IT WAS SATURDAY. THE REST OF THE WEEK HAD GONE BY QUIETLY, BOTH AT work and at home.

Powell had kept me grounded from going out in the field while he decided what to do with me. *Car-wrecker,* he'd taken to calling me, and he bitched about his budget and the cost of a new vehicle. I sighed. At least so far he hadn't given my spot to Remy like I knew he wanted to.

Since our little talk Tuesday night, Duke had been discreetly professional around me, sneaking a glance here and there, setting his hand on my hip or lower back but nothing more.

Every night, I went to bed frustrated. Thinking of Duke's expert hands while using my vibrator had become my only outlet. Having him so close, but so far, was killing me. *What is taking him so long?*

"Ready?" Constance called from outside my door.

"Almost." I checked my concealer again. The sunglasses would help hide the evidence of my accident last Monday, but it wasn't perfect. Still, the day of the family barbecue had arrived, and it was time to face the inevitable.

Constance and Terry would be outside my parents' property today. "*On standby,*" Lucas had called it. They'd be ready if Duke needed to call them in.

I applied more eyeshadow. With this little sundress, I planned to make it hard for Duke to look anywhere else. Since staying away from him hadn't motivated him to clear things up with his team quickly, maybe the temptress look would.

"Wow," Constance exclaimed when I finally opened the door. "You're going to kill him."

My eyes widened. "It's going to be warm, and this is all I had that was clean."

She raised a brow, not falling for my high-school-level deception. "I am a trained Secret Service agent. Who do you think you're fooling? I see the way you two look at each other. Dressed like this, you want him to step up and make his move."

I thought we'd been extremely discreet around the team. I guess not. "I do think he's kinda cute," I admitted.

"And he can't take his eyes off of you."

Blushing, I basked in the warmth of her words. I shouldn't have felt insecure, but it was hard not to when the man who said he wanted me seemed in no hurry to *make his move*, as she'd put it. "Why do you think he's holding back?"

She shook her head. "Why do men do half the shit they do? Because they're emotionally stunted creatures and too scared to admit it."

I giggled. "Yeah."

Duke's voice boomed from downstairs. "Terry left to get in position. Aren't you girls ready yet?"

"Coming," Constance yelled back.

Duke's eyes widened when he saw me coming down the stairs. Yup, it was the first time he'd seen me in a dress, and he liked my legs. Hot damn, did he like them.

Then, he averted his gaze. While he locked up the house, Constance and I went ahead to climb into the backseat of his SUV.

"He noticed," she commented.

"Shush."

The drive to Dad's compound went by in silence. Duke ignored us and put on his sour face.

I knew he didn't want to go to this event, but not why it was such a big deal to him. But it was his tough shit because I didn't have an alternative.

Nearing the family compound, Duke pulled to the curb behind Terry's car. Constance got out, and I moved up to the front seat.

When we reached the gate, the guard recognized me and waved us through without ID.

"You're nervous," Duke observed.

"A little."

"Explain that to me."

"Vincent told me Dad wants me to get back together with my ex."

"Why does your father get a say?"

I sighed. "You wouldn't understand." Nobody would. I turned it around on him. "You look nervous, too."

123

It didn't work. "What's this butthead ex of yours look like?" he asked.

"George is not as tall as you. Blond, longer hair last time I saw him. Scrawny by comparison. Oh, and he was a SEAL too."

"Really? A team guy, huh?" Duke snorted. "Maybe I won't break his face."

I laughed. "I'll point him out if he shows. He might not. Now wipe that scowl off your face and remember to act like my boyfriend, just in case."

After we parked, I caught movement in the curtains. I waited for Duke to open my door for me like a proper boyfriend in case it was Mom watching.

We mounted the concrete steps up to the house, and a zing went through me as Duke put his hand on the small of my back. God, that felt right. Every time he touched me was like the first time. It was scary how exciting I found it. I looked over to smile at him and realized Duke had a paper bag I hadn't noticed earlier.

When the door opened, Mom stood just inside, as I'd suspected. She looked over her glasses at me. "Serena, I didn't realize you were bringing somebody along." She hid her disappointment well.

"Mom, I'd like you to meet Duke Hawk. Duke, my mother, Marcia Benson."
Duke offered his hand.

It was a gesture she couldn't refuse.

"Duke is my boyfriend," I added, catching the twitch of Mom's eye as I did. *Score one for me.*

"A pleasure, Mrs. Benson," Duke said, whipping a rose out of the bag. "You have a lovely home, and I can see where Serena gets her beauty." He held the flower out to her. "I picked this for you. It's an American Beauty. Serena said you like roses."

Mom blushed and almost teared up taking the flower. "Why, thank you, Duke. And Marcia will do."

"Is Dad around?" I needed to get us away from Mom before I started crying at how gentlemanly Duke was.

"He had some meeting or other scheduled, and he's not back yet. Dennis can't make it. Kelly and Vincent are out back. Zach is working the grill. I'm sure your father won't miss the food. He can sniff out grilled meat ten miles away." Mom twirled the flower in her fingers.

Duke's lips curved. "A pleasure, Marcia." Then he escorted me down the hallway with my hand in his.

"What was that?" I whispered when we made it out to the back patio.

"You wanted me to act like a proper boyfriend."

"Yeah, but do you have to be so nice that she decides to adopt you?" I jumped with a yelp when he swatted my ass. "What was that for?"

"You said you didn't want me perfect."

"Let's find something that doesn't involve hitting."

"It's called spanking, and some women like it." With a strong arm around my waist, he pulled me close and kissed my ear before whispering, "Is this better?"

I sighed and nearly melted at how wonderful the contact between our bodies felt after days of longing for it. "Much better." The spanking mention didn't deserve a response.

We got through the introductions to my brothers and sister without the appearance of any more flowers, spanking, or any other weirdness.

With every glance from Duke and every touch of his hand at my back, he amped up my desire for him. After a week of keeping my distance, I wanted to drag him into my old bedroom and make him choose me over his need to look professional for his team.

As Duke asked plenty of get-to-know-you questions of my family, I intertwined my fingers with his. Here, he couldn't put artificial distance between us for appearance's sake.

When something got in my eye, I pulled off my sunglasses to wipe it away.

Kelly eyed me suspiciously, and as soon as the guys moved on to the topic of basketball and the Lakers, she pulled me aside. "What happened to your face?" She touched the bridge of her nose.

Found out. "A car accident." That part was truthful. "Please don't mention it to anybody, especially Dad. It's embarrassing, and you know how he gets."

"No worries." She laid a hand on my shoulder. "I've got your back. Just keep the sunglasses on." She looked back at the guys, and a mischievous grin appeared. "Now," she breathed. "Tell me about Duke. Is he the reason you won't return my calls?"

I pulled us farther away from them. "Yes."

She fanned her face. "He's hot. Where do I go to find another one like him?"

"Self-defense class. He's an instructor." It was the cover we'd discussed.

Duke sent a smoldering smile my way, and I waved back.

"He looks like he could lift the house off its foundation."

I nodded. "And then some." I wished I could get my hands on those muscles *right freaking now.*

Serena's brothers, Vincent and Zach, were even bigger Lakers fans than I was.

"Of course, they have a chance at the semis, if not winning the whole thing," I asserted.

Zach prodded the meat again and turned one burger. "I say all the way."

I turned back to Vincent. "Serena tells me you're looking at a new job."

"If it pans out."

"Tell me about it."

"If they like me, I'd be going to Boston to run the East Coast operations of Covington Industries. This would be the first time they trust someone outside the family with a chunk of the business."

"That's cool. Working for Bill?"

"Exactly. You know the Covingtons?" He seemed surprised.

"Yeah. Stand-up people. Hey, doesn't Liam run the Boston office?"

He moved closer and lowered his voice. "Yes, but his wife's sick, and he wants to take some leave."

"Oh, that's terrible."

"Uh-oh…" Vincent whispered.

I turned to see a man I knew wasn't a Benson. I'd spent a lot of time studying photos of Serena's family.

"Dad went through with it," Vincent mused. He elbowed Zach.

"What?"

"Dad invited Kittleman."

Ahhh… Butthead had arrived.

The man walked toward us. "Hey, Vince."

"It's Vincent," Benson replied.

"Yeah, right."

I'd had Jordy check Butthead's last few years, and they'd been unimpressive. He looked just like the idle rich kid the paperwork said he was.

"Hi, I'm Duke. You must be Georgie."

His nose wrinkled slightly. "George will do."

I dispensed with polite, deciding direct was the better option. "What are you doing here?"

He paused, clearly not expecting that. "I'm back in town and reconnecting with my girl."

The fuck you are.

Behind him, Zach rolled his eyes.

I offered my hand. "Nice to meet…"

Butthead took it.

"The ex," I added as I squeezed his sweaty hand.

He tried to pull loose, but I kept shaking and tightened my grip.

"Where's Serena?" he stuttered.

After one final squeeze, I let him go and sniffed the air. "Do you smell that?"

"What?"

I sniffed the air. "Something smells off."

Vincent hid his smile behind a cough.

My impression of Serena's father had started low, but it had just gotten lower. Lloyd Benson had abysmal standards for his daughter if he thought George "Butthead" Kittleman was deserving.

I might be in over my head, but I decided to go for it. Serena was going to be mine, and George would get nothing. Why was I denying what I'd felt from the moment the feisty woman told off Lucas? I could manage having a little fun, right?

~

SERENA

NOT LONG AFTER HE ARRIVED AT MY PARENTS', GEORGE BROKE OFF TALKING WITH THE guys and sought me out. He asked for a moment of my time, which I put off until after lunch.

At that point, my plan was to leave as soon as the meal finished. George was my past, and the attraction I felt for Duke was a hundred times greater than anything I'd ever felt for George. The sooner I got away from him the better.

Duke stayed close by while my brothers dominated the conversation.

Mom was right about Dad arriving when the burgers were ready. She'd just gone up to fetch the potato salad when my brother, Josh, stopped his monologue about the latest acquisition and stared up at the house.

"Who's that with Dad?" Vincent asked.

Duke didn't dare answer, and neither did I. Lucas Hawk, Duke's older brother, and boss, was alongside Dad as they strode our way.

"Just in time for burgers and dogs," Zach offered. "Mom's getting the potato salad."

"In a minute, Zach." Dad pointed at me as he walked up. "Munchkin, we need a word with you first."

Lucas's face was impassive, giving nothing away.

"Okay." I moved forward, and so did Duke.

Dad gave me his customary bear hug.

I stepped back. "Dad, this is my boyfriend, Duke."

Dad ignored Duke and motioned toward the old oak tree. "Just you, Munchkin."

I'd had enough of this. "Duke too."

Dad pointed a finger at Duke. "Stay. Just you, Serena."

The rest of the group stayed silent.

"No, Dad. Whatever you have to say, Duke can hear."

127

"Serena," he cautioned.

"You told me relationships should be equal. We're a package deal."

Dad took in a long breath and gave in, nodding toward the tree. "Okay." He turned to Zach. "This won't take long. Keep those burgers warm."

As we walked, I smiled at Duke. I'd won one against Dad.

Duke took my hand, but there was tension in his face.

My comment about being in a relationship with Duke had just slipped out. Had I made a mistake? When we reached the tree, I looked back to see my siblings busy with hushed conversations.

Dad turned to my new relationship partner. "Duke, right?"

"Yes, sir." They shook hands, but I sensed an undercurrent of distrust from Duke.

"Son," Dad said. "What you are about to hear is not to be discussed with anyone—not your parents, not your priest, not your dog, no one."

"Understood, sir."

Dad looked at me and took a breath. "Munchkin, Harvey Fox—"

"Stop," I cried. I couldn't go there. We couldn't ever talk about him again.

Dad ignored my plea. "He was granted parole, and I'm afraid he may be dangerous."

The words hit me like a freight train. My legs went weak, and my vision blurred. I remembered Fox's glare after the judge pronounced his sentence, but worse than that was the threat he'd mouthed as they led him away.

My longtime nightmare had become real.

CHAPTER 22

Duke

Lloyd Benson, the man who'd ruined my future years ago, hadn't recognized me. Perhaps not surprising. I'd been the poor kid, the camp counselor from the wrong family, back then. Why would he remember someone so lowly?

I looked down at Serena. As soon as her father mentioned Harvey Fox, she'd trembled and wobbled, about to faint. I grabbed her before she could fall and continued to hold her.

Talk of Harvey Fox, whoever the fuck he was, had knocked the wind out of my strong, confident woman. And a threat to her was unfuckingacceptable. "Nobody is getting to her," I practically yelled.

My declaration seemed to have stunned Serena's father. She clung to me for a few more seconds but then regained her balance and composure and straightened. "Duke, I'm okay."

I nodded and let her go, save a protective arm around her waist. She was mine to protect, regardless of where the threat originated, and everybody needed to know that.

"Munchkin, you remember Lucas from before," Benson continued.

Surprisingly, Lucas nodded at Serena.

That floored me. He'd kept from me—from all of us—that they knew each other. And Serena hadn't told me either. And what was with him calling his daughter Munchkin like she was a seven-year-old? He had to realize she found it demeaning.

That floored me. He'd kept from me—from all of us—that they knew each other. And Serena hadn't told me either.

"Dad, stop." Her words were firm.

Her arrogant father ignored her. "Listen to me, Serena. I want Lucas to put a team on you to keep you safe. Just in case."

"I'll keep her safe." Had what I said before not registered with her father? I tightened my arm around her.

Ignoring me, Lloyd Benson repeated himself. "I'm hiring Lucas to put a team on you." The man lacked the ability to deal with any challenge to his plans.

Serena shivered. Her steadfast rule was that her father not learn about the accident, about the psycho Spinelli hunting her, about her hiring us.

This conversation threatened to uncover all of that, so I improvised. "She hired us last week." It was the perfect way to hide the current assignment, by attributing it to whatever threat Harvey Fox presented.

Lucas gave me his version of a knowing smile.

I took the leap, hoping Lucas would cover for me. "When we learned of the parole—"

"I informed Serena," he filled in smoothly. "And she hired us."

Benson's eye twitched. "Why didn't you mention this?"

Lucas snarled. "I don't discuss clients with anybody, including family members." Lucas wouldn't intentionally antagonize a man as powerful as Lloyd Benson, but it didn't pay to question Lucas's ethics. He wouldn't back down against any opponent.

To defuse the tension, I added, "So you don't need to worry. We're on the case." We had successfully spun a tale to keep Serena's secret safe.

Benson looked at me like I'd sprouted a second head. "Who is *we*?"

"Duke works for me," Lucas explained. "He's heading her team. He's also my brother."

Her father looked at me and then Serena. "I thought he was your boyfriend."

It was decision time. "I'm that too." I pulled her close. "For real," I said for both Serena and Lucas's benefit.

"You're dating…" Benson pointed at me. "The brother of the man who—"

"Enough, Dad," she said forcefully. "Yes. No question about it."

"But I don't know anything about him," Benson complained. "I don't think—"

"It's not your decision to make," I interrupted, stepping forward. He needed to back off. "I'm dating your daughter. Get used to it."

Benson's eyes narrowed. He was clearly not used to being contradicted.

Lucas moved forward. "I'll vouch for my brother's character. That should be sufficient."

Benson turned to Lucas. "And you're okay with this, er, dating arrangement?"

"I married a woman I was protecting."

We all knew the story, which was why I knew Lucas would support me dating Serena.

"Is he any good?" Benson asked, not even bothering with my name.

I stiffened. The question was common, but it usually came with a heap more tact.

"Duke is a former SEAL, and there's nobody better."

"A SEAL?" Benson still had questions written all over his face. "Really?"

"Yes, sir," I answered. "DEVGRU, you probably know them as—"

"Yeah, SEAL Team Six." He straightened a little. "I was in the Navy myself, a Seabee."

"A proud branch of the Navy, sir."

Benson's grin said our Navy connection had cemented his approval. "Son, you're all right by me. But, Lucas, I want to personally approve all the other members of the team."

Serena shook her head.

Lucas got the hint. "No, Lloyd. Serena hired us, not you."

"Then you're fired from that job, and I'll hire you back."

"No, sir," I said firmly, remembering Lucas's lecture on the subject. "You didn't hire us. You can't fire us. Isn't that right, boss?"

He nodded. "That's the way it works, Lloyd. We took on a job for your daughter, and we intend to see it through."

"Serena," he pleaded.

She stiffened. "No, Dad, I'm handling this."

"I don't like it," Benson complained. "You're my daughter. I need to know what precautions are being taken."

Tough shit, I wanted to say, but I didn't. This man was clearly used to getting his way, and his daughter had just provided the hard lesson that there were things and people he couldn't buy or push around.

Serena pulled away from me and hugged her father. "I'm in good hands, Dad. The best."

He nodded.

Serena returned to my side and interlaced her fingers with mine.

God, that felt good—scary, but good. I'd claimed her, and there was no turning back now. It wasn't just that I wanted some fun with her. I really did want her as my girlfriend. Before now, I hadn't thought that possible.

"Well, then," Benson said. "I hope that burger is still warm. Lucas, care to join us?"

My brother declined, and as he turned to go, Serena held me back so we followed her father and Lucas from a distance.

"Is what you said for real?" she asked.

I didn't hesitate. "I meant it, Princess. You're mine now."

She slowed us further and whispered, "And you're mine, Studly." She rubbed her tit up against me. "As soon as we get a minute alone, I'm going to show you just what that means."

I adjusted myself. In front of her brothers was not the ideal place to be sporting a boner. Just before we reached the group, I remembered the question that had been left hanging. "Who is Harvey Fox?"

She trembled under my arm. "Not now."

❧

A FEW MINUTES LATER, I SAT NEXT TO SERENA AS THE MEAL WAS SERVED AT THE shaded table. Now everyone was focused on their food.

I tried to keep my eyes on my plate, but George Butthead Kittleman sat across the table from me. I didn't like being this close to the guy, but the investigation demanded I get a read on him as a suspect.

He laughed at something Vincent said.

I suppressed a scoff. The jerk didn't deserve another shot with Serena. He had to be the dullest tool in the shed to dump her for a job opportunity out of town, and his bravado rubbed me the wrong way. SEALs were about team-work, and none of his stories about his time in the field had included the word *team*.

After Marcia went into the house to get more chips, I gave Serena the signal we'd discussed when I needed her to try to trigger him again.

"Next week, I'm auditing Yaroslavsky," Serena said matter-of-factly, aiming her words at me. She had already woven in several of the keywords I'd requested of her.

I watched Butthead. I didn't see any reaction, so I followed up by asking her, "Do you have to travel for that?"

"Only to West Hollywood," she said. "No biggie."

Again, no reaction from the guy, which made it zero for four and meant he was not likely involved. He was just her ex, a total dickhead, and now a pain in my ass.

I finished chewing my burger.

"It was just me and this tango," Butthead said, weaving some tale for Vincent. "It could have been close, but I gave it to him, full-auto, the whole clip."

The itch I'd had about this guy came back. He knew a lot of the lingo, and I'd been focused on reading his tells for deception regarding Yaroslavsky and the notes. But now it became clear. He'd made two huge mistakes in that last sentence that proved he was no frogman, and that burned me.

As SEALs, our ammo load-out was a treasure, our lifeline, which we conserved, since we could never count on resupply. We were taught to almost always select single-round semi-auto, occasionally three-round-burst mode. Very rarely would we use full-auto, because once you were out of ammo, you were helpless. We never put more rounds into a man than it took to put him down. Those were rounds you might need for the next surprise.

Second, a clip went into a handgun, a rifle like an M4 took a mag.

It was time to find out for sure. I pushed my plate aside and leaned forward, putting my elbow on the table. "George, it's arm-wrestling time."

"No thanks."

"A SEAL is not permitted to turn down an arm-wrestle challenge from another SEAL. It's in the code. You and I both know that."

Serena's father looked on from the other end of the table with a cocked brow.

"Duke was a SEAL too," Serena mentioned, so I didn't have to.

George's eyes widened. "Uh, I'm kind of out of practice."

Yeah, dirtbag, now you're up against the real deal. "Me too." I wiggled my fingers. "Let's go. We both know there's no dishonor in losing to a fellow SEAL. Refusing a challenge? Now that's a different thing." I gave him *the* glare.

Left without an out, his sweaty hand grasped mine. Vincent counted to three, and we started.

I let him bend me back a little as he grunted and groaned, but this was going to be no contest. The guy was clearly a desk jockey.

"So you fired all our weapons in training?" I asked. "Even the fifty-cal, right?"

"Yeah," he grunted out. "That one was a beast."

Her father nodded. He'd probably actually handled the weapon.

I let Butthead gain a little, then took back a little more, prolonging the contest. "How'd you like firing the Draeger? Any trouble aiming it?"

He grunted again and shook his head. "Got the bullseye every time."

I put all I had into it and slammed his hand over and down.

He cried out in pain. "Fuck, you broke my arm."

I released my grip. "It's not broken," I scoffed. *But I might have torn a ligament.* "I should do a lot more than that to a fucking fraud like you," I yelled. "You never wore the trident. Every SEAL knows a Draeger is an underwater breathing device, not a weapon."

He cradled his elbow and stood, moving back from the table. "I... I—"

"If you ever call Serena again, I will gut you. You hear me?"

Amazingly, Lloyd Benson stayed out of it.

Butthead hightailed it away so fast I never heard a response.

The elder Benson eyed me a moment and then went back to his conversation.

Vincent chuckled. "That was entertaining."

"I never liked that guy," Zach added.

What had Serena ever seen in that twat?

"Can I feel those arm muscles?" Kelly asked.

Serena swatted her hand. "No way. He's mine."

I couldn't figure it out, so this being a day for direct questions, I asked, "What did you ever see in that guy?"

"Dad approved of him," Vincent said softly.

Lloyd didn't seem to hear.

Serena set her jaw but didn't argue. Her father had run her life in more ways than I'd imagined.

"Deny it," Zach challenged her.

"Of course, Dad approved," she whispered. "He's nice."

"And from a good family." Kelly added air quotes.

I nailed George's coffin shut. "If you go for liars."

Kelly saved Serena from that fork in the conversation. "Do you have a brother?"

Serena answered for me. "Three, but none of them are East Coast."

"Pity." Kelly shook her head.

After the meal, most people stood around with beers or wine glasses in hand to chat. Following my lead, Serena chose soft drinks instead of alcohol. And she slowly munched through almost an entire bag of chips.

Her brothers were great. But this was a crowd, and I was itching to get my woman alone.

After a time, Serena gave my hand a gentle tug. "Can I—I mean *we*—go home?"

Hearing that invitation, my cock surged. Home meant bed, and bed meant naked with this gorgeous woman. "I think that's a capital idea, Princess."

"I thought we were done with the Princess crap."

"Sure thing. If you don't like being my princess, how about Sweet Cheeks?"

"That's worse."

"Snuggles?"

"I give up. Take me home, Studly."

Snuggles it is.

She leaned close. "You have no idea how hot it was seeing you put George in his place." She fanned herself and walked over to her father. "Dad, I need to get going."

Her father's face fell. "But the afternoon is still young."

"I warned you I couldn't stay long," she chided.

"True." He opened his arms, and I let go of Serena so he could give her a goodbye hug. "See you again soon, Munchkin."

"Sure, Dad."

After shaking hands goodbye, with an arm around her waist, I led my woman away. "I can't wait to get back to your house."

With a devilish grin, she hurried me along.

CHAPTER 23

Serena

I pulled Duke up the path to the house.

I was Duke Hawk's woman now, and the burning need I had for him would not wait until we got home. After watching him demolish George, I hadn't been able to concentrate on a single thing my brothers had said. Only Duke existed for me.

Minutes ago, Kelly had commented. *"Duke is quite a…man."*

"You can't have him" had left my mouth so fast I couldn't stop the words.

She'd backed away. *"Down, girl. I'm only wishing I was as lucky as you."*

I apologized and resolved to keep food in my mouth after that to avoid more embarrassment.

When we reached the house, I pulled open the door and headed for the stairs. "My old bedroom." Bringing a boy back to my bedroom for some kissing without my parents knowing had been a frequent childhood fantasy. Even though I hadn't heard from Duke after camp, he'd starred in several of them. As a grownup, today's fantasy included more than kissing.

"Your father won't—"

"No." I cut him off. "But we should be quick before somebody notices your car is still here." I ran a finger down his chest. "But if you're too scared, we could—"

He gave my ass a swat. "I'm only afraid you'll die of embarrassment when they hear you scream my name all the way out back."

Of course, my SEAL wasn't afraid of anybody or anything. We reached the landing, and I turned us right. I was on fire with need.

"Here." I opened the door to my past, the place I'd vowed I'd never return to. Inside, I dropped my bag and turned.

Kicking the door closed behind us, Duke took me in his arms, and our bodies welded themselves to each other. His kiss consumed me—hard, deep, and wet. There was nothing soft or tentative about this afternoon. No, this was about want and need.

I struggled with his shirt as he palmed my breasts. "Duke," I moaned.

He pushed me against the door, moving from my lips to the sensitive skin of my neck. He rested a hand on my thigh and then slowly slid it up under my dress.

As his fingers ignited sparks along my skin, I made space to palm his erection. "Faster," I urged. "You better have a condom with you." He was hard and hot beneath my touch.

"A SEAL is prepared for any contingency," he mumbled as he lifted my dress over my head.

"Less talking, more doing." I pulled at his belt buckle.

While he backed up to lower his pants and sheath himself, I unhooked the strapless bra this dress required and slid my panties down, kicking them to the side.

"Are you ready? I'm not going to be able to hold back." He threw his shirt off.

I nodded confirmation and grabbed his covered length. "I can't wait one more second."

He pulled me toward the bed.

I resisted. "Door." It had always been a fantasy of mine.

"Hold on, baby. This is going to be a rough ride."

I wrapped my legs around him as he lifted me like I weighed nothing. I still wore my wedge heels.

He backed me against the door, raised me up, and brought me down on his cock, instantly filling me with sensation. "You're so fucking drenched for me, baby."

I grabbed a fistful of hair. "I told you I was turned on." I clawed at his back as he drove into me, pinning me against the wood.

The door creaked with each of his powerful thrusts.

Every time he went deep, I ground against him and nearly came apart. Since he'd eviscerated George, I'd been wound so tight, I was ready to explode. He cupped one hand under my ass, and the other went to my breast. I was a goner with the way he knew how to manipulate me.

"Serena. Marie. Benson," he croaked out with each brutal thrust. "You. Are.

Mine." He was in control, and all I could do was hold on for dear life as pleasure invaded every cell of my being.

The wood bit into my back, but that wasn't what caused my tears. They formed because of his words. I'd never been wanted like this before.

When he freed a hand and brought it to my clit, my vision blurred, and I came, screaming his name. I clawed at his back, pulling him closer to make our two bodies one, the way I felt our souls were in the moment.

He plunged in again and tensed, releasing into me with a loud groan. "Fuck, you feel so good."

I was determined to get the last word. "You're mine, Studly. And don't you forget it."

He held me against the door as our breathing slowed. "I hope I didn't hurt you."

"Nothing I can't handle." Sexually sated for the moment, all was right with the world. Luckily, I had tissues in my bag to clean up with. As he turned to put on his shirt, I saw the claw marks I'd left on him. I touched one. "I hope I didn't hurt you."

"Totally worth it."

Then, I noticed something worse. I ran my fingers over the ragged patch of scarring on his side. "What happened?"

He blew out a slow breath and placed his hand over mine. "Mission went sideways. I can't say anymore."

"Classified?"

He nodded. "Brett and Zane March, another team guy, took turns carrying me eight clicks to our evac point under fire." His eyes misted up. "I owe those guys my life."

"Your brother, Brett?"

"Yup. He's currently deployed. You'll meet him when he gets back."

I knew that with spec ops, there was always a chance his brother wouldn't come back alive, but the optimist in my man didn't allow thoughts like that.

He finished with his shirt. "We should get going."

Mom was at the base of the stairs when we descended. "Your father didn't hear a thing."

I turned beet red as I hugged her goodbye. "Thanks, Mom."

~

SERENA

THE TRIP HOME WAS EQUAL PARTS ANTICIPATION AND DREAD.

138

The continued tingle between my legs reminded me of what we'd done *and* what would come next when Duke and I could get some alone time.

All week, I'd prayed he would come to me and say the words he'd used to stand up to my father. He'd proudly proclaimed that he wanted to be with me. I might be insane for feeling this way after the short time I'd known him, but Mom once told me that the heart wants what the heart wants, and it can't be argued with.

Having Constance in the car with us on the way home allowed me to put off the conversation I had to have with Duke, the confession I had to make. Would he feel the same way once he knew the truth about me?

The mental lockbox that contained those painful memories shook and rattled around in my head, threatening to spill its ugly secrets. Thinking of all the blood turned my stomach.

Duke wanted, and now needed, to know about the Fox brothers, so there would be no avoiding the discussion about my past—about the events nobody suspected. Nobody beyond Lucas Hawk knew anything about what I'd done.

Except, of course, Harvey Fox. That thought chilled me to the bone.

After a few minutes, Constance asked Duke, "What's next?"

"Do you have time to brainstorm possibilities at the house? Because I can't help but think there's a work connection now."

"Sure thing."

My leg started trembling as my thoughts returned to Harvey Fox and the talk Duke would insist upon.

It wasn't fair. All I wanted was to curl up with my new boyfriend and lock us away for a week. Thinking about a week alone with Duke calmed me. *Yes, that would be a perfect week.* If I couldn't have that, maybe I could have a day.

I dialed Nick. "Hey, are you guys still on for Anaheim tomorrow? There's been a change in my plans."

"Yep. Does this mean you can come?"

"It sure does, me and my boyfriend." That word sounded so wonderful when I said it. I could see Duke's scrunched-up brow in the rearview mirror.

"Perfect," Nick replied.

"I want to ask my friend too. Is that okay?"

"Sure. I got plenty of tickets."

"How'd you manage that?" I asked. They were super pricey.

"Top secret, need to know."

"Okay, well, thanks." After I got off the phone, I announced, "There's been a change of plans."

"I heard," Constance said. "Where are you going?"

"Disneyland with Katelyn, my friend Gray, Nick, and his girlfriend."

"Sounds fun. I had the best time at Disneyland as a kid," Constance mused.

"You're not going," Duke countered. "It's too risky."

I added some volume. "Yes, I am."

"No."

I used my finger for emphasis. "Yes, I am, but you don't have to come along if you don't want to."

"First, we have to figure out security for the park," Constance warned me.

Duke shook his head. "I don't like it."

Constance's smile was a good counterpoint to Duke's scowl. "I can't come because they'd recognize me, but Terry and I can be floaters nearby."

"Not good enough," Duke said. "I can't cover all the approaches by myself in a place like that." His eyes moved to me. "You have to get Constance invited."

"Impossible," I said. "They think she's there to put one of them in jail."

"Work on it. Otherwise, you don't go. That's final."

Mr. Grumpypants was back. But I had a different and better idea. I dialed my friend.

"Hey, girlfriend," she answered.

"A guy at work has tickets to Disneyland. Wanna go tomorrow?"

"Disneyland?" she shrieked. "I'd love to."

"There's one catch. You're going undercover as my bodyguard's date so he can guard me without the rest of the group knowing."

"That's weird."

"Gray, you'll like him. His name is Terry Goodwin."

"That douche? No way."

"Wait, what? You know him?"

"Wish I didn't. I'll pass."

"It's only one day," I argued.

"That's one day too many with that overbearing ass."

She'd obviously been exposed to a different Terry than I had. "Santa Monica," I said calmly. I needed this, and I had leverage she couldn't refuse.

She sighed. "You suck, you know that?"

"Yeah, I know. But it'll be a fun day. We'll pick you up in the morning."

"Whatever."

After I ended the call, Duke spoke. "Is there a problem?"

"It sounds like she and Terry have some history. Not the good kind."

"Her name's Gray?"

I nodded. "Grace Brennan."

He made a face. "That could be an issue. This whole trip may not work."

"What's the problem between them?"

Duke bit his lip. "Her brother, Pete, and Terry were good friends. When Pete went missing, Terry got put in charge of the trust their parents had set up for her. It didn't go well."

I'd known Grace's brother had been assumed killed, but declared MIA when they couldn't recover Pete's body. After also losing her parents, she'd been traumatized by it. She'd chafed against the trustee of the life insurance payout, but she'd never put a name to him. He'd always been *his assholeness*, *his lordship*, or merely *the tyrant*.

I threw Duke's words back at him. "Work on it. I'm going, and that's final."

Duke shook his head, knowing I had him. "I'll deal with Terry. We still need you, Constance. You're going to be a lone floater, in disguise, so they don't recognize you."

"No problem," she answered.

~

DUKE

WHEN WE ARRIVED AT THE HOUSE, TERRY PARKED BEHIND ME.

While Constance stayed with Serena, the two of us cleared the place. I couldn't stop thinking of the Disneyland stunt Serena had just pulled. As soon as we finished, I took her into the study and shut the door.

Before I knew what was happening, she had a hand behind my neck and pulled herself up to kiss me. As soon as her soft tits hit my chest, I was a goner. I grabbed her ass to lift her up. Wrapping her legs around me, she kissed me eagerly.

I gave the kiss back to her in spades, going instantly hard and rubbing her against my length. "I want you so bad, baby."

She moaned into my mouth, then broke the kiss to nibble on my earlobe. "I want you too. I want to jump your bones again."

When she ground against me, I almost gave into the temptation to lock the door and explore that possibility right there and then. Instead, I pulled her loose. The work couldn't wait, and this could. "What were you thinking?"

Her tongue darted out to lick her lip. "I was thinking I didn't want to wait any longer to kiss you again."

"Not that. You shouldn't go to Disneyland."

"Why not?"

"It'll be crowded," I argued.

"Exactly. Because a lot of other people agree with me that it's a fun place to go."

"Crowds are dangerous. Somebody can get close without us seeing him."

"You know what you are? You're a fun-sucker-outer. You want to suck the fun out of everything."

141

This conversation had gone all wrong somehow, so I dodged. "You need to tell me how you know my boss."

Instantly, I recognized the fear in her eyes. "Next week."

"Today," I insisted.

"And you need to tell me why you hate my dad."

Checkmate. Now, we both had a place we didn't want to go.

I didn't intend to wait a week. "Tomorrow."

She sighed out her response. "Monday."

Before I could say anything else, a knock sounded on the door. "Constance said you want to brainstorm stuff."

"Yeah," I called. "In just a minute." I needed that minute—or more likely three—to get my dick back under control. "Okay, Monday."

Serena ran her hand over my crotch as she walked to the door. "A minute, huh?"

"You're not helping." When I got her alone again, she was going to pay.

It was actually three minutes before I could open the door and follow.

Serena was on her phone at the base of the stairs. "Hey, Alice, can we talk again later? We've got a meeting about to start... Great to talk to you, too." She lowered the phone before I reached her.

"You're talking to my sisters?" That was bound to cause me problems.

"Sure. Mostly Alice because Em boarded her cruise."

Emily hadn't shared with me that she'd booked a cruise.

"Alice and I are going to meet up when she comes down." That sounded like trouble.

"We don't have all day," Constance called.

CHAPTER 24

SERENA

"WANT A PIECE?" BACK DOWNSTAIRS, CONSTANCE OFFERED ME REHEATED PIZZA across the table.

"No thanks." What I really wanted was my man alone upstairs so we could continue where we'd left off. It was unavoidable now that I knew he wanted me as badly as I wanted him.

I was his—he'd said it, to my dad no less. It couldn't have been plainer than that. Well, maybe if he'd thrown me over his shoulder to cart me off, but that was a bit much to expect.

"Are you sure?" Constance asked.

Her question drew me out of my reverie. "Duke and I already ate."

"Terry and I didn't get a chance," she said around a mouthful. "Nobody delivers to a stakeout."

"I have some news." I figured it would get pretty obvious tonight. "We're now…" I added air quotes. "A couple."

Constance choked on her food. "What changed?"

"In front of my dad, he just said outright that I was his girlfriend."

"Wasn't that the cover?" she asked, confused.

"Now it's real."

"You're sure?"

Remembering a few minutes ago, I nodded. "Uh-huh."

As we waited on the guys, I contemplated our hot hide-in-my-old-bedroom sex. It didn't get more real than that. "How long will this meeting take?"

She shrugged. "Until we make some progress, I guess."

I wanted to have tonight and our not-fake date tomorrow at Disneyland before Duke learned the ugly truth about me. I only hoped we could bond enough before then that it wouldn't all come tumbling down when we had *the talk*.

Would he even want to hear the entire story or be too disgusted with me for that?

Terry, Winston, and Duke arrived with the other pizza and a tray of soft drinks.

I chose the Diet Coke and patted the seat next to me. "I saved you a seat, Studly."

Duke grimaced and rounded the table to my side. "Thanks, Snuggles."

Terry looked confused.

"They're together now," Constance explained. "Pet names are what couples do."

Terry shrugged and sat across from us. "About friggin' time."

Guess we hadn't been as discreet as we thought.

Duke dialed his phone. "Jordy, you ready?"

"Always."

"Where do we start?" Constance asked.

Duke grabbed a Coke. "First, in my opinion, we can scratch George Kittleman. He's no longer our prime suspect."

"Why is that?" Terry asked through a mouthful of pizza.

"Personal observation. No reaction to any of our trigger words, plus the fact that Serena's government car had a tracker. Also, the obsession with the USB drive doesn't fit the romantic stalker type. But we have a new name—"

"Stop," I said, cutting Duke off before he could mention Harvey Fox. I leaned over and whispered, "Remember, we can't talk about him."

"You owe me an explanation," Duke whispered back.

"Consider who?" Constance asked.

I was glad I hadn't accepted the pizza as my stomach churned. Now that these two knew there was something we were holding back, Monday's conversation was going to be an even bigger deal.

Terry leaned back. "What's going on?"

I glared at Duke.

He shook his head. "Sorry, something I learned today is confidential, and I need to get it cleared first."

Terry sat forward, glaring at Duke. "Working with an arm tied behind our backs sucks."

"Drop it," Duke commanded. "Let's get back to the basics of what we know."

Terry sighed. "It happened right after she visited the plating and chemical companies. They could be involved."

"I'm with you," Winston agreed. "Start with the ones with the most money to lose."

Duke nodded along. "So we launch Jordy on a deep dive into those two companies." He turned to me. "Who did you meet with at those two places—the decision makers, not the peons?"

"Uh, Excalibur Plating was Larry Pollock, their president. At Knife Creek Chemical, there were two, Aiden Pons, the COO, and Gabe Woodward. I don't remember his title."

Constance took notes.

Duke steepled his hands. "Yaroslavsky practically told us the source he got the info from isn't in LA anymore. That means he's either out of town—"

"Or dead," Terry finished.

Constance checked her notebook. "The body would have had to drop recently, and Winston, you didn't find any that fit the torture MO locally, right?"

"Nope. I'll expand the area."

"Good. What about that second call?" Terry brought up.

"It was to his brother in Miami," Duke answered.

Constance had been writing a note until the word Miami. "You didn't tell me he called Miami."

Duke answered. "Sorry, you weren't with us, and we might have summarized it as a call to his brother."

I got the tingle that said we'd found a thread to unravel things. "What's the significance of Miami?"

"She's not here now," Constance said, leafing through notes. "But I was told a previous EPA employee in the office relocated to Miami."

It clicked for me. "Sophia Rossi. When she left, that created the opening for my promotion. I knew she relocated to the East Coast, but nobody mentioned which city."

She looked up. "Yup, Rossi is the one, and it was definitely Miami."

Duke pointed at Winston. "First plane out. Let's find out what this woman has to say."

"Copy that. I love the beach."

Constance went back to her notes. "Let's get back to the drive. If Rossi thinks you have this drive, whatever it is, did she give you one?"

"We never talked much." I thought hard before the next part. "I'm sure she never gave me anything at all."

"This all started on Monday," Duke pointed out. "What happened last week to start this?"

"As I told you, it was my first day in the new job. I visited the two companies and was attacked on the way back to the office."

"But before that, you got a note," he reminded me.

"That's right. The note was on my car in the morning, but I'd parked down the street and thought it was meant for someone else."

"Did you change desks that morning?" Constance asked.

"Of course. I inherited Sophia's job, her files, and her workstation."

"Now something makes sense." Duke's fist came down on the table. "Constance, can you help Serena check her work area and files?"

"You got it."

"You think Sophia left something for me in the files, and that's what this is about?"

"Could be," Terry said. "Look, the timing fits. Maybe the call to Yaroslavsky's brother was to double-check on the intelligence, pressure Rossi some more, whatever. It makes a hell of a lot more sense than an ex-boyfriend."

"And the companies have the resources to get somebody like Spinelli," Constance pointed out.

I was feeling optimistic that we could find the drive and end this. "Should we go to the office tonight?"

Duke shook his head. "We should expect somebody as good as Spinelli to have eyes on us somehow. For now, Winston catches the first flight to Miami and searching the office waits until Constance can help you on Monday."

I nodded and stretched. "I'm exhausted after today."

"Rest up for your date tomorrow?" Constance kidded.

Terry perked up. "What date?"

"Oh, crap." Constance put a hand on Terry's shoulder. "I forgot to tell you, we have a date tomorrow too. You're coming along to Disneyland."

Terry turned to Duke. "Seriously? I get to date Constance?"

Constance shoved him. "In your dreams, Romeo. Your date is her friend, Grace Brennan."

"That… You gotta be kidding me," he complained. "No way. Send Jordy. I'll handle comms."

"I'm not going. No way," Jordy said over the phone. "I'm not letting Terry ruin any of my equipment."

I was determined to have my day with Duke. "I'm going. No question about it. You guys have to figure out how many extras you need for protection."

Duke side-eyed me. "Serena is the priority. Because of the crowds, we need the eyes, and they know Constance. Terry, are you admitting you can't handle her?"

"Kitty? I can handle her," Terry said without conviction. "If I have to. I'd just rather not."

Kitty was her nickname? That didn't sound as bad as Grace had made out.

Duke pointed a finger. "Suck it up. It's the job."

I pushed back from the table and stood. "You guys stay up all night figuring out the logistics if you want, but I'm going to bed."

Constance smiled. "I think we're done for tonight. What do you think, Duke?"

"Terry, you get the first shift," Duke said. "Constance, you've got the second."

"What about you?" Terry complained. "This isn't fair."

"I was on duty during that whole damned barbecue while you guys were sleeping out by the gate."

"I didn't get any sleep."

Constance stayed out of it.

Duke stood. "You should have. Now I've gotta call Lucas."

DUKE

AFTER WE BROKE THE MEETING AND SERENA WENT UPSTAIRS, I WANDERED OUTSIDE TO dial Jordy back.

"What'd you forget, Bro?"

"I've got a recent parolee we need to run down. What did he go up for, and what connection does he have to the Benson family, Serena in particular."

He sighed. "Why do you always come up with these at the end of the day?"

"It's not my fault. The name just popped up."

"What state, and who is it?"

"California, I think, and the name is Harvey Fox. How long do you think it'll take?"

"He was sent up on attempted murder charges, and there's no connection to the Bensons." Something was off. Jordy hadn't even had enough time to type the name in.

"How do you know that without looking it up?"

"I tend to remember the person convicted of attempting to kill our oldest brother."

That was a shock. "Lucas?"

"Yup. Fox copped a plea super quick, was sentenced immediately, and went straight to San Quentin."

My brother had never mentioned a thing. "Why am I just now hearing about this?"

"You have to ask Lucas. He swore me to secrecy."

147

I scratched the back of my neck. *Why would Lucas keep this from me?* "Does Brett know?"

"I didn't tell him."

I almost hung up but caught myself. "Thanks, Jordy."

"Be careful. Lucas doesn't want to talk about this." Jordy ended the call on that note.

Careful, my ass. I had to know, so I dialed.

Lucas picked up on the first ring. "I've been expecting your call."

"What's the story with you and Harvey Fox? Jordy says he got sent up for attempting to murder you."

"That's true."

"How? What happened?"

"Not important." Lucas's ability to keep conversations short didn't impress me today.

"What's the connection to Serena?"

"I don't have anything to say."

"Benson thinks he's a threat, so I damn well need to know."

I could almost hear his teeth grind. "Not my story to tell, Brother. I suggest you don't pursue this, but if you do, know it's Serena's choice what she wants to say. For her sake, do not push. I'll leave it at that."

Do not push her? What the hell was that? Even my brother was keeping something this important from me.

CHAPTER 25

SERENA

ANTICIPATION BUZZED IN MY BLOOD AS I GOT READY FOR BED. I'D KNOWN FROM THE minute he'd made a fool of George, that Duke was a completely different breed of man than any I'd dated before.

My brothers were right. I'd generally stuck to boys Dad approved of, with *boys* being the operative term.

Duke was no boy. He was all man. One with the guts to stand up to my father. One I wasn't actually sure I could handle. But I'd be damned if I didn't try. Every minute since Duke had declared I was his, I'd looked forward to tonight when we'd be away from watchful eyes.

Would I be able to put up with his bossiness, his argumentativeness? He'd say it was me being difficult, and half the time, he might be right. But that's because I knew what was good for me, and it was time I got a say in my life.

Sure, he had an issue with my dad for some reason, but at this moment, I wasn't on Team Dad either. And this afternoon, Duke had protected me from my father's overbearing instincts. Any man who would stand up to my father was either brainless or fearless, and Duke was nobody's fool.

Would tonight be as good as it had been at the beginning of the week? Would it be better? Was I ruining it by putting too much emphasis on this?

He'd expertly given me pleasure. I'd never in my life come so fast. What if I wasn't any good at returning it? Shit, what if he thought I was a mediocre lover, or even worse, a *bad* lay?

Double shit. I'd wasted the entire week. I could have been researching how to give good head—no, excellent head—or how to pull his balls. I'd read that guys liked that, or was it tickling his balls?

Was I dressed right? Should I change into a nightshirt? No shirt?

Pulling my top off, I quickly ditched my bra. That had turned him on Tuesday. Going through my closet, I looked for something loose-fitting to replicate the way I'd been dressed that day. A blue button-down was the closest thing I found.

After clicking on the closet light, I turned off the overhead room lights for the right mood.

I heard footsteps, and like Pavlov's dog, heat coiled low in my belly, eager for Duke's arrival. Looking down, I decided to undo another two buttons. As I walked to the door, the shirt opened over one breast, and I readjusted. One could never show too much cleavage when expecting one's lover, right? But hiding the nipple to tease him was best.

As soon as he knocked, I pulled the door open.

"What do you think about…" It wasn't Duke.

I pulled my shirt closed as Constance walked in.

"Oh." She raised a brow as I buttoned it back up. A smirk grew on her face. "Duke's still on the phone."

"What do I think about what?" I asked when I was no longer in danger of the shirt opening too far.

"About tomorrow. Will Grace and Terry be able to get along for a day?"

I nodded. "I hope so. Do you think she'll mess up his concentration?"

"Duke doesn't think so." Looking at me a moment, she motioned to the bed. "Can we sit?"

I nodded and sat.

She joined me. "You don't need to be nervous." Seems she'd noticed my leg tremors. "I've been doing personal protection a long time, and the guys are positively first-rate."

"I just want to have a nice time, you know, a fun day…"

"With Duke?" she filled in.

I nodded.

"What happened at your family barbecue? It seems like things changed pretty abruptly."

I explained it in the simplest way I knew. "My ex showed up, probably invited by Dad."

"Aaaaaaaawkward." She drew out the word and shook her head. "Who does that to their daughter?"

"Super awkward, but it highlighted how different Duke is from any of the boys"—I used the word intentionally—"I've dated before. Then Duke goes and tells my father he's claiming me."

"Claiming you?"

"Duke told him straight out that I was his. In my wildest dreams, I'd never imagined a guy saying that to my father. He claimed me as his girlfriend—out loud, without a care in the world for what Dad thought about it. Like in a novel." I shook my head. "He stood up to my father and flat out told him how it was going to be."

"Knowing your father's reputation, I bet that doesn't happen often."

I laughed. "Try never." My leg had stilled.

She laughed. "You're not kidding?"

"Honest to God, he did."

"Me Tarzan, you Jane," she murmured in a low voice. "Hold on. He can't do that. You get a say in this."

"You're right. I get a choice. And I choose to be his girlfriend."

Constance laid a hand on my shoulder. "I'm happy for you. Truly, I am. Duke is a stand-up guy. But..."

I waited for the catch.

"Winston tells me he doesn't do relationships."

"So?" I shrugged. We'd had sex once, so a relationship was a bit of a stretch.

"Just be careful what you expect." Constance looked up as the door opened.

"Sorry," Duke said. "I thought you were alone."

Constance stood. "I'll get out of your hair now."

"What expectations do you need to be careful about?" Duke asked after the door closed again.

I dug a fingernail into my palm. "Oh, she warned me the lines will be long and not to expect very many rides tomorrow."

"Probably true." Duke advanced on me, and the predatory look in his eyes communicated very clearly that talking about Disneyland was not on his agenda.

"She wanted to talk about how to present Terry to the group tomorrow," I added.

"I don't care." He took my hand in his and, with the other, urged my chin up.

When our gazes locked, I felt it—his heat, his desire, the connection we shared.

His hand tightened on mine. "I've been waiting for this all damned week." Apparently in my bed was different than a quickie against the door at my parents' house.

"Me too." My voice came out as a squeak as I looked up at him. I felt the intensity in his voice all the way to my toes.

"I'll ask you again, Snuggles. Are you absofuckinglutely sure about this? Because once I taste you, I just know, I'm not going to be able to stop. You and me, all night long."

I froze. *Taste me?* I'd never been talked to like that. Hell, I'd only once had a boy's mouth on me, and in spite of what I'd read in romance novels, it hadn't been special. Duke's words challenged my tattoo. Was I up to being bold enough?

He was a breath away. "So, are you?"

"Tell me, Studly, are you absofuckinglutely sure? Because once I taste you, I may not want to stop either." *How's that for being bold, Mr. Badass SEAL?*

His eyes widened. I'd surprised us both.

Taking bold further, I closed the distance. But when his lips took mine, there was no mistaking who was in charge, and it wasn't me. Urgent hands pulled me to him. With his insistent erection pressed against me, I realized he'd come in the door as revved up as I'd gotten myself contemplating how this would go. I angled my head to accept him deeper.

His tongue was hot and wickedly insistent as it probed and tangled with mine. Duke Hawk wasn't merely kissing me. His ministrations deserved another term, more possessive, more assertive, more dominant than a simple kiss.

Moaning into his mouth, I was putty in his hands as he drew out the ecstasy. This was no rush to score. Duke took his time, showing me a side of kissing that I hadn't known existed.

He broke the kiss. "You taste even better than I remembered."

I cast my eyes down. Had I misunderstood what he intended? "I thought…" I stammered.

A wicked smile curled his lips. "We'll get to that too, baby."

My pussy clenched with an image of his face between my legs. What would his stubble feel like between my thighs? Impatient to find out, I slid my hand down to cup him.

He groaned before he pulled my hand away. "Not yet."

With a firm hand in my hair, he brought us face to face, my nose touching his. "You need to learn to not argue about every damned thing."

I hooked an arm around his neck, hopped up, and wrapped my legs around him. "Do with me what you will, Studly, and I promise zero complaints." As I ground against his erection, complaining was the last thing on my mind.

A strong hand lifted my ass, pulling me to him and adding to the pressure I craved. I leaned my head back as he kissed an electric trail from my ear, down my neck, to my collarbone. Giving up on his pants, I started on the buttons of his shirt. Hot skin with a smattering of hair over hard muscle greeted me. I flinched as one of his hands slid up my side and over the cut.

"Sorry." He moved it away. "I didn't mean to hurt you."

"It's fine." I pulled his hand up to my breast and purred my appreciation as he cupped my flesh and tweaked my sensitive nipple. "I love your chest," I said, sliding my hand over the defined ridges.

He squeezed my breast. "Likewise. You have way too many clothes on," he whispered against my neck, kissing my pulse point.

"I agree," I answered as he walked us over to the bed and leaned over to drop me down. With a laugh, I stayed wrapped around him, and we tumbled onto the mattress.

He did his best to protect me from his weight, and the furious process of removing each other's clothes became a frantic race between kisses.

I lost when he got me naked by yanking my panties free, and I hadn't gotten his pants off yet.

He held my hands against the mattress at my shoulders and began kissing a trail down my body. He stopped to worship one breast—licking, sucking, and blowing air on my taut nipple—before moving on to the other.

I struggled, but only a little, as he continued down, detouring at my belly button. He skipped my pussy and lavished kisses on both my inner thighs.

I laughed. "Do you need help navigating?" His stubble grazed my inner thigh again.

"I think I know the way." A second later, his tongue split my folds on its way to my clit. Then, a finger entered me.

Groans of pleasure were all I could muster when a second finger joined the first. His tongue circled and flicked my little bud before he sucked on it. Amplified by anticipation, the simple pleasure drove me wild. Bucking my hips into him, I speared my fingers into his hair and pulled him against my heat. This was what I needed.

He looked up. Our gazes locked for a second before he sucked again, and my eyes rolled back as I fisted the sheets. My God, I'd never again doubt those authors who wrote how good this could feel. He took me right to the edge in record time.

"Come for me, baby." He crooked those fingers inside me and found that spot I thought was a myth made up to sell more copies of *Cosmo*.

I blew right past the edge and over into bliss as a red-hot orgasm crashed over me—muscle spasms, curled toes, stars behind my eyelids, all of it.

"That's it, baby. Ride the wave." He fingered and worked his magic tongue on me all through my release until I was left in a boneless heap.

I needed to work up the strength to satisfy him as well after the attention he'd just lavished on me. I took a deep breath. "Your turn, Studly. I need you inside me."

He lifted himself off and worked his jeans and boxer briefs down.

I took in the magnificence of his monster cock, thick and long.

"I'll be gentle," he said.

Once again, I chose the bold route. "I don't want gentle. I want studly."

He produced a condom and ripped the packet open.

I scooted to the edge of the bed and held out my hand. This would be a chance to get my hands on him. "What do you call him?"

Duke shrugged and handed me the condom. "Nothing."

"Nothing won't do." I rolled the condom down his length. "I'll have to think of something." I reached the root and gave him a tug. "Maybe Dino Dick."

He surged into my hand. "You've got to be kidding."

"Rex, short for T-Rex." I gave his length several strokes.

"Baby, if you keep stroking me, I'll embarrass myself before I even get inside you." He pulled my hand away. "On your hands and knees."

I wanted to be on top, to be in control, but I turned around and obliged.

He positioned himself at my entrance and eased in just a little. "I love that you're so wet, baby."

Since he hadn't been listening to me, I pushed back against him hard. The stretching sensation as I took his girth surprised me, but I held back the yelp.

"You feel so good, baby." He began to move, not hard, not fast, but slow and gentle with a hand on my breast, teasing my nipple.

I focused on the pleasure and sense of fullness that was better than any I'd experienced before. I tried to up the tempo, but his hand on my hips resisted.

"Take me, Cobra. I don't need gentle." He'd claimed me verbally, and I wanted the same physically. I shoved back against him.

With my urging, he gave in to his desires. Soon, the sound of flesh slapping against flesh filled the space. "God, baby, I'm close." Then his hand moved to my clit. "Come with me, baby."

Seconds later, I came apart for the second time, with a mind-blowing climax that set a new standard for what sex could be like. Three strong thrusts later, my orgasm pulled his from him. He tensed, and I felt the throb of his cock inside me. Yes, my man had claimed me as his.

After he took care of the condom, we snuggled. This big, powerful man gently wrapped himself around me, and I couldn't have felt more at ease, more safe.

CHAPTER 26

Duke

I WOKE WITH AN ALARM SQUAWKING AND HAIR IN MY FACE.

Serena pulled away to silence the damned noise. I'd been spooning her. Since when was I a spooner?

"We have to get up," she said.

"Go ahead." I groaned. "I'm catching a few more winks."

She pulled the covers off. "Up. I set the alarm late so you could sleep in, but we still have to pick up Grace and get down to Anaheim."

I rolled to the side of the bed and sat up. My foot landed on an empty condom wrapper. Blinking, I found it had buddies nearby—three of them. It had been a busy night, a fantastic night, to finish up a busy day.

I smiled. Telling old man Benson he could stick it if he didn't like me dating his daughter had been liberating after our encounter years ago. The risk had been worth it. Serena was mine, and I wasn't letting her go for him or anyone.

Serena moved over and rested a hand on my shoulder. Her other hand traced the scar on my lower back. "How many of these do you have?"

"Three. That was shrapnel. Then a bullet wound on my left leg."

Her fingers ran a circle around my scar. "Do they hurt?"

"That one does."

She jerked her hand away.

"When I think of the buddy I lost that day," I mean. "Freddy and I were close."

155

"I'm sorry. Can you tell me anything about it?"

"Fucking cake-eaters sent us into a real clusterfuck. The grenade that nicked me got him."

When the memory of the aftermath of his death threatened, I stood quickly, turning away. I couldn't look at Serena and have her see the real pain that day's events had triggered. "Get in the shower," I barked.

The bed shifted, and then the shower started in the bathroom.

"If you hurry, I'll let you wash my boobs."

Serena isn't Marilyn. My job here is a safe one. I made the decision to live in the present rather than the past. I grabbed a condom and walked into the bathroom. We might have to skip breakfast. They had food at the park.

As usual, traffic was heavy on the freeway as we drove down to Anaheim. Unusually, Serena was up front next to me. My dick still tingled from last night and this morning. She'd become my addiction.

We had Constance, Terry, and Grace in the back.

I checked the rearview mirror again.

"Don't you dare laugh, Duke." Constance jabbed the back of my seat. She'd certainly pulled off *different* with a frumpy top, huge sunglasses, a long wig, and a longer skirt.

I bit back my laugh but couldn't avoid the smirk. Serena turned back. "I like the look."

Normally, I was totally focused on the job, but when I put my hand on the center console and Serena covered it with hers, normal went out the window. My dick swelled, and I desperately wanted to be somewhere private with this very special woman.

"This is exciting, don't you think?" my very special woman asked. "I haven't been there in forever."

I pulled my hand away so I could concentrate on driving. "Worried is more like it." Serena shouldn't have agreed to this Disneyland outing. It would be a difficult place to maintain security with all the crowds, and we'd be unarmed.

"Kitty, how about holding hands?" Terry asked in the backseat. He and Grace hadn't agreed on how their fake-date cover was going to operate. "It would certainly be appropriate for a third date."

"First," Grace insisted. "After a few minutes with you, they'll know nobody would agree to a second date. I'd choose a very public setting like Disneyland where you'd have to behave yourself."

"Disneyland isn't a first-date place," Terry argued. "Because it would be awkward to cut it short—not that you'd want to with someone as charming as me."

"Or someone as humble," she added.

"I'd take you to a romantic dinner on our first date. Someplace with dim lighting where nobody would notice your childish nails."

"I like them," she said, displaying them in front of her. "All the better to scratch your eyes out if the situation calls for it," she added with a hiss.

I knew better than to criticize a woman's choice in nail art, even if it was multicolored and cat-themed.

Serena looked over her shoulder. "He's right, you know. How many women would choose an all-day first date?"

Grace huffed. "Okay, a second date, which I agreed to when I was too drunk to know better. And some hand-holding is allowed. But if you try to cop a feel, I'll lay you out flatter than a pancake."

Terry laughed. "You'd try."

"Or turn you into a soprano when you least expect it."

"Ouch." Terry grimaced.

When my phone rang, I put it on speaker. "What's up, Jordy?"

"I went to get a cup of coffee, and I've lost connection to the house. I'm blind."

"How's that possible?"

"I hope nobody cut the—wait… Yeah, here it is. The cable company says the internet is down in like a twenty-block area."

"Why?"

"Just a second. Keep your britches on… Got it. LAPD reports some idiot driver hit the cable company's box a few streets over, and like the good citizen he was, the guy decided to flee the scene. Typical."

"Okay. Thanks."

"Do you want to send Terry to check out the house?" Jordy asked.

"Can't. He's with us."

"You could drop him off, and he could Uber back," Jordy suggested.

I checked the rearview mirror. Constance shook her head. Terry nodded.

I agreed with Constance. A crowded space was too dangerous to give up a pair of eyes. "Send the boss."

"No can do. He's got a client meeting in Santa Barbara."

"I'm keeping Terry. Disneyland is the priority. He and Constance are both needed on this outing."

"Copy that."

"Thanks, Jordy. Keep me updated."

I ended the call and shook my head.

"What are you thinking?" Constance asked.

"I hate coincidences." My gut told me this was too many things pulling us in opposite directions all at once.

She leaned forward and patted my shoulder. "You made the right call. It's just an empty house. If you're worried, we can do an extra-careful sweep when we get back."

I nodded, but that didn't help the knot in my gut.

∿

SERENA

I WAS GIDDY AS A SCHOOLGIRL TO HAVE MY HAND IN DUKE'S AS WE WALKED ONTO Main Street in Disneyland. With a few sore muscles from last night's athletics, I wasn't looking forward to standing in a ton of lines, but that was the reality of a park like this.

"Where should we start?" Nick asked, looking at his girlfriend, Allison.

"The lady's choice," Duke said immediately, pointing at Katelyn, who was on the phone. It was a cute gesture. I'd mentioned Katelyn's depression over the loss of her fiancé and asked him to be nice to her.

"We'll be here pretty much all day," she said into the phone as she finished her call.

"You get first choice," Grace told her when she'd put the phone away.

"Oh, goodie. Space Mountain was Leo's favorite, so let's do that one."

Nick pointed the way to Tomorrowland, and we followed with Grace and Terry behind.

I didn't even have to ask. Duke held my hand or had his at the small of my back the entire time as we walked and went through the line, just like a proper date. And that's what I decided this was.

We'd been naked between the sheets, exploring each other's bodies in the dark, but somehow, his light touch in the daylight was better—in a way I couldn't put a finger on. It was more erotic, more sensual, and soothing at the same time. Maybe it was being in public in front of his team. The fact that Duke refused to break contact with me meant he was signaling that I was his to everybody around.

We boarded the ride, and his massive arm went around me, pulling me close. The ride went by in a blur as I couldn't get past the thought that I'd somehow lucked into a date with the perfect man. It would be a very long day if he kept this much bodily contact with me. Still, I intended to enjoy every single second of it.

When we exited the ride, my hormone-addled brain searched for someplace

158

secluded I could drag him, but Grace's bickering with Terry reminded me that we couldn't be alone today.

"Grace, your choice." Duke's voice boomed over the noise of the crowd.

"Yeah, Bobcat, show us what you're made of."

She pushed Terry away. "Matterhorn."

Hand in hand, we strode to one of the oldest attractions in the park. I would have chosen it as well. It had been one of my favorites as a kid. But the ride turned out to be a bit of a disappointment because the bobsleds weren't two across, so I couldn't sit with Duke next to me.

Nick had reserved a Lightning Lane time for Splash Mountain with time for lunch between now and then. It would be fun, even if it included getting wet. Still, being in line wasn't half bad. It was a typically warm Southern California morning, with bright sunshine and the gentlest of breezes.

As we ambled toward the ride, Terry pulled Duke aside for something.

Grace and I slowed at the cotton candy machine. "What do you think?" I asked her.

She nodded. "Looks yummy."

We got in line, and a guy in too-short shorts ahead of us turned around and eyed me. "It looks almost as yummy as you." *Slimeball.* He licked his lips and moved closer. "What's your name?"

Yuck, yuck, yuck. No response was the right response.

Suddenly, Duke was next to me, a protective arm tight around my shoulder. "Her name is none of your business if you want to keep your teeth," he growled.

Too-Short Shorts Guy melted backward, left the line, and scurried off.

Imagining George defending me like that was impossible, and I leaned into Duke's strength. Was it wrong to think of his possessiveness as sexy?

"Hey, guys, we need to get moving," Nick called.

"My waistline doesn't need that anyway," Grace said as we left the line.

Duke kept his arm around me as we walked. I clung to him when I noticed how many women gave him a second or third appreciative look as we passed. *Sorry, ladies. He's taken.*

We lagged behind Nick and Allison. Katelyn was recounting something about her last time here when I jerked, seeing a man in a black jacket ahead.

"What is it?" Duke demanded.

Katelyn paused her monologue. "What is what?"

Having heard the tone of Duke's question, Terry was immediately alongside us.

Looking through gaps in the crowd, the man was no longer there. "I thought I saw him."

"Where?" Duke demanded. "Terry, our six."

I pointed in the direction I'd seen him. "Black jacket."

159

Duke scanned the crowd forward while Terry turned to cover our backs. Duke pointed discreetly when Katelyn turned.

Only then did I notice Constance for the first time this morning.

She hurried to where he pointed.

Katelyn looked left and right. "Saw who?"

Duke gave her the canned explanation. "Her dipshit ex."

She waved a hand dismissively. "I never liked him."

I nodded in agreement. George was milquetoast compared to Duke. "It must have been somebody else."

"You two know each other?" Katelyn asked, pointing between the guys. It was the first time Duke had said anything to Terry.

I swallowed hard. This was bad.

"He trained me for a while," Terry explained casually, lifting his arm to flex his biceps.

"Wow," Grace cooed, playing her part as his date. She moved over to feel Terry's muscles. "He must be a miracle worker if he can get this result with a guy like you."

"It's all because of the work I put in, darlin'," Terry shot back.

Grace turned away. "Whatever you say, darlin'."

"It is," Terry insisted.

Katelyn rolled her eyes, and the question of Terry and Duke's connection seemed forgotten.

We logged another ride before lunch. Then Nick suggested the Blue Bayou restaurant and got no complaints. I hadn't had a Monte Cristo before, so Duke ordered that with fries for each of us. It was delicious, something between French toast and a grilled ham and cheese.

The others seemed oblivious that we were playing footsie under the table. Duke leaned across to wipe some ketchup off my lip. Once again, the light touch from someone so big and powerful undid me. How did I deserve a man so dreamy?

Nick and his girlfriend went to the bathroom, which I thought might be an excuse to be alone for a minute to make out.

Then Katelyn's phone rang, and she excused herself to take it.

"Do you really think you saw him?" Terry asked, now that we didn't have Katelyn listening in.

I shrugged. "It looked sort of like him, but with the distance, I could easily be mistaken. It might have been the jacket."

Duke put his food down. "We should leave to err on the safe side."

"No," I insisted. "We're not cutting this short. I'm not certain enough it was him for that."

Katelyn returned before Nick and Allison did. "What's next?"

"I think Serena and I might call it a day," Duke blurted.

Katelyn looked as mortified as I felt. "We haven't had a chance to talk."

I gave Duke my signature punch in the shoulder. "No way. You can go home alone if you feel that way."

"I drove," he pointed out.

"If you stay, I'll drive you back," Katelyn offered.

"No need," Duke said, tugging on my earlobe. "I'm not leaving my Snuggles alone."

After lunch, we hit Splash Mountain, followed by the Jungle Cruise, and my favorite of the day, Pirates of the Caribbean. Or it would have been my favorite if it hadn't been closed when we arrived.

Duke made up for it with the most romantic gesture I could have asked for. He put two quarters through the coin press, turning them into special elongated silver Disneyland coins with the Disneyland Haunted Mansion embossed on them. "Keep this with you, so you remember today."

I put the coin in my pocket.

He kept the other.

Allison was over the moon when Nick followed suit, pressing two coins for them.

Terry went next. "Here, Kitten."

Grace accepted the sliver of silver from him and tried to hide her smile, but I caught it.

Each of the rides today evoked a childlike happiness in me and an unexpected playfulness in Duke. This had resulted in too much tickling, enough hugging, and almost enough playful kissing. By the end of the day, I felt oddly naked when we weren't pressed together.

Katelyn checked her phone toward the end of the afternoon.

"What are you guys up for next?" Allison asked as she pulled close to Nick.

"I'm beat," I admitted. It was the truth. Duke had worn me out last night.

"It's too early," Katelyn complained. "We don't get here often enough to quit now."

"Riverboat," Terry suggested. "That's easy."

Nick and Allison led the say.

Terry slid an arm around Grace to follow.

Duke pulled me along after them. "That's easy enough."

Grace pulled away from Terry. He took her hand and whispered into her ear. She laughed and didn't yank free. *Progress.*

Katelyn came close a few strides later and whispered, "Leo and I started like that."

"Like what?"

"Sniping at each other as a defense mechanism."

"You think?"

"Check out the way she watches him when he's not looking."

I merely nodded. But it only took a minute for me to see an example of it.

Terry slung his arm around Grace's waist, and this time, she didn't object.

After a short walk, we strolled aboard and chose the top level near the stern of the Mark Twain riverboat. The steam puffed methodically out of the twin chimneys as the large paddle wheeler began its journey around Tom Sawyer's Island.

I leaned against the railing, snuggling up to Duke's warmth. The magic of this place was how it could transport you out of Los Angeles and into another world. Logically, I knew there were millions of people in hundreds of thousands of houses just outside the park boundaries, but I couldn't hear or see any of that now. Our existence currently included only water, trees, and the sound of the paddlewheel churning.

Nick corralled a passing couple, and they nicely took pictures of our group on all our phones. Grace changed sides, choosing not to stand next to Terry.

"If you want to go, we can call it a day," Duke mumbled into my hair after the group photo broke up.

"Thank you for coming with me."

He turned me to face him. "It's been fun for me, too."

With my breasts pressed against his chest, I became lost in the depths of his eyes and the fullness of his smile.

"Hey, lovebirds," Nick called. "We gotta get off unless you want to go around again."

Duke didn't turn us toward the stairs to exit as I expected. "You deserve days like today. That's half the reason I came."

I blinked back tears and pressed my face into his chest to hide them. When I had them under control, I turned to look out at the water again.

"And the other half?" I asked without meeting his eyes.

"I think you can guess."

"Oh, you know, us Bensons are sort of slow."

He took a deep, pained breath. "I really wanted to have a full day with you."

"We're leaving," Katelyn called from the stairs.

As we hurried to catch up, I added, "The day's not over yet."

He laughed. "Or the night."

CHAPTER 27

SERENA

WE'D DROPPED GRACE OFF ON THE WAY BACK TO MY PLACE, AND DUKE NOW USED HIS palm to unlock the door, with Terry just behind him.

I stood back, the way I'd learned was expected.

Duke stopped just inside with a raised fist. He pulled his gun.

Constance urged me back and pulled hers as well.

"We'll clear," Duke said. "Secure Serena." Then he and Terry disappeared inside and shut the door.

Constance hurried me back to Duke's SUV.

"What's going on?"

She pushed me up into it. "It's armored. Lock the doors," she barked as she closed me in.

I looked around and didn't see anybody suspicious, but that didn't stop my leg from starting up. Constance stood by the car, constantly scanning the street and the yard. It had to be ten minutes before Duke reappeared with his bite-a-lemon face. He talked to Constance for a moment before they let me out of the Suburban.

"Call Lucas and Wellbourne. We need LAPD's crime scene resources," Duke told her before he took my hand.

"What happened?" I squeaked.

"I don't think you should go inside. The house has been searched. It's a mess."

I pulled away from him. "It's my house. You're not keeping me out."

"I figured you'd say that. Brace yourself."

My stomach twisted as I followed him to the door. "Bad?"

"Very bad."

I prepared myself and pushed the door open. Terry stepped aside as I barged in. My house was trashed. The cushions of the couch were torn open and all the artwork scattered on the floor. No, I hadn't prepared myself. I bent over at the waist and almost puked.

"I warned you," Duke reminded me.

Moving to the kitchen, I found all the drawers and cupboards open. The flour was inches deep and littered with what was now garbage. Everything, literally everything, had ended up on the floor. "Why?" was my only word.

"Two options, bad and worse."

"Give me the bad one first."

"Spinelli was searching for that USB drive he's sure you have."

The destruction was near total. He'd even torn open containers in the fridge as if I'd hide something in leftover mac and cheese.

I was afraid to ask, but I did. "And the worse one?"

Duke checked that we were alone. "This was destruction done out of hate—a message. Does Harvey Fox hate you this much?"

My hand went to my mouth as I doubled over. Five seconds of slow breathing later, the urge to puke thankfully passed.

Duke put a gentle hand on my shoulder. "I'll take that as a yes."

I nodded. "He does."

"LAPD is here," Terry called.

"Thanks. We'll be out in a minute. You guys can brief them."

Steeling my resolve, we climbed up to my bedroom, where the devastation continued. Prison had probably given Fox a lot of time to think of how he was going to kill me, and yes, this was the message.

"This took a while," Duke said. "He took out the internet in the whole neighborhood to blind us."

"You think he knew we'd be gone all day?" I asked.

"Most likely."

"How?"

"Maybe he bugged the house, the car, your phone. Who knows? If that was it, Jordy will sort it out."

Looking at all the destruction, I could no longer hold back the tears.

Duke took me into his arms. "It's just things. Things are replaceable. The important truth is that you're safe."

But it wasn't only things he'd ripped from me, but also the certainty that I could be safe in my own house. Now I'd hesitate to open my front door every time, afraid of what I'd find.

A half-hour later, it got worse. "What the hell?" Dad's voice echoed through the house. "Serena?"

"He's pissed," Duke whispered into my hair.

"We have to face him."

Duke retrieved tissues from the bathroom to wipe my eyes, and we started down the stairs to face the dragon.

Dad was in the front room, berating Lucas and Constance. "What the hell kind of operation is this that something like this happens? You should have put a security system in, a good one."

Lucas stood there, looking angry, staying silent.

"We did." Constance tried a steady, even voice with Dad.

He waved his hands around. "If this can happen without you knowing, then it sucks."

"It's a top-of-the-line system," she explained. "But we lost connection with it when the internet went down in the neighborhood."

"Why wasn't anybody here to check?"

Duke stepped forward. "Because I decided against it."

"Then you're a moron. You're fired. Lucas, fire the jerk."

Lucas stoically ignored Dad.

Duke got right in Dad's face. "I didn't send someone because I prioritized your daughter's safety over the situation with the house. Our job, my job, is the safety and security of the person or people under my protection—not stuff, people, not things. I kept your daughter safe. I did my job."

Dad hadn't backed up under the assault until Duke was done. Instead of responding to Duke, he attacked his boss.

"Lucas, you're not putting enough resources on this. You're ultimately responsible."

Lucas fixed Dad with a deadly stare and pointed a finger. "Lloyd, as I explained, it's not your call, but I am getting two additional people for the job. As for responsibility, yes, I'm responsible, and in my book, Duke made the right call. We protect people, not things."

I moved up to put a supporting arm around my man. The first man I'd ever seen stand up to my father like that.

My brother Vincent walked in the door. "Wow, this is a mess."

"It's a good thing neither of you was here," Dad said. "And you're both coming home with me."

There it was, the ultimatum I'd expected.

Vincent shook his head. "No thanks. I'm going home."

"This *is* your and Serena's home," Dad insisted. "And it's not fit to live in. You're both coming with me."

"No. My other home."

Dad's eyes narrowed. "What do you mean?"

"I'm here part of the time and in Marina del Rey the rest."

Dad's expression morphed from confused to angry. "You were supposed to be living here, keeping Serena safe."

Vincent pointed my way. "Dad, open your eyes. She's not a child. She's a grownup making her own way in the world."

I loved my brother to death for defending me.

The detective who'd been interviewing Constance poked his head in. "Duke Hawk?"

Dad turned on me. "This is unbelievable, young lady. You're coming home with me." He came forward.

Duke blocked him. "She decides. Not you."

Dad tried to move around Duke. Duke shifted to stay between us.

"Out of my way," Dad bellowed.

Duke's low voice was dangerous. "Again, she decides, not you."

Duke was the first person I'd met who wasn't affected by my father's wealth or power.

"Serena," Dad pleaded.

"Dad, I'm going with Duke." I didn't know where that was or for sure that Duke wanted it, but I wouldn't allow Dad to lock me away again.

"This is not the end of this," Dad said as he stomped out, madder than I'd ever seen him.

I'd broken free, but at what cost?

After Dad left, I pointed a finger Duke's way. "This is only temporary. I'm moving back here after it's cleaned up." My most important truth was that from now on, I decided my destiny.

He growled deliciously.

~

Duke

Terry and Lieutenant Marcus Wellbourne approached after my interview with the detective. "This place is a mess," Wellbourne said. "The guy was either very thorough in his search or very angry."

"Or both. I'm going to take Serena to my place for tonight."

Terry cocked a brow. "She could stay with me. I've got more space than you."

166

I glared at him, and a growl may have escaped. No way was I letting her go with him.

He raised his hands. "It was just an offer."

Wellbourne smirked. "I'll keep the crime scene guys here as long as it takes."

"Thanks." I left them and found Constance watching over our charge upstairs.

Serena was going through clothing on the floor of her closet. "He sure has an anger issue. He ruined all my purses. I hate him."

"Why do you think Spinelli hates you so much?" Constance prodded.

I stepped back out of sight to hear her opinion and see if she mentioned Fox.

When half a minute went by, and Serena didn't answer, I rounded the corner. "There you are, my pretty."

She threw up her arms, with tears escaping her eyes. "He ruined everything."

"Remember what I said."

She sighed and put the purse down. "Yeah, things are replaceable."

Constance smiled. "Don't you think they can be repaired?"

Serena shook her head and stood. "I don't want them anymore. They'll only remind me of this, of what he did. You can have them."

Constance's face lit up. "Really?"

I suppressed a smile. Men went for flashy cars, and women for purses—and God forbid, shoes.

Serena kicked the closest one. "Help yourself. I don't want to see them again."

It was time to break this up. "Constance, I need a few minutes with Serena."

After Constance closed the door behind her, I sat on the bed. "We need to talk." I held out my hand for Serena's, and she came to sit next to me.

She hung her head. "About being my boyfriend... I hope I didn't pressure you too much."

I placed my hand over hers. "That's not a problem." It was both cute and annoying that she didn't see how strongly I felt about her, but that could wait. "What is a problem, though, is Harvey Fox."

Her head shook violently as she looked down at our joined hands. "I can't talk about it. I can't."

With a finger, I pulled her chin up to look at me. "That's not good enough."

"We agreed on tomorrow," she squeaked. Her eyes pleaded with me as her leg trembled.

To ease her fear, I wanted to give her the extra day, but I couldn't. "We have a meeting in two hours. Fox could have been the one who did this to your house, and even if he wasn't, your father thinks he's a threat. I need you to give me something to tell the team about this guy. Without information, we can't protect you."

"Tomorrow. I promise, tomorrow."

I stood. "If you won't let me protect you, then maybe it's best to take you back to your father's compound."

She looked up in horror. "You wouldn't do that."

"Try me," I challenged.

"That's not fair. You agreed to Monday. Or do you always go back on your word?"

She had checkmated me. "Right. Tomorrow. Now, this place isn't safe, so you're coming with me to my place."

She looked around the room and nodded. "Staying here would be too depressing."

∼

Nothing with Serena was easy, but a little while later, we got into the car. "My place is close."

She nodded and was silent for longer than normal.

"You're quiet," I noted as I turned onto Wilshire.

She looked out the window. "I'm still in shock at the needless destruction."

I glanced over. In the light from the street, she was beautiful, and she was mine. "He really wants that drive."

"But I don't have it."

I turned off the road. "We're here."

"Holy shit. I still can't believe you live here."

I parked, and my phone rang while I rushed to open the door for her. "What's up, Terry?"

"Do you need me?" he asked. "I hate to admit it, but I'm bushed."

"Get some rest. We're at my place about to go inside."

"Thanks, man. See ya tomorrow."

"Copy that." I hung up and grabbed Serena's bag from the trunk.

∼

Serena

When we parked at the monster tower Duke called his place, memories of how I thought I'd lost him made me shiver. The sound of the gunshot and not knowing if I'd ever see him again had almost made my heart stop.

"This time…" Duke opened the lockbox containing his gun. "I'm getting you upstairs safely."

168

I nodded and waited until he came around to open my door for me. It struck me that in all the times I'd gone anywhere with George, he'd never been this gentlemanly.

"Thank you, kind sir," I said, stepping out. "You know, you did get me inside safely last time."

He pulled my bag along with us.

I giggled as we passed the spot where he'd taken down the Russian trio.

"What's so funny?"

"I just remember the short guy saying '*We fix you,*' and then you took them down like a badass."

"I am a SEAL. It's what we do."

True to my new nickname, I snuggled closer as we walked on. "Do you have any idea how many times today I wanted to drag you off to someplace private?"

He towed me toward the door. "Me too, and when we get upstairs, I'm going to show you just how much I missed getting my hands on you."

"Watching you take down those goons was the hottest thing I've ever witnessed."

"Are you implying you're wet for me now, baby?"

"Drenched." Waves of desire rolled through me. "I need you."

"Can you be a lady until we make it upstairs?"

"I hope so."

"Good evening, Mr. Hawk, Miss Serena," Oliver said with a tip of his hat as we reached the door.

Duke returned the greeting.

We didn't make it all the way upstairs. He dropped the bag and his mouth took mine as soon as the elevator doors closed.

As we kissed, I clawed at his shirt and hair in full cavewoman mode. I couldn't get enough of him. He palmed my breast through my clothes. I wished I hadn't worn a bra, so he could feel how hard my nipples were.

I hiked up my dress and climbed him, wrapping both legs around his waist. He'd given me so many orgasms last night that I'd lost count, yet all I could think was how badly I wanted the next one. I ground against the bulge in his pants, so happy I'd worn a sundress today. "You have no idea how wet I am for you."

His response was a feral growl. When the doors opened, he squatted to get the bag and waddled us to his door with me still clamped around him.

I had let go so he could get to his keycard, but I was so turned on, I thought my heart would thump its way out of my ribcage. He opened the door and kicked it closed behind us.

My fingers were in his hair in an instant, demanding more kissing, more everything. Desire coiled between my legs, demanding to be sated. I needed one thing—Duke, my man. I reached down and cupped the giant bulge of Rex in his pants and squeezed.

He groaned and slid his hands under my ass, lifting me.

I had to pull my hand away from Rex to hang on behind his neck, but that didn't keep me from wrapping my legs around him and grinding against his erection.

He carried me sideways, swiped mail off a side table, and set me on it. I pulled at his shirt, wanting to rip it off. He pulled at mine, and in seconds, we were both topless. My breasts distracted him long enough for me to work his belt buckle free.

He growled, low and guttural. "You have the best fucking boobs."

I had trouble with the button on his jeans. "Does that mean you want to fuck my boobs?"

He pulled my breasts free of the cups. "Another time."

I lost my hold on his jeans when he cupped my breast and leaned down, taking my nipple into his mouth. I was wound so tight, the simple torture was exquisite.

Backing away, he yanked a condom from his wallet.

I released my bra while he pulled down his pants and released the Rex monster.

"Now that's what I want," I breathed.

"Are you ready, baby? I won't be able to hold back. This is going to be hard." The hot, feral look in his eyes told me his desire matched my own.

"Oh, so ready," I panted as I hiked up my dress.

He gripped my panties and, with a wicked yank, tore them off.

I gasped, surprised at how it turned me on. We'd left slow and subtle way behind and accelerated to Mach 1.

"Hang on, baby." With one hard thrust, he was deep inside. The groan he made was music to my ears. My back hit the wall, but I didn't care. I was stretched so far and filled so full, nothing else mattered.

Our gazes locked as he began a brutal rhythm. The table banged against the wall with each thrust, each delicious connection as he filled me and we became one. He delivered the relentless assault he'd promised, and I clawed at him to match his intensity.

Each push in was better than the last. "I'm almost there."

He brought his thumb to my clit, and I exploded. I gripped him with my nails as the climax rolled over me, hard and hot. "Oh, Duke. My God, my God, my God."

He sank in deep one more time, and his body locked with a groan. I felt the throb and captured his eyes, watching as his release leveled him. A minute later, there was only the panting of two satisfied lovers as I held onto him.

THAT NIGHT, DUKE'S MOVEMENT WOKE ME, AND I ROLLED TOWARD HIM IN BED. HE shook and sobbed out *"Marilyn"* several times. I realized he was having a nightmare. I shifted away. How many other women's names would I have to hear? As I lay awake, he shuddered again and murmured, "Marilyn, why?"

Suck it up, Serena. You're the one with him now. When he stilled, all I could do was wonder if *nightmare* had been the right term—or were they dreams, a longing?

I snuggled closer. I was the one with him now, and I wouldn't give him up.

CHAPTER 28

DUKE

MONDAY, I WOKE TO FIND HAIR IN FRONT OF ME AND MY ARM DRAPED OVER SERENA, with my hard dick up against her warm ass. Something had definitely shifted. For the second time in two days, I'd woken up spooning my woman. Normally, I was out of a woman's bed before falling asleep for the night, or I kicked her out of mine on the rare occasion I brought someone back here.

How long had it been? Maybe Mary, over a year ago. She was a sales rep from out of town, the two nearby hotels I considered acceptable had been booked, and a hell of a storm had made looking farther afield unappealing.

Serena shifted.

I stilled, liking the tranquility of the moment. This was a completely new experience for me, but oddly satisfying.

Her hand came up to cover mine on her boob and squeezed. "Morning." She wiggled her ass against my morning wood. "Are you this hard every morning?"

"With you in my life, I am."

She wiggled again and hummed.

The building phone on my nightstand rang.

I rolled over to pick it up. "Hello?"

"Sir…" It was our concierge downstairs. "A Mr. and Mrs. Benson are demanding to see you."

"We need to see our daughter," Lloyd Benson bellowed in the background.

172

I was tempted to send the blowhard away, but that would only create family friction for Serena. "Give me two minutes and send them up."

"Send who up?" Serena asked sleepily.

"Your parents."

She gasped and jumped out of bed. "Crap. I need more time."

SERENA

NAKED AS A JAYBIRD AND WITH HIS COCK STANDING AT ATTENTION, DUKE THREW ME my dress from yesterday. "Put this on and greet them while I get presentable." He went into the bathroom. *Presentable* had better not include an obvious erection.

Dad had taken this too far. After yesterday's blowup at my house, this was intolerable. Instead of the dress, I decided to embody the other word in my tattoo —*proud*. I was damned proud to be Duke Hawk's girlfriend. Going into his walk-in closet, I pulled a white button-down from a hanger.

Since Mom was with him, I pulled on panties but not a bra. With buttons open almost to my navel, the look was complete. I was Duke Hawk's woman, and appearing barefoot in his shirt, in his condo, with unbrushed hair, should make that crystal clear.

I waited by the door, and at the first knock, pulled it open. "Mom, Dad, what are you doing here?"

Mom's mouth opened in fly-catcher mode. "What are you—?"

I didn't let her finish. "Come in."

Dad's eyes looked past me.

"I can make coffee if you like." My man's voice came from behind me. Always the possessive one, a shirtless, barefoot Duke wrapped an arm around my waist a second later. At least he had pants on, and he wasn't sporting wood any longer.

Dad ignored Duke. "Munchkin, we're not staying," He used his practiced, master-of-the-universe voice.

Mom's gaze flicked between me and Duke. "Serena, why didn't you tell us you were attacked last week and had to go to the hospital?"

"Who—"

"Vincent 'fessed up to covering for you," Dad said before I finished the question.

"I didn't want to worry you." I aimed my words at Mom.

173

Dad looked ready to blow. "That was before Fox was paroled. What's going on?"

"We're looking into that," Duke said.

"Not good enough."

"Dad, they're looking into several leads."

"Is what happened at your house yesterday related to this?"

The creep of increasing demands had begun, and I had to stop the cycle. "That's between me and my team."

"Not good enough." He looked to Duke. "I want to know what leads you have."

"Sir, I can't divulge that without Serena's permission. We've already had this discussion. She's the client, not you."

I straightened up to be worthy of his words.

"That's bullshit. She might be your..." He motioned up my length. "I don't know what. But she's my little girl, and I have a right to know." He couldn't even bring himself to call me Duke's girlfriend.

"Serena," Mom pleaded.

Dad grasped Mom's hand. "We have a right to know."

Duke let go of me and advanced on Dad. "She used to be your little girl, but now, she is your adult daughter. She is very capable of making her own decisions."

"Munchkin, you're coming with us." Dad hadn't absorbed a single word Duke or I had said yesterday.

Duke did the unthinkable. He jabbed a finger in Dad's chest. "You're not listening. You can't dictate her life anymore. She's an adult, and you need to start treating her like one."

My God, I loved hearing him support me. Before yesterday, nobody had, not even my brothers.

Dad backed up, spluttering, "But..."

Mom's eyes were angry. "You can't talk to him like that."

"We're in my house," Duke pointed out. "And I can say anything I like. No disrespect, sir, but you're not in charge of Serena's life now. She is. It doesn't mean she doesn't love you both. But you have to respect her right to make her own decisions."

I couldn't have said it any better or any more forcefully. I came up and put my arm around Duke. "I do love you both, but I'm staying."

Dad was positively vibrating with anger. "We're not done with this."

A few seconds later, he slammed the door behind them.

I pulled in a breath. "That didn't go well."

Duke took me into his strong arms for a hug. "Give it time. It was a good start. He'd lose face if he gave in easily, but he'll come around."

"You think so?"

"Absolutely. He loves you so much he's having trouble letting you go."

I rubbed his crotch. "How about you help me shower?"

~

I REMINDED DUKE WE WERE RUNNING LATE, AND THAT SAVED ME IN THE SHOWER, BUT I didn't have the same luck at the bathroom counter when he came up behind me, still wet. His hard cock pressed up against my ass as his hands encircled me and fondled my breasts.

I moaned, watching in the mirror as his hands loved me. Closing my eyes, I reached behind me and stroked his length. "Only if you can be fast." Could a woman have too many orgasms? I'd have to look that up.

"Close your eyes and stay right there."

A moment later, I heard the tearing of the condom packet and spread my legs. I couldn't afford to be late to work.

"Now, watch your tits in the mirror." He positioned himself at my entrance and entered me with a strong push.

I did as I was told and watched my breasts flopping around as he thrust in and out. Tension quickly built inside me as he drove deep and hit a special spot on the way. The way my breasts swung with his movements was hypnotic as the pleasure built inside me. At this rate, I wasn't going to last long.

"Holy shit, you feel so damned good."

As good as it was watching my boobs, when I looked up, I caught the real show. His mesmerized look as he followed the swaying of my breasts was something else, and it amplified the feelings to know I was doing this to him. I added some side-to-side motion, and his smile increased. Yes, watching me was his catnip.

"I'm close..." He groaned as his hand found my clit.

His stroking of my little bud was like hitting the blast-off button, and I quickly came undone with a climax that convulsed around him.

After a few more savage thrusts, he locked up and unloaded inside me with a roar.

~

WHILE WE WERE MAKING BREAKFAST, I VENTURED INTO THE DANGER ZONE. "WHO IS Marilyn?" I asked.

Duke paused for a few seconds, then continued dicing the onion.

"You had a nightmare."

Chop, chop, chop.

"You seemed upset, and I want to understand. My therapist said—"

"You're not my therapist," he snapped. *Chop, chop.*

"Sorry. I only wanted to help."

He set down the knife and took a deep breath. "She died. Now, can you please get me the mushrooms?"

Feeling like the biggest jerk in town, I went to the fridge. *Nice going, Serena. Ask about the dead girlfriend, why don't you?*

Later, we sat at the table, without another mention of Marilyn, feeding each other bites of omelet while I wished I could take back the question, which had obviously caused him pain. His phone rang. It was Lucas.

"Cobra here," he answered. "Sure thing." He punched the speaker button and laid the phone down. "You're on speaker with Serena."

"I have Winston conferenced in," Lucas said. "We have a development in Florida."

"Hi, guys," Winston said.

We echoed the greeting.

Duke leaned forward. "What did you get from Rossi?"

"Nothing," Winston said. "And we're not going to. She's dead."

A coworker had been murdered. My stomach twisted, and breakfast threatened to come back up. I held my mouth and rushed to the bathroom.

Duke

I STARED AT THE CELL PHONE ON THE COUNTER FOR A SECOND. SOPHIA ROSSI BEING dead upped the stakes.

"The circumstances?" Lucas asked.

Winston sighed. "I can't know for sure until I get the coroner's report, but she was found in a canal that the Bratva here likes to use, so draw your own conclusions."

I stated mine. "It sure points to Yaroslavsky's brother doing the dirty work and getting the intel out of her. And it would explain why he said he couldn't double-check his information."

Lucas asked the next logical question. "Any clues in her apartment?"

"It's all been boxed up and sent to her parents in Oxnard."

"I don't like it," Lucas said, obviously pissed off. "We need access to that." He sounded a bit like Lloyd Benson.

"It's in transit," Winston said. "And unless you want to track down a UPS truck and hijack it, we'll have to wait until it arrives and ask her parents to take a look through it."

Lucas grumbled. "Serena, this makes it fairly certain that Rossi left you something."

"She isn't here," I said, looking toward the bathroom. "The news hit her pretty hard."

"Okay," Lucas said. "It's up to her and Constance to do a thorough check of her workspace for that drive."

"I'll tell her."

Serena returned, still a little green, but better. "Tell me what?"

"This means the search this morning with Constance is very important."

"I understand."

As we wrapped up the call, I had the feeling we'd missed an important connection.

MID-MORNING, AFTER DROPPING SERENA OFF AT WORK, I SAT IN MY FAKE LAWYER'S office and doodled factoids on a piece of paper.

My phone rang. It was Lucas.

"What's up?" I asked in greeting.

"You sure know how to make enemies, Brother."

"Who did I piss off?" It could be either Zolotarev, because I humiliated his son, or Benson, because I supported his daughter against him.

"Lloyd Benson came to see me."

"Figures."

"I just turned down an offer of a million dollars to pull you from the Benson case."

Serena's father hadn't wasted any time throwing his weight around. "Is that all?" I joked, even as it turned icy cold in the office. Benson was pissed, and he had the resources to make things pretty damned uncomfortable for me.

"No. Then he offered five million if I fired you."

Pissed was an understatement, and now I didn't know which way this conversation was going to go. "And what did you say?" I braced for bad news.

"That you're not only my best bodyguard but pretty much the fucking best in the business, and using anybody else for his daughter's protection would be putting her in danger."

Silently, I took in a deep breath. "Thanks, boss."

"After all I've done for him, he decided to piss me off. I don't give a shit how rich he is. Nofuckingbody buys me. Now go find Spinelli, and don't make me regret my words."

"Copy that." After he hung up, I stood and paced the tiny office, looking for anything I'd missed so far, but I didn't get much time to ponder before my phone rang.

"Hi, Mom," I answered. "How's Italy?" Mom and Dad were on a cruise, and I'd been checking the itinerary every two or so days.

"Wonderful so far, although the water in Venice isn't as clean as the movie people want you to believe."

"I've heard that."

She hummed. "A little birdie told me you're seeing someone."

That had to be my sisters, probably both of them.

"Really?"

"And I hear you think she's special," she said with a lilt to her voice.

"She is. Her name is Serena."

"Will you get a chance to bring her to Sunday brunch when we get back?"

Yes was the only acceptable answer in my family. "I'll need to check with her."

"Of course."

She gave me a quick rundown of their most recent stops before handing me off to Dad for a quick hello.

A half-hour later, Constance gave me the bad news—they hadn't found a USB drive anywhere in Serena's workspace. She'd even searched the breakroom.

With my doodle pad in front of me, I tapped my pen on the name Leo Gambino. Suddenly, the possible connection that had been bothering me buzzed in my head. I texted Serena.

ME: Call me when you can speak freely.

CHAPTER 29

SERENA

FIRST THING AFTER ARRIVING AT WORK, I'D MADE THE CALL AND ARRANGED FOR MY house to be cleaned up and put to rights. There were benefits to being a Benson. When I told Dad's assistant what I needed, he'd gotten on it. With the Benson name and money as a motivator, there wasn't much that couldn't be accomplished in record time. Since the house was in Dad's name, this was one time I'd gladly use family money.

A plan to move back to my house would go part way to mending fences with my parents, but how would Duke take the news?

After that, Constance and I looked high and low, but we didn't find a USB drive, which was distressing.

Later, when my man messaged me, I went into the small conference room for privacy and dialed him.

"Hi, gorgeous. Just answer yes or no—are you alone?"

Okay, so we were doing this like a thriller movie. "Yes."

"We've been summoned to Hawk Sunday brunch when my parents come back from their cruise. You can say no, or we can postpone. No pressure. You don't need to go. It's not like a super-important thing. My mom will understand if you aren't up to it. I'll under—"

"Stop it." I interrupted his nervous rambling. "I'll happily accompany you." This put us squarely in boyfriend-girlfriend, not-pretending territory. "When?"

"Uh… Okay… I'll have to check."

"Is that why you wanted me alone?"

"No. We also have new information. You mentioned earlier that your coworker Katelyn's fiancé died not too long ago."

I nodded. "Yeah. Leo passed away about six months ago. Why?"

"Where did he work?"

"Here at the EPA."

"Tell me he died of a disease."

"You're sick. No. He was in a car accident."

"Shit."

"What?"

"You were supposed to have a car accident."

The words knocked the breath out of me. The room suddenly felt chilly. I asked the unthinkable. "Are you telling me you think somebody is bumping off EPA people because we work here?"

"We're going to find out."

I decided this wasn't the best time to broach the subject of moving back to my house. After we hung up, I was still shivering. The idea that I was in danger because of my career? I'd chosen this to save families from the dangers of contaminated water. How could some ogre be against that?

If I quit, would I be safe? It didn't matter. When I pulled the picture of Carmen from my wallet again, I knew quitting was not an option. People deserved to trust that we kept their water clean.

After a minute, I went back to my desk to work, but fear made the screen go out of focus and swim in front of me.

"Serena?"

I turned to find Katelyn. "Yeah?"

"Oh dear, you look awful. Did something happen?"

I pasted on a smile. "I had a fight with my parents." It was best to stick to true things.

"I hate when that happens," she agreed. "I'd hoped we would get a chance to talk at Disneyland…"

"Sorry about that. I was bushed." From more nonstop hot sex the night before than I'd ever had in my life.

"Maybe tonight we could go out for dinner or drinks—just the two of us." She wanted girl time, and I couldn't put her off forever.

"Leo?" I asked softly.

She nodded. "I miss him so much it hurts. His death screwed me up, and now the bills are totally screwing me over."

I wanted to accept the invitation, but I remembered Duke's warnings. "Not this week, maybe next."

Her face dropped. "Yeah, whenever you can fit me into your busy schedule," she said, walking away.

My stomach twisted. I'd just won the shittiest friend award.

Powell summoned me a little while later.

"Benson, I checked the logs this morning, and I didn't see any data from your visits last week," he said when I reached his office. "You had your accident on the way back, isn't that right?"

"Yes, sir. The people at Excalibur Plating uploaded their data directly. But Knife Creek Chemical didn't provide any. They were very…" I searched for the polite word. "Difficult."

He shook his head. "I double-checked and didn't find anything for either company."

"No, I saw them upload—"

He jumped to his feet. "Are you implying I'm a liar? There's no data in the system." The vein on his temple throbbed. It was time to get out of this office before he blew.

"No, sir, not at all. They must have made a mistake I didn't catch."

He calmed slightly and sat again. "The position of external auditor is not a license to run around town and not get work done. You will not be making any more visits unsupervised. Someone will have to show you how the job is designed to be conducted, including bringing in data. Without data, we can't begin enforcement. Without enforcement…" He checked his watch. "Get out. I don't have time to teach you what we do here. I'll assign you to someone."

"Yes, sir." Turning on my heels, I scooted.

This was not my day. Practically none of the days were my day lately. Powell was a manipulative bastard, and I could see him using this to fail my probation and promote Remy.

~

JUST BEFORE THE END OF WORK, I GOT THE CALL THAT MY HOUSE WAS ALL CLEANED up, a bunch of replacement clothing had been purchased, the damaged furniture was replaced, and my kitchen was restocked. For once, I was glad the Benson name carried clout.

I hesitated before calling Duke. After almost being fired, I should want him to comfort me the way I knew he would. But I dreaded tonight even more. I'd promised to tell him the truth I never talked about. The nightmare I never wanted to revisit.

I pressed the button to call.

~

DUKE

AFTER WORK, I STARTED THE CAR.

Serena buckled in. "I'm moving back home tonight."

I hadn't expected that. "You can't. It's not safe."

"Yes, I can. The house has been all cleaned up. Terry told me himself that I have the best security system in the city."

It didn't make any sense. Her house had been completely trashed just yesterday. "How did you?"

"I'm a Benson. My dad taught me how to get things done."

If she followed her father's script, that meant throwing around money and threats. "I don't like it."

"You don't like anything," she shot back. "I can't stay at your place forever."

"One night is not forever," I pointed out.

"Please," she pleaded. "Having my own place is really an important milestone for me to maintain."

"Stay tonight, at least until Terry has a chance to check out the system." Having her in my bed was important to me, but it didn't seem right to put it that way.

She sighed and offered her hand on the console. "Okay."

After a few blocks, the fear that she'd pull her hand away eased.

She kept contact with me all the way home, a sign of trust I cherished.

❧

JUST IN CASE ZOLOTAREV WAS EVEN STUPIDER THAN I THOUGHT, I MADE A CIRCUIT OF the parking lot, checking for Russians before pulling into a slot.

When we reached the door, Oliver produced a rose from behind his back. "For the lovely lady."

Serena lit up like a Christmas tree. "Oliver, that's so thoughtful of you."

It sucked to be shown up by my own doorman.

When the elevator started its journey, I asked the question I'd waited days to have answered. "What's the deal with Harvey Fox?"

Pleading eyes looked back at me. "After dinner, please?"

❧

SERENA

. . .

I'D SUCCESSFULLY PUT OFF OUR TALK—OR RATHER MY CONFESSION—UNTIL AFTER dinner, but my time had run out. "This is really hard for me." I sat on the edge of Duke's bed and took a big breath, not sure how to start.

Duke settled beside me. "Do you remember what I told you about running from your fear?"

I nodded. "If I don't face my fear, I'll be a prisoner to it forever."

He laid his hand on mine, and I grasped it. "You have a choice to make—prisoner or not, trust me or not."

"That's not fair," I complained. "It's not that I don't trust you." Until now, I'd kept everything about those events locked away as if they didn't exist. Nobody except Lucas—and, of course, Fox—knew what had happened that day.

Duke gave my hand a gentle squeeze, pulling my attention back to him. "Then trust me with the truth."

"Okay." I'd placed my life in his hands. What else could I say?

"Start with why Harvey Fox would want to hurt you."

Images raced through my mind from the courtroom on the day of his sentencing, his vow to seek revenge, and all the blood. There'd been so much blood. I took in a breath. "He might come after me because it was my statement to the police that put him in prison."

Duke patiently waited for more.

I looked down at the floor, ashamed of what came next. "And because I killed his brother." I felt Duke jerk when I said that.

"Start with what he was convicted of," Duke said softly.

"Attempted murder."

When I didn't say any more, Duke asked, "Of whom?"

"Your brother, Lucas."

I felt Duke's breathing stop for a few seconds, as much as I heard the hitch in his breath.

His hand caressed mine. "And that's how you know Lucas?"

I nodded. "Yes." When I looked up, I didn't see horror in Duke's eyes, or judgment, even though I'd told him I'd killed another human being. That gave me the strength to go on. "I didn't tell you because Lucas is the one who found me."

"I don't understand." His words were slow, almost soothing.

"I was kidnapped." *There, I'd exposed the first secret.* I sobbed as the memories of that dark room came flooding back.

Duke held me. "I can't begin to imagine how terrifying that was, but you're safe here. Nobody's going to get to you. I won't let them."

He rocked me until I stopped sobbing. "Did Fox kidnap you?"

"His twin brother, Oscar, was the one who took me, but Harvey was part of it too. They're identical twins, and they bragged about how that meant they couldn't be caught. Harvey went around San Diego, changing outfits, credit cards, driver's licenses, girlfriends, and cars, half the time pretending to be Oscar, and half the time himself so that they both had alibis."

Duke nodded. "How long?"

"It was hard to tell time," I said, stalling and debating what to say. "A day roughly?" It had been ten brutal days, but I couldn't admit that. He'd ask about that time, about the rapes. I couldn't have this man look at me like damaged goods, in addition to being a murderer.

He ran fingers over my hand, gentle fingers that said so much. "I'm sorry."

I couldn't bring myself to tell Duke the horrid details, the darkness, the things they did to me. I'd never told anybody, not even my family.

"How come I never heard about your case?"

I let out a long breath. "Dad didn't get the cops or the FBI involved, only Lucas. They demanded three million, and Dad paid it immediately."

"So, they let you go."

I gulped down the rock lodged in my throat, thinking about that day. "No."

"Lucas found you?" he guessed.

"He did." I steadied myself for the next part. "When Dad paid the ransom, Lucas somehow followed Harvey after he picked it up." I took another breath. "When Harvey returned, Oscar picked up a knife and was about to…" I sobbed. I'd been so scared, and again, I couldn't tell Duke the truth. "Cut me loose."

"Did he?" Duke asked softly.

"Anyway, that's when Lucas came through the door." I choked up because the next part was so terrible.

Duke didn't push me.

"He didn't see Harvey behind the door, so when he came in and ordered Oscar to put his hands up, thinking he was Harvey, Harvey shot him from behind." The scene played out in slow motion. "Lucas's gun dropped to the floor, and I thought he was going to die. But Lucas turned and charged. They fought. That's when Oscar dropped the knife and went for the gun on the floor. I couldn't let him shoot Lucas again. So I grabbed the knife and stabbed him."

Duke squeezed my hand.

"My God, the blood… So much blood." I sobbed as the images I'd repressed for so long came back. "I got him in the neck."

"And Harvey vowed revenge?"

"Uh-huh. Harvey wanted a plea deal, and Dad wanted to avoid a kidnapping trial. Dad talked to the DA and got the charges dropped to attempted murder."

"Instead of kidnapping and everything else?" Duke asked incredulously. "He should have gotten life, or the needle."

"It was like I was never there. That was the price to avoid a trial, so I didn't

184

have to testify and nobody would know they could kidnap a Benson for an easy three million."

"But now he's out on the street to threaten you again, or somebody else."

"Dad made the decision to shield me." At the time, I'd loved him for it. I couldn't imagine having to recount details I hadn't even told my mother in open court.

"I can't imagine how hard that ordeal was for you. Thank you for trusting me with your truth." Duke gave me the most caring look I'd ever received. He didn't judge me, and it wasn't pity I saw, but pride.

As he gently rocked me, I thought just maybe he was right that talking about the events would get me past some of the fear. But I also felt guilty that I was too scared to share everything with him.

"I can see why he's so protective of you," Duke added after a moment.

"Hold on. It's way beyond protective. He wants to lock me in the house and never let me out. That's why I couldn't let you guys tell him about being run off the road. You saw how he was. He would have kidnapped me himself to lock me away."

"He's not doing that. You're mine, and trust me, I'll take care of you."

We leaned back on the bed, and for the longest time, he held me, stroking my hair. Slowly, my tears dried, and the memories faded. I was in my man's arms, and that was what mattered.

CHAPTER 30

SERENA

I woke Tuesday morning with Duke's arm around me, as I had for several days now. He breathed the steady rhythm of sleep into my hair.

This morning, with the hint of sunshine coming from behind the blinds, I felt completely renewed. Today was the first day of the rest of my life. I'd unloaded most of my troubled past on Duke, and he was still here.

He'd been right that facing my fear was the only way to conquer it. He hadn't seen me as the murderer I'd feared he would when he heard my story. Instead, he comforted me and understood as completely as anyone could.

His gentle lovemaking last night had confirmed the connection I craved. Yesterday, I wouldn't have believed it possible to fall completely for a man in a week's time. This morning I knew it was true. I loved Duke Hawk, bossiness, scars, and all.

Last night, he hadn't wanted to share about his past with Dad, and after all I'd put us through with my horrid truth, I'd agreed.

It didn't matter when we got to it. Duke had completely replaced my father as the man central to my well-being, central to my future.

Future. That was a concept we hadn't explored, but in my bones, I felt we had one, and it would be marvelous. How could it not be with this man?

Feeling his morning wood against me, I made a decision and turned over. "Morning, sleepyhead."

His eyes blinked open as he stretched. "Good morning, Snuggles. How are you feeling?"

There was my compassionate man. I answered by grabbing hold of Rex. "I need something."

"Really?" He rolled us, landing on top of me. And there was my caveman, always taking control.

I pushed at him with no effect. "I want to be on top." It was important that I have some control, and it was the one position in the whole book we hadn't done yet. "And I want something else."

"Gimme this, gimme that," he mimicked in falsetto.

"It's not like that, and you know it."

"Okay, baby." He rolled us so I was on top.

I got my knees under me and straddled him.

He groaned when I rubbed myself along his length. "What else is it you want?"

"It's a negative want," I said as I slid my folds over his tip.

"You're killing me here."

I leaned over and whispered in his ear. "No condom."

He jerked under me. "Are you sure? I mean, I'm clean, but…are you abso-fuckinglutely sure?"

"After George, I got tested. I haven't been with anyone since, and I get a contraceptive shot."

He watched me, his eyes asking what his lips wouldn't.

I lifted up and positioned his head at my entrance. "I'm sure." I lowered myself slowly down his length, taking every glorious inch of him. He was so hard for me and gloriously thick as he filled me completely.

His jaw clenched as his hips lifted into me. "Oh, baby. You have no idea how good you feel."

I lifted up and plunged down, rolling my hips. I was in control, complete control.

I let his hands guide me up and down, again and again, each of us groaning with the pleasure of skin-to-skin sensations. I reached behind me to grab his balls. He grunted, pleasure or pain, I didn't know, but he didn't tell me to let go. We were in it together, stroke for stroke, but I was driving this bus. Letting go of his balls, I leaned over to offer my breasts, to tease him with access to my nipples.

As I neared the precipice and pleasure radiated to every cell of my body, I took his hand and guided him to where we were joined. He found my clit, and with his talented fingers, took me up and over the edge, bliss ripping through me with amazing force. Powering up into me, he found his own release. With a roar, his entire body shook. I felt the repeated throbs of his cock as he poured into me.

When the waves receded, I collapsed forward on him and panted out the words that I knew were a risk. "I'm falling for you, Duke Hawk." I didn't dare say what I really meant.

I waited several long seconds and worried I'd blown up my chance with him. It had been less than ten days since I'd re-met Duke and learned his last name. Things had moved lightning fast. Had I made the biggest mistake of my life with a proclamation he wasn't ready for?

But then he smiled. "I'm falling for you too, Snuggles."

I didn't need any words beyond those. Still panting, I pulled his chin to face me and kissed my man. It was a new day, and yes, I was officially his and he was officially mine. Bold had paid off.

I wasn't bold enough to use the L-word, though.

Serena

IT WASN'T QUITE LUNCHTIME WHEN MY PHONE BUZZED.

> DUKE: I'm bored. Tell me something interesting.

It took me only a nanosecond to decide to fry his brain.

> ME: I'm not wearing panties.
> DUKE: Are you trying to kill me?
> ME: If I go into the conference room, maybe we could discuss what to do about it?
> DUKE: Another time, Lucas is calling.

I leaned back in my chair, fantasizing about phone sex with a big former SEAL. Would he whip it out and start pumping himself? I'd bet on it. The conference room had a partial glass wall. The question was, what could I get away with under the table?

The loud noise jolted me almost into heart-attack territory. The fire alarm's wail was annoying in the extreme.

"Everybody evacuate." Powell's voice boomed through the space. "This is not a drill."

Katelyn appeared at the door. "Come on."

Grabbing my purse, I joined her and Remy on the long trek down the stairs. The stairwell was crowded, and if someone tripped, it would probably take out a hundred of us.

"I'm thirsty," Katelyn said when we reached the door to the fresh air outside. "This is going to take a while, and there's a cold Frappuccino with my name on it at Starbucks."

"I've got to find Jacques and see what he wants," Remy said.

"True love," Katelyn noted as he strode off. "Leo and I used to be like that." Her eyes were already wet.

I changed the subject to avoid another crying session. "Starbucks sounds good, but it'll be crowded."

Katelyn began walking. "Not if we get there before they release everyone to go back inside."

Remy reappeared. "Jacques called and gave me his order."

We crossed the street, and my phone rang. I didn't recognize the number. "Hello?"

"What's going on?" Duke asked. I recognized his strong voice.

"Fire alarm. We're evacuating."

"I'm on the way. Where are you?" Heavy breathing and footsteps pegged him as running, not walking.

"Katelyn, Remy, and I are walking to Starbucks."

"Which direction?"

"Toward Ohio Avenue."

"I'll be there as soon as I can. Keep your eyes peeled." He hung up.

"Who's that?" Katelyn asked.

"Love you too," I said into the dead phone line and put the phone away. "My boyfriend." It felt good to say that and have it be real.

We crossed the street to the uncrowded side. The coffee shop beckoned two blocks away.

Suddenly, a hand came from behind and shoved Katelyn.

"What the fuck?" She toppled to the ground.

"That hurt," Remy complained as he ended up next to her.

Big, beefy arms wrapped around me, and I screamed. "Hey." I kicked behind me and connected with someone's shin—hard.

"Fuck." With a groan, his grip loosened, and I wriggled free.

He was big and built, in a black tee and black cargo pants. "No, you don't." Moving faster than I thought possible, he grabbed my wrist and yanked me toward him. He'd grabbed my bad arm, still tender from being run off the road, and it hurt like hell when he pulled. Lifting me off my feet, he carried me like a football, with my arms pinned against him and the cut on my side screaming painfully.

"Help," I yelled, but there was nobody else around.

"Let her go," Katelyn screamed.

"Yeah, let her go," Remy chimed in.

The brute ignored them and carried me toward a nearby SUV.

No. No. No. It was black, with tinted windows and no front license plate. If he got me in there, I was dead—or worse. I kicked and tried to get loose, but it was no good. I bit him through his shirt.

"Bitch." He stopped and punched my skull, then slapped me hard.

My vision blurred for a moment as pain exploded across my head. Nothing I did worked. He was too big.

But I had to get free. I'd seen the movies. If he got me in the car, I'd be raped and sex trafficked, or worse. I didn't have Liam Neeson looking over me. I saw an opening and punched his crotch.

His grip on me loosened, and I fell to my hands and knees.

"You'll pay for that," he roared as he grabbed my hair.

God, that hurt. He pulled me along, stumbling. This couldn't be the end. I was too young to die.

Then I heard an *oof,* and my attacker let go of my hair. I fell to my knees and turned to see Duke dodge the big guy's fist. Then my Duke delivered a series of rapid-fire punches to the guy's face and body. Duke was clearly skilled and almost elegant in his delivery.

The monster roared and charged. Duke dodged and kicked the monster's knee. The guy dented the parked car he landed against, but got up and hobbled toward us. The monster swung again and missed. He was no match for the former SEAL. Duke landed two more punches and a wicked kick. The big guy landed in a heap.

I didn't have Liam Neeson looking after me, but I had someone better—a SEAL, a true badass.

People were finally running this way, and I heard a siren in the distance.

"Time to go," Duke said as he extended a hand to help me up.

I took the offered hand and once again felt that zing from his touch.

Suddenly, Duke groaned and shook uncontrollably. The zing of excitement instantly became an electric shock that jerked my hand away.

Duke slumped to his knees next to me. "Gun. Waist," he mumbled through gritted teeth as he fell to the ground.

I saw two wires coming from his back and leading to… *Holy fuck.* Black Jacket Guy had appeared, and he held a yellow Taser in his hand, grinning maniacally.

"You're coming with me." He dropped the Taser and advanced.

I grabbed Duke's gun from his waist and swiveled. Mentally, I thanked Dad for making me take lessons from the master chief on handling a gun.

Black Jacket Guy glanced at the approaching crowd, then sneered and changed course to help the monster goon up off the sidewalk. "You won't shoot an unarmed man." He helped his man toward the SUV.

Flicking off the safety, I aimed and fired twice.

CHAPTER 31

Duke

THE SUV SPED AWAY.

"You ruined my fucking bag!" Katelyn screamed at the departing SUV with a finger raised in the air.

The guy with her stood there, completely useless. Remy, I think? He'd wet himself.

"Gimme that." I struggled to my knees and held out my hand for my weapon. "You shouldn't go shooting at people on a crowded street."

Serena handed it over.

I holstered it. "Good thing you missed."

"I didn't miss. I hit the radiator dead center."

A small splotch of green cooling fluid on the street where the car had been elevated my respect for her another notch. "Good thinking." The SUV would soon be toast.

I stood and helped her up before turning away. "Pull the wires out."

"What?"

"You heard me." I couldn't reach them, and I couldn't walk away trailing a Taser behind me.

She yanked.

"Fuck." It hurt like a dozen bee stings when she pulled the barbs loose.

Serena clung to me, shuddering. I stroked her back and tried to soothe her.

191

"It was Black Jacket Guy, Spinelli."

I smoothed her hair. "The big guy?"

"No, the one who Tasered you."

"He's going down."

"I can't stop shaking," she said.

"It's the adrenaline. It'll take time."

Several uniformed federal marshals arrived before we could leave. They shooed the LAPD street cops away when they learned Serena worked in their building. Assaulting a federal employee trumped whatever the locals could come up with.

Marcus Wellbourne, our friend in the LAPD, arrived after Serena had given her statement to the marshals. "You must have pissed somebody off," the lieutenant joked.

"No shit, Sherlock," Serena said. She was one unhappy camper.

"Are you going to tell me now what's cooking?" he asked.

"Not yet, but as soon as we can," I assured him. I wished I had some way we could put his resources to use, but we didn't have the kind of data the LAPD could act on—yet.

After a while, the marshals cleared us to leave.

I tapped Serena's shoulder. "I'm taking you home." Just that simple touch reminded me what her warm skin felt like under my fingers.

"No way. I'm not having some goon chase me away from my work."

"But—"

She didn't even let me finish. "We talked about this. No change to my schedule. That's the rule. You got one thing right, though, you're taking me back to my house tonight."

I didn't argue, because what was the point? Reluctantly, I handed her off to the marshals to see that she got back into the building safely. My phone rang.

"What the hell happened?" came Lucas's voice.

I explained the sequence of events.

"He hit her? Who is he?"

"No idea who the big guy is. We don't have video for facial rec. Spinelli was the second man."

"When you find the big guy, I want to be the one to make him pay."

Lucas was serious when it came to violence against women. Once overseas, he'd detoured a mission for two hours to visit a drug kingpin running a rape house. Hassan Fazel and four of his lieutenants had ended up buried under a pile of rubble.

"I'll take care of him myself."

"Why wasn't Constance with her?"

"They got separated in the evacuation."

"Where is Serena now?"

I explained Serena's insistence on going back to work, and that I'd let the marshals escort her.

Instead of a dressing down for almost losing our client, I got, "Figures. She's tough. She's been through a lot more than people realize. Keep her safe."

It wasn't the time to tell Lucas I knew what Serena had been through, so I just agreed. "Tough is right," I told him. Surviving a kidnapping and having another's death on her hands made *tough* too gentle a word.

"IT'S RUINED," KATELYN COMPLAINED AGAIN AS WE REENTERED THE BUILDING. "It's genuine, not a knockoff. I can't afford to replace it now."

I ignored the complaint.

"Shit, look at me. I'm being a terrible friend,' she said touching my shoulder. "That was scary. Are you all right? What the hell was that about?"

"No idea," I lied with a huge sigh.

Less than an hour later, Powell called me into his office.

When Katelyn joined us, I shifted to create space between us.

"Ms. Connor, I want you to take Benson here under your wing and show her how we do things, including coming back with data."

I kept my mouth shut instead of yelling, *Fuck you too, Dr. Powell, and by the way, somebody tried to knock me off like they did Leo and Sophia.*

"Yes, sir," she said with zero enthusiasm. "I'd love to. Maybe—"

Powell didn't let her finish. "Set up meetings by the day after tomorrow with the two companies she had trouble with last week."

Her open mouth said that rattled her. "I'd rather start with easier, closer companies if that's all right with—"

"Nope." He shook his head. "I want to get back on track with the two Ms. Benson didn't collect data from… Centaur…uh…" He looked at me and waved his hand.

"Excalibur Plating and Knife Creek Chemical," I filled in.

"Yes, those."

"I'm not sure the timing is practical," Katelyn tried.

"Connor," he cautioned. "We're the EPA. Tell them to make time Thursday or else."

"Yes, sir."

"And Benson," he said before we escaped the office.

I turned. "Sir?"

"You're riding with Connor until you pass probation."

After that, Katelyn mumbled curses directed Powell's way before she locked herself in the big conference room to call the companies.

Ten minutes later, Katelyn told me she had the appointments set up.

"I'll be ready."

"He's such an ass." She shook her head and went back to her computer.

It would be my first trip back to Thousand Oaks, and after the last time, I wasn't looking forward to it.

THAT EVENING, I WANDERED INTO THE KITCHEN IN BARE FEET AND MY COMFY sweats.

Duke was at the stove sautéing mushrooms with his back to me—a very enticingly naked back with a smattering of tattoos.

Before sipping from my second glass of Chablis, I surveyed the stainless appliances and stark white cabinetry of the kitchen. It was all so masculine, with offsetting black granite countertops. It suited him.

Duke raised a brow. "Easy there, slugger. Save some for dinner."

I gulped down half the glass. Tonight, I'd need more than this to quell my anxiety. "What if Katelyn tells Powell I can't cut it in the field?"

"I thought she was paired with you to help out?"

"Haven't you ever had a bad boss?

"Uh…"

"See? You don't get what office politics can be like. Powell wanted the job to go to Remy. This is his opportunity. I'm on probation. Katelyn gives me a bad report card and that combined with wrecking a car my first time out gives him what he needs to send me back to my old desk."

Duke gingerly took the glass from my hands, set it on the counter, and wrapped me up like a burrito, rocking me back and forth. "You're afraid the fix is in?"

I nodded against his shoulder.

"Then we unfix it. I'll give you a bug to wear that'll record everything so you have the evidence to fight back if you need it."

"Really?"

"Sure. Fight sneaky with sneaky."

"When?"

"Day after tomorrow."

He adopted that ate-a-lemon face of his. "I don't like it. Put it off for a week or two."

"I would if I could, but this is a command performance. And get this, I'm not allowed to wreck another government vehicle."

He laughed. "Not allowed, huh? Even with another person, I still don't like it. I obviously can't ride along with you."

"Follow us. Bring your machine gun or whatever. We're going back to the companies I visited last Monday before the accident. I'll give you the addresses and drive slow."

He sighed and squeezed a little tighter. "We'll make it work."

As he held me, my day improved remarkably. Now I had a chance.

Eventually, he let go of me. "I'm hungry. Let's get this dinner going."

A LITTLE WHILE LATER, AS WE FINISHED OUR MEAL, I SWALLOWED MY BITE OF cheesecake and patted the tabletop. "This could be fun."

"What about the terrace?" he asked.

The doorbell rang.

Duke got up. "It's probably one of my brothers."

When he opened it, a statuesque blonde sauntered in. "Lover, you didn't return any of my texts."

Lover? She was stunningly beautiful, with perfect hair and makeup, a killer dress, and heels to die for. I didn't compare, even before I'd washed my face off. I released the clip holding my hair up in a messy bun.

Duke left the door open. "Ursula, that should be a pretty clear signal I don't want to see you."

She noticed me when I stood. "Oh. You have company. Well, call me when you're done with her."

My fingers got stuck as I tried to run a hand through my hair.

"This is my girlfriend," Duke said. "I won't be calling. Now leave and forget my number."

She eyed the table. "Playing house, are we?"

I crossed my arms and raised up my boobs.

"Get out, Ursula," Duke repeated.

"That won't last. Call when you get bored of this…" She waved in my direction. "…phase." She turned.

"Oh, Ursula," I called.

She stopped.

"He's mine. If we see or hear from you again, I'll claw your eyes out."

"So American," she huffed as she left.

"Claw her eyes out?" Duke asked as he closed the door after her.

I ran and jumped up, wrapping my legs around him. "You said you'd gut George."

"And I meant it."

"Claw her eyes out is the equivalent." I wiggled against his growing erection. "Tabletop. The terrace is too far."

CHAPTER 32

DUKE

WEDNESDAY MORNING, I WAS PLAYING WITH MY DOODLE PAD AGAIN, WAITING TO hear from Terry. If any of them had been successful, the attacks on Serena would have made three EPA employees in succession, and that was the kind of coincidence I didn't believe in.

The coroner's report for Leo Gambino had been straightforward, in that his fatal injuries were consistent with a high-speed automobile crash. Now Terry was on his way to Bakersfield to see the vehicle Leo had been driving.

After lunch, Lucas joined me to wait for Terry's call. Jordy was still searching for Spinelli without any luck. He'd disappeared after the attempted abduction, along with his oversized muscle.

Lucas and I had agreed that Leo's death was our best open lead.

When one o'clock rolled around, I was getting itchy to know what Terry had found. "Should we call him?" I asked.

Lucas was laid out on the couch I'd ordered with his eyes closed. "Nope. Voltaire once said, 'Perfection is attained by slow degrees; it requires the hand of time.'"

"Translation?"

"If we rush him, he might do an adequate job. I'd rather have him check everything and make it a perfect job."

It was after four when he finally called.

I picked up my pen and answered. "Talk to me, Terry. What do we know?"

197

"It's not definitive, but it is fishy."

"What is?" He wasn't going to make this easy.

"Guess what I found?"

"Terry, I'm not interested in guessing," Lucas called from the couch.

"Sure, boss. I found paint transfer on the rear bumper. It's some flavor of black, so I'm bringing a scraping back to check for make and model."

"Thanks, Terry. Good work," Lucas said, giving him the kind of praise he didn't heap on his brothers.

Serena had been bugging me about my pleases and thank yous. Maybe it was genetic and not my fault.

"That's not all," Terry said. "He went off the road at high speed, but the airbag didn't deploy."

Lucas smiled. "Any clue why that was?"

"This is the cool part. The airbag fuse was missing."

Lucas's fist hit the table with a bang. "Great work, Terry. Thanks. See ya back here when you're able."

"Copy that."

My brother smiled. "It's about time we made some progress. Fuses don't go missing by themselves. Gambino had help dying in that crash."

It was a clue, but we still needed to figure out who and why. Or maybe the why would lead us to the who.

～

SERENA

By Wednesday afternoon, I felt safe saying things at work had gone more smoothly today than Tuesday—not a single fire alarm or kidnapping attempt.

When I said I didn't want to talk about it, people dropped their questions about me almost being snatched off the street and went back to trying to guess what and who Constance was investigating.

Near the end of the day, my phone rang. *Duke.*

"Miss me already?" I answered.

"Always," he said. "Are you somewhere you can talk?"

"Give me a second." I stood and started for the large conference room. My heart sped up, hoping he was going to take me up on yesterday's invitation for naughty phone sex.

The freaking conference room was occupied, so I ducked into an unoccupied office and closed the door. "I am now." I was already wet with anticipation.

"We think Leo Gambino may have been murdered."

198

The blood in my veins turned to ice, and I couldn't breathe. I tried for the chair behind the desk and almost didn't make it. I pulled myself up, tears threatening. He didn't want any damned stick; he wanted to kill me.

"Serena, did you hear me?"

"Uh-huh," I croaked out.

"This is good news."

"How?" I squeaked. "You're telling me he wants to kill me just because I work here."

"No," Lucas's voice came on the line. "It's good because we know more than we did yesterday, and we know he wants the drive, wherever it is. He most likely had Rossi tortured, and she told them she gave it to you."

I shook my head. "That sounds like you're telling me he plans to catch me and torture me."

Their combined silence spoke volumes.

My stomach lurched. "I'm still not hearing the good news part."

"We're not going to let that happen," Duke finally said.

"I think I'm going to puke," I said as I got up to run to the bathroom.

DUKE PICKED ME UP AFTER WORK, AS HAD BECOME OUR PATTERN, BUT THE KISS THAT started out for my coworkers' benefit had shifted to real in the last few days.

He pulled me against his solid body and stroked my hair. "I realize we freaked you out this afternoon, but you wanted to stay in the loop."

I held on as tightly as I could. "Yeah, but I didn't count on you telling me torture was now his goal."

"I've got your back, baby."

I pushed away. If the killer was targeting EPA people, I wanted to get away from here. "Let's go. Can we watch a happy movie tonight?"

"It's your house. I'd say you get to control the clicker. Anything in particular?"

"*Legally Blonde.*"

"Sure. The underdog wins the day." He was more perceptive than I'd given him credit for.

I nodded. "Yeah. Against all odds."

BACK AT HOME, NOTHING OUT OF THE ORDINARY HAPPENED. IT WAS APPROACHING dinnertime, Constance had gone home, and Duke was on a grocery run. So it was only Terry with me when the doorbell rang.

He pulled his gun. "Are you expecting anyone?" He started for the front door.

I followed. "No."

He peered through the peephole. "You've got to be kidding me."

I pushed him aside and checked the peephole myself. "Put that cannon away." I waved him back. "I forgot Grace was coming over."

He holstered the weapon. "Get rid of her."

I glared at him. "No." I pulled the door open for my best friend. "Hi, Gray."

She came in and engulfed me in our special style of hug, long and tight, the way we'd done in our trauma support group.

I stepped back and closed the door. "Grace and I are cooking together tonight."

"Does *he* have to be here?"

I looked between the two of them. "Uh…yeah."

Terry gritted his teeth. "I'm her security."

"I thought it was just the one day."

"He's on my team," I explained. "And it's more than one day."

Grace shook her head. "Keep him away from me."

"Same old Bobcat. There are those claws I remember. Maybe you should leave and make us both happy," Terry said. The name change from Kitty to Bobcat was ominous.

"No, Serena invited me," Grace spat, tossing her red hair.

I held up my hands. "Stop. I don't know what your problem is, but neither of you is leaving. Grace, I hired security for a problem I ran into, and Terry is a permanent part of the team. He stays."

Her brows creased. "I still don't get why you need a team."

"I'll explain later. Terry, Grace and I have some cooking to do. Go do some push-ups, reload your gun, or whatever."

"You can practice firing it at your head," Grace added. "It's big enough that you won't miss."

With a huff, Terry stomped away. "Lucas, we have a problem," he said into his phone as he went.

I pointed us toward the kitchen. "I thought you two were getting along better?"

Grace sighed. "He's a douche."

"I heard that, Kitty." Terry's voice carried from the other room.

She looked away and shook her head. "Make that super douche."

I shrugged. "Then let's get cooking." I needed the therapy of it.

She nodded. "I brought extra chicken breasts in case we need a redo to get it right."

I took her bag. "Good thing. We're cooking for four. Duke will be back soon."

"Do I have to cook for him?" She thumbed in Terry's direction.

I shot her a look. This was totally unlike the thoughtful and kind Grace I knew.

"Okay," she relented. "For you, girlfriend."

We unpacked the ingredients she'd brought and got everything ready. We were attempting olive-and-feta-stuffed chicken tonight. After creating the pockets in the breasts and scooping feta into a bowl, Grace addressed the elephant in the room. "You didn't mention why you needed security?"

The recipe suggested kalamata olives, but all I had were green castelvetrano ones. "Will these do?" I asked.

"If that's all we have, sure. We need to double it to twelve chopped up." She pulled the oregano from the spice rack. "You forgot about tonight, didn't you?"

I shrugged and counted the olives out on a cutting board.

"What's wrong?" she prodded.

I chopped the olives and added them to the feta. "I got run off the road a week ago Monday, and it wasn't random."

She gasped. "Is it—"

"No. He was still in prison then. Now, a teaspoon of oregano and a little pepper."

"Then?"

"He's just been paroled." I didn't have the stomach to say more.

"That sucks." She ignored the spice jar and took me into a long, tight hug. "I'm so sorry."

I shuddered into her. "I was really scared," I admitted before pulling free and straightening. "But I survived, and now I have the best team around me. Oregano?"

She measured and added it. "You better have more than *him*." She nodded toward the other room, derision in her tone.

I broke a clove off the garlic and handed it to her. "What happened with Terry?"

She shook her head. "Another time."

Terry poked his head in. "What are we having?"

"Something appropriate for you," Grace snapped. "Dog food."

"Be nice," I whispered.

"Stuffed chicken breast," she said with sugary sweetness. "I hope you like it."

Duke walked in with two grocery bags and stopped. "Hi, Grace."

"Hi."

He quietly unloaded his haul and put things away while we discussed the next steps.

"You like him," Grace teased after Duke left.

I nodded. "Duh. He's my boyfriend."

"I can tell it's more than a little."

"Where are the toothpicks?"

As we finished the prep, she brought out a surprise. "My asshole landlord is having the building tented for termites so he can sell it. Can I stay with you for a few days when that happens?"

For my best friend, there was only one possible answer. "Of course. When?"

"He hasn't told me yet, but soon."

~

"THIS IS DELICIOUS," DUKE SAID AGAIN AS THE FOUR OF US SAT AT THE TABLE EATING.

We'd stuffed and closed the chicken with toothpicks, pan-fried it on both sides, and finished it in the oven. It looked similar enough to the picture in the recipe book to be called a success. Rice pilaf and a salad completed the meal, and I was proud of it.

"I agree," Terry added. "Thank you, Serena…and Grace."

She nodded, but after a moment, Grace checked her watch. "Sorry to run, but I have to go." She stood before I could protest.

Duke turned to Terry. "Walk her to her car."

Grace glared. "That's not necessary."

"Terry will walk you to your car," Duke said in a tone that didn't invite argument. "There are dangerous people after Serena, and one of them could be out there."

Grace's mouth dropped open. "Is it that serious?"

I nodded. "Go with him."

Terry rose as ordered. "Suck it up, Kitty."

Her face contorted as she stood.

"I'll be right back," Terry said.

Duke chewed. "No hurry." He and Terry shared a look.

After the door closed behind them, I nodded toward the door. "Do you think I put her in danger by bringing her here?" That possibility was sickening.

Duke scooped up some rice. "Nope, but this will give them a chance to talk privately. Maybe it'll help."

CHAPTER 33

Duke

Thursday morning, I walked Serena into work. "One more time."

She sighed. "If we're driving and I feel threatened by another car, say so because you can hear me. You and Lucas will be behind us and come to the rescue. If something happens in the building, do what they say like a good little girl, because you may not hear me if you're not close enough."

"That's right." I hadn't included the good-little-girl part, but she'd gotten the gist of the instructions. "The mic in your bra is only good for fifty or a hundred yards. We can hear the one in the car for miles."

I waved goodbye, and a minute later, she was through security. "Safely inside," I said on comms.

"Copy that," Lucas confirmed.

"Trackers active," Jordy added.

I walked back and slid into the company Porsche Cayenne I was driving for this tail job. It didn't have the visibility of the Suburban, but that meant it blended in better. With its twin-turbo V8, it also had more speed, if that was called for. As I buckled up, Lucas gave me a wave from his Cayenne. With different colored vehicles, we'd switch up the forward and tail positions. Now, it was time to wait.

At nine o'clock, Serena and her friend Katelyn exited the building.

Serena went to the driver's side like I'd told her to, and after some discussion, the other woman went around to the passenger side.

I waited for them to pull out of the parking space and checked my phone for the tracker Jordy had supplied. It worked perfectly. One of the four icons on my screen moved with their little white car.

"Moving out," I said as I followed them.

"Taking back position," Lucas confirmed.

Jordy had to put trackers on each of the four EPA cars in the reserved section. Serena had told me they were taking Katelyn's car, but we didn't know which one that was.

If Serena had been alone, I could have followed directly behind and not risked losing her, but with her coworker along, we'd have to stay back. That was easy on the freeway, but tricky in town.

Lucas had felt it was good to learn Leo Gambino had been the first of a series of three victims. I wasn't so sure since we still had no inkling of the motive.

After three lights, I relaxed. The traffic signals were timed well enough that I wouldn't lose them. Then, a brown UPS truck pulled out in front of me and inched along before stopping again.

"Shit." I pounded the wheel as I waited for the smallest gap in the neighboring lane to get around this fucker. When I got free, the light ahead had turned red. On my phone, Serena's icon continued moving.

I pressed comms. "I missed the light. They're getting ahead of me."

"No issues," Jordy said. "I have them still on track."

"Shifting one block east to make up time," Lucas announced.

~

SERENA

KATELYN HAD GOTTEN ON THE PHONE WITH ONE OF HER CONTRACTORS THE MOMENT we started off. At least her distraction allowed me to watch for Duke's car. I only caught sight of him once.

After minutes of arguing with the guy, she hung up. "I don't feel so great." She held her stomach.

"What's wrong?"

"I had leftovers for breakfast, and they're not agreeing with me." She groaned and reclined the seat back, then put it upright again. "Stop there. The next block." She pointed ahead at the gas station with an attached Minimart. "I gotta use the bathroom, or we're going to have a big problem." She groaned again.

When we reached it, I pulled in and parked.

She quickly opened her door. "Can you buy me a Seven-up and some Saltines?" she asked as she scooted inside.

I turned off the engine and stayed in the car, watching for Duke to drive up. I waited ten seconds or so then, not seeing him, I unbuckled. "I'm going inside," I said clearly. "My friend needs my help. I'll be right back out."

I locked the car. It was a sketchy neighborhood, so I slung my purse diagonally over my chest and went inside. A girl in all black with a nose ring and a half dozen eyebrow piercings was behind the counter, jabbering on her phone.

I found the crackers near the front. The refrigerators with the soft drinks were at the back. Opening the glass door, I chose a plastic bottle with a screw top instead of a can.

Then I saw him, and my heart stopped. It was the monster who'd tried to take me off the street on Tuesday. Ducking down, I didn't think he'd seen me. But he was between me and the entrance. How did this shit keep happening to me?

Noticing an emergency exit sign high on the side wall, I let myself hope I could make it to the car. I had to get back there and to the microphone inside. *I can do this.*

Silently, I set the crackers and drink down before slinking toward that wall in a crouch.

I made it to the far aisle and shuffled down to the door. It had an alarm sign on it. That meant I'd have to sprint to the car. What if he knew Katelyn was also EPA? I didn't dare lift my head to look for him. Instead, I backtracked toward the hall with the restroom sign. I rounded the corner to the back aisle.

"There you are." His voice was as ominous as it had been before.

I turned to run, but he grabbed my ponytail and yanked. *Ow, ow, ow.* Painful didn't begin to describe it. Then, a beefy arm wrapped around me from behind.

Before I could scream, the guy clamped a rag over my mouth.

I struggled and clawed at the hands holding me, but he was way too strong. All I could get out was a muffled moan.

The rag smelled sickly sweet.

My legs felt sluggish as I stomped down, trying for his foot. I got him on the second try.

"Bitch," he swore as his hands loosened enough for me to get free.

I ran for the exit. My legs were like jelly. Making it around the corner, I rushed to the door. A push on the bar, and I'd be outside with the alarm blaring. I reached for it…

The monster grabbed the back of my shirt and jerked me toward him. The rag came up to my mouth again. My arms felt heavy and my fingers weak as I tried to pull his hand away.

Then…everything went black.

～

THE POWERFUL TWIN-TURBO ENGINE SCREAMED AS I DOWNSHIFTED AND RACED INTO the oncoming lane to pass the road boulder in my way. Whipping the wheel right again, I narrowly missed the oncoming car and got back in my lane.

Argh. My stubborn woman had refused to listen to my instructions, and I had a bad feeling about this. The episode on a sidewalk mere blocks from her building highlighted how dangerous it could be for her to be alone.

I'd accelerated as soon as I heard her say, *"I'm going inside. My friend needs my help. I'll be right back out."*

"Her location, Jordy?" I couldn't take my eyes off the road to check it myself.

"Still at the gas station. It'll be a minute before I can pull up a video feed."

"Lucas, what's your twenty?"

"I'm working on it," he said. "Too fucking many idiots on the road." I heard the crunch of metal over comms. "Fuck."

I swerved over a lane, just missing the same fate as Lucas.

Seeing the station ahead, I asked, "Jordy, update?"

"No movement. Still at the gas station."

"Three blocks out," Lucas reported.

I bottomed out the suspension hurtling into the station and screeched to a halt next to the white government econobox they'd been driving. The car was empty. "She's not in the car," I yelled as I raced to the door and flung it open. She was unprotected, and I had to get to her.

The clerk sported goth piercings and black clothing. With earbuds in her ears, she rocked to her music as she checked out a guy at the register.

Serena's coworker, Katelyn, was in line behind the guy, inhaling saltines from an open box.

Not seeing anyone else in the store, I advanced on Katelyn. "Where's Serena?"

Looking up, she startled. "What are you doing here?"

I did my best to stay calm. "Where is she? Serena."

"In the car, I guess."

"She's not. What the hell happened?"

"I almost had a big accident. Bad breakfast, I think."

I had no more time for her nonsense and went to check the aisles myself.

Lucas barged through the door. "Status?"

"Can't find her."

"Check the bathrooms."

I started with the women's and then the men's. "Bathrooms clear," I said over comms.

"Not out the back door either," Lucas replied.

"I need to see the surveillance video," I told the clerk at the register.

She pulled out one earbud. "I'm pre-law. You need a warrant for that."

My blood boiled. This was no fucking TV show. "You're about to be—"

Lucas pulled me back and laid his SIG on the counter. "Clint Eastwood once said, and I quote, 'Do you feel lucky?'" He pointed at the clerk. "Well, do you?" Lucas gave off serious don't-fuck-with-me vibes.

The girl's eyes bulged, and her face turned even more pale. She pulled out a key attached to a piece of pipe. "Anything you want. Manager's office is in the back."

Lucas took it and picked up his weapon.

I followed him to the back. "Jordy, we can't find her. We're checking internal video. Find an external feed."

"Copy that," he replied. "But it's not like on TV. It'll take some time."

"Serena doesn't have fucking time," I snapped.

CHAPTER 34

SERENA

I WOKE SLOWLY TO THE FEELING OF THE WORLD MOVING UNDERNEATH ME.

"She's still out," the monster said.

I remembered being chased and grabbed. The bumpy ride and road noise combined to give me the bad news—I was now in a car, being driven away from my radio link to Duke and the guys.

Duke would be looking for me by now. But would he get to me in time? I wished I'd listened to him and stayed in the car.

As the fog cleared, I decided to play possum for a minute and check my motor control first. My hands were duct-taped, but my feet weren't. Less than ideal for running away, but workable.

The master chief had made me practice running with my hands tied either behind me or in front. *"Practice could make the difference,"* he'd said. *"You can't afford to be off balance and fall."*

At the time, it had seemed silly in the extreme, but today, I thanked Dad for hiring him after the kidnapping and forcing those lessons on me.

I'd never considered being previously kidnapped a helpful experience, but in this instance, it certainly was. I knew from experience and the master chief that if I got a chance to escape, I'd have to act quickly and use all my might. Mentally, I recited his list of vulnerable areas. *Strike hard at the eyes, throat, groin, or knee.*

I chanced opening one eye. It took a second of blinking to focus.

Tony Spinelli, the Taser guy, was driving. We were going fast and straight next to a big truck—on the freeway, most likely—so trying to open the door and jump was off the table.

My purse was on the floor. My cell phone was zipped in the inner pocket. If they hadn't found it, Duke could track us. They did it in the movies all the time. He'd come.

I closed my eyes again as Spinelli's head turned. "It's time to put her under again."

The monster shook my shoulder.

I stayed limp.

"She's still out," he said.

"I don't trust her. Put her under again."

With only seconds to act, I sat up quickly, so quickly my head spun. I swung my elbow at the monster's throat. I caught him in the jaw instead.

"Fucking bitch." Then a bigger elbow than mine slammed into my head.

Spinelli laughed. "I told you she'd be a slippery one."

The monster grabbed my hair with one hand and pulled out a plastic bag with his other. It held the cloth he'd used on me before. I struggled against him, without success. He got it on my mouth and nose.

I held my breath for as long as I could. *Duke, I need you.*

In the end, I lost out to the darkness.

~

DUKE

THE GAS STATION SETUP WAS AN OLD VCR THAT WAS EASY TO REWIND, BUT FIGURING out how to select the camera we wanted from the eight small boxes on the screen took a minute.

"Pause it," Lucas said.

The screen held a grainy image, but it was clear enough for me. "That's the guy who grabbed her on the street Tuesday."

Lucas leaned closer to the screen. "We've gotta ID him."

I started the video again. "This isn't good enough for facial rec."

"Good girl." I watched as Serena darted away.

Lucas shifted cameras.

My gut clenched as I watched her attacker catch her again and place a rag over her mouth before she went limp.

"She tried," Lucas said.

"Yeah." It didn't make me feel any better.

The big guy then dragged her out of the building, supporting her against his side like he was helping a drunk.

Moving to the outside cameras, we watched the guy put her in the backseat of a BMW SUV and follow her in.

"Fuck." He had her, and there was also a driver involved. We couldn't see his face from this angle.

Lucas tapped his comms. "Jordy, we have her being shoved into the back of a small blue BMW SUV. The picture's poor, but probably an X3. The license is too fuzzy to make anything out. It left our position heading north."

"The tag is British Columbia," I said, pointing. "See the flag in the middle?"

"Copy that," Jordy said. Furious keyboard clicks sounded in the background. "Got it. The car continued northbound, then east ten blocks up."

"Let's go." Now we had a direction. I grabbed the office key and sprinted back to the register, slamming it down in front of the girl too entranced by her phone to notice a kidnapping in progress.

"My car's toast," Lucas said as he opened the passenger door to join me.

I looked over at his Cayenne, still venting steam from the crunched front end, and agreed. "I knew you Deltas couldn't drive."

"Fuck you."

I floored the Porsche, and its V8 burned rubber out of the gas station. "I'll be happy to give you defensive-driving lessons." The turbos whined as I raced to beat the yellow light at the next intersection.

Lucas grabbed the door handle. "You call this defensive?"

I leaned on the horn as the light turned red just before we arrived.

"My woman's in trouble. I call this warp nine."

"Jordy," Lucas said over comms. "Can you get a facial rec on the driver?"

"Already done," Jordy responded. "It's Spinelli. I don't have a usable face shot on the second guy."

When Lucas didn't respond, I added, "Thanks, Bro."

"You're welcome," came back through comms.

"Why'd he waste airtime saying that?" Lucas asked.

"The Serena effect." My woman had more of an impact on us in the last week than I'd realized.

Lucas only huffed.

I sped up to move around more slow cars. "Be okay, Serena. Be safe."

Lucas gave me a thumbs-up. "We got this."

"They got on the freeway heading north," Jordy said. "It's going to be a bitch now because we don't have much video on the freeway itself."

"Copy that," Lucas replied. "In pursuit. Jordy, get Winston and Terry spun up following us. We may need more than two shooters on this."

"Copy that. What about Constance?"

Jordy was taking this seriously because otherwise, he would have given Lucas shit if he admitted there was anything he couldn't handle by himself.

"We can't pull her and blow her cover yet. She stays at the EPA."

"What are you thinking?" I asked as I took the corner fast and the tires squealed.

"I'm thinking Spinelli is no amateur, and he wouldn't hire amateur help," Lucas said. "Four is better than two."

The Delta operator in him always planned for overwhelming force in a hostage rescue, but two against two wasn't overwhelming.

"I've got her live cell location, and it matched the freeway entrance time," Jordy said. "So we've got a lock on her. Still north on the four-oh-five."

Switching lanes, the engine roared as I added throttle and passed another two cars. "Hold on, baby. We're coming."

"It doesn't make sense. Why did he let her keep the phone?" Lucas asked.

"Maybe she hid it so he doesn't know she has it?"

"We've gotta catch that car before he finds it. Give me warp ten."

I mashed the pedal down and swerved into the oncoming lanes to get around the car ahead.

"Terry and I are on the way," Jordy announced.

"I said Winston," Lucas complained.

Jordy made a sound very close to a growl. "The shipment of Rossi's personal effects sent from Florida is arriving today. He's going to check that out. I'm your backup on this."

"I'll keep him safe," Terry said.

"You mean I'll keep you safe," Jordy scoffed. "We're good. I've got my laptop. Target is still northbound."

SERENA

"WAKE UP." IT WAS THE VOICE OF THE MONSTER WHO'D TAKEN ME. HE SHOOK MY shoulder. "Wake up, little girl."

The road noise said we were still driving, but I had no idea how long it had been. I groaned and played lethargic, blinking hard while I sat up. One breast was out of its bra cup. At least my hands were bound in front of me so I could fix it. "What's going on?" I asked, sleepily. "You can't just abduct people." My words sounded ridiculous even to me.

"My boss wants to know where the stick is," Spinelli said as he glanced back at me. "It'll go much easier for you if you tell me now before we reach his place."

"But I told you, I don't have what you want, or he wants."

He shrugged. "Don't say I didn't give you a chance for the easy way."

"But I don't know anything about it."

"Oh, you say that now, but he'll get his answer. He's very resourceful."

I pictured pliers to pull off fingernails...or dental drills like in that movie with Dustin Hoffman. Both made me want to puke.

"He'll use his little kit of drugs. You'll spill your guts, and then you're ours."

"Then you're mine." The monster grinned, looking directly at my chest. "Yeah, mine."

My stomach did a flip. The creep had fondled me while I was unconscious. *Gross, gross, gross.* Duke would come. He had to—and fast, before these two got away.

"After I test drive you," he added, "you'll fetch a pretty penny."

"No," Spinelli said, leering at me in the rearview mirror. "It's my turn to go first."

These sick fucks were the Fox brothers all over again. "Let me out now or else."

Both men laughed.

Whichever one came for me first, I was going to bite his dick off and swallow it.

"Or else what?" Spinelli smiled. "I like a woman with a little spunk."

"My boyfriend will hunt you down and bury you."

"Oh, I'm scared," the monster scoffed. "You scared, Tony?"

"After my boss gets his answers from you," Spinelli said, "you'll be ours, and your precious boyfriend will never find you. I promise you that."

I spat and got Spinelli on the cheek.

He wiped it off. "Johnson, shut her up."

Remembering Duke's advice that angry men made mistakes, I scoffed. "Johnson, huh? I bet your first name is little."

"He said quiet." Johnson's slap knocked me against the window, and pain shot across my face. Maybe now wasn't the time for Duke's advice.

"Hey. Easy with the merchandise, Brother. We want a good price. Use the needle."

Johnson? Brother? It came back to me in a rush. Winston had mentioned that Spinelli had a brother named Johnson who the FBI thought was into human trafficking. How could I get kidnapped by the one pair worse than the Fox brothers?

His slimy hand pushed my head against the window and held me there. My struggling had no effect. Then I felt the prick, and the world went black again.

CHAPTER 35

Duke

I swerved onto the left shoulder and mashed the throttle, hurtling by another two cars before rejoining the lanes.

"Careful with the shoulder," Lucas cautioned. "The crap over there can give you a flat."

"Jordy, what's the gap now?" I asked into comms.

"You're getting close. Should have visual."

Lucas craned his neck. "I don't see them."

"I've got Winston calling in," Jordy said.

"That can wait," Lucas decided. "How close?"

"Maybe fifty or a hundred yards."

As we rounded a slight bend, I could see probably a quarter-mile ahead. There were a few SUVs and a ton of sedans and pickups. "I don't see them." I changed lanes and raced forward, dodging in and out of traffic and getting a few honks in the process.

"You're really close," Jordy said.

Lucas laid his SIG in his lap and put on the headset. "I don't have anything from her body mic."

I darted around another truck.

"You should see them easy now. You're right on top of them. Twenty yards or less."

The only vehicles here were two commercial 18-wheelers, a small Toyota, and a white Ford pickup. Then a fifty-yard gap to the next vehicles.

"Check each one," Lucas said. "They could have switched cars." He palmed his weapon, though he didn't sound convinced.

We slowly passed each of them as I ignored the BMW sedan behind me flashing his high beams to get by.

"Fuck." A family in the Toyota, two grizzled truckers in the big rigs, and now an elderly couple in the pickup.

"You're within ten feet," Jordy said excitedly.

"Double fuck." An angry Lucas holstered his weapon. "Spinelli's no amateur. I should have guessed he'd pull this. We've been had. Double back at the next exit."

I mashed the pedal down and left the BMW sedan in our wake as I quickly hit a hundred.

"What happened?" Jordy asked.

"Oldest trick in the book," Lucas said. "Tie the tracker to a dog's collar and let him loose."

"Only this time, the dog was a pickup," I added, braking for the exit. "Where to?"

Lucas banged the dash. "We're on the wrong freeway. Back to the one-oh-one."

"The two companies she visited that first day are off the one-oh-one in Thousand Oaks," I finished.

"It's our best bet," he agreed. "They most likely went west to Thousand Oaks. It's not much, but it's all we have."

I accelerated down the on-ramp to go south back to the junction. Our situation wasn't great, but at least Lucas and I were on the same wavelength.

"I'm patching Winston in now," Jordy said.

"Go, Winston," I answered as I merged into the lighter southbound traffic.

"The package of Rossi's stuff arrived. I've gone through it, and found a receipt for a mailing to Serena at—"

"She claimed she didn't get anything," Lucas retorted.

I shot my brother a glare. "I believe her."

"Guys, let me finish. It went to a mailbox store. I'm on the way there now."

"Winston, she's been taken. We're trying to catch up, but the clue to where they're taking her may be in that package."

"Copy that. Flank speed," Winston replied.

My brother grimaced at the naval term, but off comms, he told me, "Sorry I doubted her."

I nodded and continued weaving through the traffic to make up time toward Thousand Oaks.

"Watch out." A man's voice came over the comm link. "Maybe I should drive if we want to get there in one piece." The voice was familiar.

"I've got to go this fast," Winston said. "Your sister's been taken."

"Faster then. Pass this guy on right."

"Winston?" I asked.

"Sorry. I've got Vincent Benson with me. He's a cosigner on the box so I can get access."

Lucas shook his head. "Keep him safe."

"Copy that."

"Copy what?" Vincent asked.

"I'm authorized to Taser you if you keep flapping your gums," Winston said. We didn't hear anything else from Vincent.

"Jordy, what's your twenty?" Lucas asked after a moment.

"Six miles behind you now."

SERENA

I WOKE ON A COUCH IN A DIMLY LIT ROOM.

"About time," Johnson complained. "I want to get this question shit over with and get to the good times."

A rock formed in my gut. *Keep it together, Benson. Escape first. Feel sorry for yourself later.*

He left the room and locked it.

I sat up. My wrists were duct-taped as before. Once again a breast was out of my bra. I fixed it. *Pervert.* He was so going to pay for that.

The door opened, and Aiden Pons, the COO of Knife Creek Chemical, entered, followed by the Spinelli brothers. I hadn't liked him that first day, and really didn't like him now.

"Cut her loose. There's no need for that. We're going to enjoy a pleasant lunch conversation with Miss Benson." Pons sounded even more pompous than at our first meeting.

Johnson grunted something but cut the tape.

"This way," Pons said, leaving the room.

I followed, rubbing at the tape residue on my wrists and watching for possible escape routes.

The brothers followed.

He led the way to an ornate dining room with a killer view of the valley below. A few acres of grapevines surrounded the house. The table was huge, and the chairs intricately carved. Lunch had been set for three—sandwiches and macaroni salad.

Maybe Pons wasn't such a bad guy. Already I preferred him to either of the Spinellis, especially the pervert Johnson.

Checking for weapons as the master chief had taught me, I came up empty. *"Know the possibilities as soon as you enter a room,"* he'd instructed. *"You never know when an opportunity will present itself."* Plastic spoons were the only utensils—no fork or knife to attack with. Even the water was in plastic cups.

"Please sit," Pons said, moving to the head of the table and indicating the chair to his right. "Tony, by the door. Johnson, you may wait outside."

Another grunt from Johnson, then the double doors closed behind him.

"This would have gone much easier if you'd agreed to my first invitation," Pons told me. "Now sit. I insist." When I didn't budge, he raised his voice. "Now."

Not seeing an advantage to resisting, I sat. My leg tremor started up instantly.

Pons's tantrum fit Dad's mold of always establishing dominance at the beginning of a meeting. "I suggest you stop checking for a weapon," he added. "Mr. Spinelli is very thorough and also an excellent shot. I doubt you can hurt me with a plastic plate before a bullet comes your way."

Spinelli grinned.

"Sorry, this is a new environment is all," I said, my eyes still darting around.

Pons sipped his water. "Eat up. I've always found negotiations are best conducted over a meal."

"No, thanks." *I don't eat with slimy assholes.*

He dabbed at his mouth with a napkin. "I assure you, the food has not been tampered with. You will find things much more enjoyable if you indulge me."

I shook my head. "I'm good." With my nerves, I wasn't sure I could hold the food down.

He slammed a fist on the table. "I will not tolerate insolence."

I flinched.

"If necessary, Mr. Spinelli will strip you bare and force-feed you like a baby."

Spinelli's chuckle got a scowl from Pons.

I picked up the sandwich and took a tentative bite. *Please, Duke, now would be an excellent time to rescue me.* I chewed slowly to stretch out whatever was going to happen and give Duke time to find me. He would find me. I knew it in my bones.

"You have the key I want."

I schooled my face. This was the first time the drive had been referred to as a key.

"Having the contents of that box out there has caused me and my associates to lose a considerable amount of time and money." His face twisted in anger. "I want it. And I want it now."

The door opened. "Yaroslavsky has arrived," Johnson said.

As if my day could get any worse. The Russian mob boss Duke had mentioned was a part of this?

"Take her upstairs," Pons commanded. "I need to talk to Igor."

Spinelli was at my side in an instant, yanking me up. So much for a pleasant lunch.

He shoved me into a spartan bedroom this time. It was clearly not a normal bedroom, as the lock clicked on a double-sided deadbolt as soon as Spinelli left. This was Pons's version of a prison cell.

Checking the window, the drop from this height didn't look too bad. I could make a rope out of the bedsheets to slide down. But when I slid the glass to the side, it stopped after three inches. A bar had been welded into the channel. Yup, this was a guest bedroom for involuntary guests.

Sliding to the side and peeking down, I saw a rotund man in a rumpled suit and two goons, one with a bald head and the other with a scary neck full of tattoos. I bent over to listen.

"How are you, Igor?" Pons said.

"Better when we have key." Igor's Russian accent was thick.

"Your brother was supposed to get it for us," Pons said.

"Where girl?"

"Upstairs."

"Where key?"

"She only just arrived, so I don't have that answer yet."

"No more room for drums. Your method too slow. Give her me, and I show how we do it in Russia. "

"Very soon, I'll be able to take your deliveries again," Pons said.

Drums? Deliveries?

"Once this EPA situation is settled," he continued, "we'll both be making money again. God, I love the EPA. Every new regulation and fee makes us more money."

The Russian laughed. "And short drive."

Taking deliveries of barrels and needing to fix the EPA situation could only mean one thing. They were making money together by avoiding the fees for the proper disposal of hazardous wastes that were supposed to be going to Nevada for processing. I'd scratch their eyes out for putting innocent families at risk by polluting our water.

"I want see her," Yaroslavsky said. "Maybe I try her and make offer. Brother always need new merchandise."

I backed away from the window as my blood ran cold. An offer from him wouldn't be to let me go. Oh no, I could guess all too well what happened to women who started that journey.

Quickly, I surveyed the room for weapons—a task I should have started as soon as the door closed. The plastic lamp was too small and flimsy. The room didn't have a chair I could break apart. The walls were bare.

Yanking open the top drawer of the nightstand, I found a silver bracelet and handcuffs—two pairs, not the gentle fur-lined kind. I slipped a pair into my back pocket. I ran my fingers over the name engraved on the bracelet and returned it to the drawer—Natasha.

Footsteps sounded from the stairwell.

"See her first," Yaroslavsky said.

"Look only. We should eat lunch first," Pons said.

Pulling open the second drawer, I found a small riding crop, some rope, and two whips. That's when I noticed the loops at the corners of the headboard. *Fuck.* This was Pons's sex dungeon, just not underground.

"You have vodka?" Yaroslavsky said from just beyond the door.

"Of course."

The only thing I could think of to do was make myself less-appealing merchandise. I scratched down my cheek as hard as I could. It hurt like hell, but it was worth it. I sat on the side of the bed, with the good side of my face toward the door.

The lock clicked, and the door opened.

"Some meat on her." The Russian laughed. "I like."

I turned my face toward the ugly fatso, letting him see the marks. The two big goons from outside stood behind him.

Yaroslavsky smiled at me. "I try after lunch."

My stomach twisted. That wasn't the reaction I'd wanted from my bloody face.

"I make offer after."

Any more words from this pig, and I'd puke all over myself.

"She's supposed to be mine." That was Johnson from the hallway. "We had a deal."

"I'm a capitalist. Highest bidder wins," Pons said with a maniacal smile.

"You can't do that. We had a deal," Johnson repeated angrily.

Pons ignored the complaint. "Tough shit. That was before my Russian friend showed an interest. Highest bidder gets delivery after I've had her for a week."

This was getting worse by the second. As much as I wanted to launch myself and claw his eyes out, I held back. This wasn't the time. I'd only get one chance, and I had to make it count.

"Lunch awaits," Pons announced.

After the door locked behind them, I rushed to the doorway and listened.

"What about us?" Johnson asked.

"You four can eat in the kitchen," Pons answered.

The Spinelli brothers and Yaroslavsky's two goons made four, meaning the hallway would be unguarded.

I replaced my shirt after taking off my bra. Biting at the tiny knot in the thread I'd used to sew the hole shut, I quickly removed the underwire. It was a procedure the master chief had made me practice until I could complete it quickly in the dark.

"Time will be of the essence," he'd said. *"And seconds could make the difference between escaping or not."*

I remembered the words well as I removed the second underwire and made the appropriate bends. Using one as the tensioner and the second as the pick, I worked the lock.

I swallowed a gasp when I felt the familiar give in the tension wire. Removing the pick wire, I carefully turned the lock and listened.

Nothing.

Slowly, I opened the door and found the hallway empty. Stepping out, I cringed at the squeak the door made closing. *Had they heard it?*

CHAPTER 36

DUKE

WE WERE STILL FIVE MILES FROM THOUSAND OAKS WHEN WINSTON CAME ON THE comms line. "Guys, it really is a USB stick, not a drive."

"What do you mean?" I asked.

"It's a USB key to a locker at the SafeStor location near here. We ran into these at the bureau. It's an electronic key that can't be copied or hacked."

That brought us closer, but we were running out of time. "We need what's in that locker."

"On the way," Winston replied. "Full afterburner."

"I don't get why Rossi would send a locker key to your girl," Lucas mused.

I shook my head and darted around another truck. "We stick to the plan until we know something more." That didn't make me feel good, because our plan of checking the two company locations was pretty feeble.

My brother nodded as we approached the freeway exit.

Excalibur Plating was closest, so that made our choice of which to check first.

"Not here," Lucas observed after we made a thorough sweep of the parking lot and adjoining streets. "Meet us at the Knife Creek address," he said into comms. "Nothing at Excalibur."

"Roger," Terry responded. "Almost at the freeway exit."

Frustrated, I hit the steering wheel. We were stuck behind traffic at a light. I looked around the guy in front of us for an opening in the oncoming lane.

"Don't even think about it," Lucas said. "Cop parked on the right, and we're not in LA. We don't have Marcus to cover for us. Get pulled over now, and we lose a half-hour minimum."

"We can't wait. My woman needs us now."

"As Zig Ziglar said…" Lucas began, starting another of his quotes, "'Be careful not to compromise what you want most for what you want now.'"

We heard a phone ringing over comms.

"Kitty, I can't talk now." It was Terry. "Seriously, I'm in the middle of something. It'll have to wait. Grace…Grace?"

"Problem?" Lucas asked before I could.

"Sorry, I forgot to turn off comms," Terry explained. He didn't say any more.

"We've got it," Winston said in my ear.

The light turned green, and we crept up to the intersection.

"Enlighten us," Lucas demanded.

"It's Aiden Pons, the COO at Knife Creek. The box has a recording of him agreeing to pay the EPA guy a ton to overlook falsified well tests on underground water quality and some test data that I'm guessing proves failures."

"Jordy, where is he right now?" I barked.

"On it."

"Who is this EPA guy?" Lucas asked.

"Don't know," Winston answered. "We have a voice, but his name isn't mentioned."

"Is every day this exciting?" Vincent asked in the background.

"Shut up or you're walking," Winston snarled.

It was several agonizing seconds before Jordy was in our ears again. "Pons is out of the office today. He has a house in the hills, which is where his cell is pinging."

Whatever Jordy did to get the cell location couldn't have been legal, but I didn't fucking care. "Address?"

He rattled it off, and I plugged it into navigation.

Lucas consulted his phone. "Guys, meet us a half mile from the house at the corner of Wild Bush Lane."

"Copy that," Terry confirmed.

My stomach finally unknotted. We had the bad guy in our sights, and the most likely location to find my woman. Now it was time to gear up and rock and roll, like the old times.

Only this wasn't just any hostage extraction, this was Serena, which meant total focus.

"We'll get her out safe. It's what we do." Lucas was on the same wavelength as me.

~

MY HEART THUNDERED IN MY CHEST AS I TIPTOED DOWN THE HALL, KEEPING MY HEELS off the hardwood to avoid noise. Breathing silently was imperative, but difficult, as amped up on adrenaline as I was. *"Silent movement is a skill,"* the master chief had said. *"Practice it."*

I hadn't, and I winced when the heel of my shoe made contact with the first step down the stairs. Somebody needed to clue this guy in that carpeted stairs were the way to go.

I stopped and slipped off my heels, ignoring the master chief's advice. *"Don't take off your shoes. Unless you have tough feet, or it's all grass, you'll injure yourself running barefoot and be caught."* I could put them back on outside. I'd already screwed up by forgetting to break off the heels.

Nearing the bottom of the stairs, I could hear Pons and the Russian nearby.

I looked around the corner and spied a door leading out the back side of the house.

Freedom beckoned, and for the first time today, a smile took over my face.

"Find a phone if you can." I ignored my instructor's words as I passed an office that most likely contained a phone. The fresh air outside was my goal. I refused to spend one extra second in this creepy house.

Reaching the door, I peered through the glass. A pool lay beyond a terrace of stone pavers, and beyond that, to the side of a small pool house, was a gate through the fence to the area of vines. That would be my escape route. A neighboring house couldn't be that far away.

The voices behind me grew louder and were joined by footsteps.

"A half hour with her, then give me your bid," Slimeball Pons said. "But that is after she and I have a chat about the key."

From my limited view through the glass, I didn't see anyone, but I had no choice. The deadbolt made a loud click when I unlocked it and pushed open the door.

Grinning with confidence, I took in a lungful of fresh air—freedom at last. With my shoes still in my hand, I hurried across the terrace and around the oval pool.

"Find her," I heard Spinelli bark.

Fuck a duck. Without daring to look back, I ducked behind the outdoor barbecue, short of the pool house.

"Check the gate. She's got to be here somewhere," he yelled.

My heart pounded as I crouched down and listened to the running boots pass on the other side of the barbecue island.

"Gate locked," a Russian-accented voice said. Then he ran back toward the house.

I slipped my shoes on. I'd have to scale the gate, and then it would be a footrace to the neighboring house and safety. Or, I could try to hide until Duke got here. He had to be on the way, didn't he?

The door to the house opened and closed, then silence.

When they didn't find me, they'd search this area again. The grapevines didn't provide enough cover to hide, so my decision was made for me—climb the gate and run through the small vineyard to the neighbor's house.

Peering over the barbecue, the coast was clear. I sprinted for the pool house. *Get to the gate and then the neighbor. Get to the neighbor.* I turned the corner at a run. "Oof." I ran smack into a nightmare.

"There you are." Johnson grabbed me.

Eyes. I tried to scratch him, but he grabbed my wrist.

Knees. I kicked at him but only hit his shin.

"Bitch." He slapped me across the face so hard my vision blurred.

Throat. I threw a punch where I thought his throat was, or at least one of them, but missed wildly. Nothing I tried worked.

He heaved me over his shoulder. "I like a little fight in a girl. You and me are going to have a lot of fun."

I kicked and hammered his back with no effect as he carried me to the house.

"Tape her to this chair," Pons ordered. The chair was big and beefy, not the kind I could tip over and break.

Tony Spinelli tossed his brother a roll of tape, and once again, nothing I did to resist worked.

Yaroslavsky sniffed my hair while Johnson taped my legs. Then he grabbed my breast and squeezed. "Ripe."

I spit at his hand but missed.

"Spirited horse make best mount," he said with a laugh.

"You stay with her while I get my kit," Pons ordered after Johnson finished.

"Sir?" A waif of a girl who couldn't be more than sixteen stood in the doorway. "Dessert is ready." She didn't even give me—a woman in obvious distress, duct-taped to a chair—a second glance.

"Thank you, Natasha. Igor, join me for pryaniki."

"Real pryaniki?"

"I think you'll like how Natasha makes them."

Yaroslavsky grinned. "We see."

Natasha? The name on the bracelet in his sex dungeon. Was the teenager a girl Pons had *bought* from Yaroslavsky?

A wave of nausea rolled over me.

CHAPTER 37

DUKE

TERRY AND JORDY ROLLED UP RIGHT BEHIND US IN A SECOND CAYENNE AT THE MEET point on Wild Bush Lane. I was already gearing up with what we carried in the back of the Cayenne.

"Terry, gear up. You're going in with us," Lucas called. "Jordy, you're on comms, and we need eyes in the sky."

"Got ya covered." Jordy pulled one of his drones from the backseat. "Here's the latest picture of Pons." He passed around his phone.

Now I had a face to go with the description of general scumbag.

Terry opened the hatch of his SUV and pulled out the same vest as I already had on—a soft, level-II model, below what I was used to for SEAL missions.

We hadn't expected a firefight and hadn't packed rifles, so today would be a handgun-only assault. Along with flashbangs and knives.

Jordy's drone buzzed and took to the air.

Lucas checked his SIG and added clips to his pockets.

I carried two and added one more. It wasn't likely to turn into a firefight, but if it did, I'd be prepared. The tiny tactical camera for seeing in rooms or around corners was next.

When Terry started screwing a suppressor on, Lucas shook his head. "We go in hot and loud. This guy is a civilian, maybe with a few hired guns, but Spinelli is likely the only one with experience. Noise is our friend against novices."

Terry nodded and removed it.

"We have no idea how many there are, or what they're carrying, so be alert and careful." Lucas looked at me to add, "No heroics, and we shoot to incapacitate." That was understood, but not always possible.

Terry pulled a flashbang from the box. "Copy that."

I nodded, knowing I would define my own level of what constituted *heroics* when it came to Serena's safety. This wasn't another SEAL mission. No, this was more important. They could be torturing Serena right now to get information she didn't have.

In the teams, I'd learned not to react to things that would turn any man's stomach, but now I almost puked into the back of the SUV. The thought of Serena being tortured was more than I could handle.

If anything happened to her, I'd burn Pons and anyone with him to the ground.

WE WORKED OUR WAY QUICKLY THROUGH THE TREES TOWARD THE OBJECTIVE.

"Jordy, confirm we have the right house," Lucas demanded.

"Screw you. I don't make mistakes," Jordy said.

Terry's eyes went wide. As a non-family member, he didn't get to say shit like that to Lucas.

"Address matches, and one of the cars out front is the Beamer that took Serena. License plate confirmed," Jordy continued.

With that, I breathed easier. Soon, I'd have her back in my arms, safe and sound. I should have told her how I felt, how much my feelings had surprised me, but I'd remedy that soon enough.

"Copy," Lucas replied. "What's the opposition situation?"

"They're not expecting company. No guards on watch. One man on a smoke break out front by the cars," Jordy said in our ears. "Beyond that, I can't get close enough to tell numbers. The north wall is the best approach, only one small window."

As we got closer, my confidence built. I had my brother, Lucas, the baddest of the Omega badasses, and Terry, who was as competent a shot as any non-spec-ops guy could be. We also had the element of surprise.

Lucas called a halt at the tree line when the house came into view.

Pons, Spinelli, and whoever else was there had no idea the hell we were prepared to rain down on them.

"Terry with me." Lucas pointed. "We'll go left. Duke, right. Jordy, keep watch."

We split and raced to the north side of the building.

"Hold," Jordy said, and we all froze along the wall. "You'll never guess who came out to talk to our smoker."

"Jordy," Lucas barked. "Now is not the time."

"Igor Yaroslavsky, and we know he never travels alone."

Shit. That would give them more shooters, not just Spinelli and his accomplice.

"We stick together," Lucas whispered. He signaled for me to take lead going around to the right.

After rounding the corner, I signaled a halt at the first window into a dining room, long table and all, but no Serena.

Then I heard her, and we halted short of the next room.

"I told you, I didn't get anything from her." It was Serena's angry voice. That was my girl, unlimited spunk regardless of the situation.

Holding the tiny tac cam up to the corner of the window, I let out a breath when I saw her on my phone.

She was taped to a chair but otherwise okay.

"This take too long," Yaroslavsky complained from the far corner. "Come."

Three men followed him out of the room. That left Pons and one armed guard.

The Pons scumbag pulled a syringe and a vial from a bag. "This will help your memory."

I hand signaled the count and direction they'd gone.

Lucas and Terry ducked and moved under the window of the next room then one room farther.

I signaled *breach on three* when they were positioned, and Lucas nodded to confirm.

No way was I letting that asswipe inject my woman with anything. Putting the camera away, I backed up for a running start, counted off three, and jumped up and into the window, shielding my face and rolling when I hit the floor inside.

Terry's flashbang sounded through the walls.

Serena screamed.

"Hold on," I yelled. For a moment, all I could see was her taped to a chair and helpless. "I'm here for you, baby." With a quick pivot, I took down the guard with two shots to the shoulder. Time at the range paid off.

Pons turned on me, wielding the syringe like a sword.

I leaped and backed up a step, kicking the groaning guard's gun into the corner. "I'll cut you loose in a second."

When Pons lunged, I knocked his arm away, landed a quick punch to the head, and brought him down with a roundhouse kick. The syringe went flying.

Shots sounded in the distance.

"Duke, look out."

226

Serena's warning was too late. Shots rang out, and I took two quick rounds in the back from a shooter I hadn't seen.

"Duke," Serena screamed.

Fuck, fuck, fuck. I'd broken rule number one of clearing a room and focused solely on Serena. The world moved in slow motion as I hit the ground, rolling.

Spinelli's ugly face grinned at me as he looked over his Beretta and fired twice more.

The hits felt like bowling balls thrown at my chest.

"Duke." Serena's cry tore at me.

Spinelli laughed maniacally and swung his gun toward her.

The pain was excruciating when I tried to pull in a breath, but my woman's safety made it irrelevant. *I am Cobra.* I lifted my SIG.

Spinelli's laughter stopped as he jerked his aim back to me. He wasn't fast enough. I returned fire with two quick shots. With a groan, he crumpled. His gun clattered to the floor.

"Duke," Serena sobbed, maybe not realizing my body armor had done its job.

Even so, when I tried to breathe, the pain was at least a twelve on the ten-point scale. It got even worse when I lifted myself off the floor. I heard gunfire as I worked through the pain to kick Spinelli's gun away and get to my woman.

"He shot you," she sobbed. "He shot you."

Pulling my knife, I cut through the tape binding her. "In. The. Vest," I grunted through painful breaths. I'd taken a hit in the vest before. But on deployment, I'd had an armor plate to spread the impact. This soft vest didn't do that.

She fell against me as I cut the last binding. "I thought he killed you," she sobbed.

"It takes a lot more than that to kill a Cobra."

She laughed, which had been my intention.

Bam. The wood floor splintered at Serena's feet.

"Hands up, or she gets the next one."

Like a fool, I'd taken my eyes off Pons.

Serena

Pons had grabbed the gun from the corner and had it aimed at us.

Duke froze. "Do as he says."

I lifted my hands, as did Duke. More shots came from another room.

Tony Spinelli moaned. "Get me a doctor."

Pons ignored him. "Two fingers only. Take out your gun and drop it," he said, like they did in the movies.

Duke moved left, away from me, lifted his gun out of his holster, and dropped it on the floor.

"Now kick it to me."

I moved right to increase the separation between us that Duke had created. When Pons kept his gun aimed at me, I implored my man, "Cobra, don't." I needed his training to kick in. "He won't shoot me. He needs what I know."

Pons laughed and shifted his aim to Duke. "Then I'll shoot him if you don't tell me right now."

I stepped to the right. "Do that, and I won't ever tell you."

He turned to aim at me. "A bullet to the liver will ensure your death, but not before my drugs get the truth out of you."

I thought I was brave, but the idea of getting shot in the stomach curdled my blood.

"No, Serena," Duke said.

Negotiating with a maniac sucked. I stepped toward him anyway. "Let him go, and I'll tell you."

He swung his gun to Duke again.

The look on Duke's face was pure pain. "Serena, stay back."

Asshole Pons wanted to pump me full of drugs, rape me, sell me to a Russian mobster, and now shoot me, on top of polluting our water. He was lower than pond scum, and I'd had enough of him.

Pons waved the gun at me. "Tell me or I'll shoot him."

I moved forward, almost close enough. "My lawyer has it. Anything happens to me, and it goes to the FBI."

Pons's face twisted in confusion.

I put my hand in my back pocket and grasped the cuffs.

He laughed. "No way."

I threw the cuffs to the side, and Pons's eyes followed, the way Duke had said they would.

I lunged forward, forcing his gun wrist up and away. "You cannot—"

He fired.

God, that was loud. *Throat.* I slammed my other fist into his throat with all my might.

He coughed and dropped the gun, bringing his hand to his neck.

Eyes. I poked him hard in the eye with my thumb. "Shoot."

His hands came up to his face.

Knee. When I kicked his knee, Pons crumpled. "My man."

Duke was by me in a second, grabbing my arm. "What the hell?"

"I'm not done." *Groin.* I kicked him hard, connecting right on target.

With a pained yell, Pons curled into a ball.

I blew out a breath. "Now I'm done."

"He could have shot you," Duke yelled in my face.

"He was about to shoot you," I yelled back. Anger still fueled me when I kicked Pons again. "Nobody gets away with that."

Duke pulled me back. "That's enough."

"Not nearly."

Lucas burst in, gun raised, and stopped.

"You're late," Duke said, picking up the gun Pons had held.

"Yaroslavsky brought six guys with him. What happened here?"

Duke pointed to the two bleeding men. "I got those two."

"After Spinelli shot you," I pointed out.

"And Serena beat the shit out of Pons here."

"You got shot four times," I yelled at my man.

Lucas's voice was concerned. "You okay?"

"The vest did its job, but it hurts like a motherfucker."

"Four, huh? You'll need x-rays."

Duke nodded.

"Jordy, roll two more ambulances," Lucas said. "No. We're good. Only bad guys."

"Let's finish up," Lucas said, pulling out zip ties and throwing one to Duke. "You get Spinelli. Who's that piece of shit?"

I cringed. "His brother, Johnson."

"Hands, Spinelli," Duke said. "Or I'll turn the woman loose on you."

I grinned. Yeah, I'd happily kick him in the soft bits.

Lucas went to Johnson. "Hands."

Johnson lifted his wrists.

Duke leaned over. "I said hands, asshole."

Spinelli didn't move.

Duke looked my way. "Want to kick him?"

Spinelli lunged up and drove a knife into my man.

I screamed as fear rolled over me.

CHAPTER 38

Duke

I'd lost my edge.

Tony Spinelli had pulled the knife from his boot and gotten me in the thigh before I could pull away.

"Fuck." I grabbed his hand.

"Fucker," Lucas yelled.

I struggled with Spinelli.

Lucas sprinted over and ended the fight with a swift kick to Spinelli's head. The fuckwit fell back, limp. I pulled the knife loose and rolled onto the floor, holding my leg. Blood spurted from between my fingers.

Serena was on me in an instant. "Hold on, Duke. I can't bear to lose you."

Lucas had gauze out a few seconds later and applied it over my fingers. "Hold this tight."

"Duke," Serena wailed.

"Get us a life-flight helo," Lucas roared into comms. "Cobra's down. He's been cut."

"How bad?" Jordy asked.

"Get it now," was Lucas's only reply as he took off his belt and cinched it tight around my leg.

"Terry, status?"

"Only minor wounds here," he announced. "You take care of Cobra. I've got everybody secured and plenty of ammo left if one of 'em moves."

Serena leaned over and kissed me. "Don't you dare leave me, Cobra."

I noticed Johnson Spinelli sprinting away. "Get him."

Lucas ignored me. "I'm not fucking leaving you, Brother."

Serena

"I love you, Cobra," I yelled as the helicopter door closed with Jordy accompanying Duke instead of me.

Duke had taken bullets and a blade to keep me safe, and it tore me apart to not be with him when he needed me.

Lucas pulled me away from the spinning rotor.

"You should have told them I was his sister," I argued.

"No way. I need to get you back to the house. Winston has the contents of the locker, and until we go through it, we won't know if we've rounded everybody up, or if someone else is still out there."

"What locker?" I asked.

"Rossi sent you an electronic key to a locker full of blackmail material on Pons."

I couldn't even begin to make sense of that, but it didn't matter. Only Duke mattered to me.

We watched as they lifted off and headed for the hospital.

"He'll be all right, won't he?"

Lucas nodded. "He'll make it. I only wish I was as tough as Duke."

Terry joined us. "The locals want to talk to Serena, get her statement."

Lucas shook his head. "Tell them to get in line. She's talking to the Feds first, at her house."

I'd explained the basics of the pollution-collusion plot to Lucas while the paramedics were treating Duke.

Terry shrugged. "I'll try that."

"Wait," I said. "There's a teenage girl inside somewhere. I think she was trafficked and is being held against her will by Pons."

Terry looked back toward the house. "I didn't see her."

"You've got to find her," I pleaded. "Her name is Natasha."

Lucas nodded when Terry looked to him for confirmation.

"Will do." Terry left at a jog.

"Let's get you inside." Lucas led me off. "We leave as soon as I give the locals a statement."

"Can we stop at the hospital?"

"No. It's not secure."

I sighed and shut up. I'd learned you didn't win an argument with Lucas Hawk.

~

DUKE

I GROGGILY PRIED MY EYES OPEN TO SEE THE TRACE ON THE MONITOR AS ITS BEEPS competed with the noise of the helo's rotors. I couldn't keep them open. I strained to hear the beeps, as that meant I was still alive.

Then the sound changed, and I was in a Blackhawk kneeling next to Freddy. *"At least the pain means I'm alive,"* he'd said.

I'd gripped his hand and yelled, *"It's going to stay that way."*

"It's cold in here." Then, he'd pulled down the oxygen mask to yell. *"Promise me you'll take care of Marilyn."*

"No need. You'll be taking care of her just fine."

"Fifteen out," the crew chief had yelled.

Freddy had squeezed my hand. *"Promise me."*

"Of course I will."

"I'm cold."

It had been over a hundred degrees on the deck in that godforsaken desert. His pain hadn't lasted fifteen minutes.

I willed my eyes open again. It wasn't a Blackhawk anymore, and we were flying over California hills. "Jordy?" I yelled through the oxygen mask.

He squeezed my hand. "Right here, Cobra."

I liked the name. I'd always admired how deadly Cobras were. "Promise me you'll take care of Serena."

"I'm leaving that to you, Bro."

"I'm cold."

"BP's dropping," the paramedic said. "Push another unit of O-neg."

"We're out."

Then things went dark.

CHAPTER 39

SERENA

MY STOMACH HAD TRIED TO TURN ITSELF INSIDE OUT ALL THE WAY BACK HOME FROM Thousand Oaks. Sure, guys hated using or hearing the L-word, but why hadn't I told Duke I loved him days ago when I had the chance? He probably hadn't heard me with the noise of the helicopter.

Terry, Constance, Winston, Lucas, and I were gathered around my kitchen island with FBI Special Agents Newson and Sanchez.

The agents were listening to the recordings again, which had come from the secure locker the USB key opened.

Then the phone on the island began to ring.

Lucas pointed. "That's Pons's phone. Winston, your turn."

Winston answered the call. "Hello?" After ten seconds or so, he checked the screen and put it down. "Unknown number. Didn't want to talk."

Jordy picked it up and started typing on his laptop. "It's a burner."

The agents went back to the recordings.

I turned to Lucas again. "Are you sure he'll be okay?" Not being able to talk to Duke was driving me crazy. Every call had gone to voicemail.

"He went into surgery. No news is good news," Lucas repeated. It was the same thing he'd told me a dozen times. Believing him was harder with every repetition.

"You're sure that's Leo Gambino?" Newson asked, pausing the recording.

I nodded. "Positive. I'm friends with his..." I stopped myself before saying fiancée. "Katelyn, the woman he was engaged to, so he was around a lot."

"Looks like he got too greedy," Sanchez said.

"And you are certain the other guy is this Aiden Pons from Knife Creek Chemical?" Newson's pen hovered over his notepad.

"Yes," I confirmed. "He's the COO there. He met with me less than two weeks ago. I know the voice, and I saw him there."

"The icing on the cake," Lucas said, "is that Serena heard Pons and Yaroslavsky discussing the conspiracy to illegally dump hazardous materials on Knife Creek's land, and Yaroslavsky said he was running out of room to store the barrels. So if you move soon, you'll catch him with the goods in one of his warehouses."

"You can testify to that effect?" Newson asked.

I nodded. "Yes, and these readings..." I tapped the monitoring-well data that had been in the locker. "...confirm that it's been going on a long time."

"We suspect," Constance said, "that Pons decided he could getter a better deal by killing Gambino and working with Rossi."

"If that's the case, how did Rossi get her hands on this material?" Sanchez asked.

"Probably found it in Gambino's things when she inherited the job," Constance guessed. "Just like Serena inherited the space from Rossi when she left."

My mind drifted to Duke again. This was the last place I wanted to be, but Lucas, the asshole, wouldn't let me go to the hospital. Even if Duke was in surgery, I wanted to be there when he got out. I wanted—no, needed—to hold his hand. There was no room for doubt. I'd fallen in love with the man, my protective, bossy Cobra.

"Isn't that true, Serena?" Constance asked, nudging me.

"What?"

"That the same workspace was passed from Gambino to Rossi, and now to you?"

I nodded. "That's right. They both worked in the same space I do now. It goes with the position."

"Maybe she left town because Pons threatened her," Terry guessed.

"We'll never know now," Constance pointed out.

"The Russians are a tough nut to crack," Newson said. "But this Pons character will roll over on them for a deal."

Lucas nodded.

"Does that mean it's over?" I asked. "I don't have to worry about any more attacks?"

Lucas rested a hand on my forearm. "Johnson Spinelli is the only loose end.

Otherwise, that's what it means. With Pons, Yaroslavsky, and Tony Spinelli arrested and the blackmail material recovered, you are no longer a threat."

"We'll have him by this time tomorrow," Sanchez predicted.

I could breathe freely now. The nightmare was finally over.

"Why would Rossi send you the key to this?" Sanchez asked.

I shook my head. "Not a clue."

The agents stared at me, waiting for more.

When the doorbell rang, Winston left to check it.

Lucas stepped in. "Maybe she knew Serena would do the right thing and turn it over."

Behind me, footsteps announced the arrival of more people. Desperate to see Duke again, I spun. I hadn't thought things could get worse. But for a second, my world stopped as Winston escorted my father in.

I hadn't wanted Dad to know anything about this.

DUKE

I OPENED MY EYES AND QUICKLY CLOSED THEM AGAINST THE BRIGHT OVERHEAD lights. The steady beeping of the monitors on the stand next to me sounded soothing. Beeps were a good sign. My leg hurt. Pain was a good sign as well. It smelled like a hospital.

It had almost killed me to see Pons pointing the gun at Serena and hear it go off when she attacked him. The rest had played out in slow motion—her hits to the throat, the eyes, and the knee had been brutally efficient. Then the kick to the balls to finish him off had been one-hundred percent my feisty woman.

I remembered seeing the knife the big Spinelli brute had pulled too late, the pain, being loaded into the helo, and then…

And then Serena had said she couldn't live without me—that she loved me.

"Hey, man. You gave us quite a scare there."

I tilted my head and found Jordy next to me.

"How's my girl?" It was the first thing that came to mind.

"With traffic, she should be at the house about now."

"I screwed up," I admitted.

Jordy shrugged. "Shit happens."

A young doctor walked in. "How are you feeling, Mr. Hawk?" she asked, looking up from the tablet she carried. "I'm Dr. Gupta if you don't remember."

I didn't. "Sorry," I said hoarsely.

"That's understandable. You lost a lot of blood, but the surgery went very well."

"Surgery?" That explained the grogginess and sore throat.

"Yes. You're a very lucky man. The knife nicked your femoral artery. A fraction of a centimeter over, and it would have transected it."

I understood how to translate the doctor-speak. I'd seen it on the battlefield. No helicopter would have been fast enough to save me with a severed artery.

"You were also lucky that your brother had the presence of mind to apply a tourniquet."

"Army training," Jordy offered.

Gupta nodded. "Your prognosis is excellent for a full recovery. Fortunately for you, the injury was approximately the size of the incision we make for a catheter insertion, and I was able to use our normal closure for that procedure. Your artery will heal quickly and quite well." She laughed. "Although you won't feel like running for a while."

I appreciated the levity. "Thanks, Doc."

"Take these for the pain." She held out her hand.

"No thanks." I hated any pain pills stronger than Advil.

She didn't pull her hand back. "Either take them or stay overnight for observation."

I hated hospitals worse than pain pills, so I swallowed them with the water she offered.

"It goes without saying, no driving for you."

"I'm driving," Jordy offered. "How long does he need to stay?"

"If things still look good in two hours, I'll discharge him then." The doctor patted my shoulder. "You have a dangerous profession, young man. Be more careful in the future."

After the doctor left, Jordy agreed. "She's right, you know? You should cut back on risks."

Jordy meant to cheer me up, but all it did was remind me of the biggest risk of all. Visions of Marilyn's lifeless body in a pool of blood filled my mind—some risks were too big. I'd almost condemned Serena to the same fate.

What if I wasn't as lucky the next time? Or I didn't have one of my brothers with me? I couldn't put her through that.

I'd disregarded the reason I didn't allow relationships in my life, and fate had almost taught me the cost of forgetting that lesson.

Serena deserved better. For her sake, I couldn't repeat the mistake.

CHAPTER 40

SERENA

"MUNCHKIN, I'VE GOT GOOD NEWS," DAD SAID. HIS FACE TURNED PERPLEXED AS HE took in the crowd.

Lucas's phone received a message. I turned, and Dad opened his arms to me. Nobody said a thing until our hug was complete.

"Or..." Sanchez murmured as I looked at the screen Lucas angled my way.

JORDY: Out of surgery - successful

I didn't know exactly what *successful* meant, but I'd take it as a win. The ordeal was over, and Duke was alive. After a deep breath, I faced Sanchez again. "Or what?"

The agent pointed a finger at me. "Rossi offered you the blackmail scam for a piece of the action."

"That's uncalled for," Constance insisted.

"What's going on here?" Dad bellowed.

"Who is this?" Sanchez demanded.

Newson backed up a step. Recognition shone in his eyes. He could see the storm brewing.

Lucas made the introduction. "This is Serena's father, Lloyd Benson, and it sounds to me like you're accusing his daughter of something criminal."

Sanchez went pale. He hadn't recognized Dad's face, but it seemed he knew

237

the name and reputation. "Not at all. Just verbalizing all the harebrained possibilities so we can discard them."

Dad's jaw clenched. "What's your name, son?"

"Uh…Special Agent Luis Sanchez." He puffed out his chest. "FBI."

I wanted this to be over. "If you don't have any more questions for me," I said firmly, "I think we're done. You have all the material that was in the locker, and that should be more than enough." I couldn't let Dad run roughshod over everybody. It would never end.

"I'd like to see that," Dad said, moving forward and stretching out his hand.

I blocked him. "No, Dad. Let them do their job now."

"But, Munchkin—"

The Munchkin comment was the last straw. "No."

"We still have some questions about the kidnapping," Sanchez said.

I could see the steam coming out of Dad's ears. "Kidnapping?"

"I'm okay," I assured him. "It was no big deal."

"We could threaten false imprisonment instead," Newson suggested.

Sanchez didn't sense the danger. "She was abducted and moved. That falls under felony kidnapping, and I want to be in a position to file charges first thing in the morning."

Dad seethed. "No. You'll do no such thing."

"That's not up to you," Sanchez said.

"Who's your boss, son?"

"Why?" Sanchez demanded.

"Never mind." Dad pulled out his phone and dialed.

I saw Newson pull Sanchez's arm.

Dad's face was flushed, and there was no stopping him now. "Cindy, get a hold of the vice president and tell him I want a meeting with whoever the hell is running the FBI office in our city."

"*Vice president?*" Sanchez mouthed.

"Of the United States," Lucas whispered.

Sanchez went pale.

I couldn't see from my vantage point, but I was ready to bet money Sanchez had wet himself.

"I think nine o'clock, my office. Thank you, Cindy." Dad ended the call. He directed his rage at the hapless agents. "There will be no discussion of kidnapping a Benson whatsoever. Unless I say otherwise, it didn't happen. Am I clear?"

Heads nodded all the way around.

"You may leave now," Dad commanded.

The two agents decided against any more questions and left with all the physical evidence Winston had brought.

As soon as the door closed, Dad turned his guns on Lucas. "Lucas, you sure screwed this up."

Lucas gritted his teeth.

"Where the hell was her supposed bodyguard while all this went down?"

Before Lucas could respond with either words or fists, I stepped between the two men. "Duke took four bullets protecting me," I yelled at my father. "That's where Duke was. Duke, Lucas, and the whole team saved me." I poked a finger in his chest. "Now you apologize."

"Munchkin, I didn't mean—"

I jabbed him again. "Yes, you did. Now apologize or get out of my house."

Dad had a rule that he didn't apologize, but he surprised me. "I'm sorry I acted inappropriately."

"Understood," Lucas replied.

"You said you had good news?" I asked him.

"We don't have to worry about Fox anymore."

That *was* good news. "Why?"

"The sheriff just told me he tried to rob a liquor store in Torrance and ran into an armed owner. He was wounded, caught, and his parole will certainly be revoked."

I thought I'd feel elated to hear news like that after what he did to me, but I didn't. Relieved maybe, but not elated. It delayed the day of reckoning, at least.

I woke up my phone to dial Duke again. He was my future, and every additional minute not knowing how he was doing or hearing from him grew more unbearable. "Lucas, why don't you tell Dad the status?"

"Lloyd, the important thing is that Serena's now out of danger…"

I left the kitchen for privacy to make my call.

It went to voicemail again.

I couldn't handle not knowing how he was.

An hour or so later, Dad had left, and Constance and I were prepping a simple dinner for the Hawk team as we all awaited news of Duke.

I still hadn't heard a response from him when Lucas came in to show me another message.

JORDY: On the way

"See?" Constance said. "He's too ornery to stay in a hospital for long."

I nodded, and then it struck me that I'd been stupid. Duke probably hadn't responded because he didn't have his phone on him. That put a smile on my face.

Then more lines of messaging showed on the phone.

> JORDY: Johnson Spinelli boarded a flight to Phoenix. Rented a car. Headed east after that. I haven't located him yet.

"Shit," Lucas swore. "I really wanted him to stick around so we could nail him."

"This means it's over, right? There aren't any more goons after me?"

Lucas nodded. "Apparently. But I'll feel better when the FBI or whoever catches the bastard."

A half-hour later, I looked over Lucas's shoulder when another message arrived.

> JORDY: Dropped Duke off at home

"I'm going over there," I announced and grabbed my purse without waiting for any damned permission. *Shit.* "I need a car." Mine was a burned-out hulk in a junkyard.

When the guys looked at each other, Constance fished keys out of her bag and threw them. "Take mine."

~

THE DRIVE OVER FELT LIKE IT TOOK FOREVER. LIQUID HEAT POOLED BETWEEN MY LEGS as I considered how to bang Duke's brains out for all he'd done for me. I also needed to come clean and tell him I'd fallen totally in love with him—right after giving him one hell of an orgasm. It was a good plan.

What would be best for him? Doggy? Bent over the couch? Me on top cupping his balls? Should I turn around and bring my vibrator?

Shit, what was I thinking? He'd been shot and knifed badly enough to need surgery. The bangfest might have to wait until he was well.

In the meantime, I'd have to settle for blowing his mind by explaining in excruciating detail all the things I intended to do to him and let him do to me. Maybe he couldn't do any of the work, and I'd have to give him the world's best blowjob while he stayed still.

I parked and power walked—jittery with excitement—into the lobby of Duke's tall building. Oliver, the doorman, was as pleasant as ever as I scooted past him.

I punched the button for his floor and butterflies filled my stomach. How had

I gotten so lucky to find a man willing to go all out in my defense, including taking bullets for me? As the floors dinged by, I had to hug myself to make sure this wasn't a dream. I couldn't have imagined a better place to end up in life than as Duke Hawk's girl.

Finally at his floor, I pressed the buzzer to his unit.

Nothing.

I knocked on the door. "Duke? Duke?" When I didn't hear anything, I upped my game to banging my fist on the door. What if he'd fallen or started bleeding and passed out?

I was about to go down to get Oliver when, "Hold on," came through the door.

~

Duke

SERENA WOULDN'T STOP BANGING ON MY DOOR.

She wouldn't like the words I was going to force myself to say, but I knew it was the right thing for her, for her long-term happiness. Everything was so much clearer now.

I shuffled gingerly to the door. "Coming." I wished I could put it off until tomorrow, give me some time to come up with the right words—the least-hurtful words to explain it to her.

After a breath, I unlocked and opened the door. "Hi. I'm not feeling so great."

She pushed the door open and barged in.

When she went in for a hug, I shook my head and put an arm out, backing away. "I've got broken ribs," I exaggerated.

"Oh." She backed away. "Sorry. I wasn't thinking." She licked her lips. "I owe you so much—"

"It's the job," I said, interrupting her and backing away for more space between us. This was going to be incredibly hard, but it had to be done.

She batted her eyelashes and lowered her gaze to my crotch. "Yeah, but I've been thinking of all the ways I could repay you." She grinned. "You didn't get shot below the belt."

I put my hands in front of me to hide the reaction she caused. "We shouldn't… We can't."

Confusion crossed her face. "I'm sorry. Since you're standing, I thought…" She waved a hand. "It doesn't matter. What are your doctor's instructions? How soon can we…you know?"

God, this was hard. Without the right, soft words to make this easier, I blurted out the harsh ones. "We can't because I'm not right for you."

Her face dropped. "What? I love you, and—"

"We have to end this," I said before she could go on. More mentions of the L-word were not the way to go. "Before—"

Anger welled up in her face. "Before what? Did you not listen to me? I fucking love you, Duke Hawk. I drove over here planning to tell you while I was banging your brains out." Her jaw clenched. "Did you hear me? I love you, and I thought you felt something for me, too."

I took in the deepest breath I could with my wounded ribs. "You're the one who's not listening. I'm not right for you."

"You're worse than my father. I'm the one who gets to decide what's right or wrong for me, not him or you."

"Your father was right." I motioned between us. "This isn't going to work. You should go."

Her face turned even redder. "You mean you don't want to put in the effort to make it work."

The words were poison on my tongue. "That's right. I don't."

The door slammed behind her with finality.

She was safe.

My world collapsed around me.

CHAPTER 41

Duke

THE NEXT MORNING, FRIDAY, I LIFTED MY HEAD. BIG MISTAKE—A SWARM OF ANGRY birds was trying to peck its way out of my skull. Settling back down into a puddle of my own drool was equally bad. This was the price I paid for doing the right thing—the thing that would save Serena. But the pain in my skull was second to the hole I'd torn in my heart. I'd never forget Serena. To save her, I'd walked away, and to save herself, she had to forget me.

I had to pee something fierce, so I levered myself up and took a long gulp of vodka from the bottle on the coffee table—hair of the dog. Hobbling, I made it to the bathroom.

"You won't feel like running for a while," the doc had said, and that was an understatement. Between my head, the bruises, and cracked ribs from the bullet hits, and the knife wound, only my toes didn't hurt.

Heading back to the couch, I grabbed the bottle for two more slugs, hating the burn as it went down. I'd know it was enough when it didn't burn anymore.

Staying shitfaced was the plan for the foreseeable future. I lifted the bottle for a fourth gulp. Alcohol, lots of it, would ease the pain, and with time, I'd learn to live without her. Time—that's what I needed. And a fuck lot more vodka.

Setting the nearly empty bottle down, I decided I could do this with class and drink out of a glass. Classy, yeah, classy drunk sounded good. So, I detoured to the kitchen before I had so much I couldn't walk. To save my eyes, I didn't turn on the light.

"Fuck," I yelled when I stubbed my toe on a damned stool and almost fell over, hopping to the counter on my heel. Fuck, my big toe felt like I'd cut it off with a dull knife, and it was my good leg too.

Keeping my injured foot off the floor, I balanced on my bad leg, ignoring the pain in my thigh as I reached for a glass in the cabinet.

"What the hell happened?" The yell hurt my head something awful.

Surprised, I jerked around. The glass slipped from my grasp, breaking on the granite edge of the counter, and fell to the floor.

Jordy laughed.

I had to put the heel of my good leg down to regain my balance. "Fuck," I yelled as I yanked it back up with a piece of glass stuck in my foot. With glass in the heel and a bum toe, that foot was now useless. It hurt like hell to hop to the side on my bad leg.

Jordy kept laughing.

"Fuck you," I said as I lifted my injured foot to the sink, turned on the water, and rinsed the injury.

"Want some help?"

"Fuck no."

He walked around and grabbed my foot anyway. "Hold still, you big pussy, or you'll jam it in farther."

I grabbed the counter edge for support. "What the fuck are you doing here, anyway?"

"I drew the short straw. You fucked up with Serena, then you started drinking and got so plastered somebody had to babysit you."

Outside of what I'd said to Serena, I didn't remember much of last night. I knew I'd started drinking—a lot. Not remembering had been the objective, and I'd gotten that part right.

The room started to sway. The extra swigs of vodka were getting to me. "I need to get to the couch."

"You need to hold still." He yanked, and blood started to flow in the water as the glass shard came out. "And then you need to go man up and fix things with Serena."

"I need more vodka and then to sleep on the couch." The idea of using the bed I'd shared with Serena was too painful.

Jordy patted my foot dry with a paper towel. "If that's what you want, get yourself there so I can bandage this. I'm not fucking carrying you."

～

"You're a fucking fool," Lucas repeated.

"Ditto that," Jordy said.

That pretty much summed up my brothers' opinions of my behavior.

They'd even brought over my sister Alice to pressure me. But she was easy to ignore. I pointed out that she hadn't even met Serena.

"But I've talked to her, and I know you well enough to know this is a mistake," she argued.

"My life, my decision," I repeated. This was going nowhere because they got no say in how I ran my life, and the risks I was and wasn't willing to take.

After Marilyn, and after the mistakes I'd made while protecting Serena, she fell into the not-willing-to-take-that-chance category—end of subject.

"Stupid and stubborn," Lucas said, pointing a finger at me. "Just like a fucking frogman."

"That's me," I agreed, not interested in prolonging the argument. They'd already taken up enough of my drinking time.

Lucas pulled away from the wall. "Since this is such a nonissue with you, I'll expect you back to work first thing Monday."

That sucked. I'd wanted to spend a good solid week drinking away my misery. "See you then," I said instead. At least I had the weekend.

SERENA

"SERENA, WAKE UP."

I blinked my eyes open on Friday morning to find Grace's caring face.

"How do you feel?" she asked. Behind her were Terry and Constance.

I pulled my covers up to my neck. "Like shit," I admitted.

I didn't drink often, but after Duke had ripped my heart out, Grace brought bottles of wine to my room and drank with me until I fell asleep. I did most of the drinking. The bottles of merlot sat almost empty on my nightstand. My headache said we should have chosen a white.

"Why are you all…"

Grace settled onto the edge of the bed. "I'm here for my bestie in her time of need."

The sentiment made me sigh.

Terry moved closer. "And because her house is being fumigated and nobody else would have her. So I stayed to keep an eye on her."

"Shut up," Grace snapped.

"And I stayed," Constance added, "to keep these two from killing each other."

The look in Terry's eyes as he gazed at Grace's ass was the opposite of homicidal. "His brothers will talk some sense into him," he assured me.

"It doesn't matter." The last thing I needed was any discussion of the fool I'd made of myself with Duke.

Constance offered a glass of orange juice. "I have to go into work for a few days so I don't blow my cover. You should call in and take the day off."

I accepted the glass and nodded. "Yeah." I needed a plan for how much to tell my boss about yesterday. The higher-ups would be apoplectic that someone in the agency had been taking bribes and probably start looking for scapegoats. To save himself, Powell would likely accuse all of us of knowing and not telling him.

"I'll stay," Grace offered. "I can print out a picture of the jerk, and we can play darts."

Terry laughed. "You carry darts around with you?"

Her head snapped around. "If you play pool, you have your own cue. I have my own darts. Plus, they can be handy. Like when you need a jerk to back off." She made a shooing motion. "Git."

Terry didn't back up. "I'll be at the office. If you need anything, call."

"Sure." I nodded. He couldn't give me the one thing I needed, though.

All I wanted was to sleep and forget my broken heart. It was my fault for mistaking lust on Duke's part for true caring, wasn't it? I'd been such a fool to think a guy like Duke could want a girl as broken as me.

But first I needed to call Powell and take the day off.

"This is my lucky set. I think you need them more than I do," Grace said as she put a plastic package of three darts in my purse. "For a while."

I didn't play, but I wasn't going to argue with the sentiment. I dialed my phone and connected to my boss.

"Fine," Powell said when I explained that maybe I had the flu. "But if it isn't cancer, I expect you first thing Monday."

Compassionate as always.

～

By mid-afternoon, I'd conquered the headache with fluids and Advil and even taken a shower and gotten dressed. In other words, I looked almost human, which was better than I felt.

Lifting the next spoonful of minestrone to my mouth, I blew on it, then swallowed. It tasted like…nothing. It was boring, just like me and the rest of the life I was doomed to live out. Even the light from the living room windows was duller than I remembered.

Two weeks with Duke had packed in more excitement than the entire rest of my life, and it was over. I was back to living in a house I didn't even own, sitting in front of a fireplace that I always planned to light and cook marshmallows over, but never had.

I still couldn't wrap my head around what had gone wrong between us. I'd thought we fit great together. The day at Disneyland had been nicer than any date I'd ever had. The nights had been fantastic. Everything had meshed until yesterday.

He'd rescued me. He'd done his job, and now that it was over, he no longer wanted me. He'd acted like he cared just to make me compliant, to keep me under control, and make his job easier.

Would things between us have worked out differently if I hadn't instantly fallen for him? If we'd taken things slowly? If we'd met outside of this strange bodyguard environment where we had to be together all the time?

My heart skipped a beat at the sound of the door being unlocked. *Could it be?*

"Sis?" my brother Vincent called from the foyer. "You ready to go?"

Elation gone, I waited until he walked into the kitchen. "Go where?"

"Back home to Mom and Dad's."

I shook my head. "Not happening."

He leaned against the wall. "I'm here to help you pack."

"Nope." I sipped another spoonful of soup.

"You're a Benson. You've given up. It's what we do, and then we go back home and hang out to forget our mistake."

"What are you talking about?"

"Grace tells me she thinks you never really liked him anyway."

I shook my head, not going for the bait. Grace wouldn't have told him that.

"So, you do like him?"

"It doesn't matter anymore." What I'd felt for Duke had gone way beyond *like*.

"If you're going to follow in my footsteps and give up, you have to go all the way and move back home." He thumbed toward the stairs. "So let's get going."

"Since when did you ever give up on anything?"

He smirked. "Not anything...anyone." His eyes shifted to the prom photo on the mantel—the one of him and Ashley Newton, the one who'd gotten away. One drunken evening, Vincent had lamented to me that he counted not going after her as the biggest mistake of his life. *"Learn from my mistake,"* he'd said. *"Don't repeat it."*

I finally understood the message I'd forgotten.

"Time to be an adult and make up your mind. Are you going to give it your best shot or give up and go home to Mom and Dad? Those are your only two choices... Well?"

"You suck." He'd ignored the curl-up-in-a-ball-and-sob-for-a-month alternative I'd been pursuing.

"Insulting me won't do you any good," he noted. "I'm staying until you make a decision."

"Why do you have to be so mean?"

He snorted. "I used to think you were tough."

"Now who's being insulting?" I closed my eyes for a minute and wished him away. Peeking, I found it hadn't worked.

He smiled smugly. We both knew he was right.

As much as I wanted to wallow, it was self-defeating, and I wasn't a quitter. I levered myself up. I'd watched how letting Ashley get away had hurt him, and that wasn't the path for me. I knew what I'd experienced with Duke, and I wasn't wrong about what he'd felt. But something had spooked him. "I'm going to go get my man back."

Nursing the coffee I'd ordered, I heard the woman next to me sigh before I saw him. Then, with a stir, every pair of female eyes in the small diner shifted to the man walking my way. Lucas Hawk had arrived. The men who noticed him shifted uncomfortably. Lucas exuded a dangerous vibe like nobody I'd ever met.

He settled into the booth across from me. "I think you're safe now."

I'd made up my mind, so direct was the order of the day. "That's not why I called. But I suspect you know that."

He shrugged. "Jordy and I both told him he's being an idiot."

The news warmed me. I didn't expect them to be opposed, but having their support had to help.

"But he's dug his feet in, and my brother can be pretty damned stubborn."

"I'm not giving up and walking away. My family invented stubborn."

My young waitress bounced up. "What can I get started for you?" she asked Lucas, complete with batting eyelashes.

"Coffee, black." Curt as always.

She added more wattage to her smile and bounced again. "Need more time with the menus?"

Lucas shook his head, ignoring her jiggling breasts.

"Thank you," I added as she left.

Lucas looked me in the eye with an intensity I wasn't used to. "I'm on your side. I think you're good for him."

"Thank you. I'm going to go see him, but he wouldn't open up to me before. And I don't know how to battle a problem I don't understand." If anybody had the key to understanding Duke, it had to be Lucas.

248

He took a deep breath. "Has he told you about Marilyn?"

I nodded. "He had a nightmare and said her name. He told me she died, but I didn't push for more. Was she an ex-girlfriend?"

"Has he told you about Freddy?"

"His SEAL friend?"

Miss Bouncy reappeared with a mug for Lucas. "Here ya go," she tried again. She'd undone a button on her blouse.

Lucas gave her a minimal smile and pulled a sugar packet. When she left, he continued, "Not just a friend. His best friend, buddy, and teammate. They were inseparable. Freddy died in helo holding Duke's hand, and let me tell you, that takes something out of you that can never be replaced."

I nodded along, though I couldn't comprehend the depth of that hurt.

Lucas stirred his coffee. "Marilyn was Freddy's wife."

"Oh." I hadn't guessed that connection. Duke clearly hadn't been honest with me about her.

"She dated Duke first. Duke introduced them." Lucas sipped from his mug.

I waited for more.

"She committed suicide after hearing of Freddy's death. Duke was the one who found her."

I cringed. "That's terrible."

"That's the threat you represent."

"You think I'm a suicide risk?" My voice went from angry to shrill. "You think I'm weak?"

He leaned forward. "Calm down."

"Yeah, right. Calm down? You have no idea what I've been through."

He gestured for me to lower my voice. "I don't think you're weak. No way, but he's not being rational. It's fear making him act this way. This business we're in is dangerous at times. He doesn't want to cause that kind of grief again."

"But I'm no weak wallflower. You, of all people, should know that."

"You're the only one who can convince him of that. Have you told him about your…experience?" he asked. "How hard it was?"

Did he suspect what had happened to me during that time? I shook my head. "Not all of it. I haven't been able to talk about it with anybody."

"Your family?"

I looked down at the table. "Nobody." I hadn't even talked with Mom about it. She knew how long I'd been held, but not what had happened to me.

"It sounds like neither of you is being completely honest."

I nodded. It was a situation I intended to change.

"I destroyed the tapes," he said after a moment.

I gasped. I'd never known they'd been recording. I was grateful to Lucas all over again.

He shifted out of the booth and stood. "It won't be easy, but if you're willing to be completely honest, I think he'll understand how strong you are."

I nodded. But was I strong enough to unlock the chest and relive it?

"I'd say the next step is up to you." He set a key on the table. "In case he won't open the door."

CHAPTER 42

DUKE

AFTER ANOTHER DOSE OF ADVIL, A GALLON OF WATER, AND AN OMELET WITH ALL THE hot sauce I could stand, I was sober, and I'd almost conquered the hangover.

Fucking Lucas hadn't given me much choice when he'd taken all the liquor away. How long would it take for memories of her to fade so I could go back to sleeping in my bed?

Maybe it would be better if I threw this one out and bought another.

The doorbell rang and rang again, forcing me up off the couch. I was so over having my family give me advice that was totally useless. "Who is it?" I demanded. Only my family was cleared past the lobby.

"It's me." Serena's voice carried through the door. "We need to talk."

At least I had a locked door between us, keeping me from making the mistake of getting lost in those pale-green eyes. "We don't have anything more to talk about."

"Yes, we do."

"No. It's over." She was safely away from me.

"Open up, Duke."

I pulled the pin on the nuclear grenade. "Leave. Ursula's on her way over." Then I walked back to my couch. *Problem solved.*

251

HE WOULDN'T, WOULD HE? THAT WAS PRETTY LOW.

With my stomach churning, I stomped to the other end of the hall—with my best smoky eye makeup, my best push-up bra paired with my sexiest red dress, and my Louboutins. I was dressed for battle, but only if I got to face him. I dialed his brother.

"Hey, Serena, can I help you?" Jordy asked.

"I need you to check a work schedule on Ursula Anders. She's a flight attendant on SAS. I want to know where she is right now." Yes, I had done my research on his blonde bombshell ex-whatever she was to him.

"Duke's Ursula?"

"That's the one." My stomach almost revolted. I hated hearing that she was that much of a fixture in Duke's life.

"Just a minute." Furious keyboard clicks came across the line. "Her flight from Frankfurt to Stockholm already landed. You know it's nine hours later in Stockholm, right?"

"Thanks a million, Jordy. I owe you."

I stomped back to Duke's door. No more Miss Nice Gal. That didn't sound right, but so what? I inserted the key and unlocked the door.

"What the hell?" Duke almost fell off the couch when I found him in the living room.

"We're talking, adult to adult, whether you like it or not."

He pointed to the door. "I said no. Now leave before Ursula gets here."

Hand on my hips, I laughed at him. "Don't try that on me. She's in Stockholm."

He didn't have an answer to that.

"I heard you when you said you didn't want me to get hurt—and I appreciate the sentiment—but I'm a grown-ass woman who can make her own decisions."

"We are not doing this. You're safe. It was fun. It's over."

Nothing new in his arguments there. Time for truth telling. "I know about Marilyn. I know you found her."

His face fell like I'd knifed him. "You don't understand."

"Lucas told me everything."

His teeth gritted in anger. "He had no right—"

"Don't blame him. I made him tell me." A mild lie because I doubted anybody could make Lucas Hawk do something he didn't want to do. "You told me you'd always be truthful with me, and you lied."

"I didn't lie."

"It sure wasn't the whole truth."

He closed his eyes and sucked in a deep breath. "I almost died in Thousand Oaks, and the next time, I might not be so lucky. I'm not putting you through that and risking…" He didn't finish, but his fear was clear.

"I am not Marilyn." I raised a hand when it looked like he might argue. "I've got more grit than that. You have no idea the hell I went through when I was kidnapped by the Fox brothers."

His brows creased. "You said it wasn't much."

"I was afraid to tell you the whole truth."

He held out his hand, and I had my first victory. "I'm sorry."

I took it and sat, angled toward him. "They had me for ten days. Ten days in total darkness."

"That's why the night lights?" he asked.

I nodded. "Darkness brings back the nightmares."

"Then why'd you tell me it was only one day?"

I swallowed hard. "Shame. It was ten days of enduring their torture. Ten days of knowing that in the end, they planned to kill me."

"But you survived."

"For ten days and nights, I listened to them on the other side of the door." I sniffled. "Every night, they fucking flipped a coin to see who got me first, and who went second. They tied me to the bed and took me every night, no matter how much I fought. I lied because I didn't want you to think—"

He took me into a hug, and I had my second victory. "Baby, the only thing I think about you is how incredibly strong you are." He rubbed my back through my sobs. "You're strong like a tiger, not backing down from any fight."

I snuggled against him. "I didn't want you to know I was damaged goods."

"I think Tiger fits you better than Snuggles."

I nodded. A tiger was bold and proud. "I'm not letting you push me away just because you're a coward."

He tensed and pushed me away. "I warned you about calling a SEAL a coward."

"Or stupid," I shot back. "And if you think I'm going to pull a Marilyn, you're stupider than dog shit."

"Leave." He pointed. "I don't think we can be together." The *I don't think* in his statement was enough wiggle room to call it another win.

"You're worse than my father," I spat.

"Don't ever compare me to him," he shot back with equal intensity.

"You're trying to run my life, just like him. Serena, do this. Serena, you can't do that."

"I don't mean it that way." His fists clenched and unclenched. I was clearly getting to him.

"You think you know better than me, and you're wrong. I love you—"

"You can't."

"I can, and I do. I'm strong enough. You know that tattoo you have? The part of the SEAL code about always getting back up? Well, Cobra, I'm that strong too. You can push me away, but I'm going to be back on your doorstep again and again until—"

"But I can't."

"Okay, sailor, admit to me that you're a stupid coward then."

"I warned you," he growled.

"Let's call Alice. You told me you can't lie to her. Tell her you don't love me."

"You're impossible."

"Read your tattoo. That's your future. Me getting back up every time you knock me down. Every single—"

His mouth covered mine, cutting off the rest of my rant.

Snaking my hands behind his neck, I kissed him back, long, deep, and filled with all the love I felt for this man.

He broke the kiss. "You're impossible."

"I'm not giving you up."

"Then I'll quit the company and—"

I straightened. "What? And become a grocery store cashier? No fucking way. I fell in love with the take-no-prisoners, badass SEAL doing the hard work others won't or can't do. That's the man you're meant to be."

"You're impossible."

"You said that. Now surrender, or do I have to throat punch you?"

He sighed. "You mentioned something about banging my brains out."

Already soaking wet, I ran my hand over the bulge in his pants. "What about your ribs? I could suck you."

"I can think of a dozen positions that will work," he said already lifting my dress over my head. "Keep the heels on."

With the fierceness of a tiger, I attacked his clothes as well, and in no time, we were both naked. His bruises were ugly, and the stitches on the inside of his leg were an angry red. I knelt in front of him.

"No. I want to—"

"Shut up." I tugged his cock and brought the head to my lips. "What part of not telling me what to do didn't you hear?"

His only response was a moan as I took him into my mouth and started working him. Wrapping my hair around his fist, he guided me up and down, almost, but not quite too deep. I wrapped tight fingers around the base of his shaft, following the movement of my mouth.

"Holy fuck, Tiger."

Cupping his balls, I gave them a light tug as I moaned around his cock. I could see his abs and thighs tensing and backed off. How would we explain to the emergency room nurse that he'd ripped the stitches he'd just gotten?

Pulling my hair, he stopped me. "Stand up, Tiger. I need to come inside you." He lifted me as if I weighed nothing. He was not as injured as I'd thought.

Wrapping my legs around him, I raked my teeth over the stubble on his neck and clawed at his back. He was mine, and I intended to mark him.

Setting me down, he spun me to face the table and pushed me over in that dominating way that turned me on. I palmed the wood and flattened myself against the cool surface, waiting for him to impale me with Rex. Instead, his tongue licked the length of my folds before returning to my clit.

He forced my legs wider, alternating between fingering and licking me in ways that built a white-hot fire within me.

Then he stood and speared me deep with one long thrust, giving me the fullness I craved. "You're so fucking wet for me, baby." He began rapid, forceful thrusts, filling me to my limit. "Baby, you feel so fucking good."

I craned my neck to look back at him. "I'm wet every time I think of you, Cobra." Yes, taking me like this, he was my deadly Cobra, my man, my SEAL.

He pushed me against the table with one hand and gripped my hips with the other, powering into me at an increasing pace. In mere minutes, I came apart, a toe-curling orgasm shuddering through me as I cried out his name.

"Fuck, baby," he roared as he shoved deep and held.

I felt the pulses of his release inside me as his climax rolled over him.

Panting loudly, he leaned over my back. "You and me, Tiger, you and me."

LATER THAT NIGHT, I PANTED ALL OVER AGAIN, MY HEART STILL POUNDING FROM MY latest orgasm. I rolled over in the sheets and closed my eyes to enjoy the post-orgasmic bliss.

Our first make-up sex had been raw and feral, the second session energetic, and the third this evening had been slow, languid lovemaking—all of them equally satisfying.

"I have something for you," he said as he gently cleaned me with a warm washcloth.

I opened my eyes and gasped.

He held open a box with a gorgeous emerald earring and necklace set. "I want you to wear these."

I levered myself up. "They're beautiful."

"To match your eyes. You have to wear them. The necklace has a tracker to keep you safe. Just in case."

I recoiled. "Didn't we just have this discussion? You can't tell me what to do."

He tensed for a second, then blew out a breath. "I'd like it," he drawled, "if you'd wear it. I'd feel better knowing you were safe."

A week ago, I would have argued about wearing an electronic leash. But today my pride at being Duke Hawk's woman overrode that. "That's sweet," I said as reeled in my man for the kiss he deserved.

Eventually, he broke the kiss. "Lucas tells me you picked the door lock and almost got away."

I nodded.

"That's pretty badass. How'd you learn that?"

"From the master chief Dad hired after I was kidnapped."

Duke was the first person I'd ever used the *kidnap* word with.

"Hmm... I'll have to thank him someday for taking care of you."

"I think you'd like him. He's no nonsense."

CHAPTER 43

SERENA

MONDAY MORNING, I FINGERED ONE OF THE EARRINGS DUKE HAD GIVEN ME AS I remembered his words. *"I love you, Tiger."* It had been a battle, but he loved me. And I was never letting him go.

Since I didn't have cancer, I was back in the office today, as demanded by his highness Dr. Powell. I'd walked by his office when I first arrived so he'd notice me, and then again, to make sure.

Luckily, Winston had made copies of what he found in the locker before turning it over to the FBI. Regardless of what happened with Aiden Pons, the material would be more than enough to get our criminal investigative division and the US Attorney's office interested in filing charges against Knife Creek, the company.

As I saw it, Pons might have been the head of the snake, but the size of the operation meant more people at the company had to have been involved. It was probably one of them who'd called Pons's phone while the FBI guys were at the house.

Katelyn bounced up and surprised me. "Ready?"

I looked up and closed the folder. "For what?"

"Another day, another site visit."

With all that had happened last week, I didn't share her enthusiasm this morning. "Where to?" I'd given Powell a request for a week off to be with Duke and relax, and that was my focus. Who knew when he'd get around to giving me an answer.

"Some little shit place down south," Katelyn said. "We're taking my car, but you can drive."

"Isn't that out of our area?"

"I don't question Powell. I just go where he sends me."

After putting away the folder, I grabbed my purse and followed her.

～

AN HOUR LATER, THE INDUSTRIAL AREA WE DROVE THROUGH BECAME INCREASINGLY sketchy.

Katelyn pointed. "Turn right down there."

It was only an alley between buildings, but I turned in as instructed.

"It's the door on the right, all the way at the end."

I stopped, and we got out. "You weren't kidding when you called this a little shit place." The rusty door had a sign hanging at an angle that read *Occidental Garlic,* an odd name.

Katelyn went in first.

The hallway was dank, with only dim light from a window above the door after it closed behind me. The slight garlic odor in the air said the sign hadn't been a joke.

Strong hands grabbed my arm. "I've got you now, pretty one."

I whipped my head around to find Johnson Spinelli. *It can't be.* He was supposed to be halfway across the country.

He clamped the same sickly sweet-smelling rag over my mouth. *Not again.* I kicked at him and pulled away. My foot connected with his shin.

"Fucking bitch." He slammed me against the wall.

My head hit hard, and pain rippled through me. I couldn't avoid sucking in a breath.

"You're not getting away this time, little bitch."

As my vision blurred, I wished we hadn't broken the clasp of Duke's necklace. He'd taken it this morning to get it repaired for me.

Johnson roughly grabbed my breast.

I willed my foot to kick the creep again, but it wouldn't move as things dimmed and the darkness sucked me back in.

～

DUKE

. . .

258

WHY DID THIS HAVE TO BE SO DIFFICULT? I SELECTED THE NEXT HAWAIIAN RESORT from the endless list. This one didn't mention dolphins either. How was I supposed to find Serena's dream vacation like this? A week in Hawaii and swimming with the dolphins had sounded simple enough.

"What's up?" Winston's voice startled me. He leaned over to check my screen. "Nice. You and Serena? You should definitely take her to the big island."

My sister Alice had told everybody that Serena and I were together again, and this morning everybody had advice for me.

"She wants to swim with the dolphins, and I can't find a place that offers that."

"Keep looking," he said. "You'll find it. By the way, the boss said he finally got ahold of your buddies, Singleton and March."

"Yeah?"

"March will be here Wednesday, but Singleton took another assignment."

One more frogman was better than none. "Thanks."

"GUYS," LUCAS YELLED FROM HIS OFFICE AN HOUR LATER. "WE HAVE A SITUATION."

Winston and I hustled in, followed by the rest of the team.

"Lloyd," Lucas said into his speakerphone setup. "Say that again. The whole team's here now, and Constance is patched in."

"I just got a ransom call," Benson said frantically.

My heart stopped.

"He has Serena and her workmate Katelyn."

My hand balled into a fist. I was going to kill whoever had taken her. "Did you talk to her?" I half yelled.

"No. They said not until I get the money together."

"He could have drugged them," Winston said.

I guessed that was meant to make me feel better. "Yeah." Hope was better than the alternative.

My gut churned as Serena's father recounted the call and then left the line to arrange for the money—two million dollars.

"What about that tracker necklace you were going to give her?" Terry asked.

I shook my head. "The clasp broke. I was going to get if fixed." I lifted it out of my pocket. It had been a victim of vigorous love-making last night.

Ten minutes later, Constance called back with specifics. "They were due to make a site visit this morning to a company in Reseda. They never arrived."

I needed hope. "Could they just be running late?"

"Not two hours late," she replied.

"And, both cellphones went dark at the same time," Jordy added.

"Constance, you said it was common for government vehicles to have trackers. Is that true of all the EPA cars, and were they driving one?"

"Yeah, but it'll take time to authorize a trace from this end."

"I can work around that," Jordy said as he rushed to his office. None of us asked how he got access to these feeds.

The whole group followed him.

I sweated as he typed, interspersing that with rapid mouse clicks.

This has to give us something.

"Got it," Jordy announced. "Car one-oh-four's track matches their phones. Now we just have to…follow it." More mouse clicks showed an increasing red line making its way south on a map on his screen.

"But that's going south, and Reseda is north," Terry pointed out.

Jordy turned in his chair. "All I know is their phones were in that car when they left the federal building."

Someone had given Constance bad info.

"There." Jordy pointed. "It stops in Long Beach. The car is still there."

Lucas patted his shoulder. "Good job, Jordy."

"Yeah, I know," Jordy pouted. "And I'm stuck here on comms."

"No." Lucas grinned. "Comms, yes, but bring your drones along. Everybody else, gear up. If the trail's hot, we're following it."

I could feel the adrenaline as we strapped on protection and checked weapons.

"Cobra," Lucas said as he slammed a clip home in his SIG. "You're with me. Jordy and Terry in car two. Winston car three. Briefing en route."

I racked the slide on my SIG and holstered it, following my brother and claiming the driver's seat when we reached the Cayenne. With the V-8 howling, we burned rubber out of the garage, and the other two Porsches followed.

"Comms check," Lucas said as he started the mission brief.

Serena

I WOKE WITH A METALLIC TASTE IN MY MOUTH. THANK GOD, IT WASN'T DARK. Squinting, I adjusted to the overhead lights and rolled on the hard floor.

"Thank goodness, you're all right," Katelyn said next to me. She stood next to the door in this small, tile-floored room. "He must have given you a bigger dose than me. I can't fucking believe this." She jiggled the doorknob. "I'm a nobody. Why kidnap me? You, I get. Your daddy has a gazillion dollars, but me? I got nobody, and I'm so far underwater I can't even see up to being dead broke."

I sat up, taking in her complaints. "Do you know where we are?"

"No fucking clue. This sucks. Chloroformed or whatever the hell that was, and now locked up in here waiting for who knows what to happen. What if I have to pee?"

"Keep your voice down." I stood and fixed my breast, which was out of my bra again. *Fucking Johnson.* "Have you heard him say anything? Do you know if he's outside or not?" I asked, stretching to get the kinks out.

She tried to force the knob with two hands. "That's why I'm freaked out. He made a call and demanded a bunch of money from your father or he'd kill us. Then after another call, he left." She rattled the knob again.

I laid a hand on her shoulder. "Calm down." I wasn't ready to tell her that what Johnson probably had planned for us was even worse.

Katelyn pulled away. "Easy for you to say." She was on the verge of hyper-ventilating. "We gotta get out of here. What if your father doesn't want to pay for me?"

"Calm down," I repeated. "We can depend on my dad. Are you sure he's gone?"

She nodded. "I heard him talking to someone. He said it would take him an hour to get there. Then he left."

I examined the lock. "I'll get us out of here."

"Really? I'm too young to die like this."

I went through the steps I'd practiced for getting my bra off and the wires out, all to Katelyn's amazement. "*Speed is everything; seconds count,*" the master chief had said. I left the bra on the floor, slipped the shirt over my head, and went to work on the lock.

Picking the cheap thing was a cinch. Putting a finger to my lips, I shushed her and stashed the wires in my pocket.

I slowly pulled open the door and hoped for no squeaks.

Johnson Spinelli's evil grin greeted me. "Very tricky, pretty girl." He sat just opposite the door with a gun pointed straight at me. The bastard had never left.

CHAPTER 44

SERENA

JOHNSON ROSE.

Bracing myself to run, I glanced left. I had a fifty percent chance of finding a door in that direction.

"She picked the lock using the underwires from her bra," Katelyn said. She pushed me into Johnson's waiting arms.

What the hell?

He grabbed my wrists and spun me around, wrapping an arm around my neck and pressing me against the wall with his horrid breath in my ear. "Try to kick me one more time, and this won't end well for you, bitch."

I relaxed. There were times to fight and times to not.

"The wires are in her back pocket," Katelyn said.

"Katelyn," I screeched.

Johnson pushed me back into the holding room.

"Why did you have to screw everything up? First that bitch Rossi, and now you." She shook her head.

"I—"

"If you'd just given me the Thousand Oaks territory like I wanted, I could have salvaged the situation. Instead, you had to go and fuck the entire thing up so nobody makes any money off Pons."

Makes money? She's deranged. "What are you talking about? Pons was

262

dumping dangerous chemicals illegally. We're the EPA. We're supposed to be preserving the groundwater."

"Oh, please. Stop that preaching shit. It's not important. My house is in ruins and being foreclosed. This oaf…" She pointed at Johnson. "Ruined my new bag."

Johnson shrugged. "Shit happens. Your share of the ransom will buy you a hundred bags."

The sick woman I'd thought was my friend just grinned at me. "Daddy is going to pay through the nose for you and just in time. I'm going to lose the house, my credit cards are maxed out, and my car got repossessed yesterday. All because you guys were against me."

"I was never—"

"Shut up," she screamed. "Fucking shut up."

Clearly, I'd have to listen to her drive the crazy train while I waited for a chance to run.

"First Powell wouldn't let me have the territory after I got rid of Leo. Then Rossi thought she'd blackmail me and Pons."

The words took a few seconds to sink in. "You killed Leo?" It was hard to fathom. "Your own fiancé?"

She snort laughed. "After you filled his head with your preachy do-gooder shit, he wanted to stop taking Pons's money and turn him in. That made him a loser and, without the bribe money, broke. I couldn't marry a broke loser. So yeah, he had to go. If Powell had only given me the accounts, everything would have been fine. Or, if he'd failed your probation when I deleted your Excalibur data, that would have worked too. But no, he didn't want to screw up your life, so he gave you more chances. But what about my life, my chances? It isn't fucking fair."

Controlling my urge to argue with her insanity wasn't easy.

"Then Sophia stole Leo's blackmail stash and used it against Pons, who sent the Russians after her. We almost had her, but she skipped town. Our Russian friends persuaded her to tell us she sent you the key."

I nearly puked, realizing Katelyn had a hand in Sophia's death as well. And all this time, I'd counted her as a friend. "Is that why you hired this guy and his brother?"

"I convinced Pons to hire them. I needed the territory, and he needed that blackmail material so we could get back in business like before. You weren't going to hand it over, so…" She shrugged. "A girl does what a girl has to do. But now, you've totally fucked it up for everybody. Nobody's going to make any money, and the only way out of my problem is your daddy's ransom money."

Two people I knew had died to feed this woman's greed, and she wanted to make me the third. None of it bothered her as much as having her fucking Gucci handbag scuffed up.

Duke, you have to find me. If only we hadn't broken the necklace.

"Make the call," Katelyn ordered.

"Yeah," Johnson said. "I wonder how much two million weighs."

"I'll be making the pickup, dickhead. You watch her until I get back."

Johnson grinned wickedly at me. "We'll be havin' a little fun."

I suppressed a shiver.

He whirled on Katelyn. "Try to double-cross me, Katie girl, and you'll regret it."

His threat backed her up a step. "We follow the plan, and we both get rich. Remember, I'm the one who got her here."

The truth of that had me tasting bile. I'd trusted her, and she'd been behind the attacks and deaths this whole time. All she cared about was money.

"Don't let her outsmart you again," Katelyn told him.

"Fuck you."

"For the right price," she snapped back.

That revolting thought had me tasting bile. I couldn't hold back. "Katelyn, you're a piece of shit."

She spun. "Maybe, but I'm going to be a rich piece of shit. And you're going to be…" She cast a glance at Johnson. "His. You deserve it for screwing up my life."

CHAPTER 45

DUKE

WE'D STOPPED AT AN INTERSECTION AWAY FROM THE LOCATION. THE BLOCK AHEAD looked deserted.

"No movement and no external guards or even cameras," Jordy reported after his drone made two circles of the building. "That's the good news. The bad news is that the building's walls are too thick to get anything on infrared, and we have five points of ingress to cover."

Lucas nodded. "Since there's only one vehicle other than the EPA car, we don't have a large group to deal with—probably two perps."

My phone vibrated.

"Records suck on buildings this old," Jordy said. "I've given you the best interior layout I can find."

Lucas checked his phone. "I hate moving without better intel, but we go with what we have. The second phone call to Benson probably already happened, and knowing him, the ransom is on the way."

I exchanged a look with Lucas. His meaning was clear. Time was our enemy. Once the kidnapper had the ransom in his hands, the hostages were more liabilities than assets.

"One person per entrance." Lucas pointed at Jordy. "That includes you. We go in slow and quiet. If you locate them, pull back, call the location, and wait for backup. We don't move without two-to-one superiority." That was his Delta training talking. "Non-lethal force—if necessary, shoot to incapacitate." That was not Delta, but his civilian status talking.

I nodded. We'd practiced the more difficult non-lethal shots at the range for months.

Terry shook his head. "We should have brought Constance."

"Hey," Jordy complained. "I can handle myself."

Terry slapped him on the shoulder. "What I mean is that without your eyes in the sky, we won't know if we get a squirter."

"Going in all the doors is the best way to avoid that," Lucas countered. "I'm on lead. Quiet entrance on my signal."

We jogged along behind Lucas to the site, splitting up to our assigned doors.

"Unlock, now," Lucas said over comms.

I checked mine. The handle turned freely, and the door creaked open an inch for me. "Cobra unlocked." One by one, we all acknowledged access.

"Enter," Lucas commanded.

I checked the layout on my phone again before lifting my M4. Wincing at the creak, I opened the door with foot pressure and started in. The musty corridor was straight and clear of people but littered with trash. A rat scurried away when I entered the first room.

"Is it all there?" a male voice came through the cracked open door of the third room ahead of me. "Okay. Nobody followed you, right?"

"Did you slit open each bundle, one at a time, and move the loose bills to our bag, checking for a tracker?... Good, and you left their bag behind?" The guy was careful. "Good. See ya soon."

I stepped into the room next to that one and whispered into comms. "I hear a perp, third room in on the right-hand side, talking to an accomplice. No eyes on hostages yet."

"Hold for backup," Lucas ordered.

"Copy," I replied.

Lucas barked orders as he always did. "Winston, egress and reenter on Cobra's door. I'll be right behind you. Terry, move forward to where your corridor intersects Cobra. Jordy, hold fast."

"Now you and me can have a little fun," the guy next door said, louder this time.

"He's threatening one of the hostages," I whispered, hoping to hell it wasn't Serena.

"Hold fast," Lucas repeated.

Screw that. It could be Serena he was threatening. "Going in." I moved slowly into the hallway, dodging boxes and papers on the floor.

"Expediting," Winston mumbled.

I heard the muffled scream before I reached the door. The hostage had obviously been gagged.

"Yeah, I'm gonna enjoy this," the sick fuck said.

I peered through the crack in the door and saw my worst nightmare. Serena's eyes shimmered with tears. Her gaze was locked on the knife in the guy's hand, her attempt to scream muffled by the tape on her mouth. She was handcuffed, and he had her backed against the wall.

"Yeah, I'm gonna enjoy this." He cut down the front of her top and tore it open the rest of the way.

Yanking this asshole limb from limb would be too kind to him, but I couldn't jump him just yet. With the knife that close to Serena, it was too dangerous. Moving as silently as I could, I opened the door wider. *Shit.* A lamp leaning against the wall next to the door started to fall, and I grabbed it with my other hand, letting my weapon fall to its sling.

Serena noticed me, and her eyes gave me away.

Johnson's head whipped around, and he moved quicker than I thought possible, sliding behind Serena with his knife at her neck. "Lift that rifle, and I slit her throat."

With my dominant right hand holding the lamp, my sidearm holstered, and my M4 hanging on its sling, I had no play here—not yet.

"Hands up and step into the room."

"Okay," I said loudly enough for Lucas and the others to hear over comms. "Put the knife down. Nobody is getting their neck slit today."

"Almost to you," Lucas said in my ear.

Serena shook her head violently as I stepped inside. With the movement, Johnson's blade scratched her skin and drew blood. Not doing that had been his one chance at living through this.

Gritting my teeth, I held the lamp and stepped forward, all my focus on the bridge of his nose, dead center of his head.

After a step, I judged the distance at four meters. Every frogman had to qualify with a handgun, including a three-meter shot to the head drawn from a holster in less than a second a half—no misses allowed. My best was seventenths of a second at five meters. All I needed was the opening. I let the lamp fall.

The noise of shattering glass should have shifted his focus to the floor for a split second—it didn't.

"Hands up," he repeated.

I flexed the fingers on my hands and slowly raised them, watching for the opening I needed.

"One hand on the scope and unclip the rifle with the other. Then let it drop."

I followed his instructions. That let me lower my hands to a better position to draw my SIG, if the opportunity came. My M4 was useless in this scenario, as it would take too long to swing into position. It clattered to the floor.

"Now the handgun."

Serena's eyes were wide with fear as she shook her head.

I kept my hands still. "I'll do anything to keep you safe, Tiger."

At the word *Tiger*, recognition shone in Serena's eyes. She kept her hands close to her body and slowly raised them, inch by inch.

"Now the handgun. Two fingers only," the dead man walking said.

"Non-lethal," Lucas said in my ear.

MY HEART THUNDERED IN MY CHEST AS DUKE DROPPED HIS RIFLE. HE'D BECOME defenseless to save me. "I'll do anything to keep you safe, Tiger."

Now, Johnson had told him to give up his handgun as well. I couldn't let this asshole hurt my man.

Tiger. I became the tiger. Bringing my hands up close to my chest, where Johnson couldn't see them, I grabbed his wrist and forearm the way I'd practiced with the master chief and swiveled, pulling the knife a few inches away as I ducked downward.

A shot rang out.

I twisted.

Two more shots in quick succession, and the knife dropped away.

I pulled free of the monster as he cried out and crumpled to the floor.

Duke was on me in a second, pulling me away from Johnson. "Hostage secured. One perp down." He kicked the knife away.

Johnson moaned loudly, writhing on the floor.

I shivered in his arms. "You came for me."

"Of course. Because you're mine, Tiger."

Lucas burst into the room, followed by Winston.

Johnson moaned again. "Fucker. I need an ambulance." He had wounds in both shoulders and one leg.

I broke loose from Duke's hold and kicked the asshole. "You're only alive because he can't shoot straight."

Duke pulled me back. "I didn't miss."

"He's right," Lucas said as he leaned over Johnson with a bandage for his leg. "Non-lethal was my order." He started on the injury. "Who else is working with you?"

Johnson spat at him.

Lucas punched his wound.

The big man screamed. "Nobody."

"Bullshit," I called.

Winston looked around. "Where's the other hostage?"

I snorted, laughing at my own stupidity. "She went to pick up the ransom. She'll be back soon."

Lucas's brow creased. "Come again?"

"She was behind the whole thing. Katelyn killed Leo, sent the Russians after Sophia, and hired this piece of shit and his brother to go after me."

Duke shook his head. "I never did like her."

"Jordy," Lucas said to the floor. "We have incoming. Katelyn Connor, co-conspirator. Winston, get the med kit from the car."

The big ex-FBI agent hustled away.

Duke pulled my shirt closed. "You're braless," he whispered in my ear. "Did he?"

"No," I said, tucking my shirt in to keep it from flowing open.

"You're shaking." He opened his arms for me. I hugged him and his lumpy body armor. His tight embrace slowly eased my tension.

Ten minutes later, Winston and Lucas were still tending to Johnson when Jordy walked in. He had a handcuffed Katelyn with a rope around her in tow.

She spat at him and turned to me. "I'm going to kill you. You ruined everything."

Jordy threw a duffle bag on the floor. "She had this."

"Damn right," she screamed. "That's my money." Her voice accelerated into dog-whistle territory.

Lucas grabbed the duct tape and shut up the shrieking Katelyn for good. "I've heard enough from you."

I bit back a laugh.

"Call Wellbourne for these two," Lucas directed. "And an ambulance."

I turned to Duke. "Do you still have that necklace? I'm fucking tired of being kidnapped."

"Sure do." He fished it out of a pocket and fastened it around my neck, tying a knot in the chain. "You're officially mine, Serena Marie Benson."

"I'm yours," I agreed. "And, you are mine."

"This will have to do until I can find a ring."

The words made my chest tight. I pushed him back. "You can't say that."

"Sure I can. You're mine now, and I plan on making it official."

Momentarily speechless, I pulled away.

"Do you guys need a minute?" Lucas called from the other room.

"No," Duke said as he inched forward. "It's taking her a minute to accept her fate."

"Fate? Maybe we should start by dating for a while."

He shrugged. "Or not."

"You can't just say we're going to get married. You've got to do this right. Get my dad's blessing, bring a ring, down on one knee, the whole bit."

He changed the subject. "How did you learn that escape move you used?"

"From the master chief who taught me to pick locks."

"Now I really have to thank this guy. What's his name."

"Master Chief Brass."

Duke froze. "Brass?" He gripped my arm. "What's his first name?"

"Fred, I think. But I wasn't allowed to call him that."

Duke's mouth dropped open.

"What?"

"That's my friend, Freddy."

"The one who…?"

He nodded. "Marilyn's husband. He died in a helo holding my hand." Tears threatened in his eyes. "He always said he'd find me a strong woman one day, and he really did."

I threw myself at Duke and hugged him. "Maybe it really is fate." The master chief had brought us together, giving me the tools to survive and be rescued by his best friend.

"I want to go home now." I had my man, and I wasn't ever letting go. Plus, I had some new ideas for positions we could try.

As he held me, I knew I'd found my partner in life, the man who cherished me as much as I did him, who would show me exciting times, stand up for me if I needed it, and protect me always.

Though hopefully, the times ahead would be a little less exciting than the last two weeks had been…

CHAPTER 46

SERENA (TWO MONTHS LATER)

DUKE HELD MY HAND AS THE COURT CLERK CALLED THE CASE. IT HAD BEEN TWO months since Duke and the Hawk team had saved me from Katelyn and Johnson Spinelli.

I recrossed my legs and squirmed with anticipation. Different courthouse, but the same hard wooden bench as I'd had for Harvey Fox's sentencing.

Duke had suggested a conservative black pantsuit for me. But being superstitious, I'd chosen the same white top, same black skirt, and same shoes that had gotten a maximum-sentence result the last time.

For moral support, my sister Kelly was in from D.C. in the row behind us, along with my parents and all my brothers except Vincent.

Vincent had taken the Covington job in Boston and couldn't make it. He had a good reason. He was being investigated by the FBI.

The agent in charge was none other than Ashley Newton, the girl he'd regretted not chasing. It couldn't get any weirder. Now she was chasing him, but with a badge and a pair of handcuffs—and not the fur-lined kind. *Talk about drama.*

Kelly leaned forward to place a hand on my shoulder. "You holding up okay?"

I nodded.

Dad whispered from behind me. "I still think this was a mistake." He didn't know how to give up on an argument.

271

"Shush now," Mom told him.

Duke had wanted to prosecute the four for a combination of conspiracy, the two kidnappings, the attempted kidnapping, and the car bomb. Multiple charges led to longer sentences, per the guidelines. But Dad had insisted I stick with his idea of keeping any mention of a Benson kidnapping out of the news.

Dad had provided leverage with the DA. But it had been my decision, and I'd sided with Duke on pressing all the charges, which Dad had a hard time swallowing.

My decision added to whatever the problem was between him and Duke. And neither would admit what the issue was.

The judge droned on for a while before telling Tony Spinelli to rise.

He stood, along with his counsel, shifting nervously.

Agreeing to Spinelli pleading guilty to a single count had been the price of getting this behind me as rapidly as possible and avoiding a trial.

I'd submitted my victim impact statement regarding Tony in written form. It hadn't been easy putting down on paper the horror that had befallen me at his hands. And maybe the judge wasn't supposed to consider it, but I'd also included the trauma of watching him stab and nearly kill my boyfriend in front of me, with a smile on his face.

"Mr. Anthony Spinelli," the judge said, "you have pled guilty to aggravated kidnapping under California Penal Code…"

I held my breath as the judge read the rest of his sentencing speech.

The defense had argued for a twenty-year sentence, which would allow him to get out in seven.

The prosecutors had argued for a life sentence.

Spinelli smiled as the judge continued. "…I hereby sentence you to life in prison—"

"Fuck you," Tony spat. "That wasn't the deal."

Seemed he'd thought the judge would go easy on him.

"Counselor, restrain your client," the judge ordered.

"I'll fucking kill you when I get out," Tony ranted.

Duke's arm came around my shoulder to tug me tight.

I smiled. This asswipe deserved every miserable year he'd now spend in prison, not just for abducting me, but for attacking my man.

"Mr. Spinelli, I wasn't done," the judge continued. "Your sentence is life in prison without the possibility of parole."

I let out the breath I'd been holding. Spinelli wasn't ever getting the chance to leave the cage he was headed for.

"That wasn't the deal," he screamed at his attorney. "You said I'd get twenty max." When he punched the poor schmuck and tried to strangle him, I grasped Duke's thigh, a silent plea for him to not get involved.

The bailiffs wrestled a swearing Tony out of the room, while the attorney he shared with his brother held a handkerchief to his nose to staunch the bleeding.

When the circus subsided, Johnson Spinelli was told to rise.

Thankfully, the sentence was the same for the pervert.

Instead of swearing at the judge, he turned around and aimed his venom at me. "I'll get you, bitch."

I sneered back and scratched my nose with her middle finger. *Take that, asshole.*

Duke glared at him. If Johnson ever escaped prison, intent on making good on his threat, he'd better hope the police caught him before Duke did.

The judge repeated the process with Pons and Katelyn. All four got life without parole.

As the three filed out the prisoner door, we stood to leave. The spectacle was complete.

"They got what they deserved, and it's over now," Duke whispered as my entire family stood and spoke over each other with pretty much the same sentiment.

I stayed glued to my man's side as we left.

When we reached the corridor outside the courtroom, he released me so my family members could have a chance to hug me one at a time.

"Love you," Mom said as she hugged me and kissed my cheek.

"Love you too."

Kelly held me loosely. "I'm so proud of you."

"Thanks."

"They deserved it," Zach told me in a one-armed hug.

I nodded.

Dennis held me tight and whispered, "I hope they die horribly in prison."

I certainly agreed when it came to Johnson.

Josh held me by the shoulders. "Chin up, Sis. Tomorrow is another day."

I nodded.

Dad gave me his standard bear hug. "Now that this is over, maybe you'd like to come along with your mother and me on a Mediterranean cruise—decompress a little."

"Thanks, Dad, but I've got work."

"You don't have to."

"Yes, I do." This was an old argument. He wanted me to rely on his money, and I wanted my independence. He might also be trying to get me away from Duke.

"Okay for now. We'll talk more later." He let me go. "Lunch is on me," he announced. "As soon as I deal with the press."

Now, it was time for the next chapter of my life, and that chapter would not be complete without Duke.

~

Duke

THE SENTENCING HEARING HADN'T BEEN ON THE COURT CALENDAR UNTIL YESTERDAY. If one ever needed confirmation that advertising spending could affect the interest level of local TV news outlets, this was it.

On the courthouse steps, Lloyd Benson stood in front of the microphones of a huge press group. "I'd like to thank the LAPD and the district attorney's office for their hard work in securing my daughter's safety and the conviction of the men responsible."

My teeth clenched. The asshole didn't mention a word about Hawk Security being the ones to rescue Serena. She had warned me that her father would take credit for the rescue and to not get worked up about it. Easier said than done.

"Our city is not a safe place for criminal scum like the men and women who were locked up today," he continued.

"Are you satisfied with the sentence?" a reporter asked.

"I would have preferred that California allow the death penalty for their crimes, but this will have to do. If the men I sent after them had been better shots, maybe today wouldn't have been necessary… But, well…"

Seething, I turned away.

Serena stroked my arm. "It's just messaging."

It was messaging all right—don't mess with Papa Benson.

Lucas turned and strode away, probably equally insulted.

"Let it be known," Benson continued, "that if any of my extended family is threatened in any way, the perpetrator will be brought to justice. I will spend every last penny of my wealth to hunt them down, and nowhere on Earth will be a safe place for them to hide." His tone was icy, and that sentiment was one I agreed with.

I towed my woman away. "I can't take any more of this bullshit—better shot my ass."

"It's just optics," she assured me.

That didn't make it sting any less. Especially since Serena expected me to secure that jerk's blessing before presenting her with the ring in my jacket pocket.

Today was not the time to approach her father, as I was likely to punch him in his smug face.

SERENA

WE WALKED TO THE PARKING GARAGE.

I knew he'd parked the Porsche to the left, but Duke kept tugging me along until we ended up in motorcycle parking.

"Ready?" he asked as he stopped in front of that big black Harley I'd seen multiple times at his place. "I promised you a ride when this was over, and now it is."

I ran my hand down my side. "I can't. Not in this skirt."

"And whose fault is that?" he asked. "I suggested the pantsuit. Snuggle close, and nobody will see a thing."

I hesitated, sorely tempted.

"Who's chicken now?" He grabbed a helmet and offered me a second one.

What the hell? I took it.

He flipped out the passenger foot pegs and mounted the bike.

Helmet in place, I flipped down the visor, hiked up my skirt, and swung my leg over.

Dad appeared. "Stop. You can't go with him."

"Ignore him," Duke said, starting the engine. "We're leaving."

"No," I yelled over the noise and dismounted, almost falling on my ass in the process. I was done with this male-ego bullshit. I was going to get to the bottom of the problem.

Duke shut down the engine. "Get back on, Tiger. We're leaving."

I didn't go for the bait. "No. We're talking to him." I knew this wouldn't be easy, so I pulled out the big threat. "Or are you scared?"

"You can't go with him," Dad pleaded. "He's not right for you."

Duke got off the Harley and removed his helmet with the meanest scowl I'd ever seen on him. "She's mine. Get over it."

I got between them. "I've had it with both of you refusing to talk to me. Now what the hell is the problem?"

Neither man spoke up.

"If I don't hear an explanation in the next five seconds, I'm walking out of here on my own." I pointed at Duke. "Not your woman." I swung to Dad. "And not your daughter."

"He had me arrested," Duke blurted.

"You deserved it," Dad insisted.

I'd never heard any of this.

"They dropped the bullshit charges," Duke spat, his face turning red. "But the arrest cost me my football scholarship."

"And rightly so, you pervert," Dad said, obviously proud of himself.

"What the hell are you two talking about?" I demanded.

"I found that note," Dad explained, "when I picked you up from summer camp."

Duke's face went even redder. "I never wrote any fucking note."

"I saw you put it in her backpack. *Meet me next Friday at the Starbucks on Langley.*" Dad pointed at me. "My God. You knew she was underage."

"I didn't write that," Duke protested.

"Hold it, Dad." I stepped up to him. It finally made sense. "You have it all wrong. I'm the one who wrote that note and gave it to him."

Dad's face fell. "You wrote it?"

I nodded. "I had a little crush." I looked over at Duke. "Even way back then."

"I stuffed that note in her backpack because I wasn't interested," Duke said, now calmer than before. "At least not then."

Dad went pale. He looked down at the ground for a long moment before finally meeting my eyes. "I'm so sorry, Munch…" He caught himself. "Serena."

"Arrested? I can't believe you." My anger ramped up my volume. "He didn't do a thing or even try."

"You're my daughter. I was protecting you. I'm sorry."

That was as much of an apology as I'd ever heard from my father, but it wasn't good enough. Shaking my head, I moved out of the way. "I'm not the one you owe an apology. Make it a good one."

He stepped forward. "Duke, I'm sorry. I hope you can accept my apology for being so wrong about you. I got carried away. Maybe you'll understand someday if you have a daughter."

Duke took a deep breath and nodded. "It's in the past, Lloyd."

That was the first time I'd heard Duke call Dad anything but *sir*.

Dad smiled, the color returning to his face. "If there's anything you ever need —anything at all I can do to make it up to you."

Duke nodded, and a few seconds later, he pulled my father aside and whispered something in his ear.

Dad glanced my way. "You got it," he said with a wide smile. "Now, I'll be on my way and leave you two kids alone."

Duke grinned suspiciously.

"What's going on?" I yelped when he lifted me up and onto the bike's seat.

"Close your eyes."

"No. Tell me—"

"Close your eyes before I paddle you."

I gave in.

"Okay. Open now."

I gasped. Duke was on one knee, holding up a gorgeous ring, a diamond flanked by emeralds on either side.

"Serena, you've made me believe that love is worth the risk."

I teared up.

"I've known since you first put my brother in his place that you were the one for me. Serena Marie Benson, will you make me the happiest frogman on Earth and marry my pathetic ass so we can have little frogman babies?"

I jumped off and into his arms. "Yes. A hundred times, yes."

"The emeralds are to match your eyes."

I blinked back tears. "It's beautiful." I offered my hand, and he slipped the ring on. I was finally where I was meant to be.

We sealed it with another kiss, and only then did I see Dad off in the corner, watching with a big fat grin on his face. I cocked my head. "What did you say to him?"

"That the only thing I wanted from him was his permission to propose to you." He handed me the helmet again. "Hurry up. I can't wait to get my fiancée home and make love to her."

"I like the sound of that." But I planned to be on top.

A minute later, we rumbled out of the garage.

As Duke gunned the engine, I waved at Dad, and we sped off. I wrapped myself tightly around Duke's hard, muscled body, flattening my breasts against his back.

The wind was in my face, the roar of the bike was loud, the vibration beneath us jolted the senses, and his body heat poured through the fabric between us.

Yes, this would be my life now, filled with new sensations, heat, and love. Duke loved me, I loved him, and I'd happily have his babies—our little frogmen.

What if we only had daughters?

EPILOGUE

THE BEST THING TO HOLD ONTO IN LIFE IS EACH OTHER. –AUDREY HEPBURN

SERENA

THE HINT OF MORNING LIGHT FILTERED INTO THE ROOM AS I WOKE WITH MY MAN'S morning wood pressed against me. Today would be my day to give back to the Hawk Security team that had done so much for me when I was in danger.

But first, I intended to personally thank my man, my protector, my fiancé.

He groaned sleepily when I rolled him over onto his back and straddled him. "Morning, Tiger."

I slid my wet folds along his length. "Cobra, are you ready to make it a very good morning?"

He grinned as he cupped my breasts. "A frogman is ready for anything."

Rising, I positioned him and got started making it a *very good morning* for us both. I started slow, but quickly ramped up, moaning as I rode Duke hard. I relished the times I got to be in charge.

He caressed my breasts, occasionally tweaking my nipples as I bounced on him. Each downstroke filled the room with the sounds of flesh meeting flesh. "You're so fucking beautiful, baby. That's it. Ride me. Take what you want."

I ground down on him, throwing my head back, lost in the pleasure that radiated to every cell in my body as he filled me.

He held off for a while, letting me drive on our combined trip to Nirvana, but he started thrusting up into me now, unwilling to wait any longer.

My release built to the shimmering white-hot heat of a climax that would destroy me. Right on the edge, I slowed down to prolong the journey and hold off the plunge over the edge a little longer.

"That's it, baby," he grunted. "Come for me." He brought his thumb to my clit and strummed.

My restraint dissolved, and suddenly, I was in freefall over that edge and into the shudders of my release. My pussy convulsed on his cock as the waves flowed over me.

A second later, he rolled us and started thrusting into me from above, hard and rapidly. Perched on locked elbows above me, he was magnificent—straining muscles under glorious tattoos. I dug my nails into his ass, urging him deeper.

With a groan bordering on a roar, he came, pulsing inside me. Instead of collapsing on top of me or off to the side, he rolled us again.

Lying on him, with Rex still inside me, I listened to the rapid beat of his heart. "I love you, Cobra."

He ran his hand over my back. "Love you back, Tiger."

"Are you looking forward to tonight?"

"Not my cup of tea, but I'll go for you."

There it was. My frogman would sacrifice himself for me. This was a small thing, but he'd already proved he'd go anywhere and do anything for me.

I really had hit the jackpot.

∿

Duke

THE DELICIOUS AROMAS HIT US AS SOON AS WE WALKED INTO CARDINELLI'S IN Westwood. Even Serena agreed this was the best Italian food in town.

"Why do we have to do this?" I complained again as we made our way to the private dining room.

"Because it's important to me," my fiancée said. "And I bet your team's looking forward to it."

"I doubt it." I checked my watch. It was too early for the surprise Bill Covington had helped me arrange.

Serena punched my shoulder.

I rubbed my arm. She was getting stronger, or I was getting more sensitive. "What was that for?"

"I can hear the grumpy in that statement, and no, you can't leave early and go to the range."

"But—"

"Are you scared of a little applause?"

I grunted

"Put up with it for me?" She patted my arm. "Please."

"Sure." As we walked up to Lucas, Terry, and Constance, I pinched her ass. She jumped. She had no idea what was coming her way in a little while.

Constance raised a brow, most likely having noticed Serena flinch. "Looking forward to this?"

"Sure," I answered. "Like going to the dentist."

When a few of Serena's coworkers joined us, the conversation devolved into small talk until Serena's friend Grace walked into the room.

Serena had been afraid she might not come.

I'd made it clear to the feisty redhead that it wasn't optional. I waved her over. She had to be here for Serena's special day.

Grace balked, probably due to Terry's presence in our group, until my glare and hand motions wore her down.

"What is Catwoman doing here?" Terry mumbled when he saw her coming our way.

"I get to invite who I want," Serena said.

I watched Terry. His eyes skated up and down Grace—twice.

"Oh, look, you invited even the B team," Grace said, giving Terry a sneer.

"At least I'm on the team, Wildcat. Maybe I'll call you when I need my sock drawer organized."

"Can't find fresh ones?" She sniffed the air. "Is that why you don't ever change them?" She turned her hand inward and admired her nails. Which resulted in her missing Terry checking out her cleavage.

"Kitty, you must be smelling the rat fur caught in your teeth."

Serena's coworker, Nick, hid a snicker.

Serena inserted herself by taking Grace's hand. "Gray, these nails are gorgeous."

She smiled and turned her hand over for an inspection. Her nails were all a shiny white today, an unusual twist for her. I'd most often seen her with several different colors on a hand. Each nail today had a different cat picture on it.

Constance *ohh*ed and *ahh*ed. "What do you think, Terry?"

Grace turned and Terry took her hand, tracing lightly down one finger. "Yeah, nice claws, Kitty."

Even I saw the tiny jolt Terry's touch caused Grace. When he excused himself, Grace tried to hide her glance at his ass as he walked away.

Constance arrived in her disguise. "I may have to leave early."

I smirked. "That's a shame, Gertrude."

"Very funny." Constance pointed at her prosthetic nose. "This thing itches. I feel sorry for those Star Trek actors who have to wear this stuff day in and day out."

~

NATURALLY, CHOOSING CARDINELLI'S RESULTED IN MUCH BETTER FOOD FOR DINNER than using a standard banquet service with the kind of rubber chicken served at weddings.

When the meal had finished and it was time for the awards, my new boss, Remy Laurent, went to the small podium and introduced Director Pacheco, the head of the entire EPA.

Work had become so much nicer since Powell's reassignment. He was now the sole occupant of the EPA's new Minot, North Dakota field office, overseeing the Superfund site there. I chuckled. That transfer couldn't have happened to a more deserving guy.

"What's so funny?" Duke asked.

"Nothing. Do trailers have good insulation?"

"I don't know, but I sort of doubt it."

I smiled. Winter would come soon enough, and the small trailer the EPA had placed in Minot would be quite chilly when the winter wind blew. None of us knew how Powell had gotten reassigned there. Dad hadn't mentioned anything, but we might have him to thank for Powell's departure.

The ceremony started, and one by one, the entire Hawk team, except Constance and the new guy, Zane March, went up to receive their EPA gold medals for exceptional service.

Fake Gertrude accepted the final one for C. Collier, thanking them on behalf of her sister. My coworkers all fell for the disguise and still had no idea Constance's real last name was Collier or that she had worked for Hawk the whole time, not CID.

After the awards, Constance left, as she'd warned us she would do.

Duke and I were chatting with Lucas and Jordy when Remy sought us out. He had the director with him, and Bill and Lauren Covington, of all people.

I hadn't even noticed the Covingtons arrive.

Duke smiled like the Cheshire Cat as Remy introduced the director to everyone.

"Miss Benson." Director Pacheco offered me a leather folder. "Instead of a simple ribbon, I thought it more appropriate to present you with this letter of appreciation for your fine work in shutting down the hazardous waste dumping scheme you uncovered."

I opened the folder and gasped. The letter was signed by both the director and the president—the president of these freaking United States. My cheeks flamed hot. "Why, thank you, sir."

After the letter was passed around, the Hawk boys, the director, and Remy wandered off, I confronted Duke about his grin. "You knew about this."

Bill laughed. "Knew? He convinced Uncle Garth to arrange it."

I grabbed my hot, thoughtful badass and kissed the hell out of him. Then I hauled off and punched his shoulder.

"What's that for?"

"For not warning me so I could get dressed up for the occasion."

"Princess, this is how surprises work."

LATER, GRACE, WINSTON, AND I WERE MINGLING WITH THE EPA SIDE OF THE ROOM when Grace's phone rang.

Her face drained of color. "Please don't hurt him," she said as she walked to the corner of the room behind the ficus.

Concerned, I discreetly followed to listen, like the nosy, concerned friend I was.

"I understand… Just don't hurt him. Okay, Langley and…"

I couldn't hear the next words clearly except for Starbucks.

"But I can't make it in a half hour… Hello?… Hello?"

It sounded bad, so I rounded the plants.

She looked blankly at her phone.

I grabbed her shoulder. "What's going on?"

Her wet eyes darted left and right. "Nothing."

"Who was that?"

She tried to go around me, but I blocked her. "You have to let me go."

"Gray, what's wrong? Talk to me."

She sniffled. "It's Elliot."

"Who's Elliot?"

Her eyes shifted to the other side of the room and back again. "I need to go."

"Who's Elliot?" I repeated.

"Uh…my newest cat, Elliot Ness. I have to go." I thought she only had two cats, Bonnie and Clyde. It finally made sense that she was upset if one of her cats was in trouble.

"Did he get loose or something?"

She nodded. "I've gotta go."

"Do you need help?" I tried.

She shook her head violently. "No, no. You stay and enjoy yourself."

I located my man across the room with Lucas, Jordy, the new guy Zane, and Terry. I'd spent too much time away from my man.

As Grace headed out, Remy surprised me. "Serena, thank you for arranging this."

$\sim$

DUKE

WE WERE STANDING AROUND, MAKING THE REQUIRED POST-AWARD SMALL TALK WHEN Terry found me, Lucas, Jordy, and Zane. He searched the room for a moment. "Have you seen Grace?"

"Which one? Kitty, Wildcat, Bobcat, or Catwoman?" I teased.

Terry's eyes were wild. "I've gotta find her."

Lucas grabbed his arm. "What's wrong?"

"I just got a call saying she's in danger."

Lucas's face turned turbulent. "In danger from whom?"

Terry shook his head. "No idea. First, her cousin called asking if I knew where she was. Then, he called again and told me to look out for her because she was in danger. He was scared shitless."

I scanned the room but didn't see her.

"Last I saw, she was talking with the Serena," Zane noted.

I swiveled to find Serena in the far corner with her new boss, Remy.

Terry took off toward her. After a few words with Serena, he hustled out the door.

Zane grabbed my attention. "Cobra, what do you think the Lakers' chances are this season?"

I shrugged. "They could go all the way, but I wouldn't put it past them to blow it."

Zane started in on his dissection of the team's weaknesses.

"What's going on with Grace and Terry?" I asked Serena when she arrived.

"Ya got me." She shrugged. "Grace got a call. She had to leave... Some problem with her new cat, and Terry went tearing out after her. I have no idea what set him off."

Lucas scowled. "He thinks she's in danger is what he told us."

Serena shook her head. "Over a cat?"

That didn't sound right to me. Terry was levelheaded. He didn't even like cats. "Maybe I should go check it out."

"No." Lucas shook his head. "Duke, it's your woman's evening. Zane, you go see if Terry needs help."

I hugged my woman to my side. Life was good. Serena had my ring on her finger and had moved in with me. Her dad and I had a deep-sea-fishing day planned, and work had slowed down to minor celebrity-protection jobs.

She looked up at me, flashing those green eyes that did me in every time. "I don't know how to thank you for this."

Bill wandered off when I chuckled. "I can think of a few ways."

"I think we should start a family."

It came out of the blue, but didn't scare me the way it could have. "That could be fun."

"Very," she purred.

"When is your dad supposed to be here?" I whispered. We couldn't leave before he got a chance to appreciate her presidential letter.

"Anytime now. He warned me he'd be late."

I turned when there was a commotion at the door.

"Call 9-1-1," Terry yelled. He carried a limp body in his arms. "She was attacked."

Lucas ran for the door, and I yanked out my phone.

Terry gently laid an unconscious Grace on the settee.

∼

THE FOLLOWING PAGES CONTAIN A PREVIEW OF *GUARDING GRACE*.

GUARDING GRACE

CHAPTER ONE

Grace

On the far side of the room, Terry Goodwin stepped away from the group he was talking with, looked my way, and nodded toward the corner again. It was unfair that a man with such a black personality looked so gorgeous.

Rolling my eyes, I gave him another subtle head shake and looked away. This distance was perfect for me. I wouldn't get a whiff of his sexy cologne again.

Where did that thought come from?

Terry's last name was laughable because, as far as I was concerned, there was nothing good about that Goodwin. His sister, Deb, however, was a sweet friend.

Terry's words to me had been as cutting as always when I'd arrived at this shindig.

"Maybe I'll call you when I need my sock drawer organized."

Ugh.

And, "Nice claws, Kitty."

I couldn't remember the last time he'd said something nice to me—not that it mattered.

My best friend, Serena Benson, had arranged this party to give medals to the team at Hawk Security that had rescued her and uncovered the hazardous-chemical-dumping scheme that threatened our local drinking water. The director of the EPA himself had handed out medals to the entire Hawk team, including Terry.

Luckily, I'd been seated at a different table than Terry for the dinner and awards. Now that we were in the stand-and-chat portion of the evening, I only had to keep my distance for maybe another half hour.

"I'm really glad you came," Serena said, snaking an arm behind her fiancé, Duke Hawk, her hot, former SEAL bodyguard and a member of Hawk Security.

I smiled. "I wouldn't miss my best friend's big night."

Serena cocked a brow, and I inwardly cringed, afraid I'd given up the surprise Duke had arranged for her.

"You look stunning this evening," Duke said before Serena could ask me anything.

"It's thanks to your lovely fiancée." I smoothed my hands down the exquisite Valentino gown. "She loaned me this dress.

Winston Evers, another member of Hawk Security, wandered over, and the conversation thankfully pivoted. When I looked back, Terry scowled at me and tried his come-hither head nod again.

I settled for sticking my tongue out at him behind a raised hand. Not as classy as I should be at an event like this, but Terry deserved it after all the aggravation he'd given me over the years.

Turning, I noticed Nick Butcher, one of Serena's coworkers, eyeing me. I pulled in a deep breath, which made my boobs almost pop out of this tight dress. If I read it right, Nick's heated gaze meant the evening might not be as boring as I'd feared.

"Want to join us?" Serena asked. "The Hawk guys are going over to Tito's to shoot some pool."

I liked Tito's, and I'd played darts there often. "Sorry, I have an early morning tomorrow." It wasn't a lie, but mostly I didn't intend to chance that Terry might also tag along.

Despite Terry's presence, I was grateful to be here this evening, and I knew how lucky I was to have my best friend still alive. Besides a car bomb attack, a sex trafficker had kidnapped Serena—twice. But she'd survived the ordeal and had come out the other side to get to her happy place, engaged to a wonderful man.

I shivered, thinking about how terrifying those days must have been for her, then couldn't help sighing over how lucky she was to have found Duke. I'd never had that kind of luck in my dating life.

I excused myself to use the ladies' room. When I returned, I noticed Terry had joined the three Hawk brothers, Duke, Lucas, and Jordy. Unfortunately, Nick was with them.

With Terry in the group, I instead headed back toward Serena, who was now talking with some EPA folks and Winston.

On the way, my phone vibrated in my purse. I pulled the device out and clicked the screen off after seeing the name—*Tyrant*, the moniker I'd given Terry years ago. It vibrated in my hand again, and I gave in, moving to the messaging app.

TYRANT: *I need to talk to you.*

TYRANT: *It's important*

I had no problem crafting a reply.

ME: *No way*

"You know," said Remy Laurent, Serena's new boss at the EPA, "wedding planning takes a long time."

He should know, he was planning his own wedding.

"Yeah," Serena said wearily.

"Have you decided on a venue?" Jacques, Remy's fiancé, asked.

Serena shook her head. "Not yet."

Winston, a big, former FBI special agent, looked disinterested, as most guys did when a discussion turned to wedding planning.

"And you need a dress," Remy added. "That can take a while. And your maid of honor and bridesmaids. And flowers, and—"

Serena held up a hand. "Later. We have to set a date first."

Remy looked heartbroken that this topic was closed. He and Jacques wandered off as I noticed Janice from work hand Terry her card.

Janice was a tall blonde, incredibly thin, on the hunt for her next husband, and not bashful about it. She figured she'd need to sleep with three or four dozen men to find the right one, or so she said. She stroked her fingers down his chest.

I turned away and half a minute later, my phone vibrated again.

Ready to kill Terry for the constant interruptions, I answered hurriedly, "I don't have time for you."

Only the creepy voice wasn't Terry's.

"We have your cousin Elliot. Do exactly as I say, or he dies."

My blood froze as I tried my best not to cry and sought privacy behind a ficus.

"Please don't hurt him." I kept my voice low.

"You will bring your phone and ATM card. Meet me in the parking lot of the Starbucks on Langley. Come alone. Do you understand?"

I shivered. I thought kidnapping for ransom only happened to rich people.

"I understand, but—"

"Be there," the creepy voice demanded.

"Just don't hurt him."

I didn't have big bucks, and obviously, they didn't think Eliot was worth much. My withdrawal limit was twenty-five hundred, and when it ticked over midnight, I guess they could double that.

"Come alone. Bring anyone, tell anyone, or call the cops, and we'll know. Then Elliot dies."

I shivered. "Langley and where? I don't know all the Starbucks."

"Look it up. There's only one."

"But that's a long way. I can't make it in a half hour."

The line was silent.

"Hello?... Hello?"

I checked the screen. *Unknown number*. And the call was over.

Serena appeared, her face concerned as she reached for my shoulder.

"What's going on?"

I held back the tears. "Nothing."

I couldn't tell her or anyone.

"Who was that?"

She blocked my way when I tried to leave.

"You have to let me go," I implored her.

"Gray, what's wrong? Talk to me."

I sniffled. "They have Elliot."

"Who's Elliot?"

I'd made a big mistake even mentioning his name. "I need to go."

"Who's Elliot?" she repeated.

"Uh..." I struggled for anything that wasn't the truth. "My newest cat, Elliot Ness. I have to go."

"Did he get loose or something?"

Seeing an opening, I nodded. "I've gotta go."

The clock was ticking down on my half hour.

"Do you need help?"

"No, no. You stay and enjoy yourself."

With that, I escaped the room.

CHAPTER 47

TERRY

"*DO YOU KNOW WHERE GRACE IS?*"

Elliot Boyle, her loser cousin, had called to ask me this question a half hour ago.

It paid to read between the lines in this line of work, and my assessment had been that he needed Grace's help for something. This was not the first time.

When I'd told him she was in the same room as I was at an awards function, he'd promptly hung up, like the little snot he was.

I'd motioned for her to come over and talk, but she only stuck her tongue out in response. Since I had no tolerance tonight for any more of Grace's snarky attitude, I'd texted her from across the room, asking for a moment of her time. I'd been polite about it.

She hadn't responded in kind, and that had ended my need to follow up on Elliot's call. He could damned well call her himself.

Sure, she looked good from a distance—bright red hair and curves for miles. No, good-looking wasn't right. I had to admit, she was a total smokeshow. Problem was, when I got close enough to talk to her, she was about as cuddly as a porcupine.

Her prickly attitude helped me keep my mind off those curves and the body I'd sworn to her dying brother I'd take care of. She'd be perfect for some guy, so long as that guy wasn't me.

Nope, not going there.

289

The evening had been excellent, as these things went, with good food and a comfortable setting. When I'd been in LAPD SWAT, awards had usually been given out while sitting on folding chairs in the sun, roasting in a dress uniform and listening to some self-important politician drone on for an hour about nothing of any interest to us cops.

Tonight was much better, but our real reward had been knowing we'd saved our buddy's girl, Serena, from the certainty of being sex-trafficked by that Spinelli asswipe. Both Spinelli brothers were locked away in San Quentin, making the world safer.

There were still a few unclaimed pieces of chocolate cheesecake on the dessert trays near me. One large piece in particular called my name. So, being the concerned citizen that I was, I quickly liberated that piece from the table in order to minimize the garbage footprint of this party.

"I saw that," Winston said, as he cruised up and snagged another one. "Good idea. These shouldn't go to waste."

We munched for a moment, but then Winston wandered away when a striking blonde coworker of Serena's caught his eye.

My phone rang again with Elliot's name on the screen. "What, Elliot?" I answered.

"You gotta watch out for Grace," he said. "You gotta protect her. She's in a shit-ton of trouble."

While he said this, I scanned the room for Grace but came up empty. "What's going on?"

"Man, they're after her. These guys don't fuckin' mess around."

"Slow down, Elliot. Who?"

"I don't suck until you pay," a woman said in the background.

"Keep her safe," Elliot said.

"Who's after her?"

"No money, no action," the annoyed woman said.

"Fuck, I gotta go."

"Shit, Elliot, tell me who is after her."

The line was silent. The little snot had hung up without telling me what I needed to know, too busy getting a blow job. God, I hated that guy.

I quickly looked from the far left to the right—still no Grace in sight. Elliot hung out with the wrong crowd and wasn't the sharpest tool in the shed, but surviving among them had probably tuned his survival instinct. The fear in his voice was not a good sign.

It took me only seconds to reach my Hawk Security coworkers, the three Hawk brothers, Lucas, Jordy and Duke, along with Winston, and Zane March our latest addition.

"Have you seen Grace?"

"Which one? Kitty, Wildcat, Bobcat, or Catwoman?" Duke joked.

I didn't have time for this shit. "I've gotta find her."

Lucas grabbed my arm. "What's wrong?"

"I just got a call saying she's in danger."

Lucas's eyes narrowed. "In danger from whom?"

I shrugged. "No idea. First, her cousin called asking if I knew where she was, and then he called back and told me to look out for her because she was in danger. The little twerp was scared shitless."

"Last I saw, she was talking with Serena," Zane said, pointing to the far side of the room.

I reached Serena quickly.

"Where's Grace?"

I almost shouted.

She startled. "She got a call. She sounded rattled and took off to meet somebody who has her cat, Elliot. It didn't make any sense."

"When?"

"Just now. What's going on?"

I sprinted for the door.

Grace didn't have a cat named Elliot. The calls instantly clicked. Somebody claiming to have Elliot lured her out to a meeting. I had to get to her first. Grace excelled at being a royal pain in my ass, but I'd promised her brother, Flynn, on his deathbed that I'd take care of her. I could not fucking fail on that promise.

Outside, I looked both ways, but I didn't see her. I accosted the closest of the two valets.

"I'm looking for a girl who just came out, about ye high, green dress, bright red hair. Which way did she go?"

He pulled an earbud out of his ear and held out his hand. "Ticket?"

I repeated myself.

The guy shrugged. "No idea."

I grabbed him by the lapels, and his eyes went wide. "Time to concentrate…" I checked his nametag. "Will."

CHAPTER 48

GRACE

I DIDN'T WANT TO SPEND THE MONEY FOR THE VALET, AND THE ONLY AVAILABLE
parking was on the side streets, so I turned left out of the restaurant toward my
car. I walked as fast as I could in these heels, retrieving my car keys from my
purse as I went.

What kind of idiot would kidnap my cousin Elliot? Nobody cared whether he
lived or died except me. A few thousand for Elliot? Life was certainly cheap to
these people.

If they knew anything about me, they would have asked for the necklace
Mom gave me. It was worth more than that.

The bright lights and traffic of the main street gave way to dim lighting and
no cars when I turned onto the side street where I'd parked.

I got the prickle at the back of my neck that any woman walking alone in the
dark sometimes got. Halfway down the block, a shadow detached from a
building ahead of me. On any other night, I would have turned around and
returned to the bright lights behind me, but Elliot needed me. I crossed to the
other side and palmed my key between my fingers as a weapon like Terry had
taught me years ago.

Terry was a former SWAT officer with the LAPD, and as terrible as his
personality was, he knew a shitload more than I did about self-defense.

Passing between the parked cars on the opposite side of the street, I lost sight
of the guy. I assumed it was a man. Dread crept up my spine as I hurried along.

He came out from between two cars. "There you are."

Heart pounding, I turned and ran.

A few steps later, he grabbed my hair and yanked.

I cried out.

Fuck, that hurt.

My scalp burned from the pain.

Beefy arms wound around me and lifted me off the ground.

"Where is fucking Spider?"

The brute slammed me against a car and spun me, pinning my arms. His breath was heavy with garlic.

Spider was Elliot's nickname with the bad crowd he hung out with.

A second skinny dude came out of the shadows. "Yeah, where is he?"

"I don't know."

Why ask about Elliot? Restrained like this, I couldn't bring my hand up to slash him like I'd been taught.

Skinny Dude yanked my purse away and rummaged through it.

"I got the phone. We can find him."

"Maybe." The big one scowled, shaking me. "Where is he hiding?"

"I told you, I don't know."

"Not good enough."

The big guy punched me in the face.

My head snapped back against the car window. Pain flashed across my cheek, and my vision blurred. I brought up the hand he'd released and slashed him across the face with my key.

He howled but didn't release his grip.

"Bitch."

He pulled back to hit me again.

My eyes had partially acclimated to the dim light. When his grip loosened, I tried to knee him, but my dress was too tight.

The brute retaliated with another punch.

My nose erupted in pain, and I tasted blood. My God, why did he have to hit so hard?

"Yeah, fuck her up good," Skinny Dude urged.

"Tell us where the little weasel—" The brute's question was cut short when a fist from nowhere landed on the side of his head.

"Get off her," Terry roared.

The big man stumbled to the side, releasing me, then regained his footing.

"Grace?"

"I'm okay," I lied.

Everything depended on me getting out of here in time to meet with the kidnapper.

"Who the fuck are you?" Skinny Dude yelled as he pulled a knife.

My heart stopped. The rules of the party tonight had been that the Hawk people would come unarmed, and this looked bad.

The big guy shook off the effect of Terry's punch and straightened. Things went from bad to worse when he pulled a knife as well and advanced.

"You guys don't want to do this," Terry warned.

The corny movie line got a laugh from Skinny Dude.

The brute kept coming. "We're going to fuck you up so—" He didn't get a chance to finish his threat before Terry launched a series of hits and kicks that made a Jackie Chan karate movie look like slow motion.

His knife hit the ground, and Terry kicked it under a car.

The brute crumpled to the ground, wheezing after a final throat punch from Terry.

Skinny Dude lunged.

Terry sidestepped and threw him against the wall. My phone clattered to the ground.

The guy bounced off the wall, turned, and ran right back into Terry's fist. His head snapped back with the sickening sound of crunching cartilage. He ended up motionless on the sidewalk.

Running footsteps approached.

"Terry," Zane called.

"Here," Terry answered, picking up Skinny Dude's knife. "These two attacked Grace."

"I have to go," I announced.

Time was slipping away, and I had to meet the kidnapper.

Terry ignored me. "Call Constance and take these two to our guest rooms at Hawk." Constance was the ex-Secret Service woman working at Hawk, and had just left the party.

I'd been inside their building and seen the holding cells they referred to as *guest accommodations*. I moved away from the car.

Terry held up a hand to block my path. "Grace got hit in the head. I'll take her to get checked out."

Zane flipped on the light of his phone. "Who are they?"

Skinny Dude was bleeding—a lot.

I felt a sickening feeling as the world went from dim to black.

Printed in Dunstable, United Kingdom